THE LAST WITNESS

A THRILLER

GLENN MEADE

HOWARD BOOKS
A Division of Simon & Schuster, Inc.

NEW YORK   NASHVILLE   LONDON   TORONTO   SYDNEY   NEW DELHI

Howard Books
A Division of Simon & Schuster, Inc.
1230 Avenue of the Americas
New York, NY 10020

First Howard Books hardcover edition August 2014

HOWARD and colophon are trademarks of Simon & Schuster, Inc.

For information about special discounts for bulk purchases, please contact Simon & Schuster Special Sales at 1-866-506-1949 or business@simonandschuster.com.

The Simon & Schuster Speakers Bureau can bring authors to your live event. For more information or to book an event, contact the Simon & Schuster Speakers Bureau at 1-866-248-3049 or visit our website at www.simonspeakers.com.

Interior design by Jaime Putorti
Jacket design by Bruce Gore
Jacket front city photograph © Getty Images
Running girl image by iStock Images

Manufactured in the United States of America

10 9 8 7 6 5 4 3 2 1

Library of Congress Cataloging-in-Publication Data

Meade, Glenn, 1957–
  The last witness : a thriller / Glenn Meade.
    pages cm
  1. Witnesses—Fiction. I. Title.
  PS3563.E16845L37 2014
  813'.54—dc23
                            2013044248
ISBN 978-1-4516-1187-8
ISBN 978-1-4516-1190-8 (ebook)

IN MEMORY OF
STEPHEN MEEHAN

FOREVER TWENTY-FIVE

Blossoms are scattered by the wind and the wind cares
   nothing,
but the blossoms of the heart no wind can touch

—YOSHIDA KENKO

TIME LINE

1989–1991

- The Berlin Wall comes down. The Soviet Union collapses.

1990–1991

- Former Soviet republics and the Baltic States declare their independence.

- The Socialist Republic of Yugoslavia begins to tear apart.

- Slobodan Milosevic, Serbia's leader, tries to rein in the Yugoslav regions of Croatia, Slovenia, and Bosnia. A bloody conflict begins as the country splits apart along ethnic/religious divides.

1992

- Reports of ethnic cleansing, concentration camps, and mass rapes, as the Serb army and militia slaughters Muslim and Christian inhabitants of towns and villages in order to create an ethnically "pure" Serb area.

- The siege of Sarajevo, in Bosnia, begins—the Serb blockade will last more than three years.

1992–1994

• Massacres committed by all sides, civilians often the victims. International peace plans fail.

1995

• 8,000 men and boys are executed by the Serbs at Srebrenica when UN safe areas in Bosnia fall to Serb forces.

• More than 250,000 are killed or wounded in the war, and a million civilians displaced.

• NATO bombs the Serb military.

• The United States forces the Serbs to join Bosnians and Croats at the peace table in Dayton, Ohio.

• War drags on in Kosovo until 2001, and NATO brands Serb leader Slobodan Milosevic a war criminal.

• Milosevic is arrested in 2001 to stand trial for war crimes but dies in prison in 2006.

PART ONE

PROLOGUE

There are many ways to reach your grave near Mostar.

You can drive by car up through resin-scented woods, or travel by bus or by train, then walk across the bridge over the bluest river in the world and climb the hill that overlooks the sixteenth-century town.

There are many ways to reach your grave, but on this day the hot summer roads are clogged with people.

For today is the Day of the Dead, when the souls here laid to rest have prayers said in their remembrance.

Today, all the local hotels are packed, for people drive from Dubrovnik and Sarajevo, from distant cities and towns, and the international media crews come from as far away as America.

They come together to pay their respects to the thousands of names and numbers, the known and the unknown, inscribed upon wood and stone that record the passing of loved ones.

Fathers and sons, mothers and daughters, brothers and sisters.

Adults and youths, children and infants.

They lie here side by side, and in different graveyards scattered across the land: Christian and Muslim, Orthodox and Jew, agnostics and unbelievers.

Some were soldiers, many were innocent civilians, and most all of them were helpless victims in a conflict not of their making.

And you, a stranger whose war this never was, are buried among them.

Your grave bears no name, simply a number. You are an unknown casualty of war, and this is where they have laid your bones.

On this day the holy men enter the cemetery and walk among the tombs, priests and mullahs and rabbis praying and chanting, and the scent of incense drenches the air.

Lines of mourners follow them. They pass your tomb.

Under a warm sun, the thoughtful among them place a flower. Children leave a toy trinket or a boiled candy. A young boy solemnly runs his hand across the smoothness of your gravestone, then giggles and runs away to join his friends.

There is no disrespect intended by his mischief, and so it should be on this day when families and friends gather to be among their departed. For when they mourn, they mourn also for you, but of you or your story they know nothing.

They can never know how much you cherished your wife; how she taught you how to love, and to trust. How she completed you, became that other half of ourselves we always seek but seldom find.

They can never know how much you worshipped your son and daughter.

How you loved to plant kisses on their necks and tickle and chase them and make them laugh. Or how you and your wife would watch them sleeping, stare down at their faces in awe and wonder: how could you both have earned the right to such happiness?

But to those mourners who wander here this day you're just a number.

They can't even know that you are a young man buried far from home, in a peaceful meadow where bees buzz and butterflies quiver and flowers drench the air with nectar. You are simply one dead among so many.

Finally, the holy men and priests move on, their prayers completed. Some families stay, to sit and talk to their dead, for their pain is etched far deeper than mere words can ever inscribe.

And when the sun fades, when the evening sky looks like fire and smoke, they will rise, some with tears in their eyes, to touch and plant kisses on the headstones before they drift away among the graves.

They will come again, upon the same day next year, or when memories haunt them.

If you could, if it was within your power, you would call them back and you would tell them how you came to lie here.

You would tell them that in your brief lifetime you loved and argued, were good and bad, imperfect and human. In short, you were just one young man among the many victims who lived and died here, and yours could be the story of any of them, condemned by the senseless brutality of war.

But your story is different.

Perhaps your story was always meant to be different.

And if you could, you would tell them what is important to know: that it doesn't matter what a man or woman is, or who they are, or by what name they call their religion, or the color of their skin or the history of the blood that flows in their veins, so long as they believe in truth and redemption and forgiveness, and in the mercy and pity that dwells in the depths of each of our souls.

And if you could, you would say to them, *please, listen to our story.*

Listen when I tell you that if you don't stand up to evil, then evil will stand up to you.

Come back with me to the beginning, to the very beginning, to where this story began.

Learn how we came to lie here.

Because if the world never learns from the lessons of its history, then it is condemned forever to repeat the sins of its past.

I

1981

This is how you find the one you'll love.

Your name is David and you're an ordinary kid—not so much a kid at twenty-one but still innocent—shy and awkward with the opposite sex, fumbling your way toward manhood.

You're a military brat on the U.S. base near Frankfurt and you love art and girls, movies and baseball. Like all young men, you don't see eye to eye with your parents.

It is the summer you and your father had a violent row that came to blows. The one that started off with a discussion of your lack of future plans and ended with him throwing a punch that bloodied your lip and sent you crashing against the wall.

You see the shame on his face.

The instant regret that he'd lost his temper and hit you.

That's something that never happened before. But you don't care. You're angry, you want him to hurt.

Your father, the military man, the special forces tough guy who's been to Panama and Grenada and every hot spot the U.S. military stomped their boots on in the last twenty years.

You never wanted to be a soldier. You never wanted to fill his shoes. You're a dreamer. You want to paint, to be an artist.

That day, you tell him you've had enough.

You tell him he doesn't control you anymore.

You tell him you're leaving the family home for good.

Your mother cries and slumps on the couch.

Your father tries to stop you. You shove him away, and leave in a rage.

You love them both, but you know it's time to stop living in your father's shadow. Besides, you want to taste the pleasure of being twenty-one, to enjoy your summer of freedom and find some Mediterranean sun and bone-white beaches and girls, and get drunk on life.

You have a longing for change. You want to find yourself, to travel your own road.

So you pack the dented Volkswagen Golf you bought with the proceeds of a part-time bar job while you sweated in college.

You pack your paints and brushes and blank canvases, a sleeping bag and an ice box for drinks, and set out one Saturday morning from Frankfurt and drive south over the Tyrol, to Switzerland and Italy. Exhilarated, you drive that little Golf all the way down Yugoslavia's Dalmatian coast, heading for sunny Greece.

But like the best-laid schemes of mice and men, things never work out the way we plan.

That night you stop in Dubrovnik, on the Dalmatian coast.

You find a cheap hotel. Across the moonlit bay, beyond a flotilla of cruise ships, lies Italy. Frommer's guide tells you that nearby Korcula Island is where Marco Polo once lived.

And that the walled town was first founded in the seventh century. But long before that it was coveted by the Romans and Greeks, and later by the Crusaders and the Byzantines.

You marvel at its beauty. You want to paint its tight cobbled streets and the way the light falls on the pale sapphire waters of the bay.

You know little about the darker side of Yugoslavia's history; how the Balkans are torn apart by centuries-old vendettas, enmities, and grievances between Serb and Croat and Bosniak. The buried hatreds that would one day wreak havoc upon your life.

For now, you love this town. The Mediterranean lifestyle appeals to you.

You stay a week. You paint in the mornings and evenings when the light is good and afterward you go for dinner and sip a glass of wine or two.

And then one evening, sitting at a restaurant called the Marco Polo—owned by a funny little man with a hunched back named Mr.

Banda, who tells you his Italian father deserted Mussolini's army to join the partisans and settle here—a waitress with cinnamon eyes serves you.

Her dark hair is tied back in a ponytail, her skin tanned against her crisp white blouse. When she leaves your table, Mr. Banda sees you stare and he smiles.

"All the men like Lana, but she never goes out with them."

"Why not?"

He shrugs. "All her free time, she studies. She wants to be a writer. And you, I've seen you paint. You want to be a painter?"

"Sure."

Mr. Banda winks. "Two artists. You like her, yes?"

You know it in your veins. It's not like you're starry-eyed and violins start to play but something happens to you, because your heart quickens.

Mr. Banda tells you Lana's from a town beyond Sarajevo, that she's an English student at the local college. That she's his best waitress.

He calls her over and introduces you.

She shakes your hand, and you can smell her hair. It smells of almonds. Something in those cinnamon eyes speaks to you.

She smiles when you compliment her on her flawless English and she tells you her mother was an English teacher and she's spoken the language since childhood. When she talks to you, it's as if you're the only person in the world.

You stay an extra week. You're normally shy with women, not good at small talk, but you finally get up the courage to ask her out.

She surprises you and accepts.

You go to a café for coffee and cake. You talk for hours. It's your last night. In the café there's even some cheesy but apt background music: KC and the Sunshine Band playing "Please Don't Go."

Afterward, you walk on the beach and talk some more: about art and books and music, about Shakespeare, a favorite of hers, and everything under the sun.

And you kiss.

It's not your first kiss—there was a certain Fräulein named Frieda back in Frankfurt who could claim that distinction, as well as a big prize for alliteration—but it sure feels like it.

And now passion has you by the throat and won't let you go.

You stay another few days.

You drive up to Mostar one afternoon and Lana brings a picnic.

This is a town she has known and loved since childhood, when her parents took her on Sunday drives. You wander among the Turkish coffeehouses, and the bazaars selling trinkets and Persian carpets.

You stand on the beautiful arched bridge that would one day be senselessly destroyed by Serb shelling and watch young men climb onto the parapet—their arms outstretched, their graceful bodies arcing as they dive from an incredible height into the bluest river you have ever seen.

Friends greet them on the riverbanks below.

An old man sells daffodils by the bridge. You buy her a bunch. Lana tells you they're her favorite flower. And that for centuries young men have come here to earn the title "Mostari" by jumping from the bridge. Some do it as a sign of their manhood. Others to show their commitment to the woman they love.

She smiles. "Or else to prove how crazy they are."

"Do women jump?"

"Sometimes. But mostly men. It's dangerous. Twenty-five meters from the bridge to the water. People have been killed."

You tell her you'll jump.

She laughs, and says you must be mad. She peels a daffodil from the bunch and lets it fall. It flutters deep down to the river and flows fast in the blue water.

You tell her you'll jump anyway. "Want to jump with me?"

She realizes you're serious.

"No! David, really, it's dangerous. The water's always icy cold, even on a hot day. The shock to the body alone can kill you if you're not fit."

You look from the bridge into the river.

"I've read about it. The trick is to jump straight, and let your arms out a little just before you hit the water. It slows your descent."

"David, to jump without practice would be crazy . . ."

"I worked as a lifeguard for three summers. I can dive. But twenty-five meters, that'll be a first."

You tear off your T-shirt, kick off your sandals, but leave on your jeans. You look down. The flowing blue water seems an awful long way. Your heart's thudding and there's a lump of fear choking your throat but you try not to show it.

"David, please, I beg you . . ."

You climb up onto the bridge. She tries to grasp your hand to stop you but she's too late. You look back at her and wink. "Wish me luck."

"David . . . !"

You jump.

The air whistles past your ears.

For a long time you plummet like a stone. The water rushes up to meet you, and you splay your hands and hit the river.

The icy cold smacks you like a brick.

When you come up gasping and sputtering for air, you wave to her.

She runs down the winding walkway to meet you on the riverbank.

You're drenched, and laughing.

She kisses your fingertips, puts them to her lips, and then wipes your face with your T-shirt. "You're insane, you know that, David Joran?"

"Maybe. But it felt terrific."

She seems genuinely happy as she slips her arm though yours, and you walk together up the hill, your jeans soggy. You find a grassy meadow and beside a gnarled olive tree you picnic on the fresh cheese, bread, vine tomatoes, and the wine she's brought from her father's farm.

As your jeans dry in the sun, she tells you about the stories she's written. They're not good, they're not bad, either, but she knows that nobody's good at the beginning. She keeps a diary she practices her writing in.

Someday she wants to write a book that will change the world.

You tell her you've always wanted to be an artist, ever since as a kid you scrawled on your parents' kitchen walls with a colorful selection of indelible markers.

And you tell her what you think is true: that she's far too pretty for you.

She looks back at you, and for the first time you see wariness in her eyes.

You think you've blown it.

She tells you she's slow to trust most men.

You tell her you feel the same.

She laughs, but when she looks into your face you know those cautious eyes of hers are not for lying.

You're a little lightheaded from the wine and you take a penknife from your pocket and you do something juvenile, something kind of dumb but you do it anyway, because you want to show her you're an artist.

You carve your names on the trunk of the olive tree. You carve the shape of a heart—you carve it pretty darned well—and chisel out two hands above it. On each side of the heart you carve your names: David, Lana.

When you've finished she looks at you.

And her eyes seem to burrow into your soul before she kisses you.

And that night, in your cheap hotel near the harbor you lie with her for the first time.

You love her face, and everything about her. You love her laugh and her voice and the way she touches your skin with her fingertips.

You hold her and talk all night. You tell her about your life. About your quarrel with your folks. She tells you about her quarrels with her own, and about her secret. You're shocked, but you still want her. You admire her honesty. And you promise never to hurt her, never to lie.

And never to speak about her secret again. That it changes nothing.

She asks if you really mean that.

You tell her that you do.

And she whispers your name in the darkness before her mouth finds yours, and you hear her muffled tears as she falls asleep in your arms.

*   *   *

In the weeks and months that follow you learn what it is to love. Now that she trusts you, she opens like a flower and teaches you.

That summer sings in you like never before. You know that you can never go back to the life you had with your parents. That something has changed. You're forging your own future.

And you know that life is a journey, because your old man always told you so, and you discover why you want to take the journey with Lana.

Because your love goes deeper than desire. She's your soul mate.

And so in the tiny church of St. Nicholas in a flurry of snow on a freezing cold Saturday in December you look at her from eyes that are proud as you both promise to love and honor.

You slip a ring on each other's fingers—two simple gold rings Mr. Banda gave you as a wedding gift, before he takes the wedding photographs.

You honeymoon in a small hotel in the hills overlooking Sarajevo. You write a postcard to your parents and tell them that you've made your life here.

You move into an apartment above Mr. Banda's restaurant. He's good to you both. The apartment's small—three tiny rooms—with narrow walls and a low ceiling that you can touch.

Mr. Banda jokes, "Now you know how I got my hunched back."

But it's warm, with a blue tiled woodstove, and best of all the accommodation comes with the jobs Mr. Banda's offered you.

Lana studies during the day and waits on tables in the evening. You help out in the kitchens cooking and doing odd jobs and paint every free moment you can—your painting is getting better—and there's always a market so long as you can sell your work to the tourists who flock to Dubrovnik. You're doing okay, you're getting by.

When the first baby comes, it's a girl.

You're fearful of parenthood, but when this helpless little wide-eyed cherub looks up at you, and suckles on your finger, you fall in love with her.

It takes longer than you could ever imagine for the next to arrive— six years—with four miscarriages in between and by then you have both almost given up hope.

This time it's a boy.

But he's tiny, barely two pounds, for he came by Caesarean eleven weeks early and the doctors didn't think he'd make it, but somehow he did, and thrives.

With his plump cheeks and dimpled smile he will lay claim to your soul. Before you know it, he's walking and talking. He's good-humored, like his sister, and because he's lived despite the odds he has a special place in your heart.

Now there are four of you in the cramped apartment, but you never knew life could be this good.

On summer days when it's warm you spend your time on the beach, and you paint and sketch while Lana and the children play in the sand with buckets and spades, their caramel bodies healthy and happy.

On winter nights when it's cold you all sleep in the double bed.

And when the children finally give in to rest, Lana huddles in beside you.

She tells you that she believes the seeds of what we'll do are sown in all of us. That you and she were destined to meet. That she loves you, that she loved you the first moment she met you, and always will no matter what life brings.

She wants you to know that.

And that she's proud to be your wife.

You both promise never to leave each other—never—no matter what.

And when she closes her eyes, you hear your family breathing as you look at their sleeping faces in the lunar light that spills its silver fingers on the floor by the bed.

And you're happier than you have ever been.

This was all before the war came.

Before the first shells shrieked like chalk across a blackboard as they fell on Dubrovnik. Before three years of siege starved and strangled Sarajevo and blood ran in the streets.

Before the ancient vendettas and grievances and ethnic cleansing cast a malignant shadow over everyone and everything in this land, destroying all that was good and decent and human.

Before you and Lana and your children were caught up in the fire-storm, and your lives were changed forever.

You recall that your father used to say that there is always a zenith in life. A moment when you reach the highest point in the arc of your happiness, and everything seems right and the angels are on your side.

If that is so, then this was that time.

For afterward you would always remember that afternoon in Mostar when you jumped from the bridge, and you carved your names upon the olive tree.

And those moonlit nights when you huddled close together for warmth, and looked with wonder on the sleeping faces of the ones you loved.

PART TWO

THE PRESENT

2

Carla Lane didn't know it, but that day would begin with life and end with death.

Nor did she know if some fleeting premonition had passed a shadow across her dreams in the weeks leading up to that afternoon, warning her of the terrible event that was about to happen.

Perhaps it had. But all she knew for certain that day was that she was excited as she came out of the doctor's office, and that she had never felt happier.

She spotted Jan waiting for her, sitting on a park bench across the street, reading a newspaper.

He looked up when he saw her. He flashed his usual lopsided smile, his fringe blowing in the wind, but then he looked more serious as he folded away his newspaper and came to meet her.

"Well? How did it go?"

She didn't speak.

"Come on, Carla, don't do this to me, honey."

"Do what?"

"Keep me in suspense. Is it good news or bad?"

"Let's put it this way. I'm going to be eating for two from now on."

His face beamed, and she knew at once why she'd married this man.

"Carla, that's terrific news." He kissed her, slid his hand around her waist, and patted her stomach. "Can they tell yet?"

"Jan, I'm only six weeks pregnant."

"How long before they can tell?"

"Four, five months, maybe. In all the excitement I forgot to ask. It doesn't matter if it's a boy or a girl, does it?"

"Not a bit. How about lunch at Barney's to celebrate? I've got a rehearsal at two, so I'm out of handcuffs until then."

A shadow flickered across Carla's face. There was something else she had to tell Jan. Something troubling her.

"What's wrong? You look distracted."

"Nothing. It'll keep until after lunch."

"We'll have a drink to celebrate. You think the doctor would mind?"

She slipped her arm through his. "Nothing stronger than a glass of sparkling water for me. From now on, Momma's strictly on the wagon."

Jan smiled, and whistled to hail a cab.

3

The restaurant on Tenth Avenue was crowded. Jan was recognized as soon as they walked in. A few people said hello and wanted to shake his hand.

Jan hated the public side of his career. Limelight was something he avoided whenever he could, but now wasn't one of those times.

Carla left her husband signing an autograph for two young couples and headed for the restroom. She overheard a customer ask the bartender, "Who's that guy who just came in?"

"Jan Lane."

"Who's he?"

"Are you kidding? Only one of the brightest young pianists on the planet. He plays all over the world. He's playing Carnegie Hall. It's been sold out for weeks."

Months, Carla was tempted to say, before stepping into the restroom and checking herself in the mirror—she was still trying to compose herself after hearing the doctor's news. *You're six weeks pregnant, Mrs. Lane.*

She put on a touch more lipstick and looked at her reflection. She had an interesting face. Her hair was chestnut brown, and with her full figure, dark eyes, and olive skin, men seemed to find her reasonably attractive.

Despite often subsisting on too much coffee and crackers, and kicking a ten-cigarette-a-day habit and putting on ten pounds, her face had held its own. And that was even after five years of countless trials and prosecutions.

She spent two of those years in private practice, the remaining three with the New York County District Attorney's Office as a prosecutor in Manhattan. Prosecuting criminals and killers, robbers and rapists, the sane and the crazies, some of them monsters whose hate crimes and brutal acts of abuse sickened her.

But law was something she always wanted to practice. Ever since she watched TV courtroom scenes on *Law & Order* as a gawky teen she could remember craving to be an attorney, to see justice done. She never knew from where that craving came, because her parents or grandparents had no connection to the law. No brushes with it, either—no criminals, fraudsters, murderers, or thieves hanging out on her family tree—not as far as she knew.

She made it into law school with her grade point average, but she had to work extra hard to graduate from Columbia, cutting herself off from everything and everyone as she tried to concentrate solely on her studies. Then, after five years as a hardworking attorney, she made a devastating discovery.

She hated law and being a lawyer.

She hated the insincerity of the profession, the opportunists and the money grabbers. She'd met decent lawyers who cared about justice, but too many were simply hired guns who didn't give a damn whether a client was innocent or guilty. Like a mortgage advisor, they'd hold your hand and be your best friend until the check arrived.

Then there were the hundreds of awful cases that sapped you.

Her last one was prosecuting a spoiled young Princeton brat who got drunk and ran over two fourteen-year-old girls in his Porsche. He'd sped away leaving their shattered bodies sprawled in the gutter. One survived; the other died in agony.

For a child to die like that filled her with a seething anger. But the accused was rich and it was his first DWI. Big bucks meant the kind of dream criminal defense team that would have made O. J. Simpson proud. The defense argued that the road was badly lit, and that the driver wasn't drunk when he hit the girls but drove home afterward and drank because of shock.

Carla fought and wanted the maximum sentence but the judge allowed the driver to plead guilty to only a misdemeanor DWI and leaving the scene of an accident. He sentenced him to fifteen days in prison and fined him five hundred dollars.

A week later the dead girl's mother committed suicide.

Carla felt sickened. Jan came home from a concert tour that day, and saw her looking morose. "It's Friday. Why the Monday face?"

She grabbed her coat. "I need a walk, Jan."

They strolled on the beach, and she told him.

"The way of the world, Carla. Nothing's fair in love and law, you of all people know that. The law's got an ugly side."

"What kind of justice is it when a mother can't face the pain of seeing her daughter's killer go free, and then kills herself? All my effort was such a waste."

"Ever heard of the definition of a total waste?"

"What is it?"

"A tour bus crammed with lawyers driving off a cliff with two empty seats."

Jan always tried to lighten things.

"Funny. But if I'm not smiling it's only because I agree with you."

"What happened to that thirst for justice?"

"It dried up, Jan. It got sapped by battling rich lawyers who get criminals off."

"Remember what Oscar Wilde said? Life is a bad quarter of an hour made up of exquisite moments. Don't waste those moments. Change jobs. At least take a break from criminal law. See how you feel a year or two from now."

"It's not that easy. It may be drudgery but it's well-paid drudgery."

"Then come work with me. I need a lawyer to negotiate contracts, and I need a manager to organize concert tours. I also need someone to fill Jessie's shoes. You'd be perfect. You can even work from home."

Jessie, his secretary PA, had left, moving to Los Angeles.

"Are you serious?"

"There's a cardinal rule in life: when anything gets to be drudgery it's time to do something else. Say yes."

She did.

She heard tales of husbands and wives working together whose marriages ended up on the skids, but working with Jan turned out to be the saving of her. A change was exactly what she needed, and she had enjoyed every exquisite moment. He was such a wise owl, sensible beyond his years.

Sometimes she would look at him and think, *How did I get this lucky?*

She first saw him at Columbia. He was walking across the campus with a bunch of friends, his fringe blowing in the wind, a lopsided smile on his face. They never met, but she heard rumors that Jan Lane was a promising musician.

Although she'd put any thought of boyfriends on the back burner while she struggled to graduate, afterward she'd had four years of lousy dates and failed relationships.

The last one took her to a party one stormy night in Greenwich Village, then wandered off to hit on a pretty blonde. Incensed, Carla flung her plastic cup of wine into a garbage bin and went to storm after him.

"Hey . . . am I playing that badly?"

She was so enraged she never noticed a guy playing a piano nearby. A spray of wine doused him. It was Jan, and he was playing Elton John's "Candle in the Wind," and playing it beautifully.

"I . . . I'm sorry, I didn't mean to."

He looked at her date moving off with the blonde.

"You came with that guy?"

"I thought I did. Now I just want to slap him."

"Big mistake. Just ignore him and put it down to a life lesson."

"And what lesson would that be?"

"That some men are about as faithful as their options."

"That's a good line. Is it yours?"

"I wish. Some writer said it." He smiled, but there was genuine caring in his voice. "Anything I can do to help?"

Carla glanced over at the rain-lashed window, the trees tossing in the storm. "Did you come here with anyone?"

"A bunch of friends, but no one in particular."

"Have you had a drink?"

"I was just about to. Why?"

"Did you drive?"

"What is this, a murder investigation?"

"Would you do me a big favor and drive me a couple of miles to where I left my car?"

"Are you serious?"

"On a night like this I could be waiting for a cab forever. I came in his car. What do you say?"

"Buy me a coffee and we've got a deal."

He drove her to her car, they found a Starbucks, and Carla bought him coffee. She discovered he was a promising concert pianist, but his modesty meant she had to drag that fact out of him. She also discovered that he liked to poke fun at himself, and he certainly didn't take his own reputation unduly seriously. They talked all evening, and he was a good listener.

It was the first time in a long while she felt comfortable with a guy.

In the following months, they dated often. She grew to love Jan's intelligence, his gentleness, his humor, and his wisdom. It almost seemed as if they'd known each other in another life, even if she knew so little about music. They married ten months later. Home became a house in Bay Shore, Long Island, an old family clapboard that overlooked the beach.

On lazy summer days when the sea was calm they loved to swim together in the waves, and afterward on the beach they would often fall asleep in each other's arms, under a parasol. She never thought much about family, before she got pregnant. It happened by accident. But Jan seemed so happy about it, too, and for that she felt relieved. Recently, she'd begun to suspect he was distracted in their relationship. He was spending more time away on tours, when she guessed he didn't need to.

He began flying home a couple of days after his concerts ended, when really he could have flown straight home the next day.

Then there was the time a couple of months back when she emptied the pockets of his suit before sending it to the dry cleaners—and found a business card for a "private gentleman's club" in New Jersey called Slick Vixens. An embossed card with the shadowed figures of two strutting, voluptuous pole dancers.

She looked up the club on the Internet.

Nothing much, but on a chat site she came across a few comment lines: "The management is pretty selective about their clientele. Men with a little class, a lot of money, and a middle-age identity crisis seems to be the common profile, or should I say the most profitable one for the owners."

The next day she decided to drive to New Jersey.

She found the club.

Freshly painted, well decorated, a single door entrance. The only giveaway a sign that said, "Happy Hour drinks half price. Beautiful girls."

Was it the kind of place where more than a lap dance could be bought?

She didn't know, but it struck her as odd. It wasn't the kind of place Jan would have hung out. Or maybe she was wrong?

Her curiosity was eating her.

She asked Jan about the card. He'd laughed it off, saying he'd been invited there by a bunch of friends but never went.

The thing was, she believed him.

She couldn't imagine Jan being unfaithful to her.

Unless . . . unless that saying had come true. That some men are about as faithful as their options.

Jan had options—lots of good-looking women in the orchestra, and admiring female fans. She tried to wipe those thoughts from her mind as she washed her hands, and dried them with a cotton hand towel.

Questions raged through her mind as she looked at her face in the mirror, and right now they seemed more important.

Will my pregnancy be normal?

Will I be a good mother?

She felt anxious.

She looked down at her hands.

She was folding and unfolding the cotton hand towel in neat squares.

As far back as she could remember, whenever she felt anxiety, she always ended up folding or unfolding a hand towel or napkin, or whatever piece of cloth came to hand.

Then she felt it: a sharp twinge in her stomach that made her jerk.

Her heart stuttered. The doctor had told her to expect changes in her body, but she felt afraid. She knew friends who suffered twinges before they miscarried. *Am I going to miscarry?*

She prayed that wouldn't happen.

She wanted to have a normal pregnancy.

She knew she had to be positive, even if her fear was moving to the panic zone.

She looked at her face in the mirror and told herself: *I'm going to be well. I'm going to have this baby.*

Then she remembered the other news she had to tell Jan.

But after lunch.

She didn't want to upset him.

She tossed the used towel in the wicker basket and went to rejoin him.

4

"If it's a boy, what will we call him?"

"I hadn't thought about it, Jan."

"If it's a girl, how about Baize, after your grandmother? Or is that too old-fashioned?"

"Don't talk about names just yet."

"Why not?"

"It's almost like bad luck."

"You think?"

Carla pushed aside her unfinished dessert. "Let's wait until nearer the baby's due. Are you nervous about tonight?"

"You know me, I'm always nervous before a concert."

"You worry too much."

"There's a whole bunch of VIPs and dignitaries—the mayor, a slew of politicians, and visiting Arab and Russian billionaires. The kind who have nothing better to do on a Friday night than listen to a klutz like me playing."

"You'll knock them dead."

"And I meant to tell you. I've got to fly to Europe in another two weeks."

"But you don't have a concert there for another five months."

"I've still got business to arrange, honey. Conductors to see."

"Nothing you can't do over the phone?"

"I wish it was that simple."

"Why don't I fly with you?"

"You really think that would be a good idea now that you're pregnant?"

"I think it's considered still okay to fly until the sixth month."

"I'd feel safer with you not taking that risk, Carla."

"Don't be silly. If it's good enough for the Academy of Family Physicians, it's good enough for me."

Jan checked his watch. "It's really just going to be a quick turn-around, a night in London, one in Paris, then fly back. But we can talk about it again."

She put a hand on his arm. "Okay. You still want me to pick you up after the concert?"

"Sure."

"I'll make supper. Try not to be late."

"Don't worry, I'll be off that stage faster than a bullet once I'm done. You know what else? I've got a plan to celebrate our news."

"What is it?"

"The last concert's tomorrow night. Why don't we pack our bags on Monday, drive up to the Catskills, and stay a week. Have some time together."

"You mean that?"

"I'll book a cabin. One with a hot tub under the stars, the works." He emptied his glass. "I better go. What's wrong?"

"There was something I wanted to talk about. But it can wait."

"Important?"

"I think so. But we'll talk tonight. I love you, Jan."

"Love you, too. See you later. Wish me luck."

There are some people who claim they have the power of premonition.

A finely tuned sixth sense that alerts them to a tragedy or an accident about to happen. Carla Lane never believed she had a sixth sense.

But that afternoon, she would recall afterward, she felt a strange sense of foreboding, a feeling that something terrible was going to happen.

She put it down to hormones, to the battle raging inside her body. And maybe her recent nightmares were part of it? They certainly seemed bizarre. She would discuss them with Jan tonight. She just hoped he wouldn't think she was crazy.

Something else bothered her. She had the distinct feeling that Jan didn't want her to travel to London with him.

And then a thought niggled her—what if Jan was seeing someone else?

What if all those delayed trips away from home added up to an affair? That the card for the "gentleman's club" foreshadowed a bigger problem? These things happened, as much as she dreaded admitting it. Husbands left wives even when they were pregnant.

Her unease distracted her all afternoon. Later, when she showered she felt a twinge in her stomach again.

When she started to pack an overnight case for them both, she was sure she felt it once more. Was it just nerves? Or was she overly sensitive of her own body now that she knew she was expecting?

Whatever it was, it distressed her that late afternoon as she laid out the table, the red candle waiting to be lit. Two crystal glasses stood on the white tablecloth, and she placed a bowl of cherries in the refrigerator, a damp cloth over them, Jan's favorite fruit.

At six, he called her.

"Tell me I'm crazy, but you know what I thought?"

"What?"

"Forget about taking the cabin on Monday."

"Why?"

"Let's do it Sunday instead. So finish packing those bags."

"How did rehearsals go?"

"Even better than I expected. Gotta go, Carla. See you after the concert."

Carnegie Hall was packed with VIPs.

Carla recognized a presidential candidate among the New York mayor's crowd, and lots of politicians and foreign dignitaries, some of their limos parked in a row on the street outside.

Jan's picture was on the posters, the one they always used, with his blond hair falling across his forehead, his arms folded, his smiling eyes pensive.

Carla arrived midway through the concert's second half and the manager recognized her and immediately led her to a seat in a private box.

Jan was playing Rachmaninov's Concerto No. 2 in C Minor, with his usual intensity and energy, the spotlight on him. She never wanted to bathe in his reflected glory, that wasn't for her, but she always felt a surge of pride whenever she watched him play.

She knew that part of the intensity in his music came from his own childhood torment, that secret well of hurt deep inside himself he never talked about. When the finale came, a storm of applause roared around the hall and everyone in Carnegie Hall rose to their feet.

Jan was called back again and again, the audience clamoring for an encore. He obliged, seating himself again at the piano. There was complete stillness and he started to play "Le Pastour" by Gabriel Grovlez.

It was so moving that the moment the last note fell the audience went wild again. Bouquets of flowers landed on the stage.

She caught Jan's eye as he went to bow. He waved up at her, gave her the usual signal with both his open palms, all fingers splayed: see you in ten minutes.

She blew him a kiss.

They always met in the parking lot near Carnegie Hall.

She parked Jan's Volvo in their reserved spot and it took her ten minutes to walk back. Jan hated the attention after a concert and always tried to slip away. He once told her that if he'd known being a concert pianist was so much show business, he'd have kept it simple and joined the circus.

VIP Mercs and limos began to start up, their engine fumes choking the lot.

Carla saw a metal door snap open, about a hundred yards away.

Jan came out, all smiles. He had changed into a pair of jeans and a sweater and jacket, and when he saw her he waved. Over his arm was draped a suit carrier for his tuxedo. She waved and hurried to join him.

Jan reached the Volvo first. Carla was fifty feet away and she flicked the remote to open the doors.

Jan went to tug open the passenger's rear door when there was a brief, sharp crack, followed by a huge flash, and then a powerful explosion thundered through the parking lot.

It lasted barely a fraction of a second.

Everything seemed to turn deathly slow and silent, as if it were happening under water, in slow motion. The car lifted; Jan's body was blown into the air. Carla felt a tremendous force punch her body, and then everything was smothered in a waterfall of dust and masonry, metal and glass.

TV news vans with satellite dishes crowded the nearby streets, cordoned off for two blocks.

No one was allowed in or out except the police and emergency crews. An NYPD Bomb Squad truck was ushered through, its lights blazing. On a corner, a uniformed cop held back the crowds of onlookers.

"Move along now, folks, move along."

A man approached, fit-looking, stocky, muscular, and flashed a Jersey police detective's ID. "Hey, Officer, what's up?"

The cop from Midtown's North Precinct barely gave the ID a glance. If he had, he still wouldn't have noticed it was a forgery. The off-duty looked like that southern actor who was once married to Angelina Jolie—Billy Bob Thornton, that was the guy. With a ready grin, a kind of goofy white smile.

"There was an explosion in a parking lot near Carnegie Hall."

"Anybody hurt?"

"I heard we're talking bodies. They're still working the scene. Some kind of bomb, maybe a terrorist thing."

"Sounds like you guys got the dirty end of the stick. Take it easy, man." The guy moved off, down an empty side street. He pulled out a black Samsung cell phone, punched the number. A click sounded.

"It's done?"

"Yeah. The problem's gone—gone for good."

5

New York

She came awake to the sound of a man's voice and her eyes flickered open.

She was lying in a hospital bed in the ICU. A cheerful doctor wearing a blue bandana and fresh green scrubs leaned across and took her pulse.

"Welcome back, Carla. We've been hoping you'd come round."

A nurse checked the drips hooked up to both her arms, an electronic monitor flickering above. Carla felt groggy, confused, a branding iron pain in her forehead.

"Can you hear me?" the doctor asked.

"Y . . . yes. Where am I?"

"Mount Sinai Hospital. How do you feel?"

"Apart from a blinding headache, confused."

He winked at her, patting her hand. "No hearing damage then, or at least we hope. You're very lucky to be still alive, young lady."

"What's going on, what happened . . . ?" She noticed small bruises on her arms and on the backs of her hands, where drips had been inserted.

"We'll get to that. For now I need to know how you feel. Where's the headache? All over, or in your temples?"

She put up a hand to massage her forehead and felt a strip of bandage across it. "Right . . . right here."

"Any other pains or aches anywhere, or blurry vision?"

"I . . . I don't think so."

The doctor held up two fingers, moved his hand from left to right a couple of feet from her face, and observed her eye movement. "Try to follow my fingers with your eyes. How many digits do you see?"

"Two."

"How about now?"

"Four."

Next, the doctor probed Carla's ears with a lighted instrument, before he went to work with his stethoscope.

She felt the cold steel on her chest. "Please, can't you tell me what happened?"

"What do you remember?"

"Jan was standing by our car . . . it . . . it seemed to catch fire. There was an explosion."

"Anything else?"

Carla felt her forehead throbbing ease a little. "Everything after that is kind of vague."

The doctor's trained eye studied a series of old, thin scars down Carla's right arm but said nothing. "You suffered some external cuts from shrapnel, all minor really, some bruises and concussion. You've been here four days."

"You . . . you're serious?"

"You've been in and out of consciousness, but mostly semi-comatose."

Carla had completely lost track of time. She recalled the intensity of the explosion, the terrible *crump*. She vaguely remembered being dragged away from the blazing car and hearing the endless bleat of ambulance sirens, but after that she'd passed out and everything afterward was ghostly, disjointed. "Where's Jan? Is he safe . . . ?" Her throat felt dry, hoarse.

The doctor finished his examination, scribbled on the chart, and hung it on the end of the bed. It was as if he hadn't heard the question, or deliberately ignored it.

"Over the next few days we'll want to make certain you suffered no permanent damage. If not, we'll release you. The good news is that your scans show no internal signs of injury."

"I . . . I'm pregnant."

"We know. We contacted your doctor. You had a letter from him in your purse."

"Will my baby be okay?"

"So far everything still looks all right, Carla. But we'll talk again. Right now, there's someone who's anxious to see you."

The door opened again after the doctor and nurse left and her grandmother came in.

School friends of Carla's used to call Baize Joran the last of the hippies—she'd been to Woodstock, and wore those old colorful kaftans if the mood took her, or sometimes a diamond stud in her nose.

For a woman touching seventy-three who smoked a half pack of herbal cigarettes a day, rarely exercised beyond a touch of light housework, and was no stranger to a bottle of wine, she usually looked terrific.

Today, Baize looked burnt-out, as if she hadn't slept in a week. Her gray hair looked even wilder than usual, and she wore no makeup. Her face was the color of ashes, her eyes raw from crying.

She flung her arms around Carla and squeezed tightly, and neither of them seemed able to let go, Carla drowning in the familiar scented haze of Baize—Elizabeth Arden perfume and the faint aroma of herbal cigarettes.

"Where's Jan?"

Her grandmother's desperate look said it all as she stepped back, still clutching her hand. "He didn't make it, Carla. I . . . I'm so sorry."

Carla looked away, and found it difficult to breathe. The reality punched her like a gunshot, carrying with it a tide of grief and disbelief. But not anger, not yet. That would come later. "Oh, dear God."

Baize gripped both her hands.

"I'm here for you, Carla, I'm right here, sweetheart. I haven't moved from outside your room since they brought you here."

Carla found it difficult to breathe, her chest tight, and suddenly whatever strength she had in her body seemed to bleed out of her. She had lost the one man she had truly loved, who mattered most in her life. Her heart felt as if it were falling into a bottomless chasm.

Baize held on to her hands, said gently, "Do you feel like talking, Carla?"

"I don't know how I feel." She wanted to cry but somehow she couldn't; it was as if her mind were in a deep freeze.

"I just wish Dan was still here. We could do with someone like him to help us through this. He was always so capable, so strong. I feel so helpless."

"Tell . . . tell me about Jan."

Baize took a paper tissue from her sleeve, dabbed her eyes. "They tried hard to save him. It seems that he took most of the force of the blast. He lasted about an hour in ER. It's all so unreal. I still can't believe it."

Carla stared back at her grandmother, speechless. Jan dead. He died and she lived.

"Honey, why didn't you tell me about the baby?"

"We . . . we'd just found out." Racked by anguish, Carla felt hysterical, in the grip of a sudden uncontrollable urge. She went to raise herself from the bed. "I want to see Jan. I want to see him *right now*. Tell them to take me to the mortuary."

Baize stopped her. "The funeral was yesterday morning, Carla."

"Jan's been buried?"

"Paul thought it better for the service to go ahead. He thought it better to bury his brother. We didn't know when you'd come round."

Carla made a fist of her hand, put it to her mouth, her eyes wet again. Every part of her body shrieked with grief. She didn't even get the chance to say goodbye.

Baize's grip tightened. "So many people attended the service. Paul's devastated. He wanted me to call him as soon as you came round."

Carla was overcome, and couldn't speak.

"It's not going to be easy in the coming days and months, sweetheart. But you have to stay strong. For your baby's sake. It's how Jan would have wanted it."

"What . . . what do the police say?"

"They interviewed me, but I couldn't tell them anything, and they've made no public statements. But a lot of VIPs attended the concert. The mayor and lots of important foreign dignitaries. The newspapers are saying it may have been a terrorist bomb. That it looks like a case of mistaken identity, and whoever was responsible picked the wrong victim."

"A bomb?"

"The police wouldn't confirm or deny it. But it makes some kind of sense. Why would anyone deliberately want to kill Jan?"

Carla looked toward the window, a sickening emptiness in the pit of her stomach. She had been trembling, and now she began to shake violently. She slid down her hand, felt where her baby was growing in her stomach. She should have felt joy, but at that moment she felt nothing, only despair. "I . . . I can't believe this . . ."

"None of us can, Carla. It's so senseless."

The door opened and the doctor with the bandana reappeared. "Mrs. Joran, sorry to intrude but I had a question for Carla."

He came over and took hold of Carla's right arm, his fingertips touching the series of thin, faintly raised scars down her arm. "When did this injury happen?"

Baize replied, "A long time ago. When Carla was eleven. Why, is anything the matter?"

"Just professional curiosity. I worked in microsurgery for a time. What happened exactly?"

Baize hesitated. "An . . . an accident. Carla cut her arm badly on a broken window pane."

The doctor let go of Carla's arm, gave a brief smile. "It's excellent work. The surgeon did a good job."

He moved back toward the door. "I'm sorry for interrupting. But we've got some more tests to do, so we'll need more time with your granddaughter, Mrs. Joran." His eyes met Carla's. "You know about Jan . . . ?"

"Yes." Carla felt the branding iron pain again.

"I always prefer that a patient has a little time to recover before they have to be told news. That isn't always possible. We did everything we could. If it's any consolation, Jan wouldn't have felt a thing. He was unconscious when they brought him in, and never regained consciousness. I'm truly sorry."

Carla said nothing. There was nothing she could say that would have changed anything. She felt fragile. As if there were thin ice beneath her feet and it could crack at any time and plunge her into freezing water.

And then the door closed and the doctor was gone.

Later that evening, two police detectives from the Midtown North Precinct came to see her.

One was named Soames; he was about fifty, with expensive white teeth.

The second detective, Reilly, had thick, wild red hair, with muscular arms, mid-thirties.

They asked about Jan's work, if he had any enemies, if he owed anyone money, had any connections to organized crime, or to a terrorist group, or knew anyone who did.

It seemed absurd to ask such questions of Jan, but the detectives wanted to know everything. They were very thorough men, probing her gently and tactfully, taking notes, but they seemed confused about a motive for the blast.

"Was it a bomb?"

"Yes, it was, ma'am. A pipe bomb under your Volvo."

"How did it get there?"

"We've no idea yet. It could have been placed there deliberately or it could have been meant for another vehicle and rolled under your car by accident. We can't tell yet how it was detonated until we find more evidence."

"My grandmother said the newspapers are claiming it was a case of mistaken identity."

White Teeth, the older of the two detectives, spread his hands. "That's really the only sensible answer we can come up with right now. There was over a hundred and fifty VIPs and dignitaries at the concert that night. Any one of them might have been a target."

"Don't you have any clues?"

Red Hair ran a hand though his Celtic mop. "Not really, Mrs. Lane. We've a lot of backgrounds to check. This is going to take time. We'll likely need to talk with you some more. We'd also appreciate it if you inform us if you need to leave the state or the country for any reason."

"Why?"

"Ma'am, until we know the reason for your husband's death, and what we're dealing with here, I'd like to know you're safe. So if you get any suspicious calls, or you feel in any kind of danger, you call us at once."

They finally left, leaving her their cards, and then Carla was alone.

She felt exhausted, every part of her racked by a powerful fatigue as if her senses were shutting down; the body's way of handling the stress and aftershock.

She looked at her hands—they were numbly folding and unfolding the corners of her blanket.

Survival was the thing, she knew. She had to get through these days, for her baby's sake. She would do whatever she had to.

Just before midnight a nurse came and took her blood pressure and gave her a mild sedative. She closed her eyes after that, her mind lingering in that place where a flimsy curtain hangs between reality and dreams.

As she lay there, on the edge of sleep, a mad, disjointed film clattered behind her closed eyes.

The parking lot near Carnegie Hall, a smiling Jan coming toward her, the explosion, a burst of white, celestial light; the faces of a small, emaciated boy staring up at her with huge sad eyes; a woman's frail hand, outstretched toward her. A bright lightbulb swinging in a dark room. A fluttering of snowflakes falling on woods on a cold winter's night.

The images floated ghostlike, as if in some distant world.

Aware that she was sobbing, she drew up her legs, her hands between her knees in the fetal position, like a child seeking the comfort of its mother's womb, until at last sleep claimed her with its velvet embrace.

PHOENIX, ARIZONA

Sunrise.

Orange rays splaying their fingers of light across the parched desert.

The man was still awake, lounging on the couch, watching the TV screen with a blank stare.

He hadn't slept all night and the glass in his hand was empty of Scotch. He scratched his unshaven jaw, stood, and checked the bottle.

A dribble remained.

He ran a hand though his hair. The cable TV was showing *The Three Stooges.* He stood there, watching the screen with sunken red eyes.

Larry hitting Moe on the head with a baseball bat and then Moe chasing Larry around in circles. He'd watched those reruns so many times as a kid and always laughed out loud at that scene. He wasn't laughing now.

Upstairs, his wife and daughters slept. Their photographs adorned the shelves. The girls aged nine and twelve. His wife, all-American, blond, beautiful. The family photos on the walls, the ranch, the art pieces scattered about the house, all attested to his perfect life.

The ranch was on five acres in a desirable subdivision, with his studio on the side. Never a hint of trouble in his life in the last twenty years.

And now this.

He swallowed the last dribble of Scotch, and tossed the bottle on the couch.

He felt drunk.

He wanted to feel even more drunk.

To forget.

There had to be something else to drink. Vodka? Wine? Windex? Scope mouthwash as a last resort.

He could have slept, given in to exhaustion and rested his tortured mind, but he knew he wanted to wallow, to feel his pain. Like a man on top of a burning building who had a rope thrown to him from a rescue helicopter, he didn't want that rope, not just yet: *Give me a moment here, okay? Let me feel the searing agony.*

He padded into the kitchen, like a sleepwalker. The suitcases were still in the corner, and looking at them made the memories crowd in on him again. He searched among the cupboards.

No alcohol.

He swore.

He needed fresh air.

He lurched toward the patio door, slid it open, the sun already warming his skin. Not branding-iron hot yet, but give it a few hours.

The rich red Arizona soil stretched to distant hills. He took a deep breath and stood there looking out at the desert sunrise, as they had often stood as kids, and felt his memories attack him. He wanted to cry. But he'd cried so much these last few days he had no tears left.

Then something odd clicked in the back of his mind.

The dog.

The dog hadn't barked.

The dog hadn't come to greet him.

The dog always barked and greeted him with a wagging tail when he came out in the morning.

Colleen's kennel was around the side of the house.

He'd made sure to leave enough food and water for while they were away. Now that he thought about it, he hadn't seen or heard Colleen when they got home last night. He'd been too distracted to take any notice. The dog often wandered off into the desert alone.

He stepped out into the yard.

Taking a deep breath of air into his lungs he stretched his arms again.

That's when he saw the black clump about fifty yards from the back of the house.

His heart beating faster, he walked out, and saw the dog lying on her side.

Colleen's mouth was open, her tongue hanging out.

A crimson gash stained the soil around the dog's neck where its throat had been cut.

The man recoiled, stumbling to the ground, and threw up.

He wiped his mouth and pushed himself up.

Suddenly he felt stone-cold sober.

And close to tears again.

He didn't want his wife and daughters to see the dog. Didn't want them to know. He looked out at the desert.

Nothing.

A few neighbors' houses nearby, but no sign of life. Not even a whisper of wind.

Frantically, he kicked over the crimson with sandy soil until the red Arizona earth covered the blood.

Then he ran to the garage to fetch the shovel.

7

The sun was struggling that day, angry white waves clawing the Long Island shoreline.

Not like the kind of days when she and Jan would swim in the sea.

Baize pulled up in the driveway and switched off the engine.

Carla looked at the yellow painted door among the row of neat detached houses overlooking the gray Atlantic.

Once, the house had offered everything she and Jan wanted: peace, comfort, the sea, a place to start a family. Now it looked empty, the curtains drawn. Jan's favorite rocking chair abandoned on the porch, next to hers.

Baize touched her arm as Carla went to climb out. "You don't have to do this, you know. Let me come with you?"

"I'd prefer to go in alone."

"Carla . . ."

"Please. I want to stay here tonight."

"You really think that's such a good idea?"

"Maybe not, but I have to."

Baize sighed. "Okay, just let me drive over to my place and grab a change of clothes and some toiletries."

Carla opened the car door.

"Give me a little while, okay? There are some things I need to do."

She put the key in the yellow door. The wood creaked as she moved inside.

Home. Not that Carla could call it home anymore, not with Jan gone, but right now it was where she had to be.

The hallway was cluttered with mail. Mostly letters addressed to Mr. and Mrs. Jan Lane. She placed them on the hall table. Glancing back, she saw Baize start the car, then roll down the window and light a herbal cigarette.

Baize waved.

She waved back, and the car drove away.

In the front room, the big old Zeiss telescope on its tripod still pointed seaward. She recalled the first day she and Jan were shown the house, by a little old real estate lady named Myrtle, in her eighties and long past retirement, and who wore a hearing aid and kept reminding them, "Just remember, I'm not completely deaf, so don't be afraid to make me an offer."

She recalled the first time they made love here.

And the last.

Now Jan was gone. She simply couldn't believe it, or the manner of his death—there was no logic to it.

But she still sensed him, in this house.

Her hand went down to touch her pregnant stomach, as if to reassure herself. That morning when she woke she felt a touch of nausea, but the doctor told her nausea and fatigue were to be expected in pregnancy.

She walked through every room, taking in the smells. In the bedroom, the big walnut bed was made up with white cotton sheets. She pulled back the curtains and sunlight drenched the room.

She remembered summer mornings when she and Jan would run out into the waves together, giggling and laughing like kids.

She felt that nothing could ease her anguish. She would never hear Jan's voice or laughter again, never see him.

She felt so desolate that a part of her felt like walking down to the sea, and pushing out into the white waves, and not coming back.

For no reason she could fathom she crossed to the closet, removed all of Jan's clothes, and flung them on the bed.

A frightening surge of anger raged through her, and it felt molten hot. She was furious at Jan being taken away from her, furious at losing him just when their life together was beginning.

Tears racked her, and she flailed her fists on the bed and tore at the clothes, until all her strength was gone and she lay there, feeling completely broken, and her eyes were red and dry.

* * *

"If it's any consolation, I felt the same way after your grandfather died."

"Tell me."

"The day they called me and told me his helicopter was shot down on a training exercise, that there was no hope, I was devastated. It felt as if my entire world had ended."

They sat in the rockers on the porch, Baize touching Carla's arm.

"You were in school. I took all Dan's clothes out of the closets, piled them high, and lay on top of them, sobbing my eyes out. It was as if I was trying to will him back."

Carla always wished she'd known her grandfather better. An army colonel, he'd died when she was sixteen. "Did you have dreams, too?"

Baize laughed. "Dreams? It was like your grandma was on crack, sweetie."

"Troubled dreams?"

"You bet. They came at me like a bayonet charge."

"Tell me."

"I guess it was because we'd been so close all our lives. Dan and I were high school sweethearts. It didn't matter that we were complete opposites. He was set on a military career, but me, I was something of a wild child. He used to jokingly call me his Yoko Ono." Baize looked across. "Why, are you having dreams?"

"More like nightmares."

"Have you been taking any medication?"

"Only folic acid for the baby. And your herbal sleeping pills at night to relax me."

"Tell me about the nightmares."

"It's like a film playing over and over in my head."

"What sort of film?"

Carla considered. "I see Jan's death. The explosion. A white light. But other images are mixed in with them. Images I've been seeing for a while now. Months maybe."

"What kind of images?"

"Strange ones. Bizarre, I guess."

"Describe the images, Carla."

"A woman with her hand outstretched is reaching toward me. A frail little boy stares up at me, as if he's pleading for something. I see a swinging lightbulb in a darkened room. I see snowflakes falling at night. It's so real, I can almost feel their coldness."

Baize looked concerned. "These people, the woman and the boy."

"What about them?"

"Could . . . could you see their faces?"

"No. I try to focus on the images, to make sense of it all, but I can't. Why?"

"But the images disturb you?"

Carla looked at her. "Of course. And they seem to be getting more frequent. I've had them on and off now for months. They're even more intense since Jan died."

"Did you ever tell Jan?"

"I meant to that day in the restaurant but I never got the chance. Why?"

Baize bit her lower lip. "I think there's someone you ought to see, Carla."

"Who?"

"Dr. Raymond Leon."

"That nice man, your therapist friend?"

"Yes."

"Why do you think that?"

"Because he helped me. And I think he can help you with the nightmares. I don't want you being troubled, especially not when you're pregnant. I'll make an appointment."

"For when?"

"Tomorrow if he can fit you in. Will you do that for me, please? It'll make me feel better knowing you're talking to someone."

"Not tomorrow."

"Why not?"

"There's something I want to do in memory of Jan. And someone I need to see."

That evening she booked the flight to Phoenix.

A Delta early bird leaving the next morning at seven.

Then she sat on her bed with the clock radio on.

Baize had placed a small wicker basket filled with fresh lavender on the nightstand, the scent calming. The music on the radio she recognized—the haunting strains of Led Zeppelin's ballad "Stairway to Heaven."

For a classical musician, she always thought Jan was a frustrated rocker at heart. It was one of his favorite pieces and it made her think of him, and suddenly she felt completely alone.

As she stood at the window she saw a young couple ramble along the beach. The man carried a little boy in his arms. The woman looked pregnant again, her belly swollen.

The couple touched their heads together as they shared a joke, and then the man leaned in to kiss the woman's cheek.

Carla stared at them as they disappeared toward the sand dunes at Cove Point, where she and Jan used to like to swim.

She turned off the radio, lay down on her bed, and closed her eyes.

A little later she swallowed one of the green herbal pills with a glass of water and curled up, praying for sleep.

8

PHOENIX, ARIZONA

She took a cab from the airport and drove north in the shimmering heat.

The ranch property was in a quiet community. It was really two houses in one: an old ranch house built more than fifty years ago, and a large modern extension with an artist's studio. A white Mustang was parked under a metal awning.

As Carla's cab drove up the dirt track, Paul came out of the studio to greet her.

He looked tired and gaunt. He was dressed in jeans and sneakers, his worn T-shirt smeared with paint and mud stains. On his wrist was a leather strap covered in turquoise beads, his long dark hair cut in a fringe.

He looked so like Jan—the same ready smile, the same determined brown eyes and handsome looks and slim artist's hands.

She almost cried as she stepped out of the car and he hugged her.

"It's good to see you, Carla. Come inside, I've got some fresh coffee brewing." He put an arm around her shoulder and led her into the house.

It was all white painted walls, and sparsely furnished with hand-carved ranch-style furniture. The studio door was open and inside looked messy, with a potter's wheel, the floor and walls crammed with bright colored pottery—plates and vases and pieces of art in pastel blues, vivid reds, striking yellows.

Out back she saw the brick-built kiln her brother-in-law had built with his own hands.

Paul had done well for himself, a beautiful wife and two pretty daughters. He had carved out a reputation as a skilled artisan and designer, with VIP clients from Hollywood and New York who flew in specially to buy his work.

In the kitchen he placed a coffeepot and some cups and chocolate-chip cookies on a tray. "You look better than the last time I saw you, in the hospital. The baby's still okay?"

"So the doctors say."

"Thank heaven for that. How've you been coping?"

"Just barely. And you?"

He smiled bravely but his eyes were bloodshot, grief showing in the tightness around his mouth, his shoulders slumped as if he were carrying a weight. "Trying to get back into work, but I just can't seem to concentrate. Let's go sit on the back porch, okay?" His face looked serious. "There are some things we need to talk about."

9

He poured their coffee. On the walls of the living room behind them were family snapshots of his wife and daughters.

"Where's everyone?"

"Kim took the girls to see their grandparents in Sedona. They ought to be back tomorrow."

Carla looked out at the desert landscape. It was stark but beautiful, dotted with cactus plants, the pastel sky so achingly blue it almost hurt her eyes.

Paul sipped his coffee. "Jan and I loved that view the first day we came here. The colors, the light. It's always been a very special place."

"Tell me about those days."

"Jan never told you?"

"He sometimes spoke about losing his parents back in Croatia. How you and he witnessed a lot of pain and horror during the war in your homeland. It affected him deeply. I think maybe it was why he was such a great musician."

"He didn't often talk about his pain, but he sure put it into his work."

"You're right. He always seemed able to draw on such a deep well of emotion to play such haunting music. For some reason I felt a connection to him because of that."

"Me, I always wanted to forget about our past, but Jan always kept a photograph he cut from a magazine and stuck on his bedroom wall to remind him of that time. Of the pain he felt, and the injustice he witnessed. He hated injustice."

Paul hesitated, looked away, then back again. "Jan was ten, I was fourteen when we came here. Our parents had been killed when the Serbs shelled our town. Our heads were so messed up by the sights we saw in the war—dead bodies, entire families shot and killed, ethnic cleansing—that it took us quite a while to settle in. For weeks we wouldn't speak at all, except to each other. Two little orphans clinging to one another for comfort and safety."

"But you found peace here?"

"It was like going from hell to paradise. We were grateful to be alive, grateful that my father's sister and her husband offered to become our guardians, instead of spending our lives in an orphanage."

He jerked his chin toward the cactus-strewn desert.

"We had some good times out there together, my kid brother and me. Our uncle would take us riding on his horses out on the desert trails. We'd see rattlesnakes, coyotes. It was like some Wild West adventure we'd seen on the movie screen in the local flea pit back in Croatia. I'm going to miss him."

Carla couldn't hold it in. She gave an anguished cry and wiped her eyes. "*Why,* Paul? Why did Jan have to die? Why would anyone want to kill him?"

Paul's face became grim. He fell silent.

"What is it?"

"Ronald Reagan, the U.S. president."

"What . . . what about him?"

"In 1987 he told the Russian leader, Mikhail Gorbachev, to tear down the Berlin Wall. It came down two years later when the Soviet Union crumbled, and everything changed. All its former satellite states were on their way to independence. Poland, the Baltic states, Czechoslovakia, and my former homeland, Croatia, which was part of Yugoslavia."

"What has this got to do with Jan's death?"

Paul looked at her. "A lot. Do you know that Yugoslavia was a manufactured state? A bunch of independent republics that were forced together by kings, or dictators. People like Marshal Tito or Slobodan Milosevic, who supported the communists."

Carla nodded, although she wasn't sure she was following.

"The main three states were Christian Orthodox Serbia, Catholic Croatia, and Bosnia, which is mostly Muslim. For hundreds of years, these three have often fought each other in bitter wars. The biggest dog in the fight was always Serbia. When Yugoslavia began to pull apart, it was led by the brutal and corrupt Serb president, Slobodan Milosevic, He had the strongest military, so he controlled the entire country.

"But all those republics now wanted independence. The country started to break apart. Milosevic ruthlessly tried to put down any revolt that threatened Serbia's power."

Paul sat back. "And this is where it gets interesting. What do you know about Balkan and Serbian organized crime?"

"Nothing. Why?"

"There's a long, long tradition of ruthless crime and banditry in that part of the world that some say can be traced back to Roman times, when mountain outlaws in the region robbed Caesar's supply trains marching east to Constantinople. Hitler's convoys invading Yugoslavia centuries later suffered the same fate. The Serb mafia make the Italian mob look like a bunch of charming old ladies."

Paul explained that it was the breakup of Yugoslavia, during a war lasting over five years, that made the Serb organized crime gangs billions in profits.

President Slobodan Milosevic desperately needed more troops to halt the breakup of Yugoslavia, and so he made the mafia an offer they couldn't refuse: amnesty for the gangster clans and a vast supply of weapons to equip their own paramilitary special forces in return for aiding the Serb army.

The mafia's job was simple: to help put down revolts in the breakaway ethnic republics—mostly regions within Croatia and Bosnia with millions of civilians who had chosen to no longer be a part of a greater Serbia. In addition, they often ethnically cleansed those regions, by either massacring the inhabitants or removing them forcibly.

The war meant more than two million displaced refugees on all sides: men, women, and children evicted from their homes, businesses, and farms. It meant evil slaughter on a massive scale—a quarter million dead and many more tortured, wounded, and injured.

Formed into mobile, well-equipped paramilitary squads—some composed of thugs and vicious crime gangs released from high-security prisons—the mafia-led units scoured the countryside, inflicting murder and mayhem on a terrified civilian population, and profiting on the battlefield by looting and stealing.

Their victims were mostly Muslims, civilians and paramilitaries alike, but Christians and Orthodox also felt their wrath.

Towns were shelled, villages torched, entire cities ransacked. Banks were robbed and their vaults emptied.

Entire ethnic groups were terrorized and executed, and their property and belongings confiscated. Even their refrigerators, washing machines, and TVs ended up being sold in Belgrade's second-hand markets.

Wealthier victims were often first forced to sign documents surrendering their homes, business premises, money, cars, and jewelry. As a final indignity, they would be charged a fee for being transported out of town, to be imprisoned or executed.

For the crime gangs quickly learned a lesson Hitler's SS had learned decades before—that wholesale slaughter can be a profitable enterprise.

Paul sat back. "Camps were also set up to imprison adult female prisoners, adolescent girls, and male and female children—and many of their fathers, brothers, and sons above the age of fourteen were destined to be callously executed."

He looked toward the desert, revulsion on his face before he turned back. "The sole purpose of the women's camps, later called 'houses of rape and horror' by war crimes prosecutors, was to provide for the sexual pleasure of the paramilitary gangs, while they carried out their murder and theft. Some rape victims were documented to be as young as seven years old."

Carla listened in grim silence, then said, "Why are you telling me all this?"

"Because there's a reason Jan was killed, and you deserve to know it."

10

"You mustn't tell anyone, not even Baize. This is just between us."

"What are you saying, Paul?"

"Jan was trying to hunt down wanted killers and bring them to justice. That's why he died."

There was a shocked silence. Carla stared back. "What killers?"

"You remember that Jan often went abroad on concerts?"

"Of course. That was work."

"Sometimes. Other times it was to talk with an organization called Families for Justice. It's a group of relatives of victims of the genocide in the former Yugoslavia who try to track down war criminals."

"What are you talking about?"

"Jan wanted to help find the brutal camp guards and executioners who carried out so many of the war crimes, the ones who escaped. Have you any idea what happened to those wanted men?"

"No."

"NATO caught the big names—the top army officers and politicians who ordered the ethnic cleansing and the butchery. We all saw the names in the headlines, the ones tried in the international courts at The Hague. People like Milosevic and his top henchman, Ratko Mladic. But many of the lesser-known thugs who carried out atrocities avoided prosecution."

"How?"

"Some vanished abroad and created new identities for themselves. Others were aided by supporters or friends. A number of the more brutal Serb paramilitary commanders had connections to organized crime, the Balkan and Russian mafias, who helped them do a disappearing act."

"Where did they disappear to?"

"Anywhere you can think of. Europe, South America, Australia, even the United States. Just like the Nazis of old, they fled like rats deserting a ship. Jan was determined to bring as many of them as he could to justice. That's what he was doing in his spare time. That's what consumed him."

"Why didn't Jan tell me all this?"

"I guess he didn't want you to be involved. There were other reasons, too."

"What reasons?"

"These were dangerous people he was hunting down. He thought you might be worried about that."

"I'm still waiting for an answer, Paul. Why did Jan die?"

"Because he got close to identifying several brutal paramilitary commanders who were never brought to trial. That's why."

"Has this got to do with your parents' deaths? How they died in the shelling? Is that why he was hunting these war criminals down?"

Paul didn't answer but his eyes welled up with tears, and he put a hand on his jaw and looked away. Finally, he said, "Yes, that was part of it. These men are just like the ones who destroyed our village and ruined our lives."

He looked at her. "I still remember that day. How we made it out alive was a miracle. Anyone who didn't flee fast enough or survived the shelling were rounded up and either executed or imprisoned."

"How do you know what Jan was doing, Paul?"

"Because he told me. What we lived though as kids made us very close. We kept no secrets from each other."

"These people paid someone to murder him?"

"I'm sure they didn't need to. They could do it themselves. Butchers like those didn't need to pay others to kill for them."

"You mean to say someone just decided to kill Jan because he was investigating them?"

"They're dangerous people, Carla. With horrific crimes in their pasts. They probably saw Jan as a threat to their freedom. A threat they decided to eliminate."

Carla sank back in the chair, shaking her head, her hand going to her mouth.

"How long have you known about this work Jan was doing?"

"Since he got involved a few years ago. I begged him to stay out of it, but Jan was determined to carry on."

"Why did he do it? Why risk his life?"

"Because he wanted to speak for the dead. Because he wanted to see these killers and torturers face the courts. He was obsessed with finding the guilty."

"Were you involved, too?"

"No, I kept my nose out of it."

"You should have told me all this before now."

"Jan insisted that I not breathe a word to you. I had to keep my promise to him."

"Why didn't you tell the police everything you've just told me?"

"Carla, you don't understand."

"Understand what?"

"I know what these people are capable of. As a boy, I witnessed their terrible crimes. I saw the villages they destroyed, the victims they butchered. Men, women, children. They're not human, they're unfeeling beasts. Like the worst of the Nazis, they showed no mercy."

"Who killed Jan? *Who?* Tell me their names."

Paul pushed himself from his chair. "I don't know their names. Jan didn't confide everything to me. But I'm pretty sure it was the same people he was trying to track down."

"Why do you say that?"

"Because Jan told me he was worried for his safety. That he'd noticed that he was being followed on a few occasions."

"Followed by whom?"

"He didn't know. But he felt certain he was being watched."

"That's not proof."

"No, it's not. But he'd had a veiled warning."

"What kind of warning?"

"A call to his cell phone a few months back."

"Tell me."

"The caller spoke in Serbian. It was a man. He told Jan not to stick his nose in where it wasn't wanted. That's all, then the man put down the phone."

"That's still not proof."

"One of his contacts in the Families for Justice called me and told me he was convinced that these people killed Jan. That others were murdered in the past, when they got too close."

"Are you going to tell the police about the men Jan was hunting? Are you going to tell them everything now?"

"No, I'm not."

"I don't understand."

Paul glanced at the family photographs on the sideboard.

"I have a wife and two young daughters to protect. I've already lost my parents and my brother to those beasts. I want no more bloodshed, no more murder. The men who killed Jan got what they wanted—his silence. They'll have no gripe with anyone else so long as we don't stick our noses in it. It's over, it's done. We have to let it be, Carla."

Anger flared in her voice. "He was your brother, for heaven's sake! How can you sit there and say that so calmly?"

"Would it help if I shouted?"

"I can't believe that you'll accept Jan's death that easily."

Paul stared back, and Carla saw the wet at the edges of his eyes. "What's easy about it? I loved him. My heart's broken. I've lost the only living relative I had. You speak as if I have a choice. But I've got none. These people are a law unto themselves. If you pursue them, or inform on them, they will find you and kill you."

"What about the police? They can protect us."

"No, they can't." He leaned forward. "Do you know what happened to the first Serb prime minister after Milosevic? A man named Zoran Dindic. It was he who sent Milosevic to trial at The Hague, then ordered the arrest of Serb war criminals with connections to organized crime."

"No, tell me."

"A Serb mafia hit man put a sniper's bullet in him. They assassinated the prime minister, for God's sake."

He shook his head. "All the mafia hoods behind that crime have still never been caught, despite Interpol, despite the FBI, and despite almost every police force on the planet out to arrest them."

He sat back again. "These men are hard and violent gangsters. Into drug smuggling, prostitution, murder, human trafficking, you name it. Cross them and there's no escaping their wrath. They've killed a prime minister. Do you think they'd stop at killing me and my family?" He glanced at her stomach. "Or a pregnant woman?"

He stood, massaging his neck. "They killed our dog. I found her in the backyard with her throat cut."

"*What?*"

"It happened while we were at Jan's funeral. I had to bury her out in the desert. I couldn't tell Kim and the girls. They think the dog ran away."

"How can you know for certain that it was a threat?"

"Come on, Carla, a blade is a favorite Balkan weapon. You're lucky if there's a single warning. After that, you're dead."

He placed a hand firmly on her shoulder. "I'm telling you what I told Jan. To stay out of it. And don't make things worse by informing the police. I love you, Carla; you're part of my family. Your safety matters to me."

He leaned down, kissed her on the forehead. "You have Jan's child to think about. Just be glad you didn't die, too, or lose your baby."

She was silent.

"Will you stay tonight?" he asked.

"I wanted to come to this place he loved so much and stay here in memory of him. But now I don't know, Paul."

"Please stay. And don't be angry with me, Carla. I'm trying to do what's best. To keep us all safe and avoid another tragedy like Jan's death."

She stared at him, hard. "And what about doing what's right?"

His mouth tightened, and he was grim-faced.

"I've made up Jan's bed in the old part of the house. The one he had as a kid and when he lived here for a time after college. He always slept in that room whenever he came back here to prepare before a concert. He called it his Arizona office. I thought you'd want to sleep there tonight."

He bent to pick up his empty coffee cup. "Maybe you'd like to have some of his personal things from his room? I think he would have wanted that."

11

It was a simple room. Sand-colored walls, a single bed, and a beige carpet.

The window looked out onto the back of the house, toward the mountains and the desert. Carla sat there, taking it all in.

White-painted bookcases were built into the walls either side of the window. Boys' adventure stories, sheet music, books on the piano and musical instruments.

A stack of old videotapes and DVDs, of the movies he'd loved as a kid: *Home Alone*, *The Addams Family*, and *The Lion King*. And the ones Jan liked when he grew older: *Casablanca, Cinema Paradiso, The Mission, Legends of the Fall.*

On a shelf was a model aircraft, and some polished stones he had picked up in the desert. On another was a pair of hand-painted plaster-cast lizards.

Buried behind some books on the shelves, some photographs were pinned with thumbtacks to a corkboard. She removed the books.

On the board was a photograph of Jan, aged about ten, sitting solemn-faced on the back porch of the house. Another of him all smiles, making sand castles on a beach.

A photograph with the school baseball team, a little older, smiling and happy. There were snapshots with his aunt and uncle and Paul at Disneyland, soon after they'd arrived in the United States. A few more of him as a young musician, and in concert.

One of the images was different, and looked as if it had been cut out of a book or magazine.

It showed lines of women and children wearing disheveled clothes, some piled onto tractors, but most of them walking, carrying their belongings on their backs as they filed past the camera. Armed Serb soldiers lining their route looked on with cold indifference.

Carla realized it was a photograph of the victims of the ethnic cleansing.

There were no tears on the faces, just gaunt despair. The kind of despair that comes when all hope is gone and prayers go unanswered.

Among the victims was a mother with a small boy and a girl wearing shabby clothes. They stared out at the camera, their wide, innocent eyes full of fear. The stark fear that only children can show when they sense danger. The mother looked fraught, her face desolate.

Carla couldn't explain it, but something about the image of the mother and her two small children made her heart stutter. The image spoke to her.

It was as if she could *feel* their hopelessness, their fear, their terror. The photograph reminded her of the haunting images of Nazi death camp victims.

She shook her head in dismay.

What kind of men could do this to innocent women and children?

What kind of men could massacre thousands of fathers and brothers and sons and mothers and daughters in cold blood and call it a justified act of war?

No wonder Jan had wanted to track down these killers.

Her fists clenched angrily as she stared at the armed men in the photograph. They were the same kind who had murdered the gentle man she had married.

And she saw him again, walking across the campus, his fringe blowing in the wind, that lopsided smile on his face. Kind, gentle Jan, who loved her and always put others first. Who had a secret in his heart she never knew about.

When she felt her eyes become wet, when she could bear it no longer, she rose and left the room, quietly closing the door after her.

"I'd like to take something from Jan's room."

Paul was sitting in the living room reading a book when she went in.

"Of course, what is it?"

"One of the photographs."

He gave a tight, sad smile. "The one on the beach?"

"No, the one of the women and children fleeing the war."

He paled visibly. "Why that?"

"I want to be reminded of what Jan did."

His hand was shaking a little as he held on to his book. "Sure. Whatever you want, Carla."

"I'll leave early tomorrow. Apologize to Kim and the girls. Give them my love."

And she turned and went back into the bedroom.

That night she lay on Jan's bed.

She used her cell phone to connect to the Internet and read more about what Paul told her of the war, and the Serb mafia.

She saw more photographs, some of them deeply disturbing: of families executed, and victims of the Serb concentration camps.

But every now and then she looked over at the photograph of the lines of fleeing families, at the mother and two small children with terror in their faces.

She couldn't keep her eyes off their image.

When she switched off her cell and undressed and lay down to sleep it still haunted her, and combined with fragments of her nightmares as the same disjointed film played out in her mind: the face of a small, emaciated boy staring up at her with huge, sad eyes; a woman's frail hand, outstretched toward her; the bright electric light swinging in a dark room. Snowflakes falling on woods on a winter's night.

In the middle of it all, she saw the small boy float closer, his mouth open in pleading, as if he was begging for her to save him, but no words came. For some reason, the vision felt like a knife in her heart.

She thought for a moment she might be going mad.

She took one of the green pills and swallowed it with a sip of water. She pulled the pillows to her face, her legs drawn up, her hands clasped together between her knees.

A little later the room started to swim, and then the first waves of sleep rolled in.

*   *   *

The next morning Paul drove her to the airport in his white Mustang.

He waited while she checked in, then escorted her to the boarding gate. "Take care of yourself, Carla. And please, don't judge me too harshly. What will you do?"

"I'm too angry to think clearly right now. But when things have calmed down I'll consider my options."

"What does that mean?"

"I don't know, Paul. My life seems upside down at the minute. If it wasn't for the baby, I'd probably have cracked before now."

"Are you going to take my advice?"

"I know I'm going to think long and hard about what you said."

"Maybe we'll talk again, once we can both think more clearly? So long, Carla."

He kissed her cheek and Carla filed toward the security barrier.

She didn't notice the man leaning against a column in the departures area.

He was fit-looking, stocky and muscular, and he was reading a newspaper as he observed them both, a pair of earphones stuck in his ears, the wires connected to his cell phone.

As Carla passed through security, the man tapped his phone and made the call.

12

NEW YORK

"Why Dr. Leon?"

Baize's Chevrolet stop-started in traffic. She hunched forward in the driver's seat. "Because he's caring, someone you'll feel safe with and can trust. Besides, you've met him before."

"Half a dozen times socially with you over the last twenty years, but otherwise I hardly know the man, so why him in particular?"

"Because he's also the best. I saw him after your grandfather died. We both knew Dr. Leon as friends for many years. If it hadn't been for him, I think I would have come apart at the seams when your grandfather died."

"You did come apart at the seams."

"Okay, so I did. But it would have been a lot worse without the doctor's help."

Baize slapped the brakes at a traffic light.

"So why all the mystery?"

"What mystery, Carla?"

"I get the feeling there's more to this. That you're not telling me everything."

"I'm just a little concerned, that's all. You know how therapists prod and probe. Sometimes they make you see aspects to yourself that you never knew, sweetheart."

"No, I don't. I've never been to one before."

Baize gave her a look, and swung the Chevrolet onto a street full of imposing houses. "Actually, you have, Carla."

"What?"

"When you were a child, you had therapy with Dr. Leon. But you don't remember, do you?"

"*No.* How old was I?"

"Eleven."

"For . . . how long did I have therapy?"

"Many months. Many long and difficult months."

"I don't understand. I ought to remember. But I don't. Why?"

Baize pulled up outside a big old house. It was built of wood and brick and looked inviting, Norman Rockwell style, the kind of place where you'd feel at ease.

"I'm sure Dr. Leon will explain. It's best you hear it from him."

Dr. Raymond Leon was a tall, elderly man with a graying Van Dyke beard and warm, wrinkled blue eyes.

He looked cheerful, one corner of his mouth raised in a permanent smile, as if he saw the world and its inhabitants with wry humor.

The house was both his home and office. He opened the door into a brightly lit suite and indicated a well worn but cozy leather chair. Carla felt at home, the room familiar, as if she'd been here before.

"It's been a while, Carla. Take a seat, it's good to see you again."

"You, too."

She expected to see the walls dressed with glass-framed academic qualifications, all stamped with shiny gilt or wax-red seals. Instead she saw a collection of family photographs, a smiling Dr. Leon in many of them, hugging his grandchildren.

On another wall she noticed framed drawings in bright, gaudy colors, some of them with weird shapes and forms, that looked as if they had been sketched by kids.

One of the drawings showed the stick figure of a crying child, the raindrop-shaped tears out of proportion to the figure. In the background lay a mass of what looked like bodies, daubed with splashes of red.

Carla shuddered: for some reason the images made her uneasy.

Dr. Leon picked up a lime-green plastic folder from his desk in the chair opposite, his legs crossed, one of his worn loafers dangling.

"May I ask you a question, Doctor?"

"Sure."

"Baize just told me I had therapy with you when I was a child. Yet for some reason I have no recollection."

"What exactly did she tell you?"

"Just that I had therapy. She didn't explain."

Dr. Leon placed the folder on the side table. "We'll talk about that shortly, Carla. But first, let me tell you something about myself professionally that you may not be aware of."

The doctor sat back, resting his hands on his knees. "I specialize in treating patients who suffer severe psychological trauma. I'm talking about life-changing accidents, postwar stress, childhood abuse, shootings, parental suicides, phobias, emotional upheavals, that sort of thing. The reality is, you suffered huge emotional trauma in your childhood."

Carla felt a strange fluttering in her chest, accompanied by a sudden feeling of apprehension. "You . . . you mean when my parents died?"

"That was only part of it, but not all."

"But I don't remember anything."

"You're not meant to, Carla."

"Why?"

"The human mind has a natural defense mechanism that suppresses unpleasant memories, especially in young people below the age of twelve."

"Can you explain?"

"People often think you can erase traumatic experiences in child patients with say, hypnotherapy treatment. But hypnotherapy might only make things worse and sometimes there really isn't any need."

"Why not?"

"One of the brain's defenses against the problems caused by trauma in childhood is to either suppress the memory or to 'split' into separate personalities, where one part carries the memory and effects of the trauma."

Dr. Leon sat back, adding, "The other part of the mind is unaware of it and is able to grow up and function fairly normally without any apparent effect. That's the part that lets us eat, sleep, move and doesn't recall anything of what happened."

"You're saying my childhood mind suppressed the trauma?"

"That was the only way it could deal with it at the time—to obliterate the bad memories, so that you could live a normal life."

"What bad memories?"

"We'll come to those. In a way you could say that the brain's hope is that when you're older you may be able to handle it better. It's one of the reasons why flashbacks to childhood traumas can occur in adulthood."

Dr. Leon sat forward again. "However, the fact you really don't remember any of it means that your mind did its job correctly. But now we're also dealing with the more recent trauma of your husband's death. Baize tells me you'd been having disturbing nightmares."

"Yes."

"She also tells me that you're pregnant."

Carla nodded.

"What kinds of images present themselves in your nightmares, Carla?"

She explained. "I guess they sound weird?"

"Not really. But sometimes long ago emotional traumas can be retriggered, causing disturbed sleep and nightmares. Tell me what you remember of your childhood."

"It—it's kind of a blur, to be honest. I have warm memories of my parents, of what they looked like, even if they're pretty hazy."

"Is that all?"

"No, I have vague recollections of some kind of family life, of days on a beach somewhere, vacations together, that sort of thing. I'm certain I felt loved. For some reason, that's a feeling I'm pretty sure of. But I don't have any particularly *bad* memories."

"For a very good reason. You were in a catatonic state when I first treated you. A kind of selective amnesia had set in to repress the bad memories."

Dr. Leon made a steeple of his fingers, touched them to his chin. "Repressing memory is not unlike hitting the delete button on your computer to get rid of an unwanted file. Does that make any sense?"

"I . . . I think so."

"Of course, the erased file may still be in your computer, only you can't recall it. But now the distress of Jan's death has upset the apple-cart."

"How?"

"It's allowed your mind to throw up fleeting glimpses from your past. Think of it as a kind of computer glitch. You look uneasy, are you okay?"

"I guess you've got me worried now."

Dr. Leon offered a smile. "I can see all this is a shock, but please, I don't want you to worry. I'm here to help."

"What were the events I lived through?"

"First, I really should explain the problem I faced when Baize told me about the nightmares."

Dr. Leon, his hands still clasped, tapped his forefinger against his lips. "I suppose it's a kind of Pandora's box situation. The lid of the box is already open a little. The question I have to ask myself is, do we wait to see what crawls out or do we open it the rest of the way ourselves?

"If we do nothing, the problem will likely worsen. So I think intervention is the best course. If the unsettling nightmares continue without some kind of explanation as to why they're happening—then they may stress you mentally and physically."

He shook his head. "We really can't let that happen. I don't want to risk anything harming your baby." Dr. Leon smiled reassuringly. "And nothing will."

Carla felt her stomach drop, and put a hand down to touch it. "Where exactly is this going, Doctor?"

"Whichever way the box is opened, you're going to be faced with some difficult truths."

"What truths?"

"You see, you're not the person you think you are, Carla."

"What—what do you mean?"

"You had another life before this, a life your mind repressed. That's why you have no real recollection of your childhood, apart from limited generic memories your own imagination will furnish as it tries to fill in the missing gaps."

"I'm not sure I follow."

"Your entire life before the age of eleven has pretty much been suppressed. The reason was your trauma. Your mind needed to shut it out, to cope, to survive. So all your memories from that period, good and bad, are buried deep, so deep you can't recall them. Perhaps even meeting me may have been all part of that unpleasant experience at the time. A good reason why you didn't recall your therapy."

A dazed Carla went to speak, her mouth open.

When no words came, Dr. Leon said, "I believe the way forward is for you to confront the truth and move on from there. Despite Jan's death you're in a safer place now than you were twenty years ago. Emotionally, you're more mature, more rational."

Leon paused. "I guess the question I have to ask you is this: Do you feel ready to face up to your past? To confront the life you never knew you had?"

"You—you make it sound as if it's a life full of terrible secrets."

"I'd be lying if I said it wasn't, Carla. But let me reassure you, I'm here to help you through it. I'll be with you every step of the way."

"Do I have any other option?"

"I guess not. But we'll need to do this gradually, over days and weeks. To do otherwise would be like pulling a bandage off a burn victim. Do it quickly and you pull away the healing flesh."

"How . . . how do we start?"

"With the truth. Let me get you something."

Dr. Leon rose and crossed to the bookshelves. He removed a gray box file, opened it, and took out a burgundy, leather-bound journal.

Carla saw that it looked old and scuffed.

"What exactly do you know about your parents, Carla?"

"Not much. They died abroad when I was young. My grandparents brought me up."

"Died where?"

"In Europe. Germany, Baize said. My grandfather was based there with the military."

"Died how?"

"In an auto wreck. Baize said I was thrown through the windshield before the car went up in flames and my mom and dad died."

"What happened to you?"

"I was badly concussed. That's why I figured I could never remember much about my life back then."

"Did you ever ask to see your parents' graves?"

"Sure. But Baize said their remains were cremated."

"Didn't you ever ask Baize about your mom and dad? About what your life was like before you came to live with your grandparents?"

"All the time. My childhood is such a blank slate."

"Tell me more about the recollections you have."

"I have a vague feeling of living abroad. Of a warm, happy family life in a strange country that was different from America."

"Nothing more specific than that?"

"Not really. The memories seem as wispy as smoke."

"You said a warm, happy family life. Did you recall brothers, sisters?"

"It's funny you should ask that. For a long time I carried an image around inside my head."

"What sort of image?"

"Of my mother with a baby in her arms. I used to have a strange feeling I may have had a younger brother. But whenever I asked Baize, she dismissed it."

"What else did Baize say?"

"Not a lot. She and my grandfather never liked talking about the past."

"Why?"

"They'd always get really uptight if I mentioned my mom or dad. My father was their only child so I guess it was hard for them, losing him. I figured they didn't like to resurrect memories."

"So you stopped asking?"

"Pretty much. The subject almost became taboo."

"Weren't you curious?"

"Are you kidding? All the time. But it seemed easier not to upset them by asking about it."

"Have you seen your parents in any photographs?"

"Just one, of my father and mother when they married."

"But no others?"

"No. Baize said my mom and dad were moving home with all our belongings when the auto wreck happened. That our family albums were destroyed in the blaze. Can I tell you a secret?"

"Sure."

"The older I got, I sort of wondered if there was more to my life back then than Baize was telling. That things were being kept from me. That maybe even there were scary reasons for Baize not talking about my parents."

"Such as?"

"Did the accident really happen? Did one of them kill the other? Did they have a suicide pact?"

"Really?"

"I wondered if unpleasant stuff like that may have caused my grandparents to avoid the subject. So I finally stopped asking in case I got that kind of answer."

"Did you ever feel as if you were missing a part of your past?"

"Doc, you're starting to bring up a lot of questions that bothered me for a long time. Questions I used to ask myself as I grew up, but never got complete answers to. That troubled me back then. The way you're talking now, they're starting to trouble me again."

"Baize had good reasons for not talking about your parents, Carla."

"What reasons?"

"You were right, your parents didn't die in an auto wreck."

An openmouthed Carla stared back. "Then how did they die?"

The doctor returned to his chair and laid the journal on his lap, resting his palms on the leather cover.

"As a first step, I want you to read some of this."

"What is it?"

"A diary. It's also the key to your past, the prime reason for your nightmares. Everything you don't know about yourself and who you really are is contained within these pages. I want you to read the first half."

He placed it on the table in front of Carla. She stared at the diary with unease.

"I'll read it alone?"

"No, I'll stay with you, sitting quietly in the background."

"Why?"

"Because it's going to be a huge shock. You'll feel emotionally affected as you read it. But it's also going to explain the truth about you."

"How—how long have I got?"

He smiled down at her gently.

"Take all the time you want—it doesn't matter if you're here all night. You're my only patient left this afternoon. I'm not going anywhere."

"Who wrote the journal?"

"Your mother wrote it, Carla. It belonged to her. You were clutching it when you were rescued, half dead from hypothermia one cold, snowy evening. The journal and a coin taped inside were the only things you had on you, apart from the ragged clothes you wore."

"Rescued from what?"

"Everything you need to know is in the diary." He momentarily put a finger to her temple. "It's already locked away up there. You're simply about to unlock it again. I'll be right here if you feel upset or overwhelmed."

Carla touched the journal. "When . . . when I read this will my bad memories come back?"

"I'm pretty sure of it. And the good ones, too."

"All together or bit by bit?"

"There's no normal in these matters, Carla."

"Explain."

"You may have to struggle to remember, or in some cases you may not. For some people their repressed memories may come over days and weeks. For others, it may happen more dramatically, as if a flood-gate opens."

Dr. Leon looked at her. "Or it can be a combination of both. But I ought to warn you that when powerful memories flood back, often the patient can feel overwhelmed."

He tapped the journal. "Reading about what happened to you will certainly trigger your subconscious. So would visiting places where you suffered your worst traumas, or experienced your intense moments of happiness in your past."

"Really?"

"Even seeing photographs from back then, or people you encountered, could have the same effect. The mind will start to connect the dots, to unravel the trauma."

Cara stared at the journal again. An icy chill rippled along her spine. She felt suddenly afraid.

Dr. Leon must have sensed her fear because he said, "Above all, you have to think of today as a kind of liberation day."

"Liberation day?"

"We're finally setting the real Carla free."

13

Carla picked up the diary.

She ran her fingers over the cover.

The leather felt scuffed in places. Something about the diary had a familiar feel to it. She opened the cover.

Taped inside the front cover was a clear plastic sleeve. Inside the sleeve was a tarnished silver dollar. She examined the coin. It was dated 1986.

On the front was Lady Liberty, and on the back the eagle and thirteen five-pointed stars. Carla replaced the coin in the flap.

She estimated that the diary contents consisted of about a hundred pages, written by hand, in English, in neat and flowing handwriting. Written in blue ink mostly, but sometimes in black. Other entries were written with different shades of pencil.

My mother's handwriting.

It felt strange to be holding the diary, and yet in another way it was comforting, like sitting in a familiar armchair. When she flicked to the back pages she saw pictures drawn inside the cover in crayon, as if by a child.

One was of a large building, guarded by stick-figure men with guns. It was all surrounded by a fuzzy-looking scrawl. Carla imagined the fuzz was meant to represent barbed wire.

Another drawing showed the side-by-side figures of a man and woman and two children, a boy and a girl. All had tears falling from their eyes.

Underneath each figure was written a name: Mama, Papa, Carla, Luka, in childish handwriting. Beside each was a small red heart drawn in crayon.

The drawing was signed: Luka.

She felt a shiver, as if someone had walked over her grave.

All of the pages seemed to have been written years before, for they bore the faintly yellow tint of age. She flicked through them.

The binding felt loose in places. Some of the entries were only a few lines; others several pages. The language appeared a touch stilted here and there, as if English wasn't the writer's mother tongue. But the entries were clearly written. Each entry bore a date. All of the dates were more than twenty years ago.

On the inside flap of the diary was inscribed in big block letters: THE DIARY OF LANA JORAN.

The first two pages were written in different-colored blue ink, and appeared to be a foreword of some kind, like it was added at a later stage. The two pages were stitched into place in the diary with coarse thread, instead of being stapled.

She looked over at Dr. Leon. He offered her a reassuring smile. "Okay so far?"

"I . . . I guess."

Carla took a deep breath, felt a catch in her chest. She settled herself into the leather couch, turned to the foreword, and began to read.

THE DIARY OF LANA JORAN

My name is Lana Joran, and this is my story.

I and my husband and our two beloved children are going to die.

I feel certain of our deaths, just as I am certain that the world will be indifferent to our suffering.

And so I write these words not in the hope that they will save us, but that this record of our torment will survive. For if the world is made witness to the brutal slaughter of so many innocents, and if my story helps prevent the murder of even one human being, then my effort will be worthwhile.

First, let me say I have come to learn that history repeats itself.

Many years ago when the Nazi concentration camps were discovered and their ovens were still warm from the bones of millions of innocent dead, the world promised genocide would never happen again.

But that promise is forgotten.

For hundreds of thousands of families like mine are forced from our homes, herded into transports or on death marches, raped and tortured, shot and beaten to death in death camps. Men, women, children, infants, exterminated on the brutal whim of yet another tyrant who lusts after power.

Make no mistake: a holocaust is happening again. I have witnessed its terrible brutality—sights that no mother or father or their children should ever see. And all the while the world stands by and does nothing.

I am afraid of death. Even when death is all around you, when it is a constant companion, you still fear dying.

I am especially afraid for my children.

That the beautiful faces I put to bed at night, that I wake to in the morning, and whom I love and cherish more than anything, will be killed by evil tormentors and executioners who place no value on human life.

There have been times when I blamed God for our misfortune. When I begged his help, cried out for him in despair. And when no help came I cursed his name. But I have come to realize that God is not to blame.

I am reminded of the query made about man's inhumanity to man in the concentration camps. The question was asked: "At Auschwitz, tell me, where was God?"

And the answer came: "Where was man?"

For it was men alone who did this evil. Not God or religion or men acting in the name of God or religion. But simply men. Men whose evil makes everyone suffer, regardless of their beliefs or race: Serb or Bosniak or Croat. Christian or Orthodox, Muslim or atheist.

There are some crimes that pass comprehension, that are beyond forgiveness or redemption. Crimes that go unpunished, and no lesson is learned from them.

All too often the men who commit these crimes are allowed to still walk among us, and to smear humankind with their evil. So I write this diary also in the hope that the men who persecuted my family will be apprehended.

That their sins will be shouted out to the world. For if they are not caught, if they are not punished, then there is no hope for any of us.

This, then, is my family's story. The story of my husband David and me, and our daughter Carla and our son Luka.

And though it will be ended by hate, it began with love.

Please God, let my words be remembered when the names of towns and cities like Sarajevo, Vukovar, and Srebrenica are mentioned. When the death camps of Omarska and Manjača, and anywhere evil was done to innocents regardless of their creed or race, are recalled among the darkest pages of humanity.

If I can achieve that, if my words live on in others, and if justice is done, then perhaps I will not fear death.

For to live in the hearts of those we leave behind is not to die.

Carla paused as she finished reading the foreword. She felt something cold and foreboding seep through her, as if she were standing outside a door beyond which something terrible had happened.

Dr. Leon asked, "Still okay?"

"I . . . I think so. I . . . I did have a brother, Luka."

"Yes. It's all in the diary, Carla. Please read on."

She began to read. The diary started with her mother describing her simple upbringing near Konjic, in the Bosnian region of Yugoslavia, midway between Mostar and Sarajevo. Then, her name was Lana Tanovic. An only child, her small-town lawyer father was a local civil prosecutor—they lived on a modest farm inherited from his parents—and her mother taught English at a nearby school. In their township, Orthodox Christian and Muslim lived side by side.

Her parents came from different backgrounds; her mother was a Christian Serb, her father a "Bosniak," of Muslim origin. They were not overly religious, although they believed in God. But they did not bring their daughter up in a traditional religious fashion.

From an early age Lana's mother taught her daughter English. By the time she was eighteen, Lana already spoke the language fluently and was accepted for college in Dubrovnik to study English.

Her dream was to be a writer, and to one day write a book that would change the world.

It was the same year Lana's mother died of breast cancer. From then on, Lana would return home from college two weekends a month, and during holidays, to visit her prosecutor father.

To help supplement the small college allowance her father gave, she found part-time work as a waitress in a restaurant owned by a man named Mr. Banda.

And it was here she met Carla's father, a young American artist.

She described in loving detail a trip they made to Mostar together, where David jumped from the bridge and carved their names on an olive tree. And how their love and affection for each other grew and was cemented by their wedding in the small church of St. Nicolas in Dubrovnik, and with the birth of her two children.

First came Marianna Carla—Marianna after her maternal grandmother, but everyone called her Carla. Her mother was overjoyed that her husband took easily to fatherhood, and they adored their daughter.

They lived in an apartment above Mr. Banda's restaurant, where her parents worked, her father painting in his spare time. When Carla's mother graduated, she found extra work giving English lessons.

Six years later came Luka. Wonderful, playful little Luka arrived eleven weeks premature. It was a difficult Caesarean birth, for the umbilical cord had caught around Luka's neck and almost starved him of oxygen. But frail Luka came crying into the word. His prematurity caused him to suffer badly from retinopathy, which left him blind in one eye.

The doctors didn't think he would live, because he was so frail, but somehow he survived and thrived.

Carla's mother described how as he grew older, Luka could never sleep without his "blankie" from his baby cot—a piece of blue cotton blanket, which he felt comforted by.

It was a happy time but their happiness would eventually be overshadowed by the siege of Dubrovnik by Serb forces in the first stages of the Balkan war. Her mother explained what happened, as Carla read on . . .

Carla is overjoyed to have a brother.

I have to make an effort to stop her from spoiling him. Luka is growing into a cheerful, playful little boy. His blind eye is milky white but it doesn't deter him from doing anything and he follows his sister everywhere, clutching her sweater or the hem of her skirt.

Once he learns to speak, he constantly begs her, "No, no leave Luka! Stay with Luka, Carla."

Luka has a giddy sense of humor, and knows he is the center of attention. When Carla asks him for a kiss, he gives a dimpled smile and runs away, giggling, puckering his angel lips, teasing her to chase him, and joking: "No, no kisses. No kisses for you today, Carla."

And then, when Carla catches him, he relents: "Well . . . well maybe just one kiss if you are good," and his giggling explodes as she scoops him up and plants kisses on his cheeks and neck.

Carla adores him. I have found everything I wished for: two beautiful children and a kind and understanding and loving husband.

What more could I ask for?

David's parents write and telephone. They talk of us all meeting in Vienna, where his father is attending a military conference. Three months later it comes true. They are anxious to meet us and the children.

We take the train and meet in Vienna and have three glorious days together in a nice hotel with wonderful food. His parents adore the children, and bring them presents.

A Barbie doll and clothes for Carla, and a Thomas the Train backpack and more clothes for Luka. And a real silver dollar each, to commemorate their births. The children are fascinated by the shiny coins.

The silver dollars minted in 1986 have a lady—Liberty—on the front and the eagle and stars on the back—thirteen five-pointed stars, Carla tells me.

Luka tells me his coin is pirate treasure, and guards it proudly in its plastic cover.

David's father warns us that there are rumors of war. That it may be wise to leave our country, and come to America.

David tells them if it gets too bad we will leave but for now we will get on with our lives. David's parents can't hide their sadness, and when we leave, David hugs his father and mother—and we promise to keep in touch. We all cry. I'm happy at least they have buried their differences and found peace.

The only shadow on our lives is this rumor of war.

Dubrovnik is besieged by Serb forces and no one can leave. We suffer food and water shortages and the electricity constantly fails. The old town is shelled, buildings destroyed, and snipers terrify us.

We are beginning to live in constant fear of death. Daily, we hear stories of ethnic cleansing, murder, and pillage.

Today a rumor goes around that there is fresh bread being sold at one of the few bakeries still working. David volunteers to go.

He's gone two hours when I hear a loud explosion. I pace the room, my nerves shattered. Another ten minutes and David has not come back. I can bear it no longer. I warn Carla to stay inside with Luka and not venture out.

"I'll be back, my darlings. Stay here."

I zigzag through the streets trying to avoid snipers. My heart's pounding when I reach the bakery. In front of me is a scene of carnage.

Medical staff attend to bodies lying around, some wounded, others dead. Legs, arms, bits of bodies are strewn in the street, awash with blood. A man is hanging over a railing, half his torso blown away.

Horrified, I freeze.

I spot David—covered in blood, bits of bone and flesh clinging to his clothes. He's upright, walking, helping others. He's not wounded, thank heavens. He tells me as people lined up for bread, a mortar shell landed, killing men, women, children. He was so far back in the line that he was only concussed. I kiss him, hug him, relieved he's alive.

The shelling ends after Christmas, when the Serbs abandon their siege.

David wants us to leave the country at once and go to America.

"I insist on it, Lana." I hear the alarm in his voice.

He calls his parents, who are anxious to send us money for air tickets.

But that day I learn my father is ill.

Too ill for him to move.

I tell David we must drive to my father's farm and try to take him back with us if he is well enough to travel.

I can't leave my father alone. I have to save him.

David's unhappy about our journey, it could be dangerous, but he will bring his American passport, which may offer us some protection.

"And then we get out of this country, okay?"

"I promise, David."

And so we say goodbye to Mr. Banda, telling him we do not know when we will return, but hopefully soon.

We set out one gray Saturday morning with some belongings.

That same morning, unknown to us, Serb tanks and paramilitaries roll north of Sarajevo to begin a murderous campaign . . .

Looking back now, I realize that our journey to save my father was a tragic mistake.

That I put the lives of my husband and children in mortal danger.

But how was I to know?

How was I to know that this was the first step of our journey into hell?

There are those who say that there has always been a war going on in these lands. That for centuries the Orthodox Christian Serbs, Catholic Croats, and Bosnian Muslim ethnic groups that mostly make up this country have always been at each other's throats.

I cannot lie—history and wars has often made us enemies, even when we share the same town or village—simply because of our ancestors' blood.

But in truth, nobody hates anybody. Only stupid people hate. We have all lived together in peace for far longer than we have fought one another.

But now the drums of war are sounding again. Tito once held the country together with an iron fist but he is long dead. Yugoslavia is splitting apart. But the evil, mad dictator Slobodan Milosevic in Belgrade is in love with power and fears losing it. So he inflames old ethnic hatreds, blaming Croats and Bosnians for ripping apart the country.

Not all Serbs support him. Many are good and decent people who oppose his rule. But it only takes a handful of rotten apples like Milosevic and his followers to ruin the entire barrel.

When all out war finally comes, it comes with a ferocious bloodletting . . .

That Saturday in our old Volkswagen, three kilometers from my town, we see broken lines of terrified civilians fleeing on the road, walking, or on tractors and trailers. I recognize neighbors. They tell us the Serb paramilitaries attacked that morning, killing dozens of townspeople and destroying homes before they withdrew. They urge us to turn back.

David and I are agonized—he says we're putting our family in jeopardy and need to leave at once—but I'm desperate to reach my father before another attack. He's sixty-five, ill and alone.

We drive past deserted homes. In the empty town I see maimed, headless bodies in the streets. David and I cringe, horrified, as we try to distract Carla and Luka from the carnage. They know something terrible is wrong.

We speed to my father's farm. The barn is smoldering, half demolished by a shell or mortar. Cattle lie dead in a field. And there, propped against the barn wall, dressed in his black prosecutor's gown, eyes wide open in death, is my father.

His throat is cut, blood stains his chest.

I can't believe the horror I am seeing. I rush to him while David remains with the children. My father was a shy man and in many ways a mystery to me, but at that moment I realize how much I loved him.

I break down, clutching his body. David is ashen-faced. He tells *the children to remain in the car but Carla sees her grandpa and screams. We hear gunfire, and our blood curdles.*

A terrified neighbor roars into the farmyard in his ancient tractor.

"Lana, you must get away from here. I came back to warn you."

"Who did this to my father?"

"Mila Shavik's paramilitaries."

Everyone in the town knew Mila Shavik. The son of a Bosnian Serb lawyer, there was bad blood between his father's family and mine.

"Shavik leads a unit called the Red Dragons. Some are local Serbs that you'll probably know. Butchers, every one. They're hellbent on killing anyone who isn't a Serb, or on their side."

More ragged bursts of gunfire sound closer.

"Leave now, Lana, they're coming back," my neighbor urges, and roars off in his tractor, leaving a cloud of diesel fumes.

Overcome, I close my father's eyes with my thumb and forefinger, and kiss his cold cheek. I want to bury him, but David drags me to the Volkswagen. "Look, Lana!"

A convoy of army trucks is heading toward the farm. David urges, "We have to get to the main road, it's our only chance."

The children are crying. David starts the car. The first truck spots us, and picks up speed. The uniformed men standing in the back take aim with their guns. My heart hammers.

A bullet explodes through our windshield, just missing Luka's head. Two more thud into the roof's metal. Carla and I scream.

Luka, terrified, pleads, "Mama, Papa . . . !"

David slams his foot to the floor.

Our engine roars like a scalded animal as we speed away from Shavik's men.

Carla paused. She noticed several pages were missing in the diary.

She looked up at Dr. Leon. "Some pages were torn out or worked loose. What happened to them?"

"I've no idea. The diary is just as I received it from Baize. Are you okay? Do you want to stop or take a break?"

"No, I want to keep going."

Carla turned the page, and carried on reading . . .

We decide that our fastest escape route back to Dubrovnik is via Sarajevo.

From there, David intends for us to leave the country.

Once, Sarajevo was called the Jerusalem of the Balkans.

With its Catholic and Orthodox churches, synagogues and mosques, it's a city of over four hundred thousand, known for its tolerance, art and culture, where Christians, Jews, and Muslims have coexisted for centuries.

But in April 1992, on the same day we enter Sarajevo, all that is about to change.

We drive there without stopping and barely make it when we hear on the radio that Serb General Stanislav Galic is sealing up the city.

Everyone inside Sarajevo is trapped in a siege.

I am still grieving for my father. I'm horrified thinking about his body lying unburied for the rats to pick at.

We find my cousin Raisa, whose small house is on Logavina Street.

She is blonde, petite—so petite she always wears high boots—and is a bundle of nerves, but happy to see us and offers to take us in.

Raisa is divorced, with an eight-year-old son, Peter. He calls David and I his aunt and uncle. They have a twitchy little spaniel, Pablo. At least Carla and Luka will have friends to play with.

Raisa has always suffered with her nerves, and chain-smokes constantly. She is worried for her son, worried about surviving.

"The shells and the snipers are driving me crazy."

When cigarettes become scarce, and she's smokeless, Raisa's nerves are as tight as violin strings. She paces the house like a restless dog.

"God forgive me, but I'd give my left leg for a smoke."

Over three hundreds shells and mortars smash into the city each day, starting at 5 a.m. It is impossible to get a full night's sleep. Everyone is red-eyed.

Yesterday two young lovers—he a Christian, she a Muslim—tried to flee the city by crossing the Vrbanja Bridge. They were mowed down by snipers. Their bodies were left to rot. People are calling them Sarajevo's Romeo and Juliet. Today, when it was dark and the snipers couldn't see, I left flowers near the bridge for them. Checkpoints and barricades are everywhere.

On a wall opposite the house someone has painted: "Welcome to the Capital of Hell."

I shiver. Something tells me it's going to get even worse.

In the streets, we all hear the rumor—Sarajevo's siege will be like another Stalingrad.

As if we needed an omen, tonight there is a violent storm. Loud and frightening, the darkness crackles with lighting and thunder.

Storms worry Luka. He clutches his piece of blue blankie, and cries, "Mama, Luka scared . . ."

I move to snuggle him but Carla says, "No, Mama, let me."

She hugs him close. "It's okay, Luka. It's nothing to worry about. Carla will keep you safe."

Luka cuddles into Carla, and clutches his blankie. He will not close his eyes without it. On restless nights, or when we're troubled by the shelling, it's a godsend. The only way Luka will sleep is holding that piece of old blanket in his hands.

Looking down at my two cherubs, I smile at how much Carla loves Luka, and how protective she is toward him. They are so close. I worry if anything were to happen to one of them, the other would be lost.

A parent is a hostage to a child. Not until they have a child of their own do children understand how a parent would sacrifice their life to protect them.

I worry desperately that we all remain safe through this siege.

They say Sarajevo has become the world's biggest concentration camp.

There is no gas, no electricity. Water is cut off for days at a time. Food is becoming scarce. Trees are being cut down for firewood.

As always, people try to fight the bleakness with grim humor.

On a wall someone has scrawled a sick joke: "What is the main difference between Sarajevo and Auschwitz? Unlike Sarajevo, at least Auschwitz had a regular gas supply."

The trams and buses have stopped.

Trains no longer leave the city, for the lines are blocked.

The only way in and out is by air. But the airport is held by Serb troops.

Rumor has it that you can buy a plane ride out if you have enough money.

But we have none, not enough anyhow. And what little we have we must keep for rations. Food is running short. Everything is running short.

Black humor seems to keep us alive. "The bad news is, your house has been half demolished by a shell. The good news is, you'll get to see it on CNN."

Even the radio station we listen to each night begins its broadcast with the words "Good evening, to all three of you who still have batteries for the radio set . . ."

There is no end to the terror and madness.

Days are spent running the gauntlet of snipers. They call it the Sarajevo Shuffle. A hesitant back-and-forward motion people make before they risk dashing across a street exposed to sniper fire.

Every movement in the street seems to attract a sniper's bullet. Elderly women trying to get some food to keep from starving, young mothers clutching children. The snipers don't care who they target.

Last night, a rocket struck near to the house. It tore slates off the roof. Now it leaks when it rains.

Raisa puffs on a butt she found in the street, and stares at the leaking roof. "Look on the bright side. At least now we can all have a shower."

Yesterday I saw some locals parade a Serb sniper they captured. He turned out to be an angel-faced fifteen-year-old boy with his uncle's old hunting rifle. The boy hid in a bell tower and shot at everyone.

They say he shot ten people dead, one a five-year-old. The boy sniper looked so innocent. I heard him cry and beg for his life as he was dragged off.

I cringe and turn away when the crowd hangs him from a lamppost, the boy's screams ringing in my ears for days.

Raisa is in one of her black moods.

She begs that if we ever go to America, we try to take her and Peter with us. David promises he will do his utmost. Raisa is jubilant.

She and Peter dance like two children, Peter excited, all giggles.

He tells David he loves to watch baseball. He shows us his rubber tennis ball he plays with, and pretends it's a baseball. He opens a school geography book and wants us to show him where in New York David's parents are from.

"Can we go to New York, Uncle David, and will you buy me a hot dog? Can I have a real baseball and will you take me to a game?"

David winks. "A hot dog and a baseball game—we've got a deal, Peter."

That night Raisa cracks open a bottle of pear brandy.

We adults get drunk. To further celebrate, Raisa smokes one of her precious cigarettes. She has bought two packs that cost her a fortune. With the siege, they have become like gold.

Raisa tells us of rumors of mass killings, Muslim and Serb. Of villages where women, young children, and babies are brutally massacred. Of adults forced to watch soldiers kill their children. There is madness on every side. I can't bear to listen to any more.

Raisa swears that if the Serbs ever completely take the city and have their revenge she would kill herself and Peter.

Another drink and she brightens. "With luck, this misery can't last forever."

She tells us a joke about a man who puts his precious cigarette behind his ear before he runs across a street that's being fired on by snipers.

Halfway across a shot rings out, and the bullet shears off the man's ear. He gets down on his knees, one hand covering his bloody wound, the other hand searching the ground.

His friend screams, "Get under cover, you idiot! You're got two ears."

Raisa slaps a hand on her boot and laughs as she gives the reply: "Hey, I don't give a damn about my ear, I'm looking for my cigarette."

The next day Raisa leaves to try to find us all some food.

Three shots ring out. Raisa comes running back, screaming. "My child . . . my child . . . for God's sake do something!'

David run out, and I follow, forcing Carla to keep Luka inside.

We see Peter lying on the street in a growing pool of blood.

Raisa let him play his pretend game of baseball in a narrow side street, not troubled by snipers. Peter threw his ball and it bounced down the street. When he ran to fetch it he was shot through the head. His left leg is twitching, he's still alive.

The dog runs to him, another shot ricochets off the pavement, and the dog scampers back.

Raisa is distraught as I and some neighbors try to hold her back. A volley of shots erupts as someone tries to pin down the sniper. Peter's body is still twitching. David runs to him and cradles him in his arms. Then another shot cracks, barely missing David as he runs back, carrying Peter.

The poor boy is already dead.

We're all inconsolable. Raisa is like a woman possessed; she screams and wails, and pleads with God. A doctor sedates her with some pills.

With the neighbors' help, we lay Peter out in his bedroom. It seems so bizarre—one day he's talking about hot dogs and baseball, and the next he's dead. All that night his spaniel, Pablo, whimpers outside Peter's room.

I hardly sleep, taking turns with David to watch over Raisa, who seems in a coma from the pills. I drift in and out of a nightmarish sleep, weeping for Peter.

As dawn creeps, I wake and Raisa is gone. My heart stutters. I find her in the bedroom where Peter's body is laid out.

She is lying across her beloved son's chest, embracing him.

Her body is still.

And then I notice the kitchen bread knife, and the congealed crimson where she cut her wrists . . .

Carla and Luka are in shock.

We are all heartbroken.

It is too dangerous to transport Raisa and Peter to the graveyard. We must bury them in the back garden for now. Neighbors help David dig the grave. We recite prayers. When it is over, the poor dog curls up in the garden, miserable, as if it knows its life is changed forever.

I worry about Carla.

At times our love was hard-won. In the past there was sometimes a distance between us, which was often my fault. There were times when I didn't want her to be so headstrong, so resolute, so independent. It often wore me down. But I overcame our distance by gradually accepting my daughter as her own person.

Always strong-willed, and quick to criticize an injustice. I remember the day I felt intensely proud of those traits.

She was nine and would ride to school on the bus, and sometimes I rode with her. Once day a young boy, Tomas, was being teased by the other children. Tomas was a little slow, mentally, and some of the children would tease him.

Carla said to me, "Why do they do that, M'ma? Why are they so cruel?"

Before I could even answer, Carla strode up the bus, sat beside Tomas, and glared at his persecutors. Every day afterward she sat next to him, befriending him. If anyone dared bother him, they had Carla to deal with.

But now I fear the brave little girl I love is becoming withdrawn by the terrible things she sees.

To shut out the hell around her, some days she sits in a corner and buries her head between her knees and cups her hands over her ears.

When Luka sees her rocking back and forth, he looks up at me and smiles his milky-eyed smile as if it is a game. Then he does the same, copying Carla, cupping his face in his hands, but peeking at her now and then through his fingers.

I tell them to think of happy things, of nice things, of good times they remember. When we played on the beach, or on my parents' farm. Dear God, do they both know how much David and I love them? How much we fret? How our hearts bleed, worrying that they will be safe?

Living in a city under siege is beginning to take its toll.

David has become quieter, more solemn, and hardly eats from all the worry.

He has not painted since we got here.

We're all getting thinner, and breaking out in sores. All we eat now are cans of tuna and vegetables and pickles in vinegar. A little oatmeal if we are lucky. Stories are spreading that people are beginning to live on grass and nettle soup. There is no meat to be had anywhere.

On balconies, instead of flowers, people grow tomatoes, herbs, or potatoes.

One day the dog, Pablo, goes missing.

A week passes and we cannot find him.

A neighbor tells me pets are being stolen for their meat.

I dare not tell the children.

It has become impossible even to go out and find food without having to risk being killed. Every day there are more ruined homes, craters, scared people hiding in basement cellars.

Today I traded Raisa's last cigarettes for a bag of carrots, a can of tuna, and a jar of pickles.

Two days later, and the last of our food is running out. David finds a tin of dog food and a few dog biscuits Raisa kept. He reads the pack.

"It says here they freshen your breath and help prevent tartar."

He smiles, nibbling at the dog biscuit. Then he uses the can opener, and scoops the soggy dog food onto a plate. It smells awful.

"You're not really going to eat that, David, are you?"

"You think I'm barking up the wrong tree?"

Typical of David to lighten the mood. I cringe at his silly joke.

"It's got protein. It'll fill me up."

He digs a spoon into the jellied mess, and swallows it down.

I know he's thinking of me and the children.

That at mealtime he'll insist he's full and that we eat his share of the food.

But of course he never says that, just smiles and winks at me.

"Woof . . ."

We burn our last few logs and lumps of coal. We are freezing.

On cold nights we all huddle under coats and blankets for warmth. We've burned everything in the stove to keep warm: kitchen chairs, bookshelves, even Raisa's boots she loved so much, and a pair of Peter's old sandals.

I feel sad, thinking of their bodies buried in the back garden.

To make it worse, the next night we hear growling. David goes out with an oil lamp. Two wild dogs are digging up the graves. One of the dogs has a hold of a rotting hand in its jaws. A horrified David gets a shovel and beats away the dogs, then reburies the hand.

I don't want to know whose hand it is, I feel so sickened.

I see how thin David has become.

He lost a tooth yesterday—because our diet is so poor.

I know there's something on his mind. "What is it, David?"

"We'll talk later, after the children are asleep."

I see the stress, the worry, his wet eyes. He sees mine.

I sob, and he puts his arms around me, and pulls me close.

And there we stand, clinging to each other, swaying in each other's arms, not like two dancers, but as fragile as young branches shaking in the wind.

That night, we lie with Carla and Luka.

The electricity is out. We light a single candle.

We gave the children our supper. David and I pretended to eat, pushing the oatmeal around our plate. Luka was ravenous and licked the plate.

David strokes their hair until they fall asleep. As always, Luka clutches his piece of blue blanket and sleeps snuggled up to Carla.

David beckons me silently into the living room. He sits me down on the couch and blows out the candle to save it. Moonlight filters through a crack in the curtains. Like shadows, we sit there. David reaches out to hold both my hands.

"Lana, if we stay here we're dead. This siege could go on for years."

"What can we do?"

"Get out of Sarajevo. Otherwise we're sitting ducks."

I fell silent.

"You know what they're saying, Lana? In Sarajevo, everyone who has a soul is leaving. Only the soulless are being left behind."

David is right. I see people wandering the streets. They look like walking dead.

"But where can we go?"

I've heard about people trying to escape over the mountains being caught and slaughtered. We're trapped.

"Lana, I met a man today. His cousin's a Serb officer. He can get us special passes for the airport bus, and plane tickets to Belgrade."

I feel my heart soar, and then it falls as quickly.

Everyone wants to escape on the aircraft that leave the city every evening. If you have money, you can buy a seat. The aircraft bring in Serb troops and supplies, and fly out anyone who can afford the outrageous prices. There's even a rumor that a unit of Mila Shavik's Red Dragons controls the airport, gangsters all of them.

"Don't joke, David. We have no money."

"He'll take the Volkswagen. And the cash we have left."

"You're serious?"

"I have an American passport. You're my wife. Our children are de facto U.S. citizens. The nearest U.S. consulate is where we're headed."

I look at David. I see how malnourished and worried he looks. His eyes are bloodshot, his lips are cracked and sore. Yet I see strength in him, a fierce determination to do whatever he must to rescue us from this madness. When I look in his eyes I still see love in them.

I touch his lips. "You know what I often think?"

"What?"

"That day on the bridge in Mostar."

"What about it?"

"I should have jumped with you."

He smiles. "Why?"

"To honor us. To show you how much I felt for you. Because I think I knew even then I loved you, just as I love you now."

His smile widens, and he looks so handsome despite his missing tooth. "Next time we're in Mostar, you can do it."

"That's a promise."

We kiss, we hug, we cry. We hold each other until our embrace is almost painful. I draw back, and rest my hand on his cheek.

"It'll be dangerous if we leave. Shavik and some of his men are from my hometown. They may recognize me. Things could take a bad turn."

I have no wish to see Mila Shavik or be recognized by his cronies.

David shoots me a meaningful look. "If we stay our children will starve to death. Or die like Peter, or by shelling. We have to take the risk. Try to change your appearance. Cut your hair short, cover your face with a headscarf."

"When do we leave."

"Tomorrow night."

14

Carla laid the diary down.

She felt astounded, if someone had struck her a blow. Reading the pages, it was as if an entire other life was trying to seep into her bones.

With great effort, she struggled to remember, forcing her mind to recollect until she felt her temples pounding.

She began to recall faces from her past.

They floated in front of her, blurred, like spirits from another world.

Her mother's face.

Her father's.

Darling little Luka's.

She felt a rush of emotion.

"I think that's enough for one day, Carla."

"W . . . what?"

"I think you've read for today. How are you?"

"Shocked . . . Stunned . . . Moved."

"We ought to talk a little about what you've read, if you feel up to it?"

She wanted to read on and yet she was afraid, afraid of what memories were hiding in the dark furrows of her mind, waiting to ambush her.

But she knew she had to continue.

"I'm sorry, I want to read all the diary."

"In one sitting? I don't think that would be wise."

"The diary belonged to my mother."

"Of course."

"Then legally it belongs to me. I want to finish what I've started."

"Carla, I'm sure it would be unwise of you, and unethical of me to allow that. We really need to approach this bit by bit. Otherwise there's a risk."

"Of what?"

"Mental overload. With the resurgence of all this trauma, you could go into deep shock, and break down."

"I still want to read it. I have to. And I want to be left alone."

"I wouldn't advise that. Remember what I said about pulling the sticking plaster off a burn victim . . . ?"

"It's my decision. Please respect it."

"Carla, no, I'm sorry . . ."

"You must respect my decision."

He sighed. "Are you really sure about this?"

"Totally."

He heard the determination in her voice. "I'm not happy. Leaving you to read alone goes against every professional instinct I have. But it seems I have no choice."

He stood reluctantly, and pointed to what looked like a small brass door buzzer screwed to the underside of his desk.

"If you need me, or if anything you read proves too upsetting, just press the buzzer. I'll be in the next room."

The doctor left, closing the door softly.

Warily, Carla picked up the diary again.

For the first time in many months I feel hope.

And excitement. That night we pack our few clothes and belongings.

We're going to Belgrade, then to America. Once we get out of here, I want to tell the world what is happening in Sarajevo, I want to shout it aloud to every newspaper or television station that will listen. I record every detail in my diary. The diary I want the world to read.

I cut my hair.

I wear an old dress, worn flat shoes.

I wrap a drab old burgundy wool cardigan around my shoulders.

I wear no makeup.

With my oldest coat and headscarf I look like I've aged twenty years.

I have lost so much weight I barely recognize myself. My cheeks are sunken, my skin ashen from months of malnourishment.

At six the next evening we carry our bags four blocks to the bus stop, David ahead of us dragging two heavy suitcases. We are wary of snipers.

I carry a rucksack on my back and a shopping bag with what little food we have left. Luka holds my hand. On his back he wears the Thomas the Train backpack his grandparents gave him. Stuffed inside is his blue blankie and a few of his treasured toys.

Carla holds his other hand and drags her pink overnight case.

When we reach the bus stop, at least two hundred people are already there, milling about with children and belongings. I panic—we won't all fit on the bus.

But three buses arrive, with a Serb officer in each. Everyone shows their documents. We are divided into groups, escorted on board, and sit at the back of the packed bus. The engine starts up.

Carla is keyed up. "Are we really going, Mama? Are we going to America?"

"Yes, sweetheart."

It is the first time I have seen her smile in months. In her palm she clutches the silver American dollar her grandparents gave her. She stares at it now and then, as if it's her ticket to freedom.

I hug her.

Luka wants a hug, too. And he wants his own silver dollar. I insist he keeps it stored in its plastic case, and inside his rucksack so he doesn't lose it. He's happy, and giggling. The children and I have never flown before.

"We going on a big airplane, Mama? Is this for my birthday?"

"Yes, Luka, for your birthday."

Today is Luka's fourth birthday. We have no cake to celebrate, no party candles, not even a present to give to give our son. All we have to give him are two hard candies I've kept in my bag for months. Luka sucks on one, delighted with himself, and gives the other one to Carla. But knowing Carla, she'll give it back to him later, when the first one's gone.

My heart soars. Perhaps David and I can give our children the best present of all—their freedom.

On the drive to the airport, my stomach churns with anticipation.

We are escorted by military policemen on motorcycles. At several checkpoints in neighborhoods near the airport, masses of people crowd into the street, wanting to escape Sarajevo. Some try to stop the driver, hitting the bus. It is a terrible sight.

Mothers lift their young children and press them to the glass, begging us to take their youngest, to save them.

All of us passengers on the bus are crying and upset, the children, too. I feel terrible for the people left behind. I have to cover Carla's and Luka's eyes from the distressing scenes as we pick up speed, leaving the crowds behind.

We hear shelling as we approach the airport gates. The Serb officer on board talks to someone on his radio. When he finishes he orders the bus drivers to pull over to the curb and switch off their engines.

We hear shelling nearby. We wait half an hour. We hear an aircraft take off, then the shelling starts up again. The Serb officer chatters on his radio.

"What's wrong?" David asks the officer.

"The runway's been damaged due to shelling. The Serb army holds the main roads so we've been given orders to drive you to Belgrade instead. Be grateful you're still getting out of this hellhole. Now be quiet."

It's a long drive to Belgrade on clogged roads, a journey that could take all night. The buses start up and head north. The signs of shelling and heavy fighting are everywhere. We are all uneasy as we pass through Serb checkpoints. The passengers on board are mostly Bosniaks, and a few Croats.

After several hours our vehicles are forced to a halt at a checkpoint. I feel a catch in my throat as truckloads of armed paramilitaries block our way.

A middle-aged woman with striking, azure blue eyes and poorly fitting dentures, and whose name is Alma, leans across from the seat opposite. She whispers palely, "Something's not right. What are they up to?"

The officer climbs off our bus and lights a cigarette. I see him grin as he chats with the paramilitary guards and nods at our vehicles. Suddenly two of the guards replace him, brandishing weapons. People protest and ask what's going on. The guards wave their guns.

"Stay in your seats, all of you. And no talking."

The buses pull out again. Instead of heading east toward Belgrade we drive west.

Everyone is worried and confused. I feel my legs shaking, my mouth dry with fear. David is angry. He approaches a guard. "We paid a lot of money for our tickets. How about you tell me what's going on here? I'm an American citizen, and my wife and children—"

The guard strikes him with the butt of his weapon.

David reels back, his forehead cut.

I rush to him.

The guard beats us back, his face an ugly grin. "I don't care who you are. You were told to sit down."

The children are crying. Adults cower in silence, everyone in shock.

Carla and Luka hug their father and won't let him go.

"Are you hurt, Papa?" Carla helps dab his cut, his blue shirt stained with blood.

"No, I'm fine, it didn't hurt, really. Don't worry."

"Why did that man do that, Papa? Why are they holding us prisoner?"

"'Cause he's a bold man," says Luka, nodding his head, as if it's self-evident. "Isn't he, Papa?"

"Yes, Luka. He's bold."

The children don't understand. How do we explain to them? This is all happening simply because I'm a Bosniak, and in this war the Serbs hate us.

David says, "We'll sort this out when we get wherever we're going. I'll speak to someone in authority, don't worry."

He clutches his American passport and tries to sound confident, but I know he's shaken by what's happened.

I'm shaken, too. Where are they taking us? Can David's passport free us? Despair settles over all the adults. We feel tricked, as if the promise of escaping Sarajevo was a hoax. And I have a sinister feeling that the Serb paramilitaries are up to something.

But what?

In darkness, four hours later, the buses halt next to a bombed bridge.

All the time I could feel my heart beating though my coat. Are we going to be killed? David squeezes my hand the entire journey.

Luka, wide-eyed, still wearing his Thomas the Train backpack, stares out of the window as the soldiers jump down off the trucks. I can feel Carla trembling when I touch her. She still clutches the silver dollar her grandparents gave her, nervously turning it over and over in her hand. I dread to think what fear is going through her young mind.

The guards, mean-faced men who scream at us, force us from the buses.

We all get off, dragging suitcases, laden with bundles and crying children. The rain pours down. We're sodden. A sign says: Omarska 10 kilometers. The guards force us to walk.

We tramp along muddy forest track, exhausted. Luka begs me for water. We have none left. David asks a guard for some.

The man scowls and tells him to keep moving. The guards beat with their rifle butts anyone who's slow.

All the mothers look desolate, terrified, and exhausted. The children cry.

A frail elderly man with a gray beard collapses. He can't keep up with us. Someone whispers in disbelief, "They . . . they're killing him. The guards are cutting the old man's throat."

I glance back and see the guards toss the man's body into a ditch.

We're all horrified. It makes me think of my father, his body left to rot, and it sinks my heart.

Another mile and a young girl soils her pants. Her mother struggles desperately to try to wash the child's garment in a stream we pass, while the guards beat and jeer the poor woman.

But all this is nothing compared to what lies ahead.

It was freezing cold and 2 a.m. when we arrive at the "camp."

Once an agricultural research laboratory, now it's ringed by barbed wire and searchlights. The windows are barred with wire grilles. Armed guards patrol the grounds with German shepherds.

Exhausted, we are marched onto a big square. The guards separate the men and boys over fourteen on one side; the women and children on the other. David is forced to line up with the men and boys. The separation of men and boys from their families causes so much anguish and wailing among us all that a Serb officer draws a leather truncheon.

He's big, with a boxer's broken nose and a slit of a mouth, and he wades into the crowd, beating men, women, and children. "Get into line! Don't speak unless you're spoken to. Be quiet for the camp commandant!"

The crowd settles and falls silent. We later learn that this brutal man is Major Boris Arkov, the camp's second in command, in charge of the guards.

Immediately a green painted door in the main building bursts open. The man who appears has a handsome, almost gentle face and he's stockier than Arkov, wears an officer's uniform, and his red beret is tilted arrogantly to one aside. He clutches a leather riding crop.

On one arm of his tunic is emblazoned an emblem: a Red Dragon.

My heart stutters.

I recognize Mila Shavik at once.

He stands under the blazing lights, hands on his hips, slapping the riding crop against his leg.

We're in the third row and I'm terrified Shavik or any of his men will recognize me from my hometown, so I keep my head down.

Shavik struts along the first row of prisoners, smacking his crop against his leg.

"You Bosniaks will be our guests until we can exchange you for Serb prisoners. While you're here you'll obey the rules or suffer punishment."

Shavik halts, staring hard at his prisoners. "Stealing, disobeying orders, or attempting to escape—all of these are serious charges, punishable by death on the orders of the district commander. Strictly women and children under fourteen will remain. Men and youths will be housed in a camp nearby. Guards, remove the male prisoners."

Cries of protest erupt from the crowd, the men and boys fearful and uncertain, the women and children crying as the guards force the men at gunpoint toward trucks parked nearby, beating anyone who protests with rifle butts. Boris Arkov wades in again with his truncheon.

Guards force a grim-faced David onto one of the trucks. "Lana, stay strong . . ."

The trucks drive back down the road. I see David's face. He waves bravely.

My heart is pounding with fear. We've heard stories of men and boys being shot by the Serbs. I'm terrified.

Luka clutches my hand and Carla's.

I hear him whisper to her, fear in his voice, "Will we be all right, Carla? Will we? Will Mama and Papa be okay, too?"

Suddenly the woman named Alma from the bus speaks up. "Commander, may I ask if we can have some food and liquids for the children?"

Boris Arkov, crimson with rage, crosses the distance between him and Alma in a second. "I thought I said not to speak unless spoken to?"

"But, sir, the children are hungry and thirsty—"

He strikes Alma a savage blow. His truncheon smacks her jaw with such force that she reels back and her bottom dentures fly out of her mouth. The guards laugh when they see the false teeth skittering across the ground.

Alma's face is cut from cheek to jaw and bleeding heavily. Arkov lashes out again, this time with his boot. "Get up. I said get up!"

Alma struggles to her feet. Arkov tears out his pistol.

Deathly silence settles over the crowd. We're certain Arkov is going to shoot Alma. I cover Luka's eyes and pull him against my leg.

Then I hear something metallic hit the ground. A moment later I realize that Carla's dropped her silver dollar and it's rolling toward Shavik's feet.

Shavik looks down as it strikes his boot. He bends, picks it up, examines it.

"Who owns this?" he demands.

Before I can stop Carla she speaks up and my heart plummets. She was always strong-willed, quick to criticize an injustice.

"I do, sir. Please, sir, don't harm the woman."

Shavik stares down at her. "Come here."

She steps toward Shavik.

"Hold out your hand."

Carla holds out her hand. Shavik places the coin gently in her palm.

"Thank you, sir."

"You're welcome." Shavik suddenly reaches out, gently strokes her hair. "What a pretty little girl. What's your name?"

"Marianna Carla Joran, sir."

I recoil as I watch his hand linger on Carla's hair. If only Shavik knew what I as her mother am thinking. I can't stop my legs shaking with fear, with revulsion.

"And what good manners you have. You know this woman?" He nods to Alma.

"Yes, sir. Please don't harm her, sir. She's a nice lady."

Shavik crosses to where the false teeth have fallen, picks them up, and hands them politely to Alma. "Yours. I believe."

The guards laugh. Shavik silences them with a look.

Alma accepts the dentures.

Then Carla says something very brave that makes my heart quake.

She looks at Shavik and says matter-of-factly, "Please, sir, the woman was only telling the truth. We've come such a long way. Everyone is hungry and thirsty, especially the children."

Shavik says nothing. Do I see his face pale with anger? In the poor light, it's hard to tell.

Boris Arkov appears to lose it. He points his pistol at Carla's head. I watch, mute with fear as Arkov's hand shakes with rage, his gun pointing at my daughter's face. Carla is terrified.

Then Arkov swings his gun back at Alma's head. "You first, you old crone."

Just when I expect she will die, Shavik lets out a roar, as if making the point that he's in charge, and not Arkov.

"Leave her, Boris. Get the prisoners back in line."

Shavik points his leather crop at Alma, her cheek cut from eye to mouth. "You heard me, madam, back in line."

He steps over to Carla next, and almost smiles. "And you, too, little girl. You've got guts, I'll give you that. But learn to do as you are told in the future; otherwise it could have some unpleasant consequences."

"Yes, sir."

Alma crawls back, grateful to be alive, and Carla burrows in to join me.

My heart is still hammering. It's a miracle no one is killed.

Shavik looks to where Carla has rejoined me.

His face lingers on mine. Do I see a flicker of recognition in his eyes, or is it my imagination? I bow my head so he can't see me. Please God, no . . .

Shavik snaps his fingers at Arkov.

"Food for the prisoners. Soup and bread."

A furious Boris Arkov has a look on his face as if he thinks Shavik's decision is insane.

"You heard me, Boris. Bring food to the dormitories. And milk for the little ones. Now have the men escort the prisoners to their quarters."

Later, Alma puts her arms around Carla and sobs, deep convulsions that rack her body.

"If it wasn't for your daughter, I wouldn't be alive. She has spirit, standing up to Shavik like that."

One of the women, a nurse, has been in the camp a week already and stitches Alma's bloodied jaw with a needle and thread, without an anesthetic. Alma faints twice, but bears up well. She's just grateful she still has her dentures.

We are all given soup and bread, and there's milk for the children, as Shavik promised.

Alma's jaw is so bad she can't eat or drink or put back in her dentures and when we finish our food she looks at me as if she wants us adults to talk. I tell Carla to take Luka to play with some other children at the end of the dormitory.

When she's gone, Alma's eyes are wary, and she tries to mutter a warning through her shrunken, bruised mouth.

"Shavik may have let me live, but I hear he's crazy. Polite one minute, deranged the next. Be careful around him in the future."

"They're both crazy, Shavik and Arkov."

The nurse dabs iodine on Alma's wound. "Shavik comes and goes here. But Arkov oversees the place most of the time. He's a complete monster."

"You know about them?" *one of the women asks.*

"They call them Cain and Abel. They're not related, but they were brought up like brothers, and they're forever at each other's throats."

"Brothers?"

The nurse says, "Boris Arkov's father is a top gangster in the Serb mafia, Ivan Arkov."

One of the women nods. "That's right. I heard Shavik's father was a lawyer who worked for Arkov. The father committed suicide when Shavik was young and Ivan Arkov took him under his wing, and treated him like a son."

"With Mila Shavik and Boris Arkov, it's like a constant power struggle between them."

"Why?"

"To be top dog of their mafia clan one day."

"Who told you all this?" the nurse asks.

"It's common knowledge. The old man, Ivan Arkov, is head of his mafia clan and controls the Red Dragons."

"What do you know about him?"

"He's so crooked they'll have to screw him into the ground when he dies. A greedy brute. All that matters to him is power and money."

"What else?"

"He's the one who tells them to steal our belongings and property from us and massacre our people. To take a life means nothing to him. His son Boris is a chip off the old block. Another heartless killer."

"And Mila Shavik?" Alma asks.

The nurse slaps the stopper back on the iodine bottle. "Shavik is simply a lackey who does Ivan Arkov's bidding."

I keep my mouth shut. I know all about Mila Shavik and his family in my hometown. And I know that's not the entire truth. But the less I tell Alma the better.

It will only disturb her.

Our first night in the camp is hell. We learn from the other prisoners that this place has a name: the Devil's Hill.

We've heard whispers about such places where people are tortured and killed in the most terrible ways. But nothing can prepare you for the reality.

The Devil's Hill houses over five hundred women and children, toddlers and young girls and boys, ranging in ages from babies in arms to thirteen.

The youngest children are frightened and filthy, and never stop crying.

The guards are brutal, heartless beasts who instill constant fear. That first night we are herded into bare dormitories. We have barely laid our heads on the bunks when at least twenty drunken guards stagger in and drag away the prettiest young women.

They are dragged outside and in through the green doors of the main building, past Shavik's office just inside the entrance.

Those green office doors will come to terrify us—once you enter, you are destined for brutal interrogation, or rape or a beating, or all three.

And sometimes death awaits you.

We hear the women's screams as they are raped all through the night.

The terror on the children's faces is too terrible to witness. I try to cover Carla's and Luka's ears to the screams but it's impossible.

I pity the poor, wailing mothers who have to listen to their young daughters being raped. One of the girls was barely fourteen.

We learn that even young boys are taken by a few more deviant guards.

It was daylight before the screams stopped.

From now on, not a night will pass without guards dragging victims away.

The things I see here, and the inhumanity, are beyond description.

Guards stare lustfully at mothers or their young daughters.

Some guards are gangsters who rob our few possessions. If a woman has jewelry or gold rings, they take them. One woman had a mouthful of gold teeth. A guard took a pliers to her mouth and pulled out her teeth.

Prisoners are either Christian or Muslim, Bosniak and Croat, but mostly Muslim.

Apart from the soup, bread, and milk the first night, for the next four days we have little food or water. Our tongues are swollen from thirst. Our children cry, but the guards ignore them.

Some women carry the lifeless bodies of their infant children who didn't survive.

The guards tell them to toss the bodies aside. When one woman refuses and swears at a guard she is dragged away. We hear her screams.

She is never seen again.

Mila Shavik has a liking for pretty young women.

Sometimes he strides into the dormitories and points out a good-looking woman in her late teens or twenties to Boris Arkov. The woman is taken to Shavik's quarters.

Shavik hasn't recognized me yet. But like many of the guards, he's often drunk, slow to recognize anyone, and for that I'm grateful.

Besides, I'm so gaunt and wretched-looking he's unlikely to remember me.

But one day Boris Arkov passes us, halts, and points to Carla with his truncheon. "What age is she?"

"Nine," I lie. Already I'm shaking.

Luka speaks up, innocently. "No, Mama, Carla is ten."

Arkov rubs his jaw and grins. "Maybe ten is old enough? What do you think, woman?"

"Sir, please . . ."

Arkov grips Carla's face between his thumb and forefinger, studying her looks. She is rigid with fear.

I want to kill Arkov.

How dare he.

How dare he talk about my daughter like that. How dare he even touch her. But I can do nothing.

Arkov lets go of Carla's face. He looks at me, a cruel glint in his eyes. "Don't worry, I'll keep a look out for her until I think she's ready."

Then he laughs aloud and walks away.

The world we live in is bizarre.

We never know how our jailers will react.

I hear a story today. A drunken guard rapes a child of twelve. She's left bloody, dazed, and crying outside a dormitory by her attacker until her frightened mother dares to come out to calm and hug her.

Shavik marches past and sees the woman and child. "What's going on?" he demands

The poor woman is too distraught to tell, and fearful the truth may condemn her.

"I asked what's going on."

Shavik's tone is so fierce the woman has no choice but to tell him.

"Which guard did this?"

The woman points a shaking finger toward a bunch of uniforms playing cards by the camp entrance gates, fifty yards away.

Shavik marches over and confronts a truculent, middle-aged guard with a fat beer gut and a drooping mustache. "You assaulted the child?"

The guard grins, wiping the back of his mouth with a grubby hand. "Defiant little brat, she was. She needed a lesson, Commandant. I gave her one."

"And what order did I give you?"

"To guard the entrance, Commandant."

"Not to leave your post, correct?"

"Well, yes, Commandant, but—"

Without a word Shavik tears out his pistol and shoots the man point-blank in the head. He slumps to the group, body twitching, blood pumping from his skull.

"No one disobeys my orders in future. They follow orders, not their own lusts. Or else they'll leave here in a box."

The guards drag the dead man away.

And every adult prisoner wonders the same question: Did Shavik kill the guard because he disobeyed orders or because he felt something for the child?

"Mama, how long are we going to stay here?"

"I don't know, my precious."

"Why are we here?"

"It's because . . . it's because these men see us as their enemies."

"Why? We've never harmed them, have we?"

"No. But they see us as different."

"How?"

"Just . . . different."

"We don't behave differently. I heard one of the women say we are Bosniaks. Are Bosniaks different? But we're not different, are we? And if we were what does it matter? We're just people."

Luka chimes in. "Yes, we're just people, Mama."

The questions go on. I'm sure every parent here has to try to answer such questions. But how can you explain over five hundred years of history to a child, when a child sees only the present?

So far we have survived the brutality around us.

But I fear our luck won't last.

For more than five hundred women and children there are six toilets and showers.

There is never hot water, except when the guards want the women to wash before they abuse them. Winter is hard and we have to wash our children in icy-cold water. The women make a roster, but sometimes there are arguments and fights.

I've heard rumors that in David's camp, the men and boys live in worse conditions and have even fewer blankets than we have. Every day—every single day—I worry about David. How is he? Is he coping? How is his health?

The questions torment me.

There is little food in the women's camp, though some days there might be fresh bread and milk and eggs. Mostly our rations consist of watery bean soup with rice and stale bread. One day, a woman complains. One of the guards undoes his fly and urinates in the soup. "Complain now, you whiner."

He laughs and strides away.

Fourteen women and six children died in the first month. All the children died of illness and malnutrition. Eight women died from internal bleeding after being raped. Victims' bodies are dumped in a pit at the edge of the camp.

The deaths of children are the hardest to deal with.

Their mothers wail and lose their minds. Two mothers who lost children ran blindly into the barbed wire and were shot by the guards, their bodies left to rot as a warning to others.

Luka no longer runs and plays and teases. Carla is listless and sad, and no longer carefree.

I try desperately to look after them, but I find my health is worsening with so little food, and I worry I will fall ill. Carla, being older, knows what is going on but Luka is totally confused. They miss their father desperately.

Carla talks about him all the time. She never stops praying and hoping that he is safe and well.

Just when we are in the depths of misery, we experience a small miracle.

Spring has come early in the first week of March. The sun shines.

The pump for the well that supplies the camp's water breaks down. Alma and I are ordered to take a load of guards' clothes down to a river to wash.

First a gruff young guard takes us to a janitor's closet in one of the hallways off the main building.

In the closet are sackfuls of foul-smelling clothes. He hands us bars of soap and warns us to do a good job or else he'll beat us.

The guard escorts us out of the camp. Alma drags two sacks. I carry Luka in my arms and Carla and I haul another two sacks.

We walk through a forest to a beautiful meadow with a shallow, gently flowing river. Butterflies float past and it's like a summer's day, a world away from the Devil's Hill.

The guard lies with his rifle against a tree and chain-smokes, watching us soaping the clothes.

Carla and Luka splash the water but Alma warns them not to make too much noise in case the guard gets irritated.

"Can we swim, Mama? Can we swim, please?"

"No, Carla. The guard wouldn't allow it."

I wasn't thinking about swimming. I was thinking about escape.

In the distance I see rooftops, a church spire. We are almost five hundred yards from the camp. We could be gone before anyone notices, if only we could disarm the guard, and tie him up or knock him unconscious.

I glance back at him. He's chewing a stem of grass, not even bothering to look at us. He's thin, and doesn't look very strong. Could Alma and I overpower him?

Then I think of David.

How could we ever leave him behind?

Before I can gather my thoughts I see Carla brazenly march up to the guard.

"Sir, we need to wash. May we bathe in the river, sir? Please?"

The guard says lazily, "Ten minutes, no more. I'll be watching, so don't try anything, you hear?"

"Yes, sir. Thank you, sir."

I take her arm. "Carla, no. Luka's had a cold."

"Please, Mama. Luka's well now."

"Carla . . ."

"But, Mama, how often do we get the chance to wash in a river?"

Alma says, "She's right, Lana. Take it while it's going, is my motto."

I give in. The gently flowing river looks tempting, and it's not too cold.

We undress, and Carla helps me remove Luka's disheveled clothes. He is overjoyed, and can't wait to splash naked in the water.

The guard watches us all naked as we wash, and really it seems so absurd.

In the midst of all this death and despair, we hold hands with Alma and rush together out into the river, scooping out armfuls of water and whooping with joy.

I feel like a child again.

As I soap Luka he gets into an excited fit of giggles and his pink little bottom runs away from me and I chase him through the water. For a few brief minutes we delight in the pleasure and the awe of being alive.

Carla begs him for a kiss. Luka chuckles and runs away.

"No, no kisses for you today," he teases.

Then Carla catches him and he laughs with joy and plants kisses on our cheeks in reward.

"I told you, Mama. He needs this," Carla says, and we all lie down in the river and let it soak our bodies, and looking up at the aching blue sky it almost feels as if we're on a beach and the waves are washing over us.

When the guard beckons, we dry ourselves with our clothes, dress, and walk back to the camp. As we approach the gates, Luka and Carla are skipping as they walk.

For the first time since we arrived in the camp, I see smiles on their faces.

I can never tell the children about my rape.

That night after bathing in the river the young guard escorting us came into our dormitory. He was joined by Boris Arkov, and both were drunk.

I can smell their vodka breath.

Carla and Luka are fast asleep. Arkov and the young guard grab me and another woman.

My heart pounds and I whimper as they drag me to their billet.

Boris Arkov beats me hard with his fists. "Shut up! Shut up, do you hear? Do as you're told or I'll kill you."

Arkov and the young guard take turns raping me. When Arkov falls into a drunk sleep, the young guard finally throws me out of the billet.

I feel defiled.

I feel beyond anger. Beyond any feeling of self-pity.

I crawl back to our dormitory and into the corner of a freezing cold shower. I find a piece of wire pot scrubber. No matter how much I scrub my raw skin under icy water with the harsh wire, I still feel dirty.

The pain between my legs feels like a fire. It takes an hour for my bleeding to stop. When I return to the dormitory and lie beside my two sleeping children I stifle my tears. I look at Carla and Luka, and I feel so ashamed.

There is an unspoken rule among the women that we never talk about what happened to us—pained glances are enough to communicate our suffering. Despite everything I'm grateful that I'm still alive and that it was me they chose and not my daughter.

Not a minute goes by when Boris Arkov's threat doesn't torment me.

How can I protect Carla? How?

I've seen Arkov take young girls to his quarters, some no more than thirteen or fourteen. Guards have raped girls as young as twelve.

I'm terrified for Carla. She's still a child.

And the guards are becoming even more cruel and debased.

Sometimes they rape mothers in front of their children. Or enter the dormitory and order a group of young women to strip. They pick the ones they want. Sometimes they pick mothers and older daughters to add to the degradation.

The next day, Arkov is drunk again. He grins as he passes me.

"Well, did you enjoy last night? Maybe next time I might try that young daughter of yours."

Luka has a low fever and a cough. I'm afraid the bathing in the river has harmed his health.

Later that afternoon, we hear shelling in the far distance.

The guards look anxious. A rumor spreads that the camp will soon be under attack from liberating Bosniak forces.

Alma confides that she thinks the guards will kill us all—we're witnesses to their crimes. I fear it may be true.

I look at Carla and Luka and ask myself what kind of men

could kill such beautiful children. But I know the answer—the same men who have raped us, degraded us, shot us, tortured us.

I long for David.

To feel him hold me, and to hold him. It is unbearable, not being able to see the one you love, or know if he is all right.

To add to our despair, these last weeks our rations of soup and bread are cut. The children are like skin and bone. Desperate women try to steal food from the guards to feed their hungry children, or willingly trade their bodies for any medicines they can get. But if they are caught stealing, they risk the wrath of Mila Shavik or Boris Arkov.

I recall a young woman who was caught stealing some chocolate from a guard to give her little boy. Shavik was away from the camp that week. Arkov was in charge, and as a guard beat her, he appeared.

Arkov slurred his words, sounding drunk as he said to the woman, "So you stole from one of my men?"

"My . . . my child was hungry, sir."

"Point out your child to me."

The woman was deathly pale.

Arkov used his truncheon to lift her chin. "I said point the child out to me."

She pointed to a boy, no more than eight. Mila crooked his finger at him. "Come here, boy."

The fearful child approached, and stared at him dumbly.

Arkov drew his pistol. "Was the chocolate good, little boy?"

When he didn't answer Arkov cocked his pistol.

The mother became distraught and begged him not to harm the child. Arkov fired into the ground in front of her, making her dance.

When he stopped shooting, a laughing Arkov grabbed a rope from one of the guards. He slipped it around the woman's neck and threw it over a wooden beam above a loading bay. In an instant he hauled the woman up, choking her.

The distraught child, watching his mother struggle to breathe, wailed and began to beat Arkov with his fists.

Arkov stared down at him. "Well, was the chocolate good? Was it worth your stupid mother's life? Don't you people understand the rules?" He stared wildly and screamed at the prisoners. "Don't you?"

Then Arkov simply staggered away drunkenly as the woman choked to death.

The boy was left there, crying beside his mother's corpse until one of the guards hauled him away and we never saw him again.

It snows, flakes falling all day. A sudden cold snap worries us. Everyone's health is frail.

More distant shelling tonight, and crackling gunfire. I try to keep Luka warm, but his nose is constantly running. For something to do, I let him draw on the back of my diary with some crayons Alma managed to find.

Luka draws a picture of the camp, guarded by men with guns. Another picture shows the figures of a man and woman and two children, a boy and a girl. All have tears falling from their eyes.

Underneath each figure Luka wrote a name: Mama, Papa, Carla, Luka. Beside each he drew a shaky red heart and signed the drawing: Luka.

It breaks my heart. When I see my son's little face look up at me with a weak, runny-nosed smile I want to cry.

Alma hears of an outbreak of pneumonia in the men's camp.

She says the words I dread. "I heard one of the ill men is an American."

This is the first news I have heard about David in months.

I despair knowing he's ill.

One of the women, the nurse, says he will need antibiotics to survive.

To make things worse, Carla has a cold, and Luka, too.

Luka's health is even more troubling. He coughs all night and has a temperature.

His chest was always weak. We should never have gone for that swim.

It is my fault, not Carla's. I allowed it.

And now I am worried sick for my children as well as my husband.

The next day, Luka's fever worsens and he starts to cough up blood.

"My chest hurts, Mama."

He looks sickly, his breathing labored. Carla and I take turns cooling Luka's fevered brow with a damp cloth. I need antibiotics, for the children and for David. I know the guards will give us nothing.

I feel so desperate with worry.

In my despair, I know I have only one vain chance.

Reveal myself to Mila Shavik and plead with him to help. Beg him on my knees and do whatever I have to in return for antibiotics.

And I know in my heart I must try to convince him to let me see David.

I tell Alma my plan, as much detail as I need to.

She looks frightened. "Catch Shavik in a bad mood and he's liable to kill you."

"His father knew mine."

"You mean they were acquaintances?"

"No. They hated each other. They came from the same village."

"For heaven's sake, Lana, don't do this. What if he kills you?"

"I'll need soap. A little makeup. Someone to help tidy my hair."

"You . . . you're going to offer yourself to Shavik?"

"I'll do whatever I have to."

Alma looks revolted, but I know she understands.

That evening I wash my hair and my body. I have no perfume, no decent clothes. I have no good underwear but scrub and wash my only change of dress. Alma loans me her cardigan.

I put on a little makeup she has managed to scrape together for me.

Carla sees me tidied up and says, "What . . . what are you doing, Mama?"

"I need to talk to someone."

"Who?"

"Mila Shavik. I need to ask him for medicines."

"I . . . I don't need medicines."

"Perhaps, but Luka and your father do."

Carla gives me the horrified look of a ten-year-old who suddenly comprehends the harsh adult ways of the world.

At that moment I am ashamed of my daughter's accusing stare.

But I know what I must do.

I kiss her forehead, leave Alma to take care of my children, and make my way to the camp office.

Behind the frosted glass, I see a lightbulb swinging above a desk and hear Shavik's gruff voice on the telephone.

The slovenly guard outside licks his lips and grins. "Well, well. All dressed up and nowhere to go. What do you want, woman?"

"To see Commandant Mila Shavik."

"Why?"

"Please tell him Lana Tanovic from Konjic wishes to see him."

Carla paused. The next page was missing.

What happened to her mother? Had Shavik raped her? Had her mother been so ashamed afterward she had ripped out the page recounting her ordeal?

Carla felt a soaring anger.

And a powerful connection to her mother.

To save her family she had risked her life, offering herself to an animal like Shavik. She hated him. Hated Shavik and his guards for the savagery they inflicted upon so many.

Carla tried to ignore the missing page. But it was almost impossible—she kept imagining the terrible humiliation her mother must have endured.

She read on.

Only a few pages remained, and the entries looked rushed . . .

It's done. I did what I had to.

What Shavik did makes me cry.

A little later he strides into our dormitory. He stares at me, not speaking. But I see a strange, unfathomable look in his eyes. I wonder if the man has a soul? He studies Carla, watching her a long time, then without a word, he tosses a bag of antibiotics at me.

He strides out again, a kind of anger in his gait.

At least he kept his word. I give Luka his antibiotics. His fever is still rising. Alma will watch over him and Carla while I bring antibiotics to David.

Shavik will allow me thirty minutes to see him—thirty minutes more than I ever expected. Shavik's on edge—like the entire camp. Distant explosions erupt all day. It can't be long before the camp is overrun.

Will we be freed? I pray that we will. That my family lives through this.

The snow still falls. A guard arrives at noon in a truck and drives me for several miles to David's camp. They call it Omarska. A big, red-bricked, disused iron-mining complex with several outbuildings.

But nothing prepares me for what I see.

It is absolutely inhuman.

I imagine it is worse than Auschwitz was. There the prisoners had barracks and bunks. There was some element of hygiene.

But at Omarska, the prisoners are kept in filthy dormitories with tightly packed metal cots, or in cattle stalls.

The camp is freezing and stinks of sweat and excrement. Each stall holds about a dozen men. They are all matchstick-thin— bones protrude from their flesh, their hair chopped tight, their eyes huge in starving faces. Despair hangs in the air like an atmosphere.

I weep as the guard escorts me down the center aisle of the stalls.

My heart pounds as I scan the prisoners for David. Gaunt faces stare back at me—husbands and sons, old men and young, boys as young as fourteen, their ribs showing through ragged clothes. They look spiritless and terrified.

They look like they should be in school, or playing football, enjoying their youth, but they huddle together like farm animals for warmth.

A few are crying and look like they have lost their minds. I see a boy no more than fifteen shake his head from side to side, crying for his mother. Everyone stares at me as if I'm an apparition. There's an air of submissive silence.

The guard checks his list and halts at a filthy stall. The stench of human excrement is awful. The male prisoners look like skeletons.

I don't recognize David at first.

He's sitting in a corner, propped against a metal rail, wearing the same blue shirt I last saw him wearing. It's caked with dirt, his blond hair matted, his parched lips cracked with a mass of sores.

My heart freezes. He is skin and bone. He looks ill. I can see his ribs through his shirt. His eyes flutter when he sees me. He can't believe it's me at first, and then he weeps.

The guard opens the gate, and I sit with David in the foul-smelling stall, but nothing matters now that I am close to him again.

I kiss his face, wipe his eyes, and clutch his bony hands. "David. My beautiful David."

He whispers hoarsely, still in shock. "Lana, it's really you . . . ?"

I'm so overcome I cannot answer.

"How are you? How . . . are the children?"

"They're well, David. We're all well."

I lie. I can't tell him the truth.

His eyes barely focus. "How did you get in . . . how did they allow you?"

"I begged and begged." I lie again. I'm so choked with tears.

He gives my hand a frail squeeze. His chest wheezes hoarsely when he speaks.

"We'll get out of this, Lana. We'll get out. We just have to stay strong."

"Yes, we will."

"I'm going to make sure you keep to your promise . . . I haven't forgotten."

"Promise?"

"The bridge . . . I want to see that jump."

He offers the ghost of a smile and winks, his eyelids fluttering.

"Of course." I caress his face.

I force him to swallow two long white pills. I have no water. I make him swallow hard, his Adam's apple bobbing.

"David, you must listen to what I tell you, it's so important. There are enough antibiotics for ten days. They will make you better. You need to take two every four hours. Can you please make sure you do that? Please?"

He nods, but I'm not convinced he'll remember. The emaciated man beside him looks more alert. I close David's hand around the pill bottle.

"Please," I tell the other man. "He's my husband. He needs to take two of these pills every four hours to get better. Can you make certain he does that? Please, I'm depending on you to remind him."

The man nods, but I wonder if he knows what time it is, let alone how long until four hours elapse.

"Yes, I'll remember. Two every four hours."

"I beg you, make sure he takes the pills. Or his health will get worse."

"Do you have pills for me?"

"Are you sick?"

"We're all sick here."

"I'm sorry. I have none for you. But I'll try to come back. I'll try to get more."

I know that it's unlikely I'll ever be allowed back but I'll say anything if it helps David. A far-off shell explodes. The prisoners murmur with fear, their nerves frayed. When two more explosions sound, the corrugated roof rattles. The nervous guard grabs my arm.

"Time's up."

"But Commander Shavik said I could have half an hour . . ."

"Didn't you hear me? We're leaving now."

He drags me out. I hold on to David's hand until our fingers stretch and part.

We always said we'd never leave each other, no matter what.

I don't want to leave him now.

My eyes can't leave his face.

We both know—we both know that we may never see each other again and the pain of that knowing shatters my heart.

The last thing I see are David's wet, desolate blue eyes stare after me as he waves a dazed and frail goodbye.

David, my beautiful, wonderful David—what will become of us?

When I return Carla asks me where I have been.

I cry the moment she asks me. I can't help it. I pretend I'm crying because I'm happy. But I know that David is so very ill. That he may not survive.

My spirit is broken but I can't show Carla that.

I say brightly, "I saw your daddy today, Carla. I saw him. I spoke with him."

She's stunned. "How—how is he?"

"He's fine, sweetheart. He is fit and healthy and he sends his love. He wants me to give you a big hug from him."

She looks at me, doubtful, but I know she wants to believe me.

I hear far-off exploding shells. We cling to each other, a fevered Luka asleep beside us.

And then the thing I'm dreading most happens.

Arkov marches into our dormitory. I smell alcohol from him.

"You're to come with me."

I stand.

"Not you. Your daughter."

"My . . . my daughter?"

"You heard me."

I've been waiting for this to happen.

"Please don't harm her."

Arkov grunts. "Do as I say. Shavik wants to see her."

"For . . . for what?"

Rage erupts on his face. "Question me again and I'll give you both a beating you won't forget."

"Mama . . ." Carla gives me a pleading, confused look, and starts to cry. "Please, I don't want to go, don't let him make me . . ."

I stroke her hair, try to calm her.

"Please, Carla, just go to Shavik. Tell him you love your brother and father. Tell him they mean everything to you. Tell him you're desperate to save them. That we need stronger antibiotics. Ask him to show mercy. You must do it, do it for your father and for Luka, for all of us."

I see tears in Carla's eyes.

Arkov clicks his fingers. "Come, on, come on, I haven't got all day."

He marches Carla away by the arm.

My soul feels shredded. My shoulders heave and I break down in tears.

By revealing myself, what have I allowed to happen?

What have I done? I've paid a terrible price for seeing Shavik. For those little white pills.

And then I cry, a torrent of tears I can't hold back.

I pace the dormitory for over an hour until Carla returns.

She looks completely dazed. Like a sleepwalker. I hug her close and try to talk to her. She barely looks at me and doesn't speak. She has tears in her eyes.

"Are you hurt? Did Shavik hurt you? What did he say to you?"

I know something happened to my daughter when she met with Shavik and it cuts me to the bone. But Carla barely shakes her head and won't talk.

A guard comes and tosses me stronger antibiotics for Luka. "What did you do to earn those, woman?"

The far-off shelling resumes. After I give Luka the pills, Alma rushes in.

"Can you hear the gunfire getting nearer? The rumor's going around that Shavik will have to evacuate us all by the morning if he and his men hope to escape."

But I'm barely listening. I watch Carla as she numbly folds and unfolds Luka's blankie—as she always does when she's frightened or upset.

Another explosion.

Luka jolts in his fevered sleep. Carla strokes his hair, his dark curls damp on his brow, his breath rasping.

Alma says, "What's wrong with Carla? She's gone very quiet."

Before I can answer, a handful of drunken guards enter the dormitory and tell everyone to prepare to leave by 6 a.m.

The women must gather their few belongings and there's total fear and panic in the air. The word goes around that Shavik doesn't have enough trucks to transport us. He has to wait until morning for more to arrive.

Carla is still silent. She worries me but frail Luka worries me even more. He's still fevered, not well enough to move any-where.

Rumors fly. "They say our troops are only ten miles away!"

In the yard beyond the barred window, the guards are pack-ing away their equipment. Drinking heavily like the cowards that they are, as if afraid of the battle to come.

Except Shavik, who's all business. I see him waving his hands and giving orders to his men.

I'm praying that the camp will be liberated soon.

But a worried Alma whispers, "Even if they move us, they'll kill us, Lana. We're only a burden—we're witnesses. We have a chance to escape now while there's panic. But we have to do it before the trucks leave tomorrow."

I think: Shavik said that we would be evacuated for our own safety.

But every day now his men are drinking, on edge, fingering their weapons. Can they be trusted to obey orders? I'm full of doubt.

When I don't respond fast enough, Alma becomes agitated. Her eyes stare at me with a wild, almost mad look.

"For heaven's sake, aren't you listening to me?"

"I hear you Alma."

"Then answer."

"I'm thinking."

"This is no time to think, it's time to act."

Alma is frantic with panic. Others begin to look at her. I grasp her shoulders.

"Alma . . . Alma . . . get a grip of yourself."

She calms, but I know that what she says makes sense.

I know our lives are at risk.

The guards are like loose cannon, capable of anything.

Now is the time to take our chances and flee.

But how?

And what about David? My poor David . . .

Later, as Carla and Luka sleep, I sit in a corner with my diary and pen.

I think long and hard.

This may be the last time I will write. My writing may even be of no consequence. But I must record all that has happened to us even if there's only a small chance that others will read my words.

The world must know. Not only what has happened, but to take hope, that the human spirit has a power that endures.

I know this to be so, despite all our tragedies.

Evil can never destroy the light of goodness that shines within us.

How can it ever?

When there is not enough darkness in the world to quench the light of one small candle . . .

A little after midnight my head hurts from thinking.

But a plan sparks in my mind.

I pack Luka's blankie and his pills inside his Thomas the Train
backpack. Luka looks wretched, his face bathed in sweat.
I don't waken the children just yet, only Alma.
"What is it?" she asks drowsily.
And I tell her—tell her what I think is our last hope of escape . . .

The writing ended abruptly. Carla flipped over the pages but they were blank, except for the childish drawings in Luka's hand at the back of the diary.

She was tormented by questions.

What happened to her mother and her father and to Luka?

She tried to think straight but it was impossible.

What happened to her in Shavik's office?

She could recall nothing, not even meeting with Shavik.

And then her mother's words in the diary rang in her mind like church bells.

It's done. I did what I had to.

What Shavik did makes me cry.

The indignity her mother must have endured at the hands of Shavik in return for the medicines.

Had she herself been assaulted, too?

She felt her temples throb with a blinding headache.

She put down the diary.

She sat back in the chair for a long time, staring at the ceiling.

Closing her eyes tightly, she slowly opened them again.

She felt sadness, pain, rage. A jumble of feelings.

She struggled hard to pull more memories from her mind.

For a time her headache felt so blinding she could barely focus.

At first, nothing came.

And then it suddenly felt as if someone had opened a floodgate and a dam broke inside her skull.

Memories washed in. They came in such an emotionally charged burst that she almost drowned in the deluge.

The time on the bus when the guard struck her father.

The long march to the camp. Luka wearing his Thomas the Train backpack as she clutched his small hand. She remembered him begging for water. And the desolate, terrified look in her mother's eyes.

She remembered all the mothers, terrified, exhausted. The little children crying. The stricken agony on her father's face, which almost seemed like shame—he must have felt so helpless he could do nothing to ease his family's suffering.

In her mind she saw again the distraught mother who stole some chocolate for her little boy and was hung by Boris Arkov, her child wailing until he was taken away and never seen again.

She saw the brutal faces of the guards, and the pitiful faces of their victims.

And that one glorious day—bathing in the river with her mother and Luka, the feel of the cold, bubbling water on her body.

It all came back.

She buried her face in her hands, sobbing.

It all felt too much to take in.

She reached under Dr. Leon's desk and pressed the buzzer.

15

"Where did you get my mother's diary?"

"I thought I explained. You had it with you when you were found. That and the silver dollar."

"Found where?"

"Wandering the streets of a deserted town four miles from the camp. You read the journal to the end?"

"Yes. Who found me?"

"NATO special forces on a reconnaissance mission in the area."

"Did I tell them what happened to me?"

"Not at once. You were shell-shocked, badly traumatized, and suffering from hypothermia."

"Was the camp overrun?"

"Yes, the same day they found you."

"What happened to Luka?"

"I've no idea, Carla. But I believe the camp was searched and found completely empty. I'm sure Baize can tell you more."

Carla collapsed back into her chair. "She—she kept all this from me, all these years."

"Baize kept silent on my instructions."

"Why?"

"I couldn't risk triggering your memory. Baize simply loves you and did as I asked her. Even if her silence came at a heavy price."

"What do you mean?"

Dr. Leon said gently, "I think I'll leave that for Baize to explain. What are you thinking, Carla? What do you feel?"

"I can't think right now. I'm still reeling."

"But you're coping?"

"No, I'm not. Not after reading so much horror."

"I know it seems inconceivable that men would inflict such depravity on other human beings. So many people were killed and tortured in your mother's homeland. Men, women, children. The savagery was terrible. Butchery not seen on a scale since the Nazis' mass killing of Jews."

She looked at Leon. "You asked what I feel. I feel angry. And ashamed."

"Why shame?"

"That I could forget my mother and father and Luka for so long."

"Not your fault, just your mind's way of coping. But you're beginning to remember, aren't you? It's starting to come back."

"Yes. Images. Recollections. Some of them clear, others kind of vague, and hazy."

"It's going to be like that in the coming days and weeks. I'm also certain the memories will get sharper. You have to be prepared for that. I'll be here to help every step of the way."

Dr. Leon removed his glasses, rubbed his eyes with a thumb and forefinger.

"If it all becomes too much, or if you need to talk to me at anytime, just remember I'm at the other end of a phone, twenty-four/seven."

"Whatever happened to Shavik and Arkov?"

"I read various reports that claimed they were dead. Others suggested they assumed new identities and vanished. So many of the minor players have never been apprehended and punished, I'm sorry to say."

He pushed his glasses back on the bridge of his nose.

"Do you recall anything about when you were summoned to see Shavik? What he did or said to you? If he harmed you?"

"No. Nothing. It's a blank."

"Of course, we have to consider there's the real possibility he physically or sexually assaulted you."

Carla felt herself recoil.

"But I have to tell you that this aspect of your case has me really confused."

"Why?"

"For example, all the perpetrators of child abuse that I have worked with were previously abused as children. Often when they reach an age where they have power, they reenact the trauma in the role of the powerful one, the abuser.

"Equally, the abuse could have the opposite effect. It may prevent them from having normal sexual relations, even when they don't remember the abuse. I've known clients who can't even look at their own genitals, and can't get any further than a fully clothed hug with the opposite sex."

"Meaning?"

"There's no indication of any of that with you. Either your memory has suppressed the abuse, or no abuse never occurred."

"But why would I suppress it if nothing happened?"

"That's what's so confusing. Something happened, I feel certain of that. What it was, I've no idea."

"The missing diary pages. Do you have any idea what they might contain?"

"No, I don't."

Leon reflected. "I remember when you first came to me."

"Remember what?"

"How for months after you arrived in this country you could relate to no one, not even to Baize and Dan. You'd hide away in your room, curled up in a ball like an addict trying to detox."

"I didn't talk much?"

"No. You seemed to remember nothing of your past, either, or want to, yet you had constant nightmares. Some nights you'd wake, screaming. You see your arm . . ."

Carla held up her scarred right arm, as Dr. Leon said, "On one occasion, you punched your hand through a glass window. You suffered deep lacerations that required major surgery. And then eventually you settled down."

"At least I know now the recent nightmares make sense. For a while I thought I was going mad. Now I'm not sure which is worse."

"What do you mean?"

"The feeling that I was going insane or knowing the truth."

She rose from her chair.

"Where are you going, Carla?"

"To see Baize. I'm sorry. I can't talk about this with you anymore today."

"That's all right. But go easy on Baize, okay? She's had a lot to deal with in the past, losing her only son and your family. We'll need to talk again, you and I. You've had a lot to take in."

"When?"

"Soon as you feel up to it. This isn't going to be easy. Working our way through everything could take a long time. But we want to make sure you're in a fit mental state before your baby arrives."

"I . . . I'd like to keep this." She picked up the diary, ran her fingers over the scuffed leather.

"Of course. It's yours."

Carla flipped toward the back pages and the crayon drawings.

Touching the faded colors with her fingertips, she faltered.

She had a blurred recollection of Luka's face—it came back like a jagged pain. A sweet little boy with an impish smile, a head of dark curls, cupid lips. His left eye cloudy white from birth. How could she ever forget a brother as darling as Luka?

How could she ever forget her mother and father? It seemed impossible that her mind could have blotted out the family she loved.

Rage started to seep in. And a gut-wrenching ache. She felt the anguish of having everything she cherished ripped away from her. She would face her grief in private, but right now she felt her body shake with anger.

"I . . . I have to know what became of Luka and my parents."

Dr. Leon pursed his lips. "I understand, Carla. But I know Baize and Dan did their utmost. They contacted relief agencies, orphanages, and displacement camps to see if your family survived, but got nowhere. We have to assume the worst. The remains of so many victims were never found. And twenty years is a long time ago now."

"I don't care how long ago it was. I need to know."

"I had a feeling you might say that. Of course, I'd prefer you stepped back a little right now. Take it one day at a time. I don't want you to overburden yourself."

"You don't understand. I feel it'll destroy me if I don't find out." She looked up at Dr. Leon. "Do you think there's any hope that Luka and my mother and father survived?"

"Honestly, I've no idea, Carla, but we have to be realistic."

He put a hand on her shoulder. "After twenty years that may be hoping too much."

16

She saw the car in her driveway.

When Carla turned the key in her front door, she found Baize seated at the patio table on the back deck, sipping from a tall iced glass, a dry martini in front of her. She looked nervous. A big, thick manila envelope lay on the table.

"I helped myself, I hope you don't mind."

Carla said nothing as she went to stand at the rail. She wrapped her arms around herself. Waves crashed on the beach, a salt tang on the breeze.

"I'm almost afraid to ask how it went with Dr. Leon." Baize stood. "I've been worried sick about you. You're still in shock, aren't you?"

"Shock doesn't even begin to describe it. I'm overwhelmed."

"I thought your appointment must have finished hours ago."

"It did. I went for a long walk."

"I tried calling you."

"I left my phone off. I needed time to think. To figure some things out."

"You read all of your mom's diary?"

"Yes."

Baize put out a hand, gently touched Carla's back. "I'm so sorry it all had to be kept a secret, sweetheart. But that's how Dr. Leon wanted it. Dan and I just followed his advice."

"I'm still angry with you. I can't help it. And I'm angry at the people who destroyed my family. Angry at the senseless brutality of it all."

Baize looked out to sea. "I went through all that years ago, Carla. The fury, the questions. I wish I could tell you different but there's no answer to any of it. Just grief. Deep, numbing grief."

"I feel I know so little about my mom and dad."

"What can I tell you?"

"Tell me about the time when they met."

"We were living in a military base near Frankfurt in Germany where Dan was posted. It wasn't exactly a happy time for any of us."

"Why not?"

"Dan and your dad were like oil and water. Dan was a spit-and-polish West Point man. I guess he hoped our son would one day follow in his footsteps. But David was an artist, a dreamer, not the military type."

"They often argued?"

"Never stopped. That didn't mean they didn't love each other. They did."

Baize offered a sad smile. "I guess they just didn't realize that the same love that keeps you together sometimes drives you apart."

She paused. "Neither of them could show their feelings for each other all that easily. The rows got worse that summer when your dad finished art college and couldn't find a proper job. And then finally everything exploded, like a bomb going off."

"What happened?"

"Dan felt David was wasting his life and needed a solid career. They fought like pit bulls, screaming and shouting. Until one day out of frustration Dan struck David—something he'd never done before. Struck him and split his lip."

"What happened?"

"David stormed out, saying he didn't want to live in his father's shadow. I begged him to stay but he said he was going to live his own life. The next thing we knew he was driving to the Greek islands. Then six months later David wrote saying he had met and married your mom in Dubrovnik. I knew then we'd lost him for good."

Baize's voice trailed off. "He seemed so young at twenty-one, still a boy. For him to leave like that, and make a life for himself so far away from us, it was hard on Dan and me. We loved David so much. But what could we do?"

She wiped her eyes with a paper tissue, sniffled, then picked up her martini, finished it in one swallow, and put down the glass.

"I know you think I sometimes drink too much. I know I do, too. But when you've lost your husband and your only son, and most of his family, sometimes cracking open a bottle seems like the only way to deaden the pain. Except it really doesn't."

Carla reached out, put a hand on Baize's. At that moment she felt she understood so much. "Tell me about Vienna."

"We had three glorious days together. It was wonderful to see you all. You were eight and Luka was walking. You probably don't remember. I brought you a Barbie doll with a pink dress."

Carla tried, but couldn't recall. Dr. Leon had worked his magic too well.

"I remember the silver dollars."

Baize smiled. "You and Luka were thrilled with them."

"Did you like my mom when you met her?"

"To be honest, I resented her. It wasn't easy losing my only child, knowing he'd made a new life for himself in a distant country. But I realized Lana was a good woman, and that she loved David. And her strength and love shine through in her diary. I know you would have been proud of her."

"You kept in touch afterward?"

Baize nodded. "After Vienna things even mellowed between Dan and your dad. Once the war started and word of the killings got out, Dan sensed big trouble ahead and begged David to leave the country. David wanted to. But then your mom's father took ill and everything changed."

Baize paused, pain creasing her face. "Afterward, Dan always felt he was partly responsible for David's death. He could never forgive himself. He always said if only he hadn't argued so much, or struck David, maybe things would have worked out differently."

Baize gave a wistful sigh. "Of course, we never found David's remains, or your mom's or Luka's. Heaven knows we tried to discover what happened to them. The refugee agencies kept lists of survivors but had no knowledge if they lived or died. That wasn't unusual."

"Why?"

"There were so many victims. At least five thousand prisoners at the Omarska camp died by execution or ill treatment, or from disease or starvation."

Baize's mouth tightened in anger. "Many of them were just young men, or schoolboys."

"Didn't they find any remains at that camp?"

"A mass grave was unearthed ten years ago a few hundred yards away by the International Commission of Missing Persons in Sarajevo. However, none of the remains matched our family DNA."

"They have my DNA?"

"Yes."

"How?"

"We sent them your blood sample years ago. They would have been able to confirm your mom's and Luka's DNA through you."

"But they never have."

"There are so many thousands of victims that have never been found, Carla. Their bodies buried in secret graves or dumped in places like the mines around Omarska."

Baize's eyes glistened. "But at least we found you. That helped ease our pain a little, knowing you survived."

Carla hugged her.

She finally drew back. "Dr. Leon said something I didn't understand."

"What?"

"That your silence came at a heavy price. What did he mean?"

Baize picked up the manila envelope, her face strained.

"Why don't we go inside? I've got something you need to see."

17

Baize placed the envelope on the kitchen table.

Carla almost felt the ground shake beneath her. "I'm not sure I can take any more revelations."

She looked down at the envelope, then at Baize, and shot her a question. *What's inside?*

Baize sat. "Jan knew. I told him."

"Told him what . . . ?"

"The truth about your past."

"You told him everything?"

"I was afraid, Carla. Afraid of what might happen if your memory ever came back. I felt Jan needed to know what he was getting into before he married you. So I told him as soon as you got engaged."

"I don't know what to say."

"I was scared about telling him at first. But Jan was a good man. I felt he'd understand. After all, he'd been through his own ordeal."

"I know now why I felt a connection to him, why the pain in his music spoke to me. What did Jan say?"

"That knowing your past made him love you all the more."

"He said that?"

"Yes."

"Who else knew?"

"Only Paul. I knew Jan and his brother were close and always confided in each other. So I figured it was best to tell them both. That way it would make it easier for Jan. He'd have someone to talk to about it if he needed to, and not feel as if he was breaking a confidence."

Baize added, "I made only one condition: that they never divulge our talk to you or to anyone else. What's wrong?"

Carla shook her head and felt a catch in her throat. *Jan knew. So that's why he was hunting down Mila Shavik.* "I . . . I regret certain things I said to Jan."

"Like?"

She closed her eyes. "I recall once telling him during an argument that he lived in an ivory tower. That he didn't really care about others."

Baize didn't answer.

"I even accused him recently of spending more time away on concert tours than I felt he needed to."

"What did he say?"

"Nothing. He just smiled, the way Jan always did. And told me he loved me and always would. I know now he cared. I know that he'd have laid down his life for me."

Her eyes wet, Carla opened her mouth to speak again, and then closed it. She avoided the temptation to explain about Jan's death. Maybe the less Baize knew the better.

"What's in the envelope?"

"When Dr. Leon treated you as a child, he had us remove all the snapshots we had of David and your mom from around the house. Except for the single photograph in your room."

"He was afraid they might spark my memory?"

"Yes."

"It's why you never spoke about Luka, or displayed his photograph. Isn't it?"

"You and he were so close. We were afraid even if you saw too many images from your past all the pain would come back. The less said the better."

Baize opened the envelope. "All the pictures Dan and I had—of David growing up, and the ones he sent us over the years, of his life with you and your mom and Luka. I kept them hidden from you. It wasn't easy keeping silent for over twenty years. But that's how it had to be."

She tilted the envelope and dozens of images in different shapes and sizes and colors cascaded out like precious jewels onto the table.

Carla saw some of her father—as a child, wet-haired on a beach, looking no more than five, and wearing blowup red plastic armbands, a grin on his face.

Another as a toddler in his parents' arms. Another about seven, making his Communion, and later as an awkward teen. In all of them that same wonderful lopsided smile she remembered.

She sifted through the other snapshots. It was as if they recorded every kiss and hug and cherished moment of her childhood.

She saw images of her on her father's lap, his arm around her mother, holding a plump-faced Luka, all of them next to an old white Volkswagen. On the back of the snapshot it said: "Dubrovnik beach."

In another, Carla was leaning in front of the bonnet, her head tilted toward her mother, locking her in an embrace. One more of her father laughing as he planted a kiss on her forehead. In yet another, she was touching noses with a smiling Luka.

There were lots of photographs of her father painting, an easel in front of him. Others of them all seated at dinner outside a restaurant, and written in felt pen at the bottom it said, " 'Dinner at Mr. Banda's. Food wonderful! Memories irreplaceable!' "

But of course photographs only offered a glimpse, and not the whole truth. They never captured the true spirit of the moment, the soul behind the image, or the real people behind the smiles.

They didn't capture the real Luka, the beautiful little boy who liked to be chased and tickled, and who was always ready to make mischief. No more than they captured the tender love behind her father's kisses, or the devoted worship in her mother's embrace.

But these photographs were all she had. The only keys she possessed to her past—the life that was long hidden from her. They were also a trigger, and this time she didn't have to struggle to recall. Her mind opened like a floodgate, as Dr. Leon predicted.

A surge of forgotten childhood memories raged through her mind like wildfire, with no order or sense to them.

An evening she spent in the hospital with her father, as he paced anxiously up and down awaiting news of Luka's birth. She remembered something that made her giggle—her father so nervous that he accepted a cigarette from another expectant father, but lit the wrong end, the filter tip going up in flames.

A time she hid in a hall closet and saw her father and mother argue, over money—the only time she recalled them ever arguing—and then when their argument was spent, she saw them kiss with such ferocity that Carla thought they would suffocate one another.

It made her cry out and burst from the closet, but it made her parents laugh as they hugged her.

Another day. A wondrous one. Her mother leading her and Luka down to the sea the first summer Luka began to walk.

They wore their bathing suits and she remembered the sparkle in her mother's eyes, as if she savored the sheer delight and the pleasure and awe of being alive and with her children.

Her mother held their hands as they ran down to the waves, rushing together into the blue sea, all of them scooping out armfuls of cool water and whooping with joy.

Overcome, she looked up.

It felt all too much.

In Baize's eyes she saw her own torment mirrored.

These were not just photographs and memories; these were the lives of her beloved family, their existence savagely ended by evil men.

"I . . . I know I loved them. Loved them so much."

"We both did, Carla."

And then Baize's arms were around her, hugging her close, rocking her, offering her a warm, soft place to fall.

18

BELGRADE

The giant Lufthansa Airbus A340 that took off from JFK Airport earlier that Friday evening powered its way across the Atlantic to its final destination in Frankfurt, Germany.

The stocky, middle-aged man wearing an expensive tailored suit who was seated comfortably in business-class seat 11A was booked on an onward connection to Belgrade. Carrying only a single piece of overnight luggage, he stayed awake all through the flight, clutching a locked briefcase that never left his sight, for it contained a priceless cargo.

When the Airbus landed in Frankfurt at 8 a.m. Saturday, within two hours the man was aboard his connecting flight. Only two photographs existed of the passenger in Interpol headquarters in Lyon, France.

One was taken while he was in a Belgrade prison serving seven years for manslaughter, and for membership in an organized crime gang. It showed a bull-necked, dark-haired young man of twenty-six, arrogant, and confident. His broken nose and slit of a mouth suggested that he wasn't someone to be crossed.

The second Interpol photograph was a grainy image taken five years later, when he was a major serving in the Serb paramilitary killing squads. No one who saw him now would recognize the man in the Interpol photographs.

More than twenty years had passed, and he was almost completely bald. He was fifty pounds heavier, and plastic surgery had restructured his chin, fixed his boxer's nose, and given him an eye-lift. His passport photo matched his new appearance and was a legitimate Austrian document, supplied by a Viennese official in return for a generous bribe.

The official had little choice—a refusal meant he would have ended up floating dead in the Danube.

The name in the document identified its owner as Bruno Neumann, which was a kind of poor joke really, for in English Neumann means "new man." The name was an alias—the passenger was in fact a member of the Serb mafia, one of the most feared and widespread organized crime groups in the world.

In reality, he was Boris Arkov, the only son of Ivan Arkov, the present head of the Arkov clan, one of a half-dozen notorious crime families that ran Yugoslavia's underworld.

Never endowed with a keen intelligence, Arkov's son preferred to use brute force, cunning, and violence.

Beginning with the cigarette, oil, and drug smuggling operations his father ran in the late 1980s with ruthless efficiency, Boris Arkov became a trusted lieutenant to his father and knew the absolute importance to the clan of *kanun*—the mafia code of loyalty—and *besa*, secrecy, and he adhered to both rigidly.

On the wanted lists of Interpol, and every country in the European Union, the role Boris Arkov played in the roster of crimes committed during the Yugoslav war in the 1990s on behalf of his father's criminal enterprise was staggering: torture, ethnic cleansing, robbery, sexual violence, drug smuggling, kidnapping, murder.

When the war finally ended, the mafia's coffers bulged with an amassed fortune that Interpol estimated at more than $5 billion from their brutal wartime escapades.

Soon, a rash of dangerous shoot-outs, bombings, and violent killings erupted on Belgrade's streets between the crime families, often because of disagreements over the division of the spoils of battle.

When the new prime minister Zoran Dindic threatened all-out war against organized crime and the mafia assassinated him, a crackdown followed.

But in reality it changed nothing, except make crime chiefs, still flush with war profits, decide it was time to expand. As one mafia clan boss put it: Serbia had become a pond too small for so many crocodiles.

The United States, South America, Europe, Scandinavia, and Australia very quickly became part of the international expansion plan—outposts in an empire that was fast on its way to rivaling the Cosa Nostra and the Russian mafia in its brutality, daring, and organization.

These foreign outposts, with ties back to the Balkan region, also became safe havens for gangsters still wanted for war crimes. With the help of new documents, backgrounds, and sometimes plastic surgery, they could begin new lives among their own clans on foreign soil, the codes of *kanun* and *besa* keeping them safe from prosecution.

By noon that day when Boris Arkov's plane touched down at Nikola Tesla Airport in Belgrade, where legally he was still a wanted man, he passed through immigration with his Austrian passport without a second glance from the border security official. Outside Arrivals he was met by two bodyguards, a pair of muscled thugs who escorted him to a waiting Merc.

One of them stashed Arkov's overnight bag in the trunk, and when he was comfortably settled in the limo's rear, Arkov stretched his legs, exhausted after the eight-hour flight spent clutching his locked briefcase. It would be a quick turnaround. He would fly back the next day.

"You had a good flight, Boris?" one of the men asked.

Arkov rubbed his eyes. "Lousy. I didn't sleep a wink. How's my old man?"

"Looking forward to seeing you."

As the limo began to drive beyond Belgrade and toward Novi Sad, Arkov allowed himself to relax in his plush leather seat, but he kept the precious briefcase clasped to his side, aware of its secret contents.

He yawned, folded his arms across his chest, and closed his eyes.

"Good. Nobody wake me until we get there."

19

Rain drenched the window as Carla sat in her study.

Two weeks passed, in which she lost all track of time.

It was as if she went through a complete shutdown. Overwhelmed by bouts of fear and rage and crying, she felt unable to function.

At times she felt as if she were standing on the edge of an abyss and about to fall in. Even the simplest things, like taking a bath or driving her car or opening mail, felt impossible. She didn't eat, and hardly slept.

On the third day Baize came to visit when her calls went unanswered. Concerned by Carla's appearance, she moved in. Cooking for her, taking care of her.

She visited Dr. Leon every second day.

On her fifth visit she said, "There's something I don't understand."

"Tell me."

"All these memories have begun to come back to me, but I still can't remember what happened in Shavik's office."

"You've tried to recall?"

"I've struggled many times."

"As I said before, it's confusing. But shame may have something to do with it."

"Shame?"

"When victims are badly abused, they often feel shame. If the feeling is very powerful, the mind can bury it so deep it's almost impossible to recall. That applies if anything happened to you that was deeply and emotionally disturbing, The mind goes into complete and total denial."

Dr. Leon sat forward, making a steeple of his fingers. "What about your escape?"

"It's—it's a kind of fog."

"Try to explain."

"I seem to recall being woken early in the morning by my mother. It was still dark. Armed soldiers were evacuating our building. There was an air of panic. All the mothers were wrapping themselves and their children up as warmly as they could. It was cold outside. I . . . I . . ."

"Go on," Leon prompted gently.

"I helped wrap up Luka. He was shivering from the fever. My mother carried him in her arms and fled with us away from the soldiers, along some corridors to an empty part of the building."

"Were you alone?"

"No, an older woman accompanied us, I think."

"The woman named Alma?"

"I don't know. Maybe."

"Please, continue."

"It's starting to come back. I remember the sounds of shelling and gunfire getting closer. Explosions shook the ground. I . . . I seem to remember my mother handing us over to Alma's care and then leaving. She wanted us to hide and then try to escape to the front lines."

"Hide where?"

"In some kind of storeroom where we once had to gather bags of laundry belonging to the guards. I think it was a janitor's closet. Yes, that's it. I remember the look on my mother's face as she left us."

"Left you?"

"Shavik and his men were gathering everyone together. For some reason my mother had to join the other prisoners. But she was desperate for Luka and I not to be rounded up." Carla paused.

"My mother looked so desolate. So pained. As if she'd never see us again."

"Anything else?"

"No. It's all foggy after that."

Dr. Leon moved behind his desk and opened the black box file from which he'd taken the diary. "The woman named Alma Dragovich mentioned in the journal. Do you remember anything about her?"

"Sort of, I think, but she's still a blur."

"An Alma Dragovich was mentioned in an interview in the *New York Times* about the Bosnian rape camps. I read the interview with interest, knowing your past. Apart from you, apparently she's the only survivor of the Devil's Hill."

From the box file, Dr. Leon took out a clipping of the article and handed it across.

"I figured there might be a reasonable chance it was the same Alma Dragovich. Maybe if you tried to find the journalist who wrote the story you could locate her, and she could help you. Assuming of course she's still alive?"

Carla took the newspaper clipping home.

There was no photograph of Alma Dragovich, just a shot of a camp with barbed wire and behind it, starved-looking women and children, with despair on their faces.

The article was written by a journalist named Max Shine and headed, "Rape Camps Horror: 20 years on, the survivors still live through hell."

The story focused on the brutality and inhuman conditions the women and children prisoners suffered in the Serb rape camps. How suicides and mental illness was high among survivors. There wasn't too much written about Alma Dragovich, except that she was the sole known survivor of the Devil's Hill, a notorious rape camp, and that her mental health was affected because of her ordeal. She claimed to have been raped and abused by the camp guards.

Carla called the *New York Times* and asked for Max Shine.

"I'm sorry, Mr. Shine's in Chicago, working on a story."

"When will he be back?"

"Try Monday."

It was the end of the second week and she felt some sort of normality return.

With it came an insatiable need to know about her parents, their experiences, and her own secret life.

A quick search on the Internet revealed that the lead agency dealing with missing victims of the war was the International Commission of Missing Persons, based in Sarajevo. Despite Baize's assurance that she provided a sample of Carla's DNA, Carla wanted to check for herself.

She verified the agencies' opening hours. Sarajevo was six hours ahead. She called, and got through to an English-speaking woman on duty, who sounded busy.

"You say you're looking for missing relatives?"

"My parents and young brother." She did her best to explain, keeping it as simple as she could, explaining that Baize had already provided Carla's DNA sample years before.

The woman said sympathetically, "If they were still alive, they probably would have been located by now. But you never know, people slip though the net, and family members who were thought to have been victims have turned up alive even decades after the war."

The woman sighed. "However, I'm afraid we're still finding victims' graves fairly often, even after all these years. In fact, I know a mass grave was discovered not so long ago near Omarska that our forensics people are still working on."

"Can you check for me, please?"

"Of course. May I have all the details?"

Carla told her everything she knew, including Luka's full name and date of birth. "Do you think there's any hope I'll ever find out what happened to my family?"

"I really can't say. But it'll be worth me double-checking if they were dealt with by the other agencies at the time, like the UN or the Red Cross or Red Crescent, especially regarding your young brother."

"Why?"

"There were considerable numbers of orphans who managed to survive. Some were found adoptive homes, or were placed with relatives willing to take them. Others, the ones whose minds were badly affected by the war, or who were badly wounded, are often still in state homes, or those run by religious and charities. Let me see if I can find anything."

"Thank you."

"It may take a little, we're very busy right now, but I'll get back to you."

* * *

On Monday she called the *New York Times* again. She asked for Max Shine and was put through. A man's gruff voice said, "Shine."

"Mr. Shine, my name is Carla Joran." She decided not to use her married name. Shine may have heard about Jan's death and she wanted to avoid discussing that topic with a journalist. "I'm calling about an article you wrote."

"Yeah? Which one. I've written lots."

"The one about the survivors of the women's rape camps, twenty years on. You mentioned a woman named Alma Dragovich. I'd like to talk with you about her."

There was a pause, as if the guy was mulling it over. "Yeah? What for?"

"I was a child prisoner in the Devil's Hill camp, Mr. Shine. I knew Alma Dragovich there. I want to contact her."

There was another silence, longer this time. "Where are you calling me from?"

"Long Island."

"You know the New York Times Building on Eighth Avenue?"

"Yes."

"There's a café called the Coffee Pot not too far away; maybe you could meet me there at five o'clock?"

20

New York
5 P.M.

Carla felt tired as she waited at a table in the Coffee Pot drinking cinnamon tea.

She placed a hand on her stomach.

The signs of pregnancy were all there.

Her breasts felt tender. She experienced morning sickness most days, and it felt like a hangover.

She told her gyno about her symptoms when she visited him that morning for a checkup.

"It's all normal," he assured her. "It could be worse. No dizziness? No cramping?"

"A few twinges."

"They may get worse." He smiled. "All part of the joy of childbearing."

She took her hand away from her stomach as a beefy man with bald, shaved head came into the café.

The place was busy but he spotted her seated alone and came over. "Carla Joran?"

"Yes."

He thrust out a hand as he sat, his blue eyes sparking with curiosity. "Max Shine."

"I'm trying to find Alma Dragovich, Mr. Shine."

"So you said. I wondered if I heard it right when you mentioned you knew her in the camp. I thought she was the only survivor of the Devil's Hill."

"It's a long story."

Shine's eyebrows rose. "Yeah? I heard that camp was pretty bad."

"Yes, it was."

He reached for a notebook in his pocket. "I covered the rape camps and the siege of Sarajevo. I've been back many times. It's never been determined what became of the other inmates, but there are suspicions they were all executed."

Carla said nothing.

"Care to tell me more? It sounds to me like maybe you've got a story to tell, Carla?"

"No, please, I'm not here to give an interview. I just need to get in touch with Alma."

"People need to hear those stories of what went on."

"I'm sorry, Mr. Shine, I'm not up to that right now. If at some time in the future I change my mind, I promise you'll be the first journalist I'll call. Can you put me in touch with Alma?"

He sat back, stretching his hands behind his bald head. "I'd hoped she could tell me a lot more about her experiences but in the end she kind of clammed up. She really didn't say too much."

"Can you help me? Where does she live? Did she return to Sarajevo?"

Shine saw the pleading in her eyes, and sat forward, put away his notebook. "I'll need to make a call first and get back to you. See if I can give you a contact phone number."

"For Alma?"

"For her son. He's a U.S. citizen. She came to live with him in New Jersey."

Carla didn't notice the stocky man who tailed her to the café.

He sat at a table drinking a latte, a newspaper open in front of him.

He glanced up now and then, observing them both, a pair of earphones stuck in his ears, the wires connected to his cell phone.

When they left, he didn't tail Carla, but followed Shine instead, tailing him as he walked back to the New York Times Building on Eight Avenue.

21

That night, unable to sleep, Carla stared at her laptop open in front of her. She watched the videos on YouTube: of young men diving off the famous rebuilt bridge at Mostar.

She saw the narrow cobbled streets where her father and mother had once walked, and the Turkish coffeehouses and bazaars.

But it was the grim images of the Serb death camps that affected her most. Disturbing photographs of emaciated inmates; gangling bodies that looked like victims in Nazi concentration camps.

Every face looked spiritless and terrified. She saw the human cost of war: gruesome photos of dead and tortured men, women, and children; they turned her stomach.

She read about the country's history and the root causes of the conflict. How for centuries ethnic and religious differences sparked intermittent orgies of violence, most recently during World War II. How Croats and Bosniaks sided with the Nazis who invaded Yugoslavia, a betrayal that cost the lives of an estimated half a million Serbs, some of them in Croat concentration camps, where they were subjected to barbarism even worse than the Nazis.

From among the Bosnian population Muslim divisions of the SS were recruited; they persecuted the Serbs, who dominated the region for centuries.

Old rivalries, ethnic hatreds, and the settling of scores kept spilling over into later generations in a cycle of violence that seemed unbreakable.

When she couldn't stomach any more images she read everything she could find on the Internet about the Serb mafia's participation in the Yugoslav wars.

The Omarska camp where her father was held was a vast human coop, an airless prison where thousands of men and youths were crammed for twenty-four hours a day, living and dying in their own filth.

Many inmates perished from poor health or went mad; those who lost their mind were usually taken away and shot, their bodies disposed of in the many iron ore mines nearby.

Prisoners were given three minutes each day to run from their quarters to a food station where they were given boiling hot, watery bean soup—often too hot to consume—and one loaf of bread between eight prisoners. Anyone who didn't complete their meal in three minutes was descended upon by packs of guards and beaten mercilessly or killed.

A favorite pastime of the guards was to bludgeon prisoners to death with sledgehammers, killing one first with a blow to the head, then forcing another prisoner to lie on the dead one, then crushing his spine with blows from the hammer until he died. In this way, they built up "piles" of corpses.

Carla shuddered.

Her father must have endured such horror every day.

It turned her stomach.

The Devil's Hill camp near Omarska was only one of dozens of places where an orgy of persecution was carried out against women and children: up to sixty thousand women, young girls, and children had been raped during the wars.

Apart from the pleasure of the guards, rapes were meant to degrade, humiliate, and intimidate.

Women who survived the camps were often unable to reclaim their marriages because of their trauma, and ended up divorced from their husbands. Other women committed suicide.

Some guards were later prosecuted, but a significant number managed to evade prison. Others were allowed serve out sentences in comfortable European prisons.

More than two million civilians were displaced during the wars, the greatest number since the Holocaust and World War II.

When she could read no more, Carla slammed shut her laptop.

She felt incensed.

Decades had passed, yet her searches on the Internet revealed that Mila Shavik and many of the guards who served in the camp were never caught.

When she googled Shavik she had found several references to him.

Wanted by the International Court of Justice in The Hague to face charges for numerous war crimes and abetting ethnic cleansing, it seems that he disappeared in the final weeks of the war.

A journalist with the *Times* of London claimed that a Serb underworld contact suggested Shavik was given a new identity and spirited abroad, like a number of other top Serb mafia war criminals. An article translated from *Der Spiegel* speculated that Shavik died in Belgrade a year after the war, but the story offered only hearsay, not solid proof.

No sightings were reported of him in the last twenty years. It was as if he had vanished from the face of the earth.

Her mind remained shut to what happened to her in his office, but the question racked her mind: What became of Mila Shavik?

Was he still alive?

Did he ever lay awake at night and think of the evil he committed, the innocent lives he destroyed?

She doubted it.

A mirror hung on the wall opposite. Carla looked at herself, and saw her fury. She felt so powerless at the injustice—that a criminal like Shavik was never hunted down and prosecuted.

She balled her fist, slammed it hard on the study desk.

She hated these men. Hated what they did.

She could never forgive them.

Never.

Especially Shavik.

And her mother and father and poor, darling Luka.

Whatever became of them?

On the study desk were scattered some of Baize's photographs. Next to them was the single framed photograph of her parents, her only keepsake.

It was taken on their wedding day. They were dressed up, smiling for the camera. They looked so handsome and young.

Her father tall and blond and tanned, with a smile that lit his face.

Her mother dark-haired, with glittering, happy eyes and tanned skin.

Next to it was one of the photographs from Baize's pile. For some reason it was one Carla wanted to keep: a happy photograph of her and Luka and her mom and dad on a Dubrovnik beach.

Carla looked at the snapshots for a long time. She felt a flutter of nervous apprehension in her stomach. Would she ever learn her family's fate?

Would she ever know if they had lived or died?

Even if by some miracle they survived, Luka would be a grown man by now, in his twenties.

It seemed so strange to think of her little brother as an adult.

Somehow she doubted her family had lived. That thought seared her to the bone. But she couldn't give up hope.

She was determined to know what happened to her mother, father, and brother.

She placed the photograph taken on Dubrovnik beach in a large business-size envelope.

She wondered again about the missing pages. Had they simply fallen out, or were they deliberately removed? She marked the pages with the slip of paper containing the phone number for Alma Dragovich's son.

She stood.

As she did so she noticed Jan's brown leather attaché case propped beside the desk. The one he used for concerts and business trips. They both shared the study—the walls plastered with framed concert programs, and photographs of her and Jan together, younger, on vacation.

She picked up the attaché case. It had a combination lock. She tried the catch. It was locked. It wasn't like Jan to lock things.

She didn't know the combination.

She went down to the kitchen and found a long-nosed metal pliers in one of the drawers. She returned and used them to force the latch open.

Inside the case she found lots of sheet music, a half-full bottle of water, a handful of pencils, a pencil sharpener, and two worn rubber erasers.

She also found an unmarked envelope in one of the leather pockets. She opened it.

Inside was a single page. She unfolded it.

The handwriting in ballpoint ink was Jan's.

Mila Shavik.
Boris Arkov (alias Neumann?)
Both living in Atlantic City, New Jersey, under Serb mafia
    aliases.

Below the lines was what looked like a phone number and the word
Angel.

She felt a stab like a stiletto prod her heart.

Mila Shavik in America?

And Boris Arkov?

She was astonished.

Who gave Jan this information?

And who or what was Angel? It sounded like a woman's name. It
was after 3 a.m., too late to call the number. She never remembered
Jan talking about anyone named Angel. She heard footsteps.

She folded the page.

Baize came in, carrying a cup of hot chocolate. Witnessing Carla's
shutdown, her bouts of rage and crying, she insisted on staying over
until she felt better. Her eyes drifted to the attaché case.

"I couldn't sleep and heard a noise. Is everything all right, honey?
What are you doing up so late?"

"Thinking." Carla replaced the page and closed the attaché case.

"About the diary?"

"Yes."

"What's wrong, Carla?"

"There are some missing pages. Do you know anything about
them?"

"No, I don't. We gave the diary to Dr. Leon before he treated you.
That was the last time I saw it until now."

Carla thought about how to say this next part.

"Don't be offended if you don't see me for a little while."

"Why?"

"I feel I need to take some time out. Maybe take a vacation. Be on
my own for a little while."

"Really?"

"There's a lot I need to reflect on. So don't fret if I don't call."

"I understand. It might be a good idea. You'll be okay?"

"I'll be fine. Don't worry."

"If you do need to talk, or you need company, just call me, okay? Or
talk to Dr. Leon. He's a good man."

"I've got a feeling I'll be talking to him for quite a while."

"What are you going to do, Carla?"

"I'll think about it tomorrow. Right now, I just need to get some more sleep."

"Me, too, sweetheart."

Baize kissed her forehead before she padded back down the hall.

Carla turned to her reflection in the mirror, the question still echoing in her mind. *What are you going to do, Carla?*

This time, she gave her honest answers.

"First, I'm going to find out what happened to my family."

With fierce intensity, Carla stared back at her image in the mirror.

"Then I'm going to track down Mila Shavik."

PART THREE

22

BELGRADE

It was a beautiful old stone house at Novi Sad, overlooking the Danube.

Once the summer residence of a fifteenth-century Serb prince, the two-hundred-acre mountain estate had its own centuries-old Orthodox monastery and was one of many homes belonging to Ivan Arkov, the present head of the Arkov mafia clan.

A dapper, slim man with a Van Dyke beard and a polka-dot bow tie, at seventy-two he looked more like a kindly college professor than a mafia godfather. But appearances hid a sadistic streak.

When an underling named Milan Jurisic stole clan money, he was made an example of: Jurisic was tracked down to Spain's Costa Brava, tortured and beaten to death with a hammer, then his body put through an industrial chopper.

According to Interpol sources, underworld rumors claimed the thieving gangster was cooked in a stew, and his killers even ate part of him for lunch. Whether the rumor was true or not, one fact was known but never proven: Ivan Arkov had a macabre mask fashioned from the victim's facial skin and kept as a grisly memento.

Few knew the true extent of the brutal crimes Arkov, a widower, secretly directed during the Yugoslav wars. And now, from his mountain lair, Arkov ran an international criminal operation from which he had derived an estimated net worth of more than half a billion U.S. dollars.

As far as evidence of his criminal conspiracy went, he was flameproof. He never gave a written order, and he directed his lieutenants to do likewise. Not a shred of criminal evidence led back to him. Much of his money came from a raft of legitimate businesses he ran in tandem with the illegitimate ones whose ownership could not be traced to him.

An army of clever and expensive accountants, lawyers, and tax advisors made sure his real fortune stayed hidden offshore. And his powerful connections among politicians and the country's elite, along with his cunning arm's-length distance from his crimes, meant arrest was an unlikely option.

Besides, more than twenty years had passed since the genocidal war, and in all that time Arkov had never been indicted for a single crime.

When the limo carrying his son drove up that afternoon, Arkov senior was outdoors enjoying the sunshine and tending to his vineyard. Boris Arkov came over and kissed his father on both cheeks, Serbian style.

"You're looking well. All this mountain air must be agreeing with you."

By the swimming pool, three young women wearing tiny bright-colored bikinis lay tanning themselves on sun loungers. The younger Arkov flicked them an admiring glance.

His father snipped off a thick bunch of juicy red grapes with a pruning shears and tossed both in a wicker basket.

For more than fifty years he'd led this life and never tired of it. The power, the money—the life of luxury, the beautiful women—and the danger of always having to be one step ahead of the law. Like a deadly chess game, one that never failed to excite him. But instead of chess pieces, you wagered your life.

The older man eyed the briefcase, far more interested in its contents than the beautiful women. He wiped his hands vigorously on a cotton towel.

"Never mind the skirt. You've got everything we need?"

"It's all here, Father."

They sat at a table at the far end of the pool, well away from the sunbathing beauties.

A bodyguard brought one of Ivan Arkov's own homemade wines and poured.

His son rolled the glass, sniffed, and finally sipped, letting the pale liquid wash over his tongue. He smiled his satisfaction.

"I love it, Father. Excellent. Lemony, with a hint of gooseberries on the nose."

In truth, Arkov junior resisted the urge to spit the stuff into the pool. It tasted like something a dog might spray on a lamppost. His father was a lot of things, but he was not a winemaker.

The old man swirled his glass, sipped, and nodded. "I prefer the red, but the white's been good this year."

"You'll have to produce your own label. Like that guy who did the *Godfather* movies."

"Coppola?"

"Yeah, him."

"I tried his stuff once. Wasn't to my taste. For me, he should have stuck to making movies." The old man put down his glass. "Let me see the figures."

His son thumbed open the briefcase and removed its precious cargo: an Apple laptop. He switched it on, and when it booted up, the old man handed him a black memory stick.

His son slipped it into the side port, fiddled with the Apple's mouse, and the screen began to fill with pictograms and data.

"Computers baffle me. You're sure it's all safe?"

"Your flash drive holds the decoder. No one can read the data without it. Shavik is a hundred percent certain that it's safe."

"That's good enough for me."

When the screen was loaded, Arkov handed over the Mac.

His father slipped on a pair of reading glasses. It was all here, the profit reports for the last four months for North America, in graphs and pie charts.

All of it far too sensitive to send encrypted over the Internet, in case the FBI or Interpol intercepted the data. Hence his son's visits at least three times a year.

The head of the Arkov clan nodded, slipped off his reading glasses, and slid across the laptop. "Everything looks good. We can go over the details later. For now, let's turn to the matter that's been troubling me."

"All taken care of. The guy's dust."

"Did you consult with Mila?"

"He wasn't entirely happy about it. He wanted to first give the guy a tough warning, but I told him we had no option."

"Explain."

"The guy was asking too many questions. We think he was working with the usual groups that give us trouble. We blew up his car at the Carnegie Hall in New York."

"Who was he?"

"A musician whose family was originally from Croatia. He was sniffing around, trying to get information on me and Shavik."

"What about the police and FBI?"

"They'll never trace the blast back to us. There were so many VIPs at the concert: Arab, Russian, Ukrainian, even a couple of wealthy Iraqis. Any one of them could have been the target."

Boris Arkov paused. "What's wrong, Father? You don't look happy."

"Are you expecting any more trouble?"

"The man's wife survived. She wasn't a target. But we don't think she's a concern."

"Why?"

"We've kept a watch on her, and the guy's only other family is his brother."

"Thinking isn't good enough. Be certain. The woman's occupation?"

"She's a former prosecutor."

"I don't like it already. A woman with her legal background could be trouble. Watch her more carefully."

The old man fell silent, then pointed a finger at his son. "And tell Mila I want both of you to be ready to extract yourselves from the United States, just in case."

"Father?"

"The slightest whiff that the police or FBI are on to you, you'll vanish. Prepare whatever temporary travel documents and safe houses may be needed."

"Mila won't like that. He's spent a lot of years building the U.S. businesses for you."

"And he does an excellent job. But I don't care what he does or doesn't like. What I care about is our entire North American operation."

The clan head tossed down his glasses. "Besides, I don't like controversy, and I don't like trouble. Both are bad for business. Meantime, both of you lie low. Whatever must be done, you do it discreetly. I don't want any red flags being waved. Pass it on."

"May I ask a question, Father?"

"Ask away."

"When will I assume more responsibility within the clan? If you passed away tomorrow the family needs to be prepared to carry on."

"Mila will be able to do that. I have absolute faith in him."

Boris Arkov's jaw tightened. "And what about me?"

"You may despise Mila, but once you put your differences aside for the sake of family loyalty, anything is possible. Can't you see that loyalty is strength, Boris?"

"Yes, Father."

"I took Mila into our house and cared for him as a son. His dead father was my good friend. I know there's always been friction between you. But I've tried to teach you that the clan comes first. Even if at times I had to beat it into you. On the other hand, Mila always grasped the point of loyalty right away."

"With respect, you didn't answer my question."

His father reflected. "Admit it, Mila's so clever he could run the business blindfold. That's why he's heading the American operation. That's why he's your boss. Live with it, but more importantly, continue to learn from him."

"Blood isn't thicker than water?"

The old man heard the sullenness in his son's voice, stood, slapped a hand on his shoulder. "It's good that you're impatient, Boris. No doubt you'll have your turn when my time comes. But don't be in such a hurry to bury me. I still have a few years left in me yet."

He jerked his head toward the swimming pool. "You want to pick some company for the evening?"

Boris Arkov eyed the three sunbathing beauties, his fatigue forgotten, his concerns eased. "I wouldn't say no."

"If there's any hint of trouble from this man's wife . . ."

"She'll be dealt with."

23

TRENTON, NEW JERSEY

The address was in a row of suburban terraced houses.

A gritty working-class neighborhood flanked by a tired-looking redbrick industrial plant and a FedEx depot.

House number 1276 was neat and well kept, with freshly painted gray siding, the American flag hanging proudly if limply on the screened porch.

A white van was parked in the driveway. On the side was inscribed:

The best for less.
Larry Dragovich. International Plumber.

New York, London, Paris, New Jersey
(but mostly New Jersey)

At least someone had a sense of humor.

Carla sat there in her car for several minutes, almost too afraid to walk up the front path. Her sense of anticipation was gnawing inside her.

Was it the same Alma? Would she remember her? And what if she didn't want to remember? She imagined that so many victims who lived through the genocide preferred to forget.

She called the number for Angel that morning, at nine. A woman's sexy voice kicked in. "Hey, honeys, Angel here. Leave your number."

She sounded young and sassy.

Who *was* she? How did Jan know her?

As Carla sat there, the front door of the house opened.

A man came down the porch steps, opened the garage door, and began to remove armfuls of small cardboard boxes and load them into the van. Stocky, in his forties, with a thick dark mustache and long graying hair tied in a ponytail, he wore a loose-fitting sleeveless T-shirt.

That morning when she called the number Max Shine gave her, it rang out until the answering message: "Hi, this is Larry Dragovich Plumbing. Leave your message and I'll get right back to you."

Carla didn't call back but checked the name and number online, and got the New Jersey address. Larry the plumber worked from home.

She decided that instead of phoning again, she would drive there. She wanted to meet Alma Dragovich face-to-face.

She saw the man close the garage door and take a couple of more boxes to the van, as if it was his final load. Carla felt her legs weaken as she locked her car and went up the footpath.

"Larry Dragovich?"

The man leaned back out of the van. "Yeah?"

His brown eyes were wary, and his hands looked like hammers from hard manual labor, black hairs sprouting from his back and neck.

"I wonder if I could speak to Alma Dragovich? I believe she lives here."

"Why, what about? What's up?"

"I was hoping she could help me, Mr. Dragovich. Are you her son?"

He nodded, stood there saying nothing, waiting for Carla to explain.

"I . . . I knew your mother a long time ago, when I was a child."

His eyes sparked. "Hey, are you the lady from the old country? The one Max Shine called me about?"

"Yes. Do you think I could speak with her? I was hoping she'd remember me."

He smiled, slid shut the van door. "Sure, come on inside."

A fat, silver ornamental samovar sat in a corner like a plump Buddha.

Family photographs cluttered every shelf. On a tray on top of a sideboard stood bottles of plum and pear brandy and some shot glasses. All very ethnic.

"I hope I'm not disturbing you?"

"Naw, not at all. I had to come back to load up some supplies. My wife's at work; my youngest kids are in high school."

"How's your mom?"

Larry shrugged. "She has her good days and bad. Her memory comes and goes. She's getting on. Seventy-seven last birthday. How do you know her?"

"That's a long story. Have you got a couple of hours?"

He answered with a smile. "If only. I got to leave shortly."

"You say your mom's memory isn't good?"

"Some days she remembers what kind of sandwiches she packed for my school lunch over thirty years ago. Others, she looks at me like I'm some punk who just broke into the house to rob her."

He shrugged. "Sometimes you just have to be very patient with her. But today she's in good form. At least my wife's a nurse and helps care for her."

He filled a coffeemaker. "So, are you from Sarajevo?"

"No, I spent most of my childhood in Dubrovnik. But my mother was from Konjic, not too far from Sarajevo."

"I know it well. I left to come to Jersey and work for my uncle almost thirty years ago. But maybe I knew your family? Carla, you say?"

"Carla Joran. But my mother's family name was Tanovic back then."

He grinned. "Hey, mine wasn't Larry, either. But it's a lot easier to write on the side of a van than Slavoljub Dragovich. Mom's upstairs in her room, watching TV. She likes *The Ricki Lake Show*. Let me get her. Coffee won't be long."

"Does your mom speak English? It's been a long time since I spoke my mother's language. I wouldn't understand."

"She speaks English pretty well. My wife or kids don't understand a word of Serbo-Croat, so she's got to. I'll make sure to tell her."

"Thank you."

"Sure." He winked, opened the door, and disappeared upstairs.

Carla wandered around the room. The aroma of fresh coffee scented the air.

She studied the photographs on the shelves. Sons and daughters and extended family, Larry and his wife, a plump, dark-haired woman with a cheerful smile. Snapshots of old Sarajevo.

She noticed a worn family photograph taken outside a typical Yugoslav house and vineyard: whitewashed walls and a red pantiled roof. It jolted a memory out of thin air.

Of her father up a ladder fixing the roof on her grandfather's farm one afternoon as Carla walked up the pathway from school.

She remembered her father waving, tossing away the hammer and sliding down the ladder, his blond hair bleached white by the sun, his face a warm smile, his arms open wide to greet her.

"Hey, how's my Balkan princess?"

She struggled to recollect more but all she remembered was a feeling of love and safety in his arms. Her emotions soared. She knew she adored her father.

She heard footsteps, and pushed away the memory. Slow, clunky footsteps as if someone was being helped down the stairs.

Carla switched off her cell phone and slipped it into her purse. She didn't want any distraction.

The living room door opened.

An old woman stood in the doorway. Her strong, peasant face was deeply wrinkled, her hair almost snow white.

She looked dazed, in a trance. It seemed grief had aged her, a ghost of torment in her striking blue eyes. A long scar ran down the right side of her face.

Carla felt a kick in her chest.

There was no mistaking that scar.

Alma. She remembered.

Alma muttered something in Serbo-Croat. Larry said, "English, Mom, remember, Carla doesn't speak the old language too good."

"Carla . . . Carla it's you, isn't it? My son told me. Carla Joran. I thought I was hearing things when he said the name."

The old woman was transformed as she studied Carla. Her face came alive, and her hand went to her mouth, covering dentures that were overly white.

Carla said, "You remember me?"

A single tear rolled down the old woman's face.

Carla felt her own eyes moisten.

Alma opened her arms wide. Carla let herself go, as Alma's arms wrapped around her.

And just as she had twenty years before, the old woman started to cry, deep, convulsive sobs that racked her entire body.

24

Carla stood there for a long time, hugging Alma.

When both of them finally wiped their eyes, Larry led them to the sofa and helped seat his mother.

Carla sat, clutching Alma's hands.

Larry smiled nervously, an uncertain tremor in his voice, as if he didn't quite know if this emotional get-together was good news or bad. "You okay, Mom?"

Alma took a tissue from a box on the coffee table, then handed the box to Carla.

"Yes . . . yes, I'm fine. Carla's an old friend, I'm just so happy to see her. This is the young girl who saved me. This is her."

Larry smiled. "Yeah? You're serious? Hey, you don't get reunions like this too often. How about a plum brandy to celebrate?"

Before Carla could answer, the coffee was forgotten and Larry filled three shot glasses, one for each of them, setting them down on the coffee table.

"Mom, Carla, your health. *Zivjeli!*"

Alma fumbled with her glass; Carla left hers aside. This didn't quite seem like an occasion to celebrate with alcohol. Besides, she was pregnant.

Larry seemed to sense something, too, but it didn't stop him knocking his glass back in one swallow. He slapped it on the coffee table.

"Hey, I'll leave you girls to talk. Me, I got a living to earn. Mom, I've got some deliveries to make. I'll be back in less than an hour, tops. You'll be okay?"

"I'll be fine. Go, do what you have to."

"You need me, just call." He mimicked putting a phone to his ear, and gave a thumbs-up sign. "Great to meet you, Carla. I hope we get to talk again soon? Maybe you'd come to dinner?"

"Thank you."

Larry left. They heard the van start up, reverse, and drive away.

Alma said, "He's a good son. My eldest, the only one alive. He found me through the Red-Crescent, and brought me here. His brother, sister, father . . . they're all gone, dead in the war. How have you been, Carla?"

"Surviving. How about you?"

Alma smiled. "Older, grayer, but as well as can be expected." She let go of Carla's hands just long enough to wipe her eyes with the tissue. "I've thought of you often, Carla."

"I'm so glad you remembered me."

"How could I forget the girl who saved my life?"

Carla wondered if she should tell Alma the truth: *I forgot all about you.* She decided it best not to complicate things.

"It's wonderful to see you, too."

Alma gave a nervous laugh. "I . . . I think I will have that drink after all. Seeing you, it's like seeing a ghost. So many years have passed. So many faces lost. But not yours, thankfully."

Alma lifted the glass to her lips, barely sipped, then replaced it on the table.

"However did you find me?"

"You gave an interview in a newspaper. I got your son's address."

Alma spread her hands in a helpless gesture.

"That interview. You know, I didn't want to do it. But my son got to know the journalist, and he persuaded me. I'm glad now he did, even if I didn't say much. It's painful to remember."

Alma put down her glass. "The journalist said it was important to remind the world of the terrible inhumanity that was done in our country. But so many who lived through the genocide prefer to forget, you know."

Alma looked into her face. "In my dreams I often see those I knew and loved. My husband, my sons, my daughter, my friends and neighbors, all those who have passed. I've seen your face, too, so many times. I often wondered if you survived and were still alive. And now look at you."

She squeezed Carla's hand. "You look wonderful. You have an American accent. How did you come here, how did you come to America? With your parents? Did any of your family survive?"

"My American grandparents adopted me. I haven't seen my family since the day I last saw you."

A spark died at once in Alma's face, as if a switch were thrown.

"I . . . I'm so sorry. I was told I was the only known survivor of the camp but of course I never wanted to believe it."

"Who told you that?"

"The war crimes investigators who interviewed me. They told me they never discovered what happened to all the other women and children Shavik evacuated that day but they feared the worst. At least I know now you survived."

"Alma, that's why I wanted to talk with you. You're the only person I know who last saw Luka and my mother alive that day at the camp. Larry mentioned that sometimes your memory isn't always good. But you do remember my mother?"

"Yes, yes I do. Of course."

"And Luka, my little brother?"

Alma looked flustered. "Y . . . yes, Luka . . . such a cute, sweet little boy."

"That day's events are foggy to me, Alma. It was so much trauma. Do you remember what happened? Can you help me recall?"

Alma fell quiet.

"Alma, I recall my mother wanted you to hide with Luka in the janitor's closet until Shavik and his men had gone. Then she wanted us to escape through one of the windows and try to reach the front lines."

Alma was completely silent, as if she was numbed. The stillness hung heavy in the air.

"What is it, Alma?"

Alma didn't speak, a look close to terror in her eyes.

"Alma, I need to know what happened to Luka."

Alma's lips began to tremble. "I . . . I don't like thinking about those days at the camp. They . . . they upset me."

"I understand, Alma, but this is so very important. Can you tell me what you recall? Can you try?"

25

"You *never* saw Luka again after you left the camp?"

"Never. Not since the day we were all separated."

"My poor Carla."

"I don't know if he lived or died. Or what happened to my parents."

Alma put a hand to her scarred cheek. "Have . . . haven't you looked for them?"

"Others have, but without success. So much time has passed that it's unlikely my parents lived. But Luka was with you. I know the building was shelled, I remember that much. Yet you survived. I thought that if you survived, then Luka may have survived, too."

Carla saw a terrified look on Alma's face. As if she was standing outside a door she feared to open.

"What's wrong, Alma?"

She didn't reply.

"Alma, if there's something I need to be told, even if it's bad, you have to tell me. I know it may be very difficult for you but I need to know what happened that day the camp was evacuated."

"It's—it's just that sometimes I can recall clearly, even when I don't want to. Other days it's all a blank, as if my mind is forcing me to forget."

"Can you try to cast your mind back?"

Alma fell silent.

The silence grew between them.

Carla was conscious of the terrible void. She tried to fill it.

"Do you remember when the gunfire and shelling gradually came closer to the camp the day before the evacuation?"

"Yes."

"What do you remember?"

"The weather was getting worse. It began to snow. The guards became agitated. We could overhear them talking among themselves. Some of them wanted to flee. They were worried."

"About what, Alma?" Carla prompted.

"That their crimes against us would be discovered. One of the women claimed she heard the guards say they would kill us all before they left."

"So there would be no witnesses?"

Alma nodded. "All of us started to panic. We feared for our lives, and the lives of the children."

"What else, Alma? What else do you recall?"

"Mila Shavik strode into the dormitory and announced that because of the enemy shelling we would be evacuated early the next morning for our own safety."

Alma faltered.

Carla tried to keep the conversation moving, afraid to let it die.

"Don't stop, Alma. Please."

"But nobody believed Shavik. They were still afraid they were going to be killed. The guards were drinking heavily, and getting more edgy."

Alma looked at her.

"That's why your mother wanted me to hide Luka and you in the janitor's closet, hoping you wouldn't be missed in the chaos and that we could eventually escape."

"Please tell me what you recall."

"Early the next morning during the evacuation there was chaos, everyone was frightened, and the children were wailing. Shavik and his guards started to herd everyone out of the building. That's when your mother became desperate and decided it was time to act."

Alma's eyes narrowed, as if the intensity of the memory was becoming painful.

"She thrust Luka into my arms and pushed us back into the building, toward one of the corridors that led to the janitor's closet. Luka was crying, holding his hands out for his mother. You tried to soothe him. Your mother placed something in your hands, a book."

"The diary she used to write."

"Yes, that was it. She told you not to lose it. That it was important."

"Why didn't my mother come with us?"

"She felt certain Shavik would know if she disappeared. At least if he saw her there, in all the panic he might not notice you and Luka were gone."

In a flash of memory Carla remembered her mother's face as they parted, her terrifying look of despair and fear. She was wearing her old overcoat, a burgundy cardigan and headscarf, her expression desolate with worry. She recalled Luka crying, his tiny hands reaching out for their mother. The memory cut into her heart, sharp as broken glass.

She forced her tears away. The last thing she needed now was to crumple in front of Alma, who started to speak again.

"I held you and Luka by the hands and ran with you along the corridor toward the janitor's closet. We ran quickly. Because we could hear the guards moving through the building, trying to empty it."

More fragments of memories began to return, and they urged Carla on. "It's coming back to me. And all the time the sound of shelling was getting closer."

"Yes. As we approached the closet you spotted an open window at the end of the hall."

"I could see more snow falling beyond the window."

"That's right. It was cold outside, freezing. You thought little Luka was too feverish, too ill to move any further."

Alma squeezed her hand.

"So you decided we might stand a better chance if you left us hiding in the closet and you fled alone to the front lines. That way you could bring back help."

"But . . . but the guards were coming."

"Yes, they were coming closer, so you had to act fast. You hugged Luka, and kissed him. He was pleading with you to keep him safe, begging you to come back, and not to forget him. The last thing you said to him was that you'd come back for him; you promised him that." Alma paused. "Then you left us. You were sobbing, too, I remember that."

Carla remembered. Luka holding on to her, not wanting her to go. It was pitiful, Luka's face full of fear, clutching her. She had to pry his tiny, determined fingers away, refusing to let her go; she had to uncurl them one by one as he cried. She felt his sobs, his fear, his panic, his terror, all growing within her again.

Carla closed her eyes. It felt wretched, remembering their last few words.

"Carla, please . . . Carla don't leave me, please . . ."

"I'll come back for you, Luka, I promise. Carla will come back. Don't be afraid."

She opened her eyes. She wanted to break down, fought it, the effort enormous.

"What . . . what happened after I left?"

"I opened the closet door. That's when I got a shock."

"What do you mean?"

"The closet was full. Other children were already hiding there. Perhaps their mothers hid them with the same intention, hoping they'd survive. Or the children were frightened of the shelling, I don't know. But they looked petrified."

"How many children?"

"Three, I think, maybe four. I remember a boy of eight or nine, and a girl of four or five, and another small boy. They were crying. The closet was crowded. I had to force myself in between them, and close the door. It was claustrophobic."

Alma reflected. "We heard the sound of trucks starting up outside and moving off. The children started to get even more upset, realizing their mothers were on board."

"And Luka?"

"He was inconsolable. He just wanted his mother and you. That's when we all heard the noise."

"What noise?"

"Someone approaching. I heard boots march down the corridor. My heart was in my mouth with fear."

Carla shivered. She could hear that sound, too.

Alma said, "That's when Luka really started to cry. He was distraught, trying to get out of the dark closet."

Carla stiffened, felt her stomach heave.

Alma went on, "I heard the footsteps getting closer. I had to restrain Luka to keep him quiet. To put my hand over the poor child's mouth, and tell the other children to be silent."

Alma nervously brushed away a strand of hair. "There were bullet holes in the closet wall. Some of them looked out onto the corridor. I peered out and saw Shavik. He had a pistol in his hand. He was opening doors along the corridor, checking inside. He looked livid. As if he was searching for us."

"What . . . what did he do?"

"The shelling started up again. Shavik was getting more agitated, and fired his pistol in the air. He was opening doors faster, as if he was anxious to find us. He fired his pistol into the ceiling a few times, as if he was enraged. That only made the children worse."

Alma paused. "Then the shelling suddenly collapsed part of the hallway roof."

"And?"

"I heard more shooting, lots of it, off in the distance. I thought Shavik would find us and finish us off, but he ran out of the building, like a coward. Then I heard a vehicle drive off."

Alma looked at her.

"I told the children to wait while I went to see if Shavik and his men were gone. Luka was still crying. He was terribly distressed, trying to force his way out of the closet.

"I told the eldest boy to hold on to him while I squeezed out to take a look. I'd gone about twenty yards down the hall when I thought I heard Luka behind me, as if he'd escaped."

"Did he?"

"I couldn't tell. As I turned back to check another shell hit farther along the hall. There was a huge explosion, dust and rubble everywhere. I woke up two days later with internal bleeding in a temporary hospital somewhere in the mountains. I was lucky to be alive."

"What . . . what about Luka?"

"I asked a nun who was tending to me in the hospital. She told me they had a number of child patients who'd been brought from different camps. All were being treated in the hospital's intensive care unit. I begged her to take me to see them."

Alma paused. "One of the children I saw was a badly injured little boy. He was heavily bandaged."

Carla waited, silent, for Alma to fill the void.

"I think it was Luka."

"Why do you think the boy was Luka?"

"He looked the same age, the same build."

"Is that all?"

"He had the same color hair. And when I called out his name, he definitely reacted. Though he seemed half comatose, not fully conscious. The nurse said he'd suffered shrapnel injuries but was expected to live."

"Did you tell anyone about the children hiding in the storeroom?"

"I told one of the senior nurses."

"Did they send someone to search the building?"

"I don't know."

"Surely they must have checked?"

"I'm sure they did once the camp was overrun."

"Didn't you see the boy again to make sure it was Luka?"

"No, I never got the chance."

"Why not?"

"It was so overcrowded they moved me to a proper hospital."

Out in the driveway she heard Larry's van return, and the engine switched off.

Moments later the key was turned in the hall door. Footsteps sounded, the door into the front room was open a few inches.

Alma reached out and squeezed her hand. "Your mama was such a good woman. I'm so sorry you never saw her again. It was a terrible time. Even those who survived the torture and rapes in other camps were never right afterward."

Alma tapped a finger to her temple. "Never right up here. Do you know what I mean?"

Carla looked into Alma's face.

The old woman's eyes misted, as if she was still grappling with terrifying images from her memory.

"Alma, I need you to be very sure that the boy you saw in the hospital was Luka."

Carla waited, let her words sink in. "Can you be sure, Alma? Can you be sure that it was definitely him?"

Alma looked in a trance, as if she was staring into the past again. The pause seemed endless. Finally, she met her stare.

"Yes, I'm positive it was Luka. I'm certain I saw him alive."

26

"Did you and my mom have a good talk?"

Larry walked her to the end of the driveway, hands stuck in his work jeans.

He said something, but Carla barely listened. Alma's words still rang in her ears: *Yes, I'm positive it was Luka. I'm certain I saw him alive.*

It was a blinding ray of hope. Her heart soared.

Luka, where are you now?

Would you remember me?

"I . . . I'm sorry?"

"You and my mom, did you have a good talk?"

"Yes, yes, thank you."

"The door was open a crack when I got back. I heard my mom talking about someone named Luka."

"My younger brother."

"Yeah?"

She told Larry.

"So you lost your family, too. That's really tough."

"When I learned your mom was alive, I hoped she might be able to help me."

"What did she tell you?"

"That she saw my brother. That he was alive. It's given me such hope."

Carla could hardly contain her excitement.

Larry chewed on his lower lip a moment. "You did well to get my mom to talk. Usually she clams up if someone brings up the war."

"I can understand."

"Even if she does talk about it, she's not right for days afterward. She probably won't sleep tonight. She'll have nightmares about the camp."

"Larry, I'm so sorry, forgive me. But I desperately needed her help."

"How were you to know? What will you do about your brother?"

"Check with the refugee agencies, for a start. My grandparents went that route in the past, without success. Maybe I'll have better luck."

"How old was your brother back then?"

"Four."

Larry halted on the driveway, rested a palm on the back of his van, and jerked his chin back toward his house. "I was living here with my uncle when the ethnic cleansing started. Soon as I saw all the news reports I called my family and begged them all to get the heck out of there. But things turned sour pretty quickly. Only my mom survived."

"Yes, Alma told me. I'm so sorry."

"My young brother, Dario, was a week away from his fourteenth birthday. They executed him and my father soon after they were separated from my mom and sister. Dario was a tall boy for his age, so they put him with the men. Emila was only eighteen. God only knows what she went through before they killed her."

Anguish braided his voice. "Dozens more of our relatives died at Srebrenica."

He looked at Carla. "Before the war, you know, we lived peacefully with our neighbors. Nobody bothered anyone. Religious or ethnic differences really didn't matter. Kids played together. Adults socialized. We sang together, danced together, went to weddings and funerals together."

He took a deep breath, let it out. "Then that evil slimeball, Milosevic, turns the clock back centuries by churning up hatred, and by scaremongering. He pitted friends against friends, neighbors against neighbors. All because he was afraid of losing power."

He paused, touched Carla's arm. "You, know, I saw Ratko Mladic on TV when he was on trial for killing those eight thousand men and boys at Srebrenica. He was smirking at the camera, denying he was responsible for a single civilian death. Then he mocks the living and the dead by making a throat-cutting gesture at the victims' relatives who were in court."

Larry let out a deep sigh. "What kind of men can kill children like that, I ask you? May that beast rot in hell. Him and all the other butchers like him."

They reached the driveway's end. Larry halted, his eyes filling with emotion.

What kind of men could kill children like that? Carla had no answer. Except one. *The kind of men she wanted to find—and destroy.*

She touched his arm. "Thanks for letting me meet your mom. I hope it doesn't upset her too much."

Larry wiped his eyes with his sleeve. "That's why I wanted to walk out with you."

"Pardon?"

"My mom may seem rational at times but really she's not."

"She—she seemed pretty clearheaded to me."

"It seems that way often enough but really her mind's gone."

Larry blinked a couple of times, and looked kind of lost. "The war totally messed up her head. She imagines things, you see. Hears voices. There's an old saying in our part of the world—when the wind blows, the dead whisper your name. You ever hear that saying?"

"No."

"It's like that way with my mom, only all the time."

"What do you mean?"

"She has these imagined conversations with my father and sister and brother every night. Talks to them like they're still alive, in the next room. She hears their voices, you see. Really believes they're here, in the house. You can't convince her otherwise."

Larry took a deep breath, let it out in a frustrated sigh. "The docs say it's not unusual when you've suffered massive trauma the way she did, that your mind gets messed up. The pre-dementia doesn't help either."

"She has pre-dementia?"

"That's what the doc says. She's supposed to take her meds, because they can help stop the voices in her head, but most times she won't take them. I'm guessing that she likes the voices. They comfort her, if that makes sense?"

"Yes."

"Anyway, my wife will tell you the same—Mom's lost her marbles. She doesn't know what the heck she's saying half the time. She'll tell you things she only imagines, but in her mind she believes they're true."

"But . . . she seemed certain she saw Luka."

"She's certain she sees lots of things. Last week she was certain she saw my father in the frozen food aisles in Walmart and insisted we go look for him."

Larry met Carla's stare. "So whatever my mom tells you, really you need to take it with a grain of salt."

27

NEW YORK

Driving home, in the silence of the car, Carla felt like weeping.

Had Alma only imagined seeing Luka at the hospital all those years ago?

Was Larry right? Was his mother's mind no longer sound? Alma *seemed* sound of mind, but Larry's words threw her. As much as her spirits soared just a short while ago, they sank now, down a deep well of despair.

And a disturbing thought upset her—of her brother trapped in that tiny airless closet, with no food and water, his body wasting away until he perished. It was too much to bear.

She felt so distracted that she had to pull over. Coasting onto a suburban street, she halted at the curb, her engine running.

"No!"

She screamed out her disappointment, slamming the steering wheel with her fists until her knuckles bleached. She buried her face in her arms, her optimism completely shattered.

As she sat there, not moving, she felt overcome. It took her a few minutes to get a grip of herself.

When she did, she wiped her eyes and turned back on her cell. Moments later it beeped twice.

It was a missed call from Jan's brother, with a voice mail.

"Carla, it's Paul. I'm in town and I need to meet up. It's really urgent. Can you call me when you get this?"

She didn't feel like talking but Paul had said it was urgent. She sat upright, wiping her face with a tissue, and punched in his number. It rang out and Paul's voice message kicked in.

"Hi, I'm busy right now but please leave your name and number and I'll get back."

"Paul, it's Carla. Call me again when you get a chance."

She sat there for several minutes more, gripping the steering wheel with bitter disappointment. And yet it was strange, because she still felt a glimmer of hope.

She told herself: there's always a chance that Alma really *did* see Luka. That her memory of that day wasn't fogged by a disturbed mind.

She tried to perk up.

Wasn't a tiny glimmer of something better than the cold certainty of nothing?

And with that thought she pulled out from the curb.

When she got home she made a fresh pot of coffee and sat at her study desk in front of her laptop.

She still had no idea about how she would go about finding Mila Shavik.

On the desk in front of her lay Baize's envelope stuffed with photographs. Carla spread out the images on the desk: it still seared her heart to look at her parents' and Luka's faces.

In several of the snapshots of Dan and Baize, her grandfather was in uniform.

Carla thought: *If he was alive he would have known how to go about hunting down a war criminal like Shavik.*

In some of the photographs her grandfather posed with his special forces comrades. One of them stood out—Ronnie Kilgore was a dark-haired young sergeant in his early twenties with an easy smile.

She remembered him as an occasional visitor to her grandparents' home when they lived near Fort Bragg in North Carolina. Carla recalled a vague kind of teenage crush on him, until one day she overheard Baize say that Ronnie Kilgore was getting married.

And then a thought struck her and sent her pulse racing.

She found the cardboard storage box in the attic.

After her grandfather's death she had helped Baize go through his personal belongings. Baize insisted she take some of Dan's things to remember him by.

Carla kept a pair of his reading glasses, a few service medals, and one of the many photograph albums with snapshots taken of Dan in various battle zones around the world: Panama, Grenada, Desert Storm.

But what she remembered most was the handful of letters she kept.

There were so many Baize stacked them in several thick piles. A bunch were from Dan's former army buddies, men he'd served with who wrote condolence letters.

She found the one she was looking for among a wad of envelopes held together with a thick rubber band.

The letter wasn't written on plain paper like the others but had a logo in blue ink at the top of the page: an image of a motorboat plowing through waves.

> *Dear Mrs. Joran,*
>
> *I just wanted to write and say how honored I was to serve with Dan.*
>
> *He was a wonderful, humane man—one of the finest officers I've ever known—and he'll be sorely missed by his friends and comrades. As you know, I had the honor to serve under your husband for over ten years, and I was also proud to call him a close personal friend.*
>
> *There were many occasions in battle when I owed my life to Dan, as did so many of our comrades, and we're forever grateful to him.*
>
> *Please know that your husband will always be in the hearts and prayers of those who knew, admired, and loved him. If there's ever any way I can help, don't hesitate to contact me.*
>
> *My deepest sympathies.*

It was signed Ronnie Kilgore, the writing firm and bold.

The headed paper had a phone number and the address was Kilgore's Union County Marina, Union County, Tennessee.

She dialed the number. A woman's chirpy southern voice answered. "Kilgore's Marina."

"I'd like to speak with Ronnie, please."

"Ronnie's not here. He'll be back tomorrow. Can I say who's calling?"

"No . . . no, it's fine. I'll call again. Thank you."

She ended the call. She didn't really know what she was going to say to the man. All she knew was that a vague plan was forming in the back of her head, one that might help her find Mila Shavik.

Her cell chirped. It was Paul.

"Carla? Sorry I missed your call. But I'm in Manhattan on short notice to meet a corporate client. Any chance we could meet?"

"What's so important?"

"I'd prefer not to talk about it over the phone."

"Why?"

"What I have to say would be better face-to-face."

"Now you have me worried."

"Sorry, I don't mean to. Are you by any chance free for an early dinner, or a drink?"

"How early?"

"Five p.m. Do you know Fitzer's on Lexington Avenue?"

"It is that important?"

"You bet."

28

New York

Carla arrived just before five.

Fitzer's was already busy, and she spotted Paul alone at a private booth. He stood when he saw her, and kissed her on the cheek.

"Thanks for coming. What'll you have to drink, Carla?"

"A seltzer, please."

The waiter came and Paul ordered her seltzer and another Scotch on the rocks for himself. When the waiter left, Paul sipped his drink. He was a little flushed, as if he'd already had a couple, and he looked uncomfortable.

"So, what's this about, Paul?"

"I guess I ought to start by saying I'm aware that you know Baize confided about your past to me."

"You spoke with Baize?"

"She called me today. I guess she's worried about you. She said you went to see the therapist who once treated you. That he gave you a diary to read."

"You read my mother's diary?"

"No, but Baize told Jan and I you had it in your possession when they found you."

"Did Baize ask you to speak with me?"

Paul toyed with his swizzle stick.

"No, she didn't, Carla. But I wanted to remind you."

"Of what?"

"That the men who killed Jan are hard and violent gangsters."

"Come on, Paul, don't you think I know that?"

"You seemed noncommittal the last time we spoke."

"So?"

"Afterward I had a funny feeling. Call it an intuition."

"Intuition about what?"

"That you might try to avenge Jan's death in some way."

"Why did you think that?"

"You're a lawyer. Injustice enrages you. Jan always said that."

"What else did he say?"

"That you'd walk over broken glass to ensure that justice triumphed over the guilty."

"The law doesn't always triumph. Killers are not always caught. Sometimes they get away scot-free."

"That's the part that worried me."

"Why?"

"That somehow you might decide to take the law into your own hands."

"What gave you that impression?"

"You've always been a determined woman, Carla. You loved Jan. Loved him enough to want to see his killers punished."

"Want is not a crime."

"No, but I felt I had to make it absolutely clear you understand these people won't hesitate to kill you and your baby if you make trouble for them."

"Listen, I've read all I need to about the Serb mafia's involvement in drug smuggling, prostitution, human trafficking, murder, and fraud. Enough to do me a lifetime."

"Then please, steer well clear of them."

"I heard your warning the first time, Paul. Is that why you wanted to see me?"

He took a big mouthful of Scotch. "No. It's something I didn't tell you when we last met. I guess you know that to this day there are still digs going on to unearth massacre sites?"

"Yes, I know."

"The International Commission on Missing Persons, the ICMP, in Sarajevo oversees many of the forensic excavations. They keep DNA data banks of the victims they've discovered."

"I know that, too. I spoke to them the other day."

"You did?"

"Baize gave them a sample of my DNA years ago in the hopes they would find a link to my family. I wanted to check up on it. The woman said she'll get back to me."

"And did she?"

"Not yet. Why?"

"Jan often kept in touch with the commission, hoping they might eventually turn up news about your family. Baize had told him about giving your DNA sample."

"Spit it out, Paul. I'm not in the mood for suspense."

"Jan was planning to fly to Europe this week."

"Why?"

"Carla, I didn't tell Baize, and I think it's best we don't until we know the facts. But no doubt the commission will confirm it to you."

"Confirm what?"

"Jan learned that a mass grave site was discovered near Omarska recently."

"I know. The woman told me."

"That's all you learned?"

"Like I said, she promised to get back. Why?"

Paul put down his glass. "No doubt she'll get around to telling you what they told Jan. I thought it only right to tell you, face-to-face. I figured maybe you'd want to make travel arrangements."

"For what reason?"

"They've got a DNA match to your family, Carla."

29

NEW JERSEY

That same afternoon a Lufthansa Airbus A340 touched down at JFK from Frankfurt after a bumpy eight-hour flight across the Atlantic.

Two hours later passenger Boris Arkov was cruising in his GMC Denali along Highway 9, past Atlantic City, and heading in the direction of Cape May.

America's oldest seaside resort was popular since the early 1800s. Turreted Gothic mansions, charming summer cottages, and rambling Victorian townhouses with white picket fences. He turned off the highway and drove toward a row of impressive beach houses overlooking Delaware Bay, yachts and sailboats riding the water.

Arkov's cell rang. He answered gruffly. "Yeah?"

A male voice said, "It's about the woman."

"I'm listening."

The caller spoke for several minutes, until Arkov said, "Good job. Keep on it. I want to know if anything else important turns up."

And Arkov flicked off his cell phone and grinned to himself.

The Cape May property was a large terra-cotta-colored stucco built on a sandy inlet facing the bay. It was ringed by a high wall, the entrance from the main road protected by tall steel gates with security cameras.

Arkov pressed the intercom buzzer.

Moments later the motorized security camera swung left and right as a bodyguard inside the house observed the visitor's arrival, and then the gate yawned open.

Arkov moved through the impressive marble hallway and walked out to the back of the house, past the swimming pool.

A rockery with steps led down to a wrought iron gate, inlaid with the design of an imperial eagle. Past the exit was a private boardwalk.

The property had its own boat dock jutting into the inlet. A polished black powerboat with a massive Mercury engine was tied up.

All part of the owner's contingency plans, Arkov knew.

If ever a hasty getaway was needed, the powerboat was just one of several ways of escape. A quick call to a trusty clan member farther up the coast and a safe house was at their disposal.

He entered the code and slipped out the gate.

A burly middle-aged man stood at the edge of the boardwalk, a fishing rod in his hand.

Mila Shavik wore white linen trousers rolled up to the knees, and a pale blue Tommy Bahama shirt. He jerked the rod a few times, trying to entice a bite.

"Any luck with dinner?" Arkov asked, joining him.

Shavik kicked at the blue plastic bucket beside him on the boardwalk, and it splashed water. "Today is not a good day. You don't have the patience for fishing, do you, Boris?"

Mila Shavik's English was fluent but his accent unmistakably Slavic. His tanned, lived-in face had deep creases. His pale gray eyes were washed out looking and his mouth was set hard with discontent, almost as if he'd seen too much of life and was wearied by it.

"It never was my thing," Arkov replied.

Shavik flicked the rod again. "You should try it sometime. You'll learn that skill and patience have their reward."

Arkov lit a cigarette, took a drag. "Give it a rest. You're beginning to sound like my old man."

Shavik was acutely aware of the sullen tone in Arkov's voice, a hint of the uneasy resentment that existed between son and adopted son.

"Well, did you enjoy the wine? What did your father have you try? Red or white?"

"The white."

"Last year I tried the white. I had stomach cramps for two days. When I got back to New York, I didn't need a limo, I needed an ambulance."

"He's happy with the figures; that's all that's important. He'll meet us when he flies in to do the pickup."

"And the other business?"

"He thinks we need to lie low."

"Any lower and I'll be on my back."

"He wants us to be ready to leave the U.S. as a precaution."

"*What?*"

"It worries him the woman could create problems."

"Why?"

"She's a trained prosecutor."

"So?"

"She may start sniffing around. If she does and there's the slightest hint that the police or FBI are on to us, we're to do our disappearing act."

"Explain."

Arkov held up his cell phone. "I got a call while I was on the way here. One of the guys I'm using to tail her."

"What about it?"

"She was seen talking with a well-known *New York Times* journalist in a coffee shop in New York. He's written about the Serb mafia before, and covered the war back home. Talking to a journalist like that, she's got to be making connections to us. That makes me nervous."

Shavik slammed a fist hard on the boardwalk's wooden rail.

"I'm going nowhere."

"It's an order, Mila."

"No stupid woman is going to destroy the life I've made here."

"I'm just telling you what my father said."

"And I say my running days are over."

"You'd defy my father?"

"I've put over fifteen years into growing the business here." Shavik laid the rod on the rail, and held up his hands. "Worked these fingers to the bone day and night to build Ivan's empire for him. There'll be no more running."

"Then we better be prepared to take care of the woman."

Shavik switched to his native Serbo-Croat, speaking more rapidly. "Get all the information you can on her."

"We still have some stuff on the husband."

"Use that, too. What about the musician's brother in Arizona?"

Arkov grinned. "Billy cut the throat of the guy's dog, as a friendly warning. I don't think he's the kind who'll bother us. But the woman's a different matter. A former prosecutor's bound to be plucky."

"Find out everything—her phone numbers, her favorite restaurants, her employer, who her relatives are. Every detail, I don't care how. Right down to the name of the man who mows her lawn. Does she have kids?"

"Not that we know of. You want me to find out if there's anyone we can use as leverage? A close relative or friend, parents, a family member . . . ?"

"Whatever, but it must be handled skilfully, so it doesn't look deliberate. If it looks like someone's harmed the wife or relatives of Jan Lane so soon after the explosion it could alert the feds."

"Any other thoughts?"

"Try to focus just on the woman for now. She's a grieving wife. If need be, we can always make it look like suicide."

Shavik's rod jerked violently. He reeled in the line. Seconds later he had a mackerel wriggling on the end of his hook.

He flicked open a long, frightening-looking blade. There was the sound of gristle and bone being cut, and a wash of blood as the mackerel's head was severed, and the fish expertly gutted.

Shavik flung the fish in the bucket of water, tossed guts into the sea

near the powerboat. A rare smile creased his lips as he turned back to
Arkov.

"See. All things come to a man who waits."

30

KNOXVILLE, TENNESSEE
11 A.M.

She hired a car from the Hertz desk at McGhee Tyson Airport and
drove north on Interstate 75, the Smoky Mountains in the distance.

When she reached Union County it was after lunch, the sky cloud-
less and hot. She came around a bend in the narrow road, passing a
clutter of lakeside cabins and camping trailers, some of them in need
of a little more affection, and maybe a lick of paint.

A notice on one of them proclaimed, "Welcome to a little bit of
Hillbilly Heaven."

Another said, "Banjo lessons. Treat those fingers to a good plucking!"

Up ahead she saw a sign: KILGORE'S UNION COUNTY MARINA.

The marina was a little tired-looking in places, but that seemed
all part of its charm. The lakeshore was very beautiful, peppered with
wooden holiday cabins and more trailers. Pontoon boats and leisure
craft bobbed out on the water or were berthed under metal-roofed
docks, and a few dozen houseboats floated out on the lake.

As Carla parked the hire car she saw a blond woman busy working
one of the dock's gas pumps, filling a customer's boat.

She looked about thirty, very pretty, and wore jeans and a white
cotton top.

Next to her was a pale-looking boy in a wheelchair who was no
more than twelve or thirteen. He wore beach shorts and a heavy metal
T-shirt.

After the blond woman noticed Carla, she finished pumping gas, wiped her hands on a rag, and came over. The boy followed her, palming the chair's wheels.

"Can I help you, honey?" the woman asked.

"I'm looking for Ronnie Kilgore."

"Who's asking?"

"My name's Carla Lane."

The woman put her hands on her hips. "Ronnie expecting you?"

"No. But I need to talk with him."

"About what?"

"It's private?"

"He a friend of yours?"

"Not exactly, but we've met."

The woman raised an eye. "You're not with Internal Revenue, are ya?"

"No, I'm not."

"Ronnie ain't here right now. He's gone to Knoxville on business."

"Is there somewhere I can wait?"

"You could be doing some waiting, honey. He usually doesn't get back until after eight, or even later."

Carla sensed an instant dislike in the woman's tone. She noticed a sign in one of the cabin windows. ASK ABOUT OUR SPECIAL WEEKLY RATES.

"You have a cabin for hire?"

"You fixing on staying?"

"I may."

"Come into the office."

She led Carla to the dock office. The boy followed, maneuvering his wheelchair through the widened door.

On the office desk was a plaque with a dummy grenade. A ticket that said "Number 1" was tied with string onto the grenade pin, and a sign on the bottom of the plaque said: COMPLAINT DEPARTMENT. PICK A NUMBER.

The woman consulted the black leather-bound guest book. "I've got a cabin. It'll be a little cheaper if you stay more than one night."

"I'll take it."

"Just one night?"

"It depends."

"On what, honey?"

"On when I get to talk to Ronnie."

The woman shrugged, turned to the boy. "Go get the lady some fresh sheets and towels, Josh."

"Yes, ma'am."

The boy wheeled himself toward a storeroom at the back.

The woman slapped shut the guest book. "There's a Food Lion and a Dollar General nearby where you can get some groceries if you need them, or there's a restaurant here at the dock. We fix breakfast and snacks. For dinner, you've got a couple of bars in the area, or you can drive into Harrogate or LaFollette. Let me show you the cabin."

She led Carla across the gravel to one of the A-frame wooden cabins, steps leading up to the front door.

The rooms were simple, fresh and clean, and there was a small balcony. A panoramic window looked out onto the lake.

"This one's got a pretty view if you like sunsets. Where you from?"

"New York."

"I thought so. We don't get too many New Yorkers in these parts. Most of our customers come from Kentucky, Ohio, or Tennessee."

"The cabin's fine. I'll take it." She wrote on a slip of paper.

"Could you give this to Ronnie when he gets back, and tell him I'd like to see him?"

The woman nodded, took the note. "I'll get the paperwork done and you can sign in."

Carla looked out at the view. It was exceptional. A smoky haze swathed the forested slopes, the lake calm as a mirror. There was something about the landscape that brought back echoes of her mother's homeland: misted mountains and deep gorges, thick forests and calm lakes.

"It's really very beautiful."

The woman smiled for the first time. "Yeah. We call it the Redneck Riviera around these parts."

* * *

Carla signed the guest book, and the woman led her back to the cabin, where she changed the bed linen and left fresh towels. "I'll give you a holler when Ronnie gets back."

"What's your name?"

"Regan Kilgore."

"Thank you."

"Sure." The woman nodded and was gone. She seemed a little more pleasant, but Carla sensed a wariness about her.

When she finished unpacking her overnight bag she showered and washed her hair, then went out onto the balcony. Regan and Josh were busy getting ready to give a lick of paint to an old houseboat.

A couple of bass boats drifted by lazily on the lake as fishermen flicked their rods. She felt tired after the early start and the drive, and decided to nap for a few hours.

First, she phoned Paul. He answered on the second ring.

"Carla? Have you booked your flight?"

"I fly out to Dubrovnik tomorrow night, via Rome."

"I contacted the International Commission on Missing Persons; they're overseeing the excavation."

"And?"

"A guy named Kelly will meet you at the airport and drive you to the site the next morning. I guess you'll need to book a hotel in Dubrovnik."

"Did you find out the location of the site?"

"It's only a couple of miles from the Devil's Hill."

Her heart instantly felt as if it was dropping into a bottomless pit.

"Are you okay, Carla?"

"Y—yes."

"I know it'll be difficult." Pause. "Are you still there, Carla?"

"Yes."

"You take care. Give me a call at any time if you need me. Okay?"

The line clicked.

* * *

She shut off her phone and laid it on the nightstand.

The very thought of what she had to do made her quake. To have to go anywhere near the Devil's Hill again . . .

It was a nightmare she was dreading.

She felt drained, emotionally and physically.

She knew part of it had to do with being pregnant.

Morning sickness greeted her each day now when she climbed out of bed, a nauseous feeling in the pit of her stomach.

Fatigue washed over her again.

She felt she needed to rest.

As she turned back into the bedroom, she saw Josh in the wheelchair down on the dock, staring up at her through the patio window.

He gave her a shy wave.

She waved back.

The boy turned away and she went toward the bed.

Lying there, she placed a hand on her stomach. She imagined she felt a slight swell. It felt such a comfort.

A joy to counter all the heartbreak.

At least she had that.

At least she had Jan's baby growing inside her.

31

She woke to the sound of knocking on her cabin door.

The knocking ceased, then started again. "I'm coming. Hold your horses."

Carla dragged on a pair of Levi's and a T-shirt and ran a hand through her tousled hair. As she opened the door she was still buttoning her jeans.

The man who stood there was in his mid-forties. Tall and reasonably attractive, with the kind of self-assured look that most women would find instantly appealing.

His dark hair had a touch of gray at the sides and he wore jeans, cowboy boots, and a Stetson cowboy hat, his shirt open at the neck. A pair of worn buck leather gloves was tucked into the silver buckle on his jean's belt.

His handshake was firm. "Carla. It's sure been a while. I'm guessing you must have been no more than sixteen the last time we met."

His voice was deep and masculine, a southern hint to it. Brown eyes and high cheekbones suggested a hint of Native American somewhere in his genes. She guessed he didn't miss much, either, for his eyes seemed to take her in with a single look.

"It's good to see you again, Ronnie."

He smiled. "And you. Regan said you wanted to see me."

Carla noticed a dark-colored Ram pickup parked outside her cabin, the truck bed laden with packing crates and dock provisions. A hunting rifle hung from a pair of hooks in back of the vehicle's cabin. "Is there somewhere we could talk in private?"

"Has this got something to do with Dan?"

"No. It hasn't."

Ronnie pushed back his hat. "I guess the dock's as good a place as any. How about we meet down there in thirty minutes? That'll give me time to unload my truck and have a shower."

She was standing on the dock, admiring the sunset, when she heard the footsteps on the wooden boards.

He had showered, his hair glistening wet, and changed into a fresh short-sleeve shirt and jeans. "You ever been in this part of the country before, Carla?"

"No, I haven't."

"How'd you find me?"

"I found a letter you wrote to Baize after my grandfather's death."

"You mind me asking what exactly brings you here?"

She took a deep breath, not knowing where to start, and then she plunged in. She gave him just the bare facts he needed to know.

He looked at her before he spoke.

"I'm sorry to hear about your husband. He seemed like a very gifted man."

"You heard about Jan?"

"I watched a TV news report about his death. But I guess I'm still at a loss as to why you wanted to meet with me."

"I need your help, Ronnie."

He didn't speak.

"I got the impression you and my grandfather were close friends."

He stayed silent, waiting for her to carry on.

"I'm not quite sure what exactly you both did while serving in the special forces. I can only imagine."

"Imagine what?"

"Maybe it sounds as if I've seen too many movies. But I'm guessing my grandfather served with the kind of special forces units you hear about being used to hunt down wanted terrorists."

"Dan told you that?"

"No, he never spoke about his work. But I'm not stupid. I can put two and two together."

"Meaning?"

"Maybe he even killed people. Except I could never see him as a coldhearted killer. To me he was always a decent, caring human being."

"Yes, he was."

"But did he kill people?"

"Heck of a question. Dan was a soldier. He did what he had to do."

"Which was?"

"He did his duty. I still don't see where this is going."

"I'm here to ask you to help me hunt down two men."

"Why?"

"They're dangerous war criminals. They murdered my husband. Maybe the rest of my family, too."

She tried to explain as best she could.

It took a while, and Ronnie listened.

"Dan mentioned you were in one of those rape camps. Is that right?"

"Yes. Why would he tell you that?"

"I know that what happened to his family tore his heart out, just as much as losing David did. And never knowing where his only son was buried only made it worse. It left him a haunted man. Lost, broken. He needed to talk."

"What else did he tell you?"

"That you were traumatized and needed therapy."

Ronnie fell quiet, the silence like a dead weight, until he said, "Assuming you could find these men, then what?"

"I want information from them."

"And if you got it?"

"Then I want to see these scum handed over to the law and punished."

"You're deadly serious, aren't you? You mean to hunt them down. All by yourself if need be."

"I want justice. And yes, I had therapy a long time ago but I'm not just out for revenge like some crazy woman, in case you think that."

"Dan always spoke highly of you. He never gave me that impression."

"So, will you help me?"

"Carla, the police and federal agencies are paid to deal with the kind of criminals you're talking about."

"Don't you think I know that?"

"Then tell them and let justice take its course."

"It's been over twenty years. These people are never going to face justice."

"Why do you say that?"

"Because they're cowards, and cowards always run and hide. Do you know what percentage of wanted killers who committed genocide have been caught in the last twenty years?"

"No."

"A conservative estimate would be less than thirty percent. Why should I put my faith in a justice system that's flawed?"

"You really believe that?"

"You're talking to a lawyer."

"Then you're the first honest one I've met."

"If there's a threat of being found out, these men will simply do what they've done before—flee and invent new identities."

"That's what you think?"

"I guarantee it. They're probably working on it right now, after killing Jan. It could be another twenty years before they're found. Or maybe never. That's why I have to find them, and very soon."

Ronnie didn't speak.

"One of the two men is Mila Shavik. I believe he may be responsible for my parents' deaths, and for Jan's. The other man is Boris Arkov, but really he's just a lackey. Shavik was in charge of the camp. I want to see them punished."

He stood still, not moving, his eyes never leaving her face.

"Do me a favor?" he said.

"What?"

"Let me think about it. Regan tells me you're staying tonight."

"Yes."

"You're welcome to join us for supper."

"I got the feeling Regan wasn't too keen on me."

He laughed. "She's a kitty cat behind it all, so pay her no need. She always acts a little gruff at first with Yankee visitors."

"You make it sound like the Civil War's still going on down south."

He tipped his hat, added a smile. "Some might say you never spoke a truer word."

32

Regan's place was one of the older cabins facing the lake.

Carla showered and changed clothes, and dabbed on some perfume.

The cabin interior had a homely feel, the table already set with pitchers of iced tea and water. When Carla knocked and Ronnie led

her in, Regan was coming out of the kitchen carrying a steaming cas-
serole dish.

"It's nothing fancy—chicken and dumplings, collard greens and
mashed potatoes, and if you're good company, afterward pecan pie
and ice cream."

"Can I help?"

"It's all done, honey, just grab yourself a seat and put on a nosebag."

Ronnie brought in some more serving dishes. "In case you two
haven't been formerly introduced, say hello to Miss Carla, Josh."

"Ma'am." The boy pushed himself away from an electronic keyboard
in a corner, wheeled over to the table, and politely offered a handshake.

"Pleased to meet you, Josh."

Ronnie began passing around a dish of mashed potatoes as they all
sat. "Josh wants to be a musician. He plays the keyboard, like his mom
used to. He writes some songs, too. He's pretty good."

"I'll have to hear you play, Josh," Carla offered.

The boy blushed. "Naw, I'm really not that good."

Ronnie took a forkful of dumpling. "Yeah, and my boy's modest,
too."

"Dad . . ."

"Listen to this, boy. Tell him, Carla."

"My husband was a concert pianist. He played all over the world."

Josh perked up. "Yeah? Is he famous?"

"I guess you could say he was."

Ronnie said, "New York, London, Paris, Rome. You name it. He
recorded CDs too, Josh."

The boy whistled. "Yeah? That's really cool."

Regan said, "Got any good advice for this boy here?"

"Jan always said you could succeed at anything so long as you
wanted it badly enough. You just had to be prepared to work at it day
and night. I guess that means lots of practice, Josh."

Regan shook her head in mock despair. "Josh never stops playing
that darned electronic piano. I hear some of the neighbors are thinking
of getting a court order against him for noise disturbance."

Josh blushed. "Very funny . . ."

"I've got one even funnier. Maybe I ought to become an organ donor and give that keyboard to charity?"

Carla winked playfully at Josh. "Another piece of advice is never to pay attention to the critics."

"Does your husband still play, Miss Carla?"

"No, Josh. He died a few weeks ago."

There was an awkward silence around the table, Regan and Josh looking at Ronnie, who touched Carla's arm. "I guess I should have explained."

"No, please. I didn't mean to put a damper on things."

"You didn't, honey." Regan patted her hand.

When it came time for dessert, Ronnie wiped his mouth with his napkin and rose. "Would you all excuse me awhile?"

He peered out at the evening sky, and grabbed a flashlight from the hall table.

"Is everything okay?"

He smiled back at Carla. "Sure, but a storm's due later tonight and I need to check everything's well anchored. Besides, it'll give you and Regan a chance to do some girl talk over dessert."

After dessert, Carla helped Regan wash the dishes.

They left Josh playing the keyboard in the front room and moved out to the veranda. Crickets sounded, and fireflies sparked in the balmy twilight, like exploding stars in some distant universe.

Down by the lake Carla saw Ronnie wielding a powerful flashlight as he eased himself down into a motorboat. She heard the motor sputter as he headed toward some houseboats.

The noise was drowned by Josh playing a soft rock number.

"You sure impressed Josh."

"You think?"

"Anything to do with music gets him fired up."

Carla saw a firefly burst into light a few feet away, and then fade. "How much did Ronnie tell you about me?"

"Other than you're related to an old army buddy, nothing. But I'm sure sorry to hear about your husband. I guess it hasn't been easy."

Carla looked out at the lake and mountains tinted dark orange by the dying sunset. She hadn't felt such a sense of peace in quite a while.

"How long have you lived here?"

"All my life. Daddy owned the dock since I was a kid."

"You and Ronnie took it over?"

She nodded. "After Daddy passed away. For Ronnie it's a full-time job. Me, I only help out in summer and holidays. In real life I'm a teacher at the local middle school."

"It seems idyllic. A special place."

"Hey, don't think it's all dreamy sunsets. In peak season you'll work your fanny ragged. Then there's the local entertainment."

"What about it?"

"There ain't none, honey. It's a choice between a few local bars, boating on the lake, fishing on the lake, or shooting yourself in the foot for something to do—probably down by the lake. Oh, and did I mention the lake?"

Carla smiled. "Still, there's almost something spiritual about this place.'"

"All this land used to be a haunt of the Cherokee and Shawnee nations. A lot of locals have Indian blood—I guess there was more fraternizing with the natives than the history books would have you believe."

Regan jerked her head. "Over that way Daniel Boone blazed the settler trail into the Appalachian Mountains in the 1700s."

"Really?"

"Sometimes when I need to clear my head I like to put on my hiking boots and walk some of those mountain trails."

"What's up there?"

"All kinds of wildlife. Eagles, snakes, bears."

"Isn't that dangerous?"

Regan lifted her blouse, revealing a small silvered .38 revolver tucked into a black leather holster on the belt of her jeans. "A shot in the air and most wild animals will run scared."

"Some guys, too, I bet?"

She gave an easy laugh. "Pretty much everyone around here carries a gun, honey. It's the southern settler mentality—you cut your teeth on firearms from the cradle. The principle being that the best person to take care of you is likely to be yourself."

"Your husband doesn't worry about you hiking dangerous trails on your own?"

"Worry? All Dwayne worries about is if he's got enough beer money. I got sense and left that idiot years ago."

"Dwayne . . . ?"

Regan laughed out loud, and put a hand to her mouth. "Oh, I get it. You thought Ronnie and me? No, Ronnie's my brother."

"And Josh's mom?"

"Annie was just a simple country girl, and a loving mother, even if she did have a truckload of problems."

"What problems were those?"

"She was always kind of a lost soul. She could never handle Ronnie's long periods away when he got deployed. No more than she could handle her drinking when his absence drove her to it."

"What happened?"

"She was over the limit one night and smashed her car into a wall. Josh's spine and legs were broken. By the time they cut his momma out she was gone."

"That—that must have been terrible."

"It ripped Ronnie's heart to shreds. I guess he still feels to blame for Annie's death, and for Josh being the way he is. It's a pretty big cross to bear when a man loves his son like crazy."

Josh's music carried on the air, this time a soft ballad.

Regan said, "Annie used to play some nights when Ronnie was deployed abroad; that's how Josh started playing. Annie would get bored, so she bought the keyboard at a pawnshop in Harrogate and tried to teach herself. I always used to think it was kind of sad, her cooped in up here, just playing that thing for company."

"How's Josh coping?"

"It's been five years since his momma passed. Sometimes he sits up in bed like he's still waiting for her footsteps to come up the cabin steps, the way she used to. I've known nights when he wakes, crying out for her."

"And Ronnie?"

"I don't think he's ever looked at a woman since. He sure hasn't gone out with one."

"He seems like a solid guy."

"Here's the weird thing. Ronnie may look like a redneck with that pickup and those cowboy boots. But he graduated in psychology, top of his class."

"From where?"

"Vanderbilt. Never think it, would you? Broke Daddy's heart when Ronnie upped and joined the military after graduating from one of the South's top colleges. Ronnie never even wanted to be an officer. I could never figure it out."

"He quit the army?"

"Resigned to look after Josh. He did the right thing, but if you ask me he's still carrying a lot of guilt around for what happened."

Regan rose, dusted her jeans. "Well, I've got some ironing to finish before I turn in."

"Thanks for dinner."

"You're still leaving tomorrow?"

"I guess so. I've got a flight to catch in the evening."

"Where to?"

"Europe."

"Lucky for some. You need anyone to carry your luggage, you let me know. Well, it's been nice meeting you, Carla."

"And you."

Regan smiled, offered her hand. "I'll make a point of listening to your husband's music. It'll make a change."

"From what?"

"Listening to Josh. And the country and western cry-in-your-beer stuff I'm used to in the local bar most Friday nights."

33

Carla showered before bed.

She toweled herself dry, dragged on her nightgown, then looked at the phone number for Angel she had copied down from Jan's briefcase. She called it again.

This time the woman's voice answered. "Yeah?"

"Is that Angel?"

"Who is this?"

The woman's voice sounded defensive, hoarse from sleep or cigarettes, she couldn't tell which. A radio or TV was on in the background, the noise fading as it was turned down.

"Angel, my name is Carla Lane."

There was total silence.

"Are you still there?"

Carla could hear the woman breathing. Five more seconds passed, the silence unbearable.

"Angel, my husband was Jan Lane."

"I know who you are. Listen, you don't *ever* call me on this number again, do you hear me?"

"Just who are you?"

"You don't know?"

"If I did I wouldn't be asking. But I can always find out."

"How?"

"By giving the police your number."

"Listen, that really wouldn't be a good idea. Not unless you want more trouble than you can handle."

"Then you and I need to talk."

"About what?"

"I think you know what."

A few moments' silence. "I'll call you back in five minutes."

"Let me give you my number."

"I've already got it."

And the line hummed dead.

Five minutes passed.

And another five.

I know who you are. How did the woman know her number? Had it simply showed up on her cell when she made the call or did the woman mean she already had it?

By the time fifteen minutes passed, Carla knew the woman wasn't going to call her back. She went to call the number again just as a knock came on her door. The wind gusted, rattling the glass.

"Who's there?"

"It's me, Ronnie."

She opened the door and he stood there, carrying the flashlight, the trees behind him tossed by the wind. The night sky stained black and blue with inky clouds.

He tipped his hat. "You got everything you need?"

"Yes, thanks."

He looked straight into her eyes. "I just wanted to make sure, Carla."

"Of what?"

"You really know what you're doing."

"What do you mean?"

"Hunting these men down."

"Yes, I'm very sure."

"You know what I figure? That you really need to think this through. That your mind's being clouded by revenge. You want to settle scores."

"I'll be the judge of that."

"I'm sure you will. But the problem with settling scores is that it's always emotional, and likely to impair your judgment. Are you ready for the consequences if things go wrong?"

"Such as?"

"The men you're hunting coming after you, maybe even killing you."

Carla fell silent.

"Aren't you afraid, Carla?"

"The thought of confronting Shavik frightens me half to death. I know the savagery he's capable of. But I have to do it."

"Won't you at least think all this through a little more?"

"I already have."

He paused. "How do I contact you?"

"I've got a flight to catch tomorrow night from New York to Rome, with a connection to Dubrovnik, so I'll be gone a few days. But you can always reach me on my cell." She jotted on a piece of paper and handed it to him.

"Why the trip?"

"They matched my DNA to remains they found at a massacre site not far from the camp."

"I'm sorry. Did they find your father?"

"I don't know. I've been too terrified to ask who they've found."

Distant thunder rumbled.

"You better get some sleep. You'll need it with all the traveling."

The strain showed, her voice full of emotion. "To be honest, I'm dreading going anywhere near the camp."

"I can understand that, too."

"I never thought such horror and cruelty could exist in the world. It's the one place I never want to return to."

She bit her lip hard, as if the words she spoke were the most painful she'd ever uttered.

He touched her arm. "We'll talk about it some more when you get back, okay?"

He opened the cabin door. A warm gust blew across the veranda.

"The storm ought to break in the middle of the night. If your electricity is knocked out, there's a flashlight in the nightstand drawer."

"Thanks, Ronnie."

His eyes lingered on her face as he tipped his hat again.

"One more thing. Shavik's top of your list, right?"

"Yes."

"And Arkov?"

"He's just a pawn. I'm after the king."

* * *

She watched from the window as he walked toward his cabin.

He seemed like a good man, a man she could trust. Her cell rang. She answered.

Angel, sounding angry this time. "How did you get my number?"

"I found it written in Jan's briefcase."

"Is that all you found?"

"What do you mean?"

"Any papers? Or notes?"

"No. Just some names written down. What kind of notes do you mean?"

Angel didn't answer the questions, but she heard her swear.

"Did you tell the police your husband had my number?"

"No."

"What *did* you tell them?"

"Nothing. I knew nothing until I found your name."

"What are you going to tell the police now?"

"I don't know. First, I want us to meet and talk. You and me, face-to-face."

"Are you crazy? I can't do that. It's too risky."

"Why?"

Carla heard no reply.

"Goodbye, Angel. I guess next time you'll be hearing from the cops after they trace you through your number. You can explain to them."

"No, wait! Look . . . I'll meet. Say when."

She got into JFK the next morning. Her flight to Europe didn't leave until 7 p.m. "Early tomorrow afternoon. I'm assuming from your cell number you're near New York?"

"Near enough."

"Let's meet somewhere in Manhattan."

A brief silence. "The Metropolitan Museum of Art. Ten minutes before I'll text you what section we'll meet in."

"When?"

"Noon. Come alone. If I see anyone with you, you can forget it, I'll walk away."

"How will I know you?"

"You won't. I'll know you."

Carla lay on the bed, trying to sleep.

She thought of Jan as her hand caressed her stomach.

Through a crack in the curtain she saw the night was dark and ominous. She could feel the air pressure change. It would be a violent storm.

The kind of storm that used to scare Luka so much, just like when the shelling became terrifying.

When he'd cling to her, frightened, holding his piece of blue blanket for comfort.

She took two of the green pills, flicked out the light, and fell asleep just after midnight, wondering about Angel.

Who was she?

What was her relationship to Jan?

Why did Jan feel the need to keep his connection to her a secret?

Was there more to their relationship?

Recently or in the past?

The questions tormented her until finally she drifted off to sleep.

A little after 2 a.m. she woke with a start.

A ferocious storm raged outside.

Gusts shrieked, thunder exploded, lightning flashed.

When she closed her eyes again she thought she could hear little Luka's voice, silenced for so long, cry out to her in the wind, pleading with her to keep him safe, begging her not to forget him.

And there, lying in the dark, feeling a tear stream down her face, Carla promised that she never would.

PART FOUR

34

She was beautiful.

Tall, blond, leggy, with great cheekbones.

Her hair looked like it might be a wig. She reminded Carla of an expensive call girl she once subpoenaed as a witness, who went by the name of Destiny Star.

Angel carried a faux leopard skin purse, and wore a beige coat and black high heels. Her legs looked tanned, her make up a little overdone with a slash of bright pink lipstick.

She was also the only adult woman Carla saw in that section of the Met. The others a gaggle of schoolkids and their male teacher. They passed her, heading toward the museum store.

Angel was reading a catalog when she looked up, eyeing Carla and scanning the hallway. She jerked her head to indicate a gallery on the right.

Carla followed.

The gallery was empty except for Angel, studying a painting by some eighteenth-century artist with a French-sounding name Carla had never heard of. Angel's dyed blond hair job looked expensive. Thick faux ivory bracelets on each wrist, she wore a classy gold watch with some costume rings. They exchanged a quick nod.

She guessed Angel was about her own age, except she had a dancer's figure, curves in all the right places. Ivory-painted nails matched her bracelets and she clutched a leather purse. You only needed one word to describe Angel.

Sex.

Carla had visited the museum once when she was in high school. She remembered almost nothing about the trip, except a cute dark-haired boy named Brad. She went a few times after that with Jan, whenever Paul visited New York.

"So, tell me what's been going on with you and Jan."

Angel stared back at her.

"You're giving me a look, Mrs. Lane."

"What kind of look?"

"Like I was having an affair with your husband."

"Were you?"

"Do you really need an answer to that question?"

"Right this minute I feel I do."

"Jan and I were friends."

"Friends?"

Carla felt a catch in her heart. Angel's accent was Jersey. But there was a hint of another one in the background, only she couldn't tell from where. All she knew was she felt an instant dislike toward this woman.

"It's really a long story, Mrs. Lane."

"I've got time."

"What was between Jan and me wasn't an affair. It was something else."

"Really? What's something else?"

"We'll get to that, I promise. You and I have more in common than you might think."

"I kind of doubt it." Carla's stare lingered on Angel's face as it turned to look at the painting. She had great cheekbones, a perfect profile.

"Why meet here?"

"I studied art in college. The Met is also where Jan and I used to meet."

"Come again?"

"Don't rush me, Mrs. Lane. It's been hard enough for me to meet you here, face-to-face, believe me."

"Why is it that all of a sudden my legs are shaking? And why am I thinking that art isn't what you do for a living?"

"Is what I do so important?"

"Humor me, Angel. I'm trying to get a handle on this."

"I work in a club."

"I'm assuming not a golf club?"

"Got a sense of humor, haven't you?"

"It's sarcasm."

"I'm a stripper."

"Stripper?"

"Stripper, lap dancer. You could have added hooker once upon a time but that's all in the past, as they say."

Carla felt her heart race, letting it all sink in.

The silence lingered.

"Is that where you met Jan, in the strip club?"

"Sometimes."

Angel gently bit her lower lip, leaving it shiny pink.

Carla felt a rush of blood pounding in her temples.

"Tell me how you and Jan came to meet."

"The circumstances?"

"Everything you think might be relevant."

"We first met a long time ago."

"How long?"

"Do you know anything about Franz Yakov, Mrs. Lane?"

Before Carla could reply, Angel looked back at the painting and said, "He was an artist. He used to say—"

"That there's always a secret part of our lives we keep hidden until the day we die. Or at least until we're found out."

Angel looked back at her, impressed, one plucked eyebrow raised. "That's right."

"Jan told me that quote. Maybe he told it to you, too?"

"Yes, he did. We both had secrets. Not the kind that you share."

"If this is going somewhere, I'd like to get to it, fast. Because right now, all I'm getting is a headache."

"I loved Jan."

"What . . . ?"

"When I saw on the TV news that he died, I cried, believe me."

"Loved him?"

"He was a good, kind, and decent man. A very brave man."

"Kind, good, decent, and brave, I can take. Even the crying. It's the love bit that has me worried."

"I meant I loved and admired him as a human being."

"And I loved and admired him as a husband. So let's cut to the chase here, Angel, and put me out of my misery. Where's this leading?"

"I think you're the only one who can answer that. What do you want from me, Mrs. Lane? You made the call."

Carla remembered the names scrawled on the paper with Angel's. "Apart from the truth about you and Jan, probably the same thing Jan wanted. Help in finding the men he was hunting down, trying to bring to justice. I'm assuming you know about them?"

Silence.

"Don't you?"

A tiny nod. "I helped Jan in whatever way I could."

"Helped him how?"

"With information."

"What kind?"

"About the men he was looking for. I also told Jan he should be very careful. But he wasn't, unfortunately."

"Explain."

"Simply *looking* for these people puts your life in danger. Probe too much and they'll get to hear about it. They have eyes and ears everywhere, including paid informers in the police. I warned Jan."

Angel looked at her. "Once they know they're being watched, that someone's becoming interested in their activities, they'll act ruthlessly and kill whoever's nosing into their affairs. I told Jan that."

Angel paused. "Like there was this guy, a small-time journalist with a local paper. He used to play pool in one of the bars where they'd hang out. He's playing one day and hears their accents. He starts asking where they're from, their backgrounds, what they do. It's really not a big deal, but he's really curious, asking the wrong questions."

"And?"

"A few days later they found him with his hands nailed down on the pool table, like he'd been crucified. The police were called. The guy wouldn't say a word about who did it, wouldn't press charges. Claimed it was a little DIY accident. You understand?"

"I'm beginning to. Will you help me?"

"Nothing deters you, does it?"

"I won't allow myself to be intimidated by people like that. I saw enough of them in the courts."

"Jan said you were a lawyer. I'm guessing if I don't help you'll involve the police, right?"

"You're bright, I'll give you that."

"And you're being smart."

"Something about you brings out the worst in me, Angel. I don't know why. Or maybe I do but I'm afraid to say. And let's just avoid any misunderstanding. By men you mean Boris Arkov and Mila Shavik, right?"

"Yes. Do you really need to ask?"

"What's that supposed to mean?"

"Jan told me about your experience in the camp."

"You're saying he did it because of me?"

"Probably. But a lot of innocent people suffered because of those two. Jan simply wanted justice. And by the way, don't contact the police, you'll get nowhere."

"Why's that?"

"Because both men will vanish if they learn from their informers they're being watched by the police. I've no idea if their investigation's going anywhere. But I bet if it suddenly did, Shavik and Arkov would disappear."

"You sound very sure of that."

"I'd take bets on it. They may be even planning to flee right now. So we may not have much of a window."

"We?"

"I'll help you, because of Jan."

"No other reason?"

"Because I promised I'd help him bring those men to justice."

"That's telling me nothing. Why did you offer?"

"We don't need to talk about that right now."

"Did you two have a shared past?"

"How perceptive of you, Mrs. Lane."

"Tell me."

Angel looked at her watch. "That's a story meant for another day. Right now, I have to be someplace. I have one question for you."

"Ask away."

"What do you intend to do with Shavik and Arkov?"

"See that they pay for their crimes. Every last one."

Angel considered. "Good." She turned to go. "Once I have some useful information I'll contact you. We can meet. But as they say in show business, don't call me, I'll call you."

"Why can't you help me now?"

"After what they did to Jan, I need to protect myself. And please, don't try to follow me, check up on me, or find out where I live. That would only put us both in grave danger."

Angel started to move away. Carla clutched her arm. "Not so fast. Give me something to make me believe I can trust you."

"I know one of the men responsible for Jan's death."

"Who?"

"The man I live with."

"Who's that?"

"Mila Shavik."

35

Baize pulled into the driveway.

There was no sign of Carla's Ford.

She hardly ever parked in the garage, but Baize checked anyway, letting herself into the house and disabling the alarm.

The garage was empty.

When she moved into the kitchen she opened the refrigerator.

Some yogurt, milk, cheese, a few cans of Diet Coke, and a bottle of white wine. From the looks of it, Carla hadn't visited the supermarket recently.

Baize climbed the stairs.

She didn't like to be nosy, but she was concerned—concerned because Carla hardly called her in the last three days, or answered all her calls. And when she did answer she didn't say a whole lot.

Then last night she had called to say she was flying to Europe for a few days.

"Why?"

"Just some legal stuff I need to notarize, to do with Jan."

She sounded somber. Baize tried to call her back three times that morning but her calls went straight to Carla's voice mail.

In Carla's study, she noticed the old photographs of herself and Dan spread out on the desk.

They brought back good memories, made her smile.

Next to the photos was a letter.

She picked it up, and frowned, a little puzzled.

A letter of condolence written by one of Dan's army buddies in Tennessee.

She heard a vehicle pull up outside in the street.

A man climbed out of a gray van. He wore overalls and walked up the driveway, carrying an official-looking clipboard.

The doorbell rang.

"Hi, Mrs. Carla Lane?"

Baize stared back at him warily.

The man smiled, showed his ID. Glasses, dark hair slicked back, a teeny bit of an overbite.

"I'm with the phone company. Got a call about a faulty line."

"You're talking to the wrong woman."

"Ma'am?"

"Carla's my granddaughter but she's not here right now. There's a problem with her line?"

"It seems to be intermittent, ma'am. Could be a loose wire, something simple like that. I might need to hang a meter on all the phone sockets room to room, and make sure we've got a signal, ya with me, ma'am?"

"No, you're blinding me with science."

"She didn't mention any problems?"

"No. But I've left messages that she doesn't answer. The same with her cell."

The man was handsome in a quirky sort of way. Kind of like that actor Billy Bob Thornton, only better-looking.

"I don't know about the cell, ma'am, but she may not get the land-line calls because the line's intermittent. Are you okay for me to check it out?"

"May I see your ID again?"

"You sure can." He presented it once more and smiled. "Yeah, that's me, unfortunately."

The ID looked official, a bland-faced corporate mug shot.

Baize handed it back. "How long will it take?"

"Coming up to lunchtime, feeling pretty hungry, so I'm hoping not too long."

Billy Davix went room to room, leaving the elderly woman making coffee.

He took his time. The glasses, the hair slicked back, the overalls, all part of his act. He always liked this part of the job, pretending to be someone he wasn't. It gave him a big kick, just like his acting days.

He fitted audio bugs in the three house phones: in the living room, bedroom, and study. The trick was to be slick and slow, no rush, not go like a rocket.

Eagles may soar, but weasels don't get sucked into jet engines.

On the study desk he noticed the photographs and correspondence. He plucked a miniature video camera from his tool kit and took some close-up footage of the letter and photographs.

He saw the attaché case on the floor.

He opened it. Reams of sheet music, pencils, eraser, and a pencil sharpener. He saw the envelope, unfolded the page inside, saw the names, and his eyebrows twitched.

He smiled, held the camera over the page, and then popped it back in the attaché.

As he checked all the study drawers, he listened for any sound coming up the stairs.

In the drawers, he found a bunch of computer printouts and bills, including one from the phone company with her cell phone number. He found a couple of more letters from a doctor's office, and a copy of a hospital bill.

He used the camera again.

Five minutes later he was down the stairs and back in the kitchen, carrying his meter and tools.

"I think I found the problem, ma'am."

"Good for you, Einstein. What was it?"

"Loose wire in one of the sockets."

"Great. Maybe now my granddaughter will answer my calls when she gets back."

"When will that be, ma'am?"

"I don't know. She said she'd be abroad for a few days. Maybe she isn't answering her cell messages because she hasn't got coverage."

"Could be. Where is she?"

"Somewhere in darkest Europe, that's all I know. Care for some coffee?"

He gave her the Billy Bob grin. "No, thank you, ma'am, but I sure appreciate the offer. Any more trouble and you just holler."

36

DUBROVNIK

From the air she saw pale blue sea.

Carla stared out the window at the Dalmatian coast as the Al Italia Airbus descended. Mediterranean-looking villages with red pantiled roofs clung to cliffs and mountainsides, and everywhere there were deep gorges and rolling hills of thick forest.

She felt a flux of emotions: fear, anxiety, uncertainty. Her heart beat wildly. A part of her felt she was coming home. Another part of her dreaded what lay ahead. Her palms perspired, she felt palpitations.

She wasn't over the shock of Angel's revelation.

How could she live with Mila Shavik? How could she live with a man who was a killer, a brutal, wanted war criminal? How could she and yet agree to betray him?

Fear gnawed at her. Could she really trust Angel?

She didn't think so.

What if Angel played a part in Jan's death?

What if she was being tricked, lured to her own death?

Carla felt confused, on edge.

The aircraft shook as it descended through the clouds. She closed her eyes. When she opened them again she glimpsed the pale sandstone walls and cobbled streets of ancient Dubrovnik, the bay scattered with palm trees and cruise ships.

Down there, somewhere, was the street and restaurant where her parents first met. Where she and Luka lived the first years of their lives.

Where her ghosts walked.

Ten minutes later the aircraft tires shrieked as they kissed the runway.

When Carla retrieved her luggage from the baggage carousel, she didn't noticed the two casually dressed young men watching her from across the hall. One of them wore a black Nikon camera dangling around his neck.

He snapped off three quick shots of Carla when she wasn't looking.

"Mrs. Lane?"

The man who met in the arrivals area looked in his fifties, with a friendly face and tired, baggy eyes. He carried a white page on which he'd written her name in black marker: Carla Lane.

"My name's Sean Kelly. I'm a forensic pathologist working with the International Commission on Missing Persons."

"Mr. Kelly. Are you English?"

He smiled charmingly as they shook hands. "Irish, but I'll forgive the insult. If you'll come this way, please, my car's in the parking lot."

He took her suitcase and led her to an old blue Renault with a dented front fender.

He opened the passenger door for her. Tossed on the backseat was a rolled-up pair of work trousers and some muddy work boots.

Kelly climbed into the driver's seat. "I've got business here in Dubrovnik this afternoon so I believe I'll be driving you to the site in the morning. It's a long drive, about seven hours."

"Thank you."

"Some of the victims' remains have already been moved to storage near Omarska, in Sanski Most."

"Are we going there?"

"No, the excavations are still ongoing at the site, where we've set up a temporary mortuary. Have you visited Dubrovnik before, Mrs. Lane?"

"As a child."

"You made hotel arrangements?"

"The Hotel Villa Dubrovnik."

"I know it well." Kelly drove toward the city.

"The remains you found whose DNA matched mine, who did they belong to?"

"We made a positive match with a female the same age as your mother."

Carla felt a pang of grief cut her like a blade. "Are . . . are you certain?"

Kelly's green eyes glinted with pity. "The mother-to-daughter DNA link is a very strong one. Our threshold for any match is 99.95 percent probability, so I'm afraid there's no doubt." Kelly glanced across. "I couldn't help but wonder about your American accent. Have you lived there long?"

"Since I was a child. I was adopted by my father's family."

"I see. Well, we'll try to make the whole process here as smooth as possible. I'm sure you're apprehensive."

"Tell me how the bodies were found."

"A farmer plowing a field came across some human bones."

Kelly slowed as he went around a bend.

"It was sheer luck. Part of my job involves studying satellite aerial photography taken by the Americans during the conflict, looking for evidence of massacre sites. Believe it or not, there are still sites undiscovered, even twenty years later."

"Why has it taken so long so long?"

"Often killings happened in remote locations. Anything from single families to entire villages, to thousands of victims killed over days or weeks. In some cases there are no witnesses left alive to come forward. Which is a problem, because until we have at least some intelligence to begin the search, we don't know where to look. So burial sites will probably still turn up by accident for many decades to come."

Kelly shook his head. "To tell the truth, I've been working here on and off for many years now and it doesn't get any easier. It's a tough part of the job, having to confirm a victim's death to relatives."

"May I ask you a question?"

"Of course."

"Were any remains of children found at the site?"

"Yes, quite a few."

Carla's heart sank. "Did my DNA match any of them?"

"Pardon?"

"My four-year-old brother was imprisoned in the camp. I've never known if he lived or died."

"Dear Lord, I'm very sorry to hear that. But none of the children were a match with your DNA, at least none of them so far."

"So far?"

"There's a smaller burial site nearby. We think they may be a different batch of victims, who died from ill health, or possibly at another camp, but we're not sure yet. We haven't excavated that site."

"When will you?"

"There's a whole procedure to go through, involving the Missing Persons' Institute, the police, the pathologist, and the local prosecutor. It could be another week or maybe more."

Kelly pulled up outside the Hotel Villa Dubrovnik, high up in the hills on the edge of the old town, with magnificent views of the port.

"Here we are, Mrs. Lane." He took her luggage from the car and led her toward the hotel.

"I was told the massacre site wasn't far from the women's camp?"

"That's right. Roughly about two miles."

"How did the victims die?"

Kelly seemed to hold back.

"Please, I need to know."

"I can only tell you what we can assume from the evidence."

"Tell me."

"The women and children were being transported on trucks from a nearby camp called the Devil's Hill. We think they were being driven to some other destination."

Kelly's cheek twitched with a look of discomfort.

"From the way gunshot wounds were inflicted on a number of the women, we suspect they may have tried to escape by jumping off, perhaps as the trucks slowed or stopped, or got stuck. We found cranial fragments and shell casings on the other side from the road from the grave. So the guards must have opened fire on them from above."

"And then?"

"Then all hell probably broke loose and they decided to finish everyone off. All the remaining women and children were shot at reasonably close range. There were bullets and shell casings beside the grave."

"They were buried where they died?"

"Pretty much. The field's next to the road. At some stage their killers brought in an excavator to gouge out a mass grave, to cover up their crime."

Carla fell silent for a time. "Is the Devil's Hill camp still there?"

"Yes, it's still intact, even if parts of it were destroyed by shelling."

Kelly added, "There was talk of it being knocked down some years ago, but relatives wanted it kept as a kind of memorial. Though it's just left abandoned. You've heard about the camp?"

"I escaped from there as it was being evacuated."

"I . . . I didn't know. I understood there was only one living survivor, an elderly woman who now lives in America."

"Alma Dragovich?"

"Yes."

"I know her."

Kelly frowned. "If you don't mind me asking, why didn't you come forward as a witness before now?"

"It's a long story, Mr. Kelly. Can we can talk about it another time?"

"Of course. How about I pick you up at eight a.m.?"

Across the street, the two young men sat in a gray BMW, watching Carla and Kelly talking outside the hotel.

The passenger aimed the Nikon camera.

He clicked off at least a dozen good shots of the pair as they talked, then another three as Carla stepped in through the hotel entrance.

37

Carla showered, threw on the hotel bathrobe, and went to stand on the tiny balcony.

A warm breeze blew. The Hotel Villa Dubrovnik was a rambling place, the walls covered with jasmine and bougainvillea. Stretched out below her was the old town where she had spent much of her childhood.

Something in her bones felt familiar with everything she could see and taste and smell: the bustling sidewalks crowded with tourists, the twisting narrow streets, the tangy salt air, the shrieks of seagulls. The town's old fort perched on top of cliffs, waves crashing into the rocks below.

A couple of huge cruise ships squatted in the glassy harbor. It felt like a bizarre homecoming—it made her feel both crestfallen and elated. Crestfallen because she knew with certainty now that her mother was dead.

Had her father met a similar fate? If he'd lived, he'd have made contact with the refugee agencies. That seemed unlikely to have happened after so long. It crushed her, made her sad.

And yet she felt a powerful sense of hope that Luka might be alive. She wanted to think nothing but positive thoughts.

Luka would be a young man now, in his mid-twenties. It seemed so strange to think that in the blink of an eye her little brother might have gone from being a child to a grown man.

She felt like weeping for all those missing years.

Where are you, Luka? Who has taken care of you? Who has loved you with your mama and papa and your sister gone? Who put you to sleep all those nights and tucked you in? She felt her emotions flare.

Noise drifted up from the town. Somewhere in those streets crowded with tourists was Mr. Banda's restaurant. She wondered if it was still in business. She threw on a pair of jeans and a T-shirt, draped a sweater over her shoulders, and went down to the reception desk.

The young man on duty smiled. "Madam."

"Do you know of a restaurant called the Marco Polo?"

"In the old town? Yes. The food's excellent and not expensive, but it's always busy."

"Would you book me a table?"

"Of course. Let me give you directions."

The streets were bedlam, lined with shops and trader's stalls. Kiosks sold trinkets and cigarettes and postcards. In cafés and restaurants, waiters ran in every direction, carrying trays balanced above their heads.

It felt strange to think that over thirty years ago her father walked these same streets the evening he met her mother.

She recognized familiar names on shops and directions on signposts, as words and phrases came back to her, like fragments of a long-forgotten school poem.

A sign said: PLAŽA. Beach. She remembered that.

She followed the sign. The streets grew quieter, less crowded. A gray BMW coasted past her, with two young men inside.

The passenger was coarse-faced, his muscled chest bulging under his polo shirt. A leather jacket lay across his knees, a camera on top. As the BMW passed her, the passenger looked away.

The car disappeared around a corner. As it did so, the driver gave a brief glance back at her, but didn't make eye contact.

Carla shivered. The man's look didn't feel like an admiring glance.

It felt like something a little more sinister.

Or was it just her imagination?

She tried to bury the thought as she hurried on.

The beach looked so familiar.

A wonderful memory blossomed in her mind. A sunny day she and Luka posed for a picture, laughing and eating ice cream and touching noses.

The same beach where her parents strolled soon after they met.

Where on that wondrous day her mother led her and Luka down to the sea in their bathing suits, the first summer her brother began to walk. Her mama holding their hands as they rushed together into the blue waves.

Memories washed over Carla.

Sitting on the sand with Luka and her parents, having a picnic of fresh baked bread and cheese. Luka, giggling and tugging on her sleeve as he tried to nibble the top of her bread roll.

The memories comforted and stung.

She forced herself to shut them off before she felt completely overwhelmed.

Turning back, she wiped her eyes and pushed her way through the swarming backstreets.

She found Marco Polo in a small square facing a bubbling fountain.

Tables and chairs spilled out onto the pavement, the tables lit with flickering white candles set in small glasses. In one corner, artificial vines threaded through a wooden trellis to form a canopy.

Harried waiters passed her, until one eventually guided her to her table near the entrance. He handed her the wine list. "Zdravo!"

"Zdravo!" Hi. She understood that much.

She ordered a plate of spaghetti with pesto. When the waiter went away with her order she studied the restaurant.

She noticed a lean, balding man with bushy eyebrows, his shirt open to reveal too much chest hair. He was operating the cash register and seemed to be in charge, snapping his fingers at the waiters.

Carla waited until he passed her table.

"Excuse me, do you speak English?"

"Of course. I'm the manager, is everything all right?"

"I'm looking for Mr. Banda."

"Mr. Banda isn't here. May I help you?"

"Can you tell me where he is?"

"I'm afraid he doesn't come down to the restaurant very often. Mr. Banda's been ill for years." He jerked his head toward some windows above the awning. "He's upstairs in his room."

"Will you do something for me?"

"Madam?"

Carla took a notebook from her purse. She wrote on a page, folded the paper.

"Could you give him this note and tell him I'd very much like to meet him?"

38

Ten minutes passed.

Carla's gaze lingered on the rooms above the restaurant. She felt vague memories, as delicate as smoke, forming in her mind. Her father letting her make a colorful mess as she spread paints upon his canvas.

She and Luka helping her mother bake a cake, the air rich with the smell of dried fruit and spices.

The wispy memories vanished as her eyes shifted to an old man descending the restaurant stairs, the manager guiding him.

She remembered Mr. Banda the moment she set eyes on him.

When she was a child he looked old and craggy. Now he looked even older, his hair snow white, his back almost bent double.

He used a wooden cane to walk, his left arm stiff, as if he'd had a stroke, one leg dragging. When he reached the bottom of the stairs he nodded to a few patrons and stopped once, to kiss a woman's hand. Then he shuffled over to Carla, escorted by the manager.

"This is the young lady, Mr. Banda."

Hooded eyes under bushy eyebrows studied her. Carla thought Mr. Banda looked like one of the grumpy old men in the Muppets, his big lips turned down in a disapproving frown. He clutched her note.

"So you're Lana and David's daughter, Carla?" He spoke in Serbo-Croat.

Carla was certain she could understand, but said, "Could we speak in English, Mr. Banda? I'm afraid my memory of my mother's language isn't good. But I hope you remember me?"

Mr. Banda's lips parted in a huge smile that lit up his face, and this time he answered in English.

"Remember you? This body may look old, but up here . . ." He tapped his temple with his finger as if he were knocking in a nail. "Up here, I'm still in fantastic shape, with the mind of a twenty-five-year-old. Of course I remember you. It's good to meet you again, Carla, and after so long."

He shook her hand warmly, patted it, and accepted her hug.

"It must be twenty years. You always looked so much like your mother. She was a beautiful person."

He turned to the manager. "Wine, Philip. A good bottle, from the cellars."

"Of course."

The manager left.

"You're probably wondering why I'm here?"

"Whatever the reason, it's wonderful to see you again. I loved your parents; they were always such good people."

"Can you tell me a little about the time we lived here? About my mother and father back then?"

Resting one hand on the top of his cane, Mr. Banda nodded up toward the restaurant windows, a TV flickering behind one of them.

"They lived up there for over ten years. See that window? Do you remember that time?"

"Vaguely."

"To me it only seems like yesterday. Your father used to sit over there and paint." He pointed to the bubbling stone fountain across the square.

"Sometimes you'd sit on his knee and distract him. He pretended to be annoyed, but of course he loved it. He adored you. And Luka, too."

He leaned closer on his cane. "Artists are supposed to be . . . how do you say? *Raspet.* Tormented, isn't that so?"

"So they say."

"But your father was always a happy man, who felt his life was complete. And why wouldn't he? He had a wonderful wife, two beautiful children."

Mr. Banda stared up at the windows, as if he were looking back into the past.

"Your mother came here to work and study. And sometimes she would help me improve my English in her spare time. She was barely a month here when she met your father. Your parents, they were blessed. They were so good for each other."

"You think so?"

"Of that I'm certain. I often wondered what became of you all. Your parents promised to write after they left but as the weeks and months passed I heard nothing from them. I'm not complaining, of course; people have their lives to lead. You have an American accent, I think. You're American now?"

"Yes."

His eyes sparkled. "So, you all went to America after all. Good. Tell me all the news. How are your parents? Alive and well, I hope? Did they have more children? Where are they living in America?"

She paused, the words almost too difficult to speak. "They're dead, Mr. Banda. My parents were killed during the war."

The old man slumped back in his chair as if someone stabbed him, his shock instant. His mouth hung open, his face ashen. "No . . . not Lana and David. Please . . . no, it can't be true?"

"We were trying to flee Sarajevo when we were rounded up. My father may have died in Omarska camp, but I can't know for certain. My mother, Luka, and I were in a camp nearby."

Spittle frothed at the corners of the old man's mouth.

"May God forgive whoever harmed them. May God forgive their killers." His eyes were wet and he took a paper tissue from his pocket, wiped them, then dabbed his mouth.

"My poor child, I'm so sorry. I loved them both. They were like a son and daughter to me. I often wondered why they never wrote, what became of them."

His bony hand reached out and gripped Carla's wrist. "You must tell me. Tell me what happened to David, and to my beautiful Lana. Tell me everything . . ."

Diners came and went. Glasses clinked, waiters scurried past, carrying steaming plates and dishes. Mr. Banda listened, in a daze, unaware of what has going on around him.

In the middle of it all the manager came with a bottle of wine and two glasses, and set them down. The wine remained untouched.

Carla told him as much as she needed to. Not everything, for that would have only complicated things, and what would be the point?

Mr. Banda's mouth trembled.

"I . . . I don't know what to say. I feel so distressed." He wiped his eyes again. "It must have been dreadful for you. The camp, your parents' deaths, and now this, returning to witness your mother's remains."

He placed both hands on his cane.

"The evil people who kill and maim, they never think of families who have to deal with a lifetime of sorrow. They never think of anything, except hate. But what did hate ever achieve?"

He reached across, touched her hand. "You say you've learned that Luka may have survived?"

"Yes."

"Dear God, I hope so."

"I'll do all I can to find him. Whatever it takes."

"You poor child. And dear, innocent Luka. So many children lost parents, so many orphans. It's many years since the war, yet still I see young men and women who lost entire families and they wander these streets like lost souls."

His wrinkled hand kneaded hers. "If there's anything I can do to help, anything at all, you only have to ask."

"Thank you."

Streetlamps were coming on, glowing amber as the evening sun was dying.

"Please, come with me upstairs." Mr. Banda went to rise, and Carla moved to help him.

"There's something I want to show you. Something I think you ought to see."

Mr. Banda shuffled into the apartment and switched on the light.

Carla looked around her, wandering into the rooms.

It all felt so familiar.

The double bed tucked into a corner. The blackened woodstove fringed by pale blue tiles. A varnished pine kitchen table that shone like polished glass.

Simple, clean, cozy. Comforting smells drifted up from the restaurant kitchen: garlic, olive oil, oregano and other spices.

Mr. Banda sat on one of the pine chairs. "You remember?"

"I . . . I'm not sure."

"That same bed is where you were born. And remember Luka's birth at the hospital? We thought he wouldn't live. The young doctor who delivered him wasn't long out of medical school."

Mr. Banda smiled. "I think that night he wished he had settled for being a car mechanic, like his brother."

Carla touched the stove's blue tiles, ran her fingers over the glassy smoothness.

She closed her eyes tightly, and fought to remember.

Fragments seeped in.

Images of achingly wonderful memories.

Supper on Saturday evenings, of roast chicken and herb stuffing, her parents sharing a bottle of wine and talking and laughing across the shiny pine table.

Carla sitting on her father's knee, listening rapt as he told her about America.

Other fragments came back to life, like ship's flotsam bobbing to the surface. She recalled her mother, her sleeves rolled up, bent over a pile of ironing, steam rising as she pressed the clothes.

A winter's night before Christmas, snow falling, the sound of church bells echoing through the old town, and she and her mother bathing a giggling Luka in a big old zinc bath by the stove.

And afterward, rocking Luka asleep in her arms, as he said sleepily, "Volim te, Carla." *I love you, Carla.*

Twenty years were peeled away, as if they had never existed.

Overcome, she wanted to cry into her hands with such a terrible despair.

"I left everything as it was when we renovated the restaurant, just gave the walls a fresh coat of paint. But that's not why I asked you here, Carla."

Mr. Banda led her down a hallway to his own living room. It had the same blue-tiled stove, the same straw-color walls, decked with old family photos. A big TV was on, its sound muted.

He shuffled over to one of the walls, where a painting hung.

"See."

Carla saw it was a portrait of her father's, about the size of a brief-case.

A wonderful, colorful image, of all of them together on the beach, the old town walls in the background. Luka playing in the sand, his curly mop of hair the color of ink; Carla in a bathing costume, chubby with puppy fat; her mother wearing a pale blue summer frock, her hands on her hips in mock dismay as she looked at Carla's father, who was scratching his head with frustration as he tried to unfold a wood-and-cloth deck chair.

The image made Carla smile.

It was a fun painting, lighthearted, in the style of a seaside postcard, an idyllic family moment frozen in time.

"Your father had me take a photograph of you all posing on the beach, then used it to paint this. I always thought he'd come back for it, because it's such a personal portrait. I've treasured it, but of course it really belongs to you. I know your father would have wanted you to have it."

"Mr. Banda, you don't have to . . ."

"I insist. Where are you staying?"

"The Hotel Villa Dubrovnik."

"Better still, give me your home address. I'll have it properly wrapped and shipped to your home."

"Thank you."

She wrote out her address. He kissed his cheek. His bony hand gripped hers. "I wish you luck, Carla. I wish you all the luck finding Luka."

"You're the only credible witness to survive the Devil's Hill camp. Are you aware of that, Mrs. Lane?"

The Renault strained up a mountain road, and Kelly added, "As far as we know all the other victims are dead, apart from Mrs. Dragovich."

"And her mental state may not hold up in court."

"Exactly. That's why your testimony could be vital to any future prosecution."

Kelly looked across. "I hate to say this, but your life could even be in danger. If any of the war criminals still at large who committed these terrible acts ever find out, they may want to kill you. You may have to become a protected witness. Do you understand?"

"Yes, I'm a lawyer."

"A lawyer?"

"Try not to say it as if I've got leprosy, Mr. Kelly."

"I . . . I wasn't. I just wasn't aware . . ."

"I'm kidding. Mocking my profession can be a habit of mine. I get what you're saying. Mind if I open the window?"

"Not at all. Give the handle a good jerk."

Carla jerked the handle and let in fresh air.

They left Dubrovnik far behind and drove up through rocky gorges and heavily wooded mountains, the air drenched with the smell of pine sap. She remembered that fragrance, as if it was ingrained in her.

They crossed the border from Croatia into Bosnia, and took several rest stops during the long drive. Kelly passed villages still gouged by bullet holes and artillery shells, and the remains of burned-out farms and houses.

"For all its exquisite scenery, this place has such a dark past, Mrs. Lane."

"Do we drive near the Omarska camp?"

"Near enough. We pass it on the way to the site."

"It's where my father was imprisoned. I'd like to see it if you don't mind."

"You can't get in."

"Why not?"

"The camp was part of an iron ore mine that's now owned by the Indian mining company, AcelorMittal, in partnership with the local government."

"So?"

"There are memorials in most surrounding towns and villages but to this day none's been erected to the victims who perished there. And they don't exactly encourage visitors."

"Why not?"

"The region is still predominantly Serb, and the local council would prefer to put that ugly part of their history behind them. As well as that, most of the old buildings where the prisoners were kept are torn down. But I can drive by, if that's what you want."

Carla felt her stomach tighten. The more miles the Renault ate up, the more apprehensive she grew.

When hours later they came around a bend she saw a large industrial mining complex—several large buildings, including an ore smelter.

Surrounded by a barbed-wire fence, security guards manned the gates.

"That's Omarska. The mines are still being worked—despite the fact that it's estimated thousands of bodies are still missing. We only found several hundred."

"Tell me."

"Many had been starved or shot to death, or dead from ill health. They say it was as bad as Auschwitz."

"What happened to all the others?"

"I've no doubt most of them are buried in the huge mounds of spoil heaps scattered around the mines."

Carla saw hills of old mining debris sprinkled around the landscape. She thought about her father and how he must have suffered. Was he buried here, somewhere in the mounds of debris?

She felt a violent shiver. The prospect was too terrible to contemplate.

"Will you take me to see the Devil's Hill?"

"Are you really sure you want to do that?"

"It's the last thing I want to do, believe me."

"Then why do what you're dreading?"

"Because I feel compelled to."

"Okay, but first we'll see the site where the bodies were found. After that, if you still feel up to it I'll take you there."

40

Kelly slowed and turned the Renault onto a forest track.

"We found the bodies buried at the end of this track, in a field beside the woods. The team's still working there."

He stopped in a clearing. Several cars and four-wheel drives were parked there.

The terrain looked familiar to Carla.

Hilly woods on one side, a valley on the other. A couple of miles down the valley she could just make out a clump of gray concrete buildings. She felt a thudding sensation, as if someone were pounding her chest with a hammer.

"The Devil's Hill?"

"Yes. It occurred to me that while you were there you must have known the dreaded Mila Shavik."

"Yes, I met him."

"They've never managed to find him, even after all these years. Of course, he could be dead by now. I've heard rumors to that effect."

"He's not dead, Mr. Kelly."

"You sound very certain of that."

"I've no doubt he's still in hiding, like so many of the others who scurried away like cowardly rats."

They stepped out of the Renault.

The track led to a field, a hundred yards away. She felt her palms perspire again, and her legs began to shake.

She remembered the nighttime death march to the camp, when the old man who couldn't keep up had his throat cut by the guards. It was on a forest track just like this. Memories of that terrible night came back, and they terrified her.

She felt Kelly's hand gently touch hers.

She opened her eyes. They felt moist.

"Do you think you'll be all right?"

"I . . . I don't know."

Kelly kept a firm grip on her hand as they approached the field.

A noisy electric generator hummed. A huge white canvas tent was erected, a gray van parked beside it. A couple of Porta Potties were nearby, with rows of shovels and picks stacked at the side.

A Toyota Land Cruiser had a trailer hitched to the back. It held a muddied, mini yellow JCB excavator, its grab like a hooked claw.

A local police car was parked nearby, two uniformed officers seated at a plastic trestle table in front of the tent, drinking coffee.

Carla trembled with distress.

She thought of how her mother must have met her death somewhere along this track.

Frightened, knowing her end had come. Knowing that she would never see her children or husband again. And all those other mothers and children. What terror had they gone through?

She touched her stomach.

Now that she was pregnant with her own baby, she truly understood the depths of their fear. Not for themselves, but for their children. Her blood curdled.

A half-dozen men and women, some wearing white overalls and using hand trowels, were excavating a wide, deep trench at the edge of the field.

A few of them worked with wire sifters, carefully examining the removed clay and stones. Another man stood over the trench, adjusting a camera on a tripod. Faces looked up, watching her arrival.

As Kelly led her toward the tent, Carla recoiled.

In a corner of the trench she saw a tangle of skulls, bones, and rib cages exposed above the soil, some with parts of clothing or shoes still attached. Most looked like the remains of adults, but others appeared to be children.

As if to prove it, a girl's faded blue shoe poked through a knot of bones.

Carla put a hand to her mouth, stifled a cry.

She felt Kelly's arm slide around her waist for support. "We'll try and get this over with as quickly as we can."

Kelly pulled aside the tent flap.

It was huge inside, with no groundsheet. A portable fan was on. Meshed vents around the walls allowed air to circulate. Even so, a stench of freshly dug earth and human decay filled their nostrils.

Half a dozen metal tables were laid side by side. On several human remains were laid out: parts of skeletons, skulls and bones, bits of rotted clothing and footwear. On others were unzipped body bags. Carla saw a complete skeleton in one, while others held a jumble of bones.

Kelly gestured to rows of metal shelves stacked with more body bags, each with tags attached.

"We've found ninety-seven victims in all in this location. Sixty-three women and thirty-four adolescents, children, and infants. Of the children, twenty were female, and fourteen were male."

He stopped beside a table. It contained a grim exhibit of bones and a single adult skull, stained brown in places. An obscene bullet hole went through the back of the crown, exiting at the front. At the bottom of the table was a plastic basin containing what looked like a clump of dried-up clothing. A tag on the body bag lying by the exhibit said: O26B.

Kelly said, "These are the remains that gave us a positive match. They were among the first we excavated."

Staring down at the pitiful skull and bones and ragged bits of clothing, she could hardly stand, her legs were shaking so much. Shock and a terrible anger registered on Carla's face.

Is this all that remains of my mother?

She caressed the top of skull with her fingertips. She felt its coldness seep into her.

She closed her eyes, pictured her mother's face, her smiling, calm eyes, and remembered her warmth, her spirit, her generosity.

She opened her eyes again. They were blurred, felt wet.

At that moment she wanted to scream, to call out to God and curse him, but she knew that no God did this; nor did any religion.

Just men.

Brutal, callous, evil men.

She recalled the lines in her mother's diary after she visited Shavik in his office.

It's done. I did what I had to.

What Shavik did makes me cry.

If she had a gun and Mila Shavik was in front of her, she would have shot him without a shred of mercy.

She hated him with a powerful intensity.

She put a hand to her mouth to stifle a cry.

Kelly said, "I'm sorry this is so distressing."

He indicated the clump of dried clothing.

"What we've got here are bits of clothing and personal items found on or near the remains. Things often get jumbled up in mass grave sites, so we can never be sure who they belonged to. We've cleaned away the mud and decay as best we can."

Kelly picked up a pair of short metal tongs from the table and used it to separate the items.

"Do you recognize anything at all?" he asked gently.

Carla saw a rusted cheap bracelet, some shreds of clothing, a broken, corroded earring, and what looked like a young girl's plastic hair clasp.

"No."

"The clothing is mostly rotted away. But sometimes people discover a personal item, like a piece of jewelry that they like to have as a keepsake. Difficult as this is, please take your time. Use the tongs if you wish."

Kelly laid the tongs down in front of her.

Carla stared at the pile. It was such a tangled mess she couldn't tell what it contained.

Her hands shook as she picked up the tongs. She sifted delicately, separating a piece of a patterned summer dress from what looked like a cheap headscarf.

She recognized nothing.

Perhaps they're wrong about my mother? Perhaps it's not her at all?

Her heart began to soar with hope.

And then it plummeted.

Embedded in the pile, she spotted the lump of wool.

So dark it was almost black, the color of dried blood. The same color as the burgundy cardigan her mother wore the last time she saw her.

Carla put a hand to her throat.

"Are—are you all right?" Kelly asked.

She lurched toward the exit.

41

"You're all right now, girl, you're all right. Here, drink some water."

Kelly's charming Irish accent calmed her, his hand firmly patting her face.

She felt shaken, and lightheaded. She was sitting on a fold-up chair outside the tent. A female colleague of Kelly's offered her a bottle of ice-cold water.

Carla took a swallow.

Kelly said to the woman, "Thanks, Jane, you're a pet."

The woman left. A thermos flask lay beside Kelly and he screwed it open.

"I'd offer you a sip of whiskey if I had some. A shot of Jameson is a great one to steady the nerves, but all I have is tea, I'm afraid. Will you have a drop?"

Carla shook her head.

Kelly filled his mug. The sun beat down. He wiped his brow with the back of his hand.

"Every time I'm there to help someone see their dead, they either faint or lose their head completely. Sorry if I patted your face too hard, but you were getting a bit wobbly and I thought you might pass out."

He pulled a pack of Marlboros from his pocket and offered one to Carla.

She declined. Kelly lit a cigarette, touching it to the flame from a plastic lighter. "I never hit a woman in my life until I came to work here. Now it's almost a regular event. I've become a right brute, so I have."

Carla clenched her fists so tightly the skin was bone white. She felt a powerful sense of grief and anger that made her seethe.

"How could they kill women and children like that? How . . . how could they just bulldoze the corpses into a pit, the way you'd bulldoze garbage? How?"

Kelly took a drag on his cigarette. "I know, it's hard to make sense of it all. And so many of them were children of tender years."

He blew out smoke with a sigh that sounded like an ache. "It's been truly awful, the work here. I've seen atrocities committed by all sides—Croats, Bosniaks, Serbs."

He paused. "I've excavated the remains of adults, children, and infants who've been shot, or beheaded, or strangled, or had their throats cut. I've even seen the remains of unborn babies ripped from their mothers' wombs. The depravity is almost beyond comprehension."

"So much evil, and for what, Mr. Kelly?"

"On the surface, it always looks to the world as if it's all about religion—about the endless conflict between Christian and Muslim. But the majority of Serbs, Croats, and Bosnians were decent people who wanted nothing to do with killing."

He looked at her. "In rural areas like these there are certainly feuds that have gone on for centuries, split down mostly ethnic lines. Feuds between towns, ethnic groups, even families. They're almost like hillbilly feuds—the Hatfields and McCoys—only far more savage. But it's not just about that."

"Then what is it about?"

"Hatred and intolerance are certainly part of it. And sheer cruelty. But like the Nazis or the Japanese military class during World War Two it's mostly about arrogance—maybe the worst sin of all, because it makes some people see others as less than human, as inferior enemies deserving of torture and death."

Kelly jabbed a finger toward the pit. "That's what that's all about. And because they can get away with it, because the rule of law has broken down. It's in human nature. As for the Serb mafia involvement, it was about making a profit under the guise of patriotism—stealing people's homes and land, their possessions and valuables, and often killing their victims. But rest assured the prosecutors will gather all the evidence they can. If justice can be done, it will."

"Do you really believe that, Mr. Kelly? Do you believe with all your heart that all the killers who did this will be caught and punished?"

Her voice sounded hard, demanding.

Kelly chewed his bottom lip a moment, picked at a fleck of tobacco, and flicked it away. "No. I don't think all of them will."

"At least you're honest."

He tapped ash from his cigarette. "The bits of wool . . . ?"

"My mother wore a cardigan that same color."

"You may think it pointless, but the authorities will be grateful for whatever you can tell them in a witness statement. It doesn't have to be today. But they'd like to have it for the record."

She followed Kelly's stare down the valley toward the Devil's Hill.

"It's probably wise you don't go near that place now."

"You've seen the camp?"

"I went in to have a look a few years back and it gave even me the creeps."

"Does anybody go near it?"

"I wouldn't think so. It's all boarded up."

"But you can still get in?"

"Sure."

"How did it look inside?"

"A bit of mess. There's no electricity, and parts of the building were caved in with bomb rubble."

"They left it as it was?"

"Pretty much as they found it. The authorities no doubt had enough to be doing elsewhere, rebuilding towns and villages."

"On . . . on the ground floor were some corridors. One of them led to a janitor's closet."

"I don't remember, to tell you the truth."

"Do you know if the entire building was searched?"

"I have absolutely no idea. Why?"

42

Carla saw the collection of concrete buildings with pebble-and-mortar-coated walls and black slate roofs.

Bits of an old army truck were scattered in a meadow, a corroded engine block and a mangled fender. The camp's barbed-wire fence all rusted now.

As the Toyota Land Cruiser drove up the entrance road, she felt her stomach turn.

The camp was just as she remembered it, except parts of the roof were caved in by gaping shell holes. Chunks of masonry were gouged from the walls, stitched by bullet holes.

Her legs began to shake again.

Kelly braked as they approached a metal gate at the camp entrance. In the back of the Land Cruiser sat two of his male colleagues.

One of them jumped out and slid the gate's metal bolt.

Kelly hit the accelerator, and drove the Toyota through, pulling the small JCB excavator on the trailer.

They stopped at the front entrance.

Windows were covered with rotting plywood, the assembly square in front of the main building blanketed with weeds and thick clumps of wild grass.

Carla saw the green double entrance doors, the paint flaking and weathered.

One of the doors was hanging off its hinges.

Kelly said, "Are you really sure you want to go through with this? In all likelihood, the place was searched, considering it was a war crimes' scene."

"But we don't know for sure."

"No. But I'd assume—"

"I can't assume anything."

Carla felt apprehensive as they stepped out of the Land Cruiser. Approaching the double green doors, Kelly and his men carried flashlights.

The sun was out, the day hot. Crickets chirped, a smell of rotting wood corroding the air.

The green doors and the pebble-coated walls on either side were scarred with bullet holes. Carla turned to look around the camp square.

The tendons on her neck felt taut. Images flooded in. She tried to fight them off, but they were too powerful.

She recalled arriving in the camp in the cold and dark early hours, tired and hungry. She remembered the cries of despair as the men and boys were separated from their families, and her father being taken away.

The look on his face as the truck drove off. He was waving bravely through what must have been a terrible fear. For some reason she recalled seeing tears running down his face. Were they tears of helplessness and shame that he could do nothing to protect his family?

Where are you, beloved Papa? What became of you? Will I ever see your kind and smiling face again?

Other images floated in. Boris Arkov striking Alma the savage blow that cut her from cheek to jaw, her dentures shuttling across the ground.

And Carla dropping the silver dollar, seeing it roll toward Shavik's feet, a distraction that may have saved Alma's life.

Her stomach knotted as she recalled the humiliation of the mothers and girls dragged away by the guards that first night, and the livid terror on her mother's face, fearful that they might be next.

She recalled the brutality of Mila Shavik's men, and again came the questions.

How could any man abuse mothers and children like that, in front of each other? How could they let children starve and mothers fret themselves half to death with worry and revulsion? How could they rape and murder their victims so callously?

Some of the men must have been fathers themselves. Some must have had children and infants they loved, or mothers and daughters and sons they adored.

Was it all because the victims were simply of a different culture, or religion? How did that make the victims any less human?

Another memory intruded. Standing there on the square that first night, clutching Luka's hand as he wore his Thomas the Train backpack. His little face was wide-eyed and openmouthed with fear, looking lost as he squeezed her hand tightly, fright in his voice as he whispered to her.

"Will we be all right, Carla? Will we? Will Mama and Papa be okay, too?"

His fearful questions rang again in her ears.

She was afraid to move beyond the green door hanging off its hinges.

Afraid to take that first step.

Afraid to think of what could lie ahead.

What if Alma was wrong?

What if her tormented mind only imagined seeing Luka at the hospital? What if Luka and the other children were killed by the shelling?

Disturbing questions raged through her mind.

In despair, Carla placed her palm against the bullet-gouged wall and took several deep breaths, as if to prepare herself.

She felt fingers touch her arm. She looked around.

Kelly didn't speak, but his soft eyes flicked to the green doors, then back again, asking her the question.

Are you ready?

She nodded.

Kelly's flashlight sprang on.

He pushed aside the hanging door, the hinges groaned, and they stepped inside.

43

Broken glass crunched beneath their feet.

A stench of rotted wood filled the hallway.

Carla's eyes adjusted to the dimness, as Kelly and his men waved their flashlights. The entrance hallway looked smaller than she remembered.

It was covered in dust, debris, and shattered glass.

She saw discarded sardine and tuna cans, rusted and empty.

Old wooden ammunition crates with Russian markings lay scattered about, as well as spent cartridge cases. A scrunched-up rotted blouse lay tossed in a corner, next to a man's shriveled green sock.

This was the hallway through which women were dragged for interrogation or rape or beatings.

Just inside the hallway on the left was a main office, the door's frosted glass pane smashed.

Shavik's office, no doubt. She felt a chill down her spine.

Strange that still she could not remember a single thing about their meeting on the evening before she escaped.

Perhaps it was just as well. Even the thought of being face-to-face with Shavik repulsed her.

As they moved deeper into the building, more light began to filter from shattered windows and shell holes in the roof. Kelly and his men turned off their flashlights.

Carla saw a thick layer of dust cover the ground, some of the walls caked with graffiti. "Murderers go to Hell!" "Walk with the devil, die with the devil!"

They passed rooms with rusted metal beds, no doubt where the guards raped women. On some of the walls crude sexual symbols were drawn.

They came to a crossroads of corridors.

Two led left, and two right.

Kelly shone his flashlight. Mounds of bomb wreckage choked one corridor on each side, blocking them with fallen masonry and rubble. Bombs had shattered the ceilings, and electrical cables hung down like thin black snakes.

These two corridors looked impossible to penetrate.

Shafts of light filled the other two corridors, some of the doors along the passageways missing or smashed off their hinges.

Carla felt her breathing quicken, her pulse drumming in her ears.

Kelly gestured with the flashlight. "Do you remember which one?"

"I . . . I think it's this way."

She picked her way down the left corridor, Kelly and the others following.

Where a door was closed, Carla opened it, the hinges creaking.

In several rooms were rusting steel filing cabinets and shattered furniture. Behind one door was an electrical switch room, the wires a mess, hanging like spaghetti.

But no janitor's closet.

"I was wrong. This isn't the one. I has to be the next corridor—the one that's blocked."

Kelly shouted to his colleagues. "Go get the JCB digger, boys! Knock down the front doors if you have to, but get that bloody thing in here, pronto."

Carla moved back to the mouth of the next corridor. It was blocked by a huge mound of wreckage.

She felt certain this was the one that led to the closet.

She began to lift pieces of debris from the mound. A shower of ceiling plaster and dust fell from above.

Kelly said, "Steady on, girl. I don't like the look of that ceiling. It could cave in. Wait until the digger arrives."

But she was barely listening. She grasped a shattered plank of wood and cast it aside.

"Didn't you hear me?"

Ignoring Kelly, she moved a slab of ceiling plaster next. She worked furiously, in a kind of fearful desperation.

Kelly tried to stop her but she pushed him aside forcefully. Outside, they heard the JCB start up, and then came a crashing sound, as if the men had rammed the digger through the entrance doors.

Carla kept working, frantically. She coughed and sputtered.

The plaster dust was like a film of talcum powder, and it covered bumps of debris on the floor. Her right foot hit something hard, shaking off some of the dust—a soldier's old boot.

Then she stepped on something soft.

She nudged it with the tip of her shoe, and saw a flash of blue and red. A shiver ripped through her heart.

She dropped to her knees, brushed the dust off the object.

She recognized the Thomas the Train motif, the little blue engine with huge eyes and a smile.

"What's wrong?" Kelly asked.

"My—my brother's backpack . . ." Her breath came in gasps as she examined it.

The zipper was open. Fear pounding her chest, she turned the rucksack upside down. The contents tumbled out.

A rusted tin of sardines. A shabby pair of boy's underwear and undershirt.

A shiny stone, a piece of string. The kind of things infinitely important to a small boy.

A 1986 silver dollar coin in a plastic case.

The last thing to tumble out was a piece of a blue material.

Luka's comforter.

His blankie . . .

She squeezed the piece of cotton, began to tremble, a cry building inside her, and her eyes felt wet.

She scrabbled again at the debris, grasping huge chunks of masonry. A noise roared in her ears as the men arrived with the JCB.

Kelly grabbed ahold of her shoulders. "Please, move back. We'll have it cleared in no time."

The machine's claw plowed into the mound. In no more than two minutes it cleared a path through the rubble, leaving only a cloud of choking dust.

They seemed the longest two minutes in Carla's life.

She was trembling so much she could hardly breathe, from the dust, from dread, and she had to hold her sides.

Once the digger broke through, the driver backed it up, leaving a gap wide enough to step through.

Kelly turned on his flashlight. A corridor lay beyond.

Doors either side. Some ripped off their hinges, others intact.

"Stop! Stop the bloody machine . . . !" Kelly made a cutting gesture to his neck.

The driver killed the noisy engine.

Silence engulfed them.

Kelly, his face covered in dust, his arm over his mouth and nose, looked back at Carla.

Her eyes were wide, afraid.

Without a word, she grabbed the flashlight from Kelly and stumbled through the gap.

The flashlight sliced through the dusty air like a silver blade.

She saw that the debris had been right up against a door.

She shone the light on its grimy engraved sign: DOMAR.

She remembered the word.

Janitor.

She gripped the handle, twisted.

The closet door wouldn't budge. Debris was scattered at the bottom of the door and she kicked it away.

She jerked the handle again. It still didn't move.

Kelly was behind her now. "Here, let me try . . ."

He turned the handle, yanked hard, and Carla heard a splintering crack. The wood appeared to be jammed or swollen in its frame.

Kelly yanked again. The door creaked open an inch or two, then stuck.

Before Kelly could yank it again, Carla slid the fingers of both her hands into the gap of the door frame and pulled with all her strength.

The door groaned and cracked open.

A moldy odor hit them. Carla couldn't speak. She felt bile rise in her throat and clasped a hand to her mouth to muffle a gasp.

"Step back, Carla. Do as I say, please," Kelly urged, and tried to pull her away, but she fought him off desperately.

Inside the storeroom she saw the mummified remains of several children.

Some were curled up on the floor; some were standing. Their empty eye sockets were huge gaping holes, and their features were beyond recognition.

The bodies still had hair and clothes, but the garments were shriveled up, a mottled brown color. One of the bodies was of a little girl, her long hair plaited down to her waist.

Another was a little boy with dark locks. Carla felt a strange fluttering in her chest, as if her heart was about to stop.

She gave a cry that sounded like a strangled moan.

Then she sank on her knees to the floor and screamed.

For her mother, for her father, for Luka.

A terrible scream that seemed to echo throughout the building, like a cry from all the souls of all the dead who had ever perished there.

PART FIVE

44

The man who called himself Billy Davix admired the pole dancer's legs as she swung them around the steel bar, her blond hair flailing the air.

Music blared, a Rolling Stones number.

A waitress came over and placed a vodka-and-tonic on Billy's table. All the women working in the bar were terrific lookers, even in the low lighting of the private club.

"Can I get you anything else, sir?"

Billy peeled some bills from his wallet and nodded to the pole dancer. "Yeah, how about the new girl?"

"You've got expensive tastes."

"You're right there, baby. Do me a favor and tell the man upstairs that Billy is here to see him."

"Sure."

Billy watched the woman's retreating figure beneath her tight skirt. The private club did pretty good business. Only Wednesday evening, but buzzing.

Some of the women at the bar looked like the hookers they were; too much lipstick and makeup and cheap flashy clothes. Tonight the male patrons were Russian and Serb mostly, tough-looking guys wearing leather jackets.

Billy could never understand the leather jacket thing with mobsters. As if it was the ultimate symbol of success. His old man was the same. First thing he did when he came to the States when Billy was four, his old man bought himself a black leather jacket. How tacky could you get?

Dumb. It made you stand out like a thug.

Dobrashin, Arkov's bodyguard, waddled over to the table. Another leather jacket. Built like a sumo wrestler, the effects of too many steroids.

His nose looked like it had been hammered into his face, his arms swollen with energy.

He was from one of the 'stans—Uzbekistan, Turkmenistan, wherever—an Asiatic hint in his slanting eyes.

He sorta reminded Billy of that ukulele-playing Hawaiian guy, Israel something, who had a hit with "Somewhere over the Rainbow."

Despite Dobrashin's ferocious size, Billy knew he could waste him, no problem.

"The boss said to go right on up."

Arkov sat behind the laptop on his desk and indicated the seat opposite.

"Take a seat, Billy."

Billy knew his old man's cousin was wanted by Interpol and half the cops on the planet, but Billy also knew the supreme importance of *kanun*—loyalty—and *besa,* secrecy.

His old man worked for Arkov's people for years as an enforcer, doing what he did best, muscle and mayhem, until a heart attack whacked him at fifty-six as he watched *The Sopranos*. His mom buried his old man in his shiny leather jacket, dazzling white shirt with white tie, slicked black hair—Billy thought his old man looked like a penguin in the coffin.

Billy preferred a tailor-made suit or casual jacket. That way, you didn't stand out like a mobster from central casting.

Billy never finished high school, but six years with the U.S. Marines gave vent to his natural aggression and gave him all the education he needed. Except the weird thing was, if Billy had his way, he would have liked to have been an actor.

Everyone told him he looked like Billy Bob Thornton, only better-looking. He even tried walking the boards but all he'd had to show for twelve months of sweat and poverty were a crappy TV battery commercial alongside the Energizer Bunny, a bit part in his old man's favorite show, *The Sopranos,* and a month wearing tights with the rent-a-crowd in *Hamlet.*

The entire world's a stage and he didn't get cast in a decent role. Thanks a bunch, but crime paid better.

Arkov came around slowly from behind his desk and sat on the edge. The office blinds were drawn, the light on overhead.

Arkov splashed Scotch into a crystal tumbler. "So what's the story with the woman?"

"You mind if I ask why you've got me watching her?"

"Patience, Billy. Give me the story first. It's why I pay you and the boys."

Billy removed a manila envelope from inside his coat pocket, and unfolded a sheaf of photograph copies and pages. "It's all in here. Including some hard copy of stills from the video I took."

Arkov took the envelope but tossed it on the desk. "I'm a one-sheet man, Billy. Tell me."

"She lives alone. She wasn't there when I called to bug the phone. But her grandmother was."

"Where was she?"

"Abroad. Guess where?"

"I'm past guessing."

"The old country. Dubrovnik."

Arkov raised his eyes.

"You certain about that?"

"Yeah, I saw a printout of an airline booking in her name. JFK to Rome, Rome to Dubrovnik. I put a copy in the envelope."

"Any idea why she went there?"

"Nope, not yet. But I'm working on it—I've asked our people back home to keep their eyes and ears open."

Billy plucked one of the sheets from the envelope and handed it over. "Meanwhile, this ought to interest you. I found two names in a note in her study. Your name is on it, and Mila Shavik's."

Arkov flushed, and his hand shook as he read the page. "Keep going."

"That's basically it. No one's used her home phone since I bugged it, so I figure she's still away."

"You're saying you don't know where she is?"

Billy smiled. "I didn't say that. She also had a flight booked via Atlanta, to Knoxville, on her return."

"So where is she?"

"I'm guessing down south somewhere, in hicksville, East Tennessee."

"What's she doing there?"

"No idea, but I came across this in her study."

He handed over a photo of a letter with a logo.

"It's from a guy in Tennessee. He runs a marina."

"How do you know?"

"I called the number on the logo."

"What's the connection between her and him?"

"Too early to say. But I've got something else on her."

"What?"

"There was some medical correspondence from her doctor and her insurance company in her study."

"So?"

"I called the hospital where she was a patient after the blast. I pretended I was from the insurance company."

"And?"

"She's pregnant."

"Why's that important?"

Billy smiled. "You said to look for a weakness, something we could exploit. That's a major. We can get any information from her you want with that one, if we need to. A woman will do anything to protect her baby."

"But it doesn't tell us where she is."

"I've got a plan to find her."

Arkov drained his Scotch, slapped down the glass.

"Just be careful. We don't want the feds alerted and all over us like a butt rash, as the Americans say."

"And after that?"

"You'll do what you did to her husband. You'll kill her."

45

After Billy left, the side door opened and Shavik strode in.

"You heard everything?" Arkov opened the envelope, handed it over.

"I heard." Shavik examined the contents, then tossed the envelope on the table. "Lane's widow is up to something by going to Dubrovnik. She's got to be."

"But what?"

"The big question."

"There was a knock on the office door and Arkov went to open it. Shavik's bodyguard Dobrashin stood there, a locked briefcase in his hand.

"For you, boss."

He took it, and the bodyguard left.

Arkov crossed to behind his desk and took out a harmless-looking slim metal rod hidden in a compartment in his desk.

He knelt on the floor and inserted the rod deep into what looked like a wood knothole in the floorboards. He turned it and lifted a false panel, revealing a sturdy safe.

Shavik tossed him the keys to the briefcase. "You're confident Billy can handle this thing discreetly?"

Arkov grinned and unlocked the briefcase, revealing thick stacks of hundred-dollar bills and two heavy leather pouches. He untied one of the pouches, spilling out the contents to reveal a glittering stash of diamonds.

"Billy's an actor. He can play any part that's needed. How much is in here?"

"Just over two million in cash and stones."

Arkov grinned. "That'll be six million this quarter. The old man's going to be happy."

"Did he call?"

"Right before you arrived. Says he's got some important family stuff to discuss when he gets here."

"About what?"

"He didn't say."

Shavik crossed to the window, parted the blinds, and looked out absently at the New Jersey landscape.

Arkov refilled the pouch, opened the floor safe, and dropped in the cash and diamonds.

"What's up, Mila?"

"I'm thinking."

"You ever wonder what we're going to do with all this money when the old man finally goes?"

"Why?"

"He's getting on. We've got to start thinking about the future."

"Spit it out."

"Building the business. More power, more territory. The future we used to talk about in the old days when we were dealing with those scum in the camps."

"This isn't the old days, Boris. They're long gone."

Arkov grinned, locking the safe. "But time's still on our side. The future's still bright."

"You just pay close attention to the business in hand, Boris. Or maybe you won't have a future. Unless it's playing someone's girlfriend in a federal prison. We need to deal with the woman. Now show me her photograph."

Arkov didn't like the rebuke and his grin vanished, replaced by a sullen look.

He slid open a desk drawer, plucked out a file, and threw a photograph on the desk. A copy of a newspaper shot of Carla Lane and her husband, dressed up for a concert.

"A lawyer you said?"

"She was with the public prosecutor's office until she went to work for her husband."

Shavik studied the woman's features. She was pretty. Something about her was oddly familiar, but he couldn't put a finger on it.

"Lawyers are always trouble. I want to know what she was doing in Dubrovnik. And about her background. Who she was before she married the nosy musician."

"I'm already on it."

Shavik tossed down the photograph, rubbed his chin. "Something worries me about her. A feeling in my gut we could be looking at trouble."

"That's what my old man said. Because she's a lawyer?"

"Maybe."

"Keep the photograph if you like, I've got copies. There's something else you need to see."

Arkov turned round his laptop so that it faced Shavik.

"What is it?"

Arkov grinned. "A video you're not going to like."

46

Tennessee

Ronnie tossed a bag of tools into the boat.

He saw a white Toyota Camry pull up at the dock office, and Carla climbed out. She wore sunglasses, the evening rays still strong, and her hair was tied back. She walked down to join him.

"Hey. When did you get back?"

She kept her sunglasses on, but there was no mistaking the strain in her face.

"This afternoon. I got a rental car in Knoxville. Where's Regan?"

"Gone to visit a friend with Josh."

He jumped aboard the boat, held out his hand to her. "I've got some houseboats to check out. Want to join me?"

* * *

He headed out along the lake, checking the houseboat anchor lines as he went.

The wind popped the canvas awning over their heads. The sun was out, hot and sticky, but dark clouds bubbled in the distance, a smell of rain on the air.

"You saw the remains?"

"Yes."

Carla looked out at the lake, and bit her lip. Ronnie killed the engine and the boat drifted.

"Whose were they?"

She faltered.

"Whose, Carla?"

"My . . . my mother's and . . ."

"Who else?"

She didn't speak as she took off her sunglasses.

He saw her eyes. They welled up with tears, red and swollen, dark rings as if she hadn't slept in days. She put her hands to her face and sobbed so hard her body shook. She felt his arm around her shoulder.

"Just take your time and tell me everything."

47

They sat there, the boat gently rocking against the dock.

"There's no question it was your mom?"

"Her DNA matched mine."

Ronnie clasped her hand in his.

She stared back at him, as if mesmerized by her own thoughts.

"Seeing what was left of her was bad enough. But the children's remains . . . it was just so pitiful. I can never forget it. Not ever."

She wiped her eyes, her voice hoarse. "Kelly didn't want me to look. There was a faint odor. He pushed me away."

"What did you see?"

"The skeletons of two small children about Luka's size, aged four or five, were curled up on the floor. Two older children were in standing positions."

"What age?"

"I can't say. I only know they were older. The flesh had shriveled up, the bodies mummified and unrecognizable. It was heartbreaking. It sent me over the edge. I've hardly slept since."

She stopped, the words choking in her throat.

"We all just stood there for a time, horrified, until Kelly pulled me away."

"Could they tell if either of the younger children was Luka?"

"Not yet, not positively. Kelly needs to verify the DNA."

"You're not hopeful."

"How could I be? One of the smaller children had dark hair, like Luka. I can't seem to fool myself into believing he's still alive, no matter how hard I try."

She looked at him. "Seeing the bodies brought it all back. That last day, when I left my mother, and how I hugged and kissed Luka. I remembered . . ."

"What?"

"How he clung to me. How he pleaded with me to keep him safe, and not to forget him. The last thing I told him was that I'd come back for him. I failed him, Ronnie. I failed Luka."

Her voice cracked. "I'll never forget his little face, so full of fear, not wanting to let me go. I . . . I had to pry away his fingers."

She closed her wet eyes.

She felt Ronnie's hand fall on her shoulder again, but this time he said nothing.

"How?" she said. "How could they have missed the children? How could they not have found the bodies?"

"I can't answer that, Carla."

Her face looked up, full of pain. "What makes it worse is know-ing what Luka and the others must have gone through. The hor-ror of dying slowly in that small space with barely enough air to breathe, of being entombed alive. And it's all my fault. All of it was my fault."

"Why do you say that?"

"Luka getting sick was my fault. I insisted that Mother let us bathe in the river one day. If I hadn't done that, Luka wouldn't have fallen ill."

"You don't know that."

"Yes I do."

"Carla . . ."

"It was all my fault Luka was left behind. I should have taken him with me, even though he was ill."

He heard the plaintive sound in her voice, like an animal cry of pain.

"You're not responsible for Luka's death."

"Then why am I feeling like this?"

"You've got survivor's guilt, that's all. You feel guilty that you sur-vived and Luka didn't."

"No, it was my fault. Nothing will make me change my mind."

"Did you contact Baize?"

"I called her as soon as I got myself together. I had to talk with somebody."

"How did she take it?"

"I think she was hoping they'd find my father's remains and she'd finally have closure. But when I told her about Luka she was devas-tated."

Carla rubbed her eyes with her thumb and forefinger.

"I called her twice again that night, and twice yesterday. She was still in shock. I'll call her again tomorrow. Right now I'm too stressed to talk about it anymore. I've hardly slept in three days."

"Shouldn't you be with Baize right now?"

"Maybe I should. But there are other things I need to do."

"Such as?"

She looked at him, and vehemence blazed in her eyes.

"I'm not just going to hunt down Shavik."

"What do you mean?"

"I'm going to kill him."

48

Ronnie eased the boat back into the dock and tied it up.

"You mean that?"

"I want to kill him so badly. What he did to my mother, my family, I won't let that go unpunished. I want Arkov dead, too. I want to do it myself." Her eyes met his. "So will you teach me to do that? To kill them?"

"Have you ever killed anyone, Carla?"

"No, of course not."

"To kill someone, up close, to feel their last breath on your face, and hear the life going out of them, that's maybe the most heart-wrenching experience you can ever have, if you're in any way half human."

He shook his head. "It doesn't matter if the man or woman you kill is an evil serial killer or a brutal terrorist. If you have a shred of humanity, even killing someone like Shavik can take a huge bite out of your soul."

"I'm not worried about that. My killing would be just. I'm not a soldier obeying orders. A man like you could train me to kill. Will you do that?"

"I'm not a gun for hire. You've come to the wrong man."

"Why?"

"Because asking me to help you to kill another human being is asking too much. I've put those days behind me. I'm done with killing and I've paid the price."

"What price?"

"Believe me, there's always a price. You need to really think this through. What if you're caught trying to kill these men, or after doing it? You could face life in prison."

She didn't answer. He looked at her.

"If I helped you, I could wind up joining you behind bars as an accessory. Even if the men you kill are the scum of the earth it's still murder."

"You don't get it, Ronnie."

"I get it. I understand your need to confront these killers. But there will always be evil people who don't deserve to walk this earth. You need to step back. Think hard about what you're getting into."

"I won't change my mind. And I really don't think you do get it, Ronnie."

"Why?"

She met his stare. "When Jan was killed, I felt as if someone punched a hole in my heart. Then I found out about my past, and the hole got bigger. Now, with Luka, I feel like whatever remained of my heart was ripped out. That I'll never be able to heal, not ever."

He stayed silent. The silence seemed endless.

She seemed to lose it then, and exploded, pounding the boat's handrail with her fist. "Don't you see? I can't let the same killers who destroyed Jan and my family get away with their crimes. I can't let them. Shavik and his kind, they shouldn't be free to walk this earth. They're worse than animals."

"It's still revenge, Carla. It's killing someone to settle scores."

"So what if it is? But it's not just that. It goes deeper."

"How deep?"

"I don't want a child of mine to grow up to have their lives destroyed by people like Shavik and Arkov."

She looked into his face.

"I wouldn't want anyone's child to know the fear and terror I went through, Ronnie. So long as men like these are allowed to walk this earth, they're capable of doing to others what they did to me."

From her bag, she took the piece of blue blanket and clutched it fiercely in her hand.

"Look—look at what I have left of my brother. A small, frail, beautiful little boy, and this is what I have left to remind me of him. What if they were your son's bones that lay in that closet? How would you feel then?"

He fell silent again. She stared at him.

"I hate pleading but I don't have time to find someone else. All I'm asking is a week—a week of your time. Could it be done in a week?"

"It's not long enough. You'd just about cover the basics."

"Any more time and I'd be taking the risk of Shavik and Arkov fleeing the country."

"How do you know?"

"Angel tipped me off. She warned me I may not have much of a window, and I have a gut feeling she's right." Her face darkened. "Just looking at you I know what you're thinking, Ronnie."

"What?"

"That you're all Josh has. That if something went horribly wrong and we were caught or were implicated, you'd destroy Josh's life. Destroy both your lives."

"I love him, Carla. I can't let him down. I did once before and I promised my boy I'd never do it again."

"I understand. I wouldn't ask you unless I was desperate."

She looked into his face.

"I'd never tell on you, Ronnie. Never. I'd never tell anyone you helped me. I'm not asking you to kill for me. Just show me how to do it."

"I'd still be involved. I'd still be putting my life on the line. Josh's, too."

"So you won't do it?"

"I can't, Carla."

His lips pressed together and then he looked out over the lake.

Carla stumbled off the boat. "It's okay. Let me out here, please."

"Carla . . ."

"Let me out."

And she jumped onto the dock, hurrying along the boardwalk toward her car.

49

He caught up with her.

"Hold your horses."

"Goodbye, Ronnie."

She ignored him, went to open her car door.

He gripped her arm.

"Wait. I know it's against my better judgment. I know it's a huge risk. That if it goes wrong, there'll be a big price to pay. But I'll help you."

There was a strange, disturbing intimacy between them now, standing there together on the dock, the smell of rain on the evening air.

"Why? What changed your mind?"

"Because maybe I owe it to Dan. I wouldn't be here if it wasn't for him. Countless times he watched my back. I know he'd want me to watch yours. But there's one thing I won't do."

"What?"

"I won't kill for you, Carla. I won't ever do that. But I will teach you what you need to know."

"You said we always pay a price. Did you mean that?"

"Yes, I did. Once we take a life it's as if there's an avenging angel watching over our shoulder, ready to exact payment from us."

"And what price will I pay?"

"You could end up haunted by what you've done. Or corrupted by the very people you despise. I really can't say, but when the time comes, you'll know."

"You've seen it happen?"

"Lots of times. Guys I served with, I've seen them pay."

"How?"

"In busted marriages, in ruined lives. I've known some to turn to drugs or alcohol. Or others to put a gun to their heads."

"They were soldiers. They were acting under orders. Me, I believe in what I'm doing. I believe I have a just cause."

"It doesn't matter. You'll still pay."

"You've killed men before?"

"Yes."

"And what price did you pay?"

She hit raw bone, saw it in his face. "What happened to Josh was part of the price. His mom's death, too."

"How can you know that?"

"I know, believe me."

"Then why hasn't Shavik been repaid?"

"How do you know he already hasn't?"

"Somehow I doubt he lies awake at night thinking of the evil he's done."

He fixed her with a steady gaze. "You won't be the same person after you take a life. You'll be changed by it. Don't say you haven't been warned."

She didn't speak for a moment, considering his words.

"I meant what I said. I won't compromise you, Ronnie. No one has to know."

"Are you still afraid of facing Shavik?"

"More than ever. Now that I've seen what he's capable of—massacring women and children."

"You've got guts, I'll give you that."

"I wish I did, Ronnie, but I don't. I'm scared. Maybe more scared than I've ever been in my life. But I can't let Shavik get away with his crimes. I can't dishonor all those dead."

"Use the cabin you stayed in and try to get a good night's sleep. We've lots to do, and very little time to do it."

"When do we start?"

"We already have."

That night the rain came again.

A drenching summer downpour that pounded on the roof. Flashes of lightning sizzled and thundered in the night sky.

Carla lay on her back, her hands on her stomach, staring out at the storm.

She couldn't forget the sight of the small skeletons in the closet.

The pathetic pieces of clothing and desiccated flesh that had once been beloved children. The little girl with the braids to her waist. And darling Luka, the sight of his dark hair still vivid in her mind.

From her handbag, she took out a manila envelope. From inside, she removed the piece of blue blanket that had been her brother's comfort, and the photo of her and Luka and her mom and dad on the Dubrovnik beach.

She clutched both in her hands and stared down at them, her eyes brimming.

Her heart felt broken, shattered beyond repair.

In her mind she heard Luka's tiny voice cry out to her again in the dark.

When she could bear it no more, when she felt her body shake with convulsions, she turned her face into the pillow.

50

Ronnie drove the Ram toward a meadow.

Seated next to him in the pickup, Carla felt a powerful fear growing in her, and was afraid to tell him why.

A couple of bleached wooden picnic benches were set up in a corner of the meadow. A hundred yards away a ridge of earth formed the backstop for a shooting range.

At various distances toward the ridge were an assortment of metal and paper targets, some in the shape of a human torso. Ronnie turned off the engine and Carla followed him, climbing out of the cab.

"I'm impressed. Your own private shooting range."

"I haven't used it much in the last few years. Let's get the stuff unloaded."

He went around to the rear and let down the tailgate. A charcoal-colored, heavy plastic Pelican trunk with a combination padlock lay in the back.

When he unlocked the lid, Carla saw a selection of firearms packed in gray protective foam. A half-dozen handguns in different calibers, along with an AR assault rifle, a Heckler & Koch MP5 machine pistol, a bolt-action sniper rifle with a telescope, and a Remington pump-action shotgun.

From the pickup he grabbed two green metal cans and a black canvas range bag. He laid them next to the weapons. Carla recoiled at the sight of the firearms.

"What's wrong?" he asked.

"Guns scare me. I hate them. I even find it hard to watch TV when there's shooting involved. I . . . I was afraid to tell you that."

"Sounds like we're off to a terrific start."

Ronnie laid out the weapons on the tables.

Carla said, "Anything to do with war and weapons makes me sick to the pit of my stomach."

"I understand, but you'll have to get over that fear if you want to do this. Think of firearms as a tool you have to master to get the job done, that's all."

"What's in the green cans?"

"Ammo."

"And the bag?"

"A first-aid kit. Just in case."

"Of what?"

"You'll need to know how to treat a gunshot wound. In case you're ever hit, or shoot yourself by accident. Accidents have a lousy habit of happening where firearms are concerned."

"I get it. Guns are dangerous."

"Follow the four cardinal rules and you'll always be safe."

"And they are?"

"We'll get to them."

Carla spread her hands at the assortment of guns. "Why so many?"

"Your weapon may jam, or misfire. If you can't clear it and reload it you may have to use another, whatever's at hand."

"You mean one I'm not familiar with?"

"Right. So you'll need to get to know more than one gun. Know what Vivaldi once said?"

"The Vivaldi?"

He smiled. "Yeah, the composer. Not some hillbilly marksman in these parts by the same name."

"Tell me."

"Everything's down to balance. Everything—music, physics, math, life, the universe, relationships, you name it. The same applies with shooting—it's all down to balance, the right stance. And to grip, which is really the same thing. Get both of those right and hitting the target is just about practice."

"So what are the four cardinal rules?"

He held up four fingers, touched each in turn as he made his point.

"One, treat all guns as if they're always loaded. Two, never point the gun barrel at anything you're not willing to kill. Three, keep your finger off the trigger until your sights are on the target and you're ready to shoot. Four, always be sure of your target and your backstop."

He pointed to the ridge of earth at the end of the range. "That's why the berm is there as a backstop. We don't want stray shots or ricochets. Likewise, in a shoot-out, you don't want to kill innocent bystanders in the background."

He picked up a worn-looking black pistol, removed the magazine, and began to load it with a handful of cartridges from one of the ammunition boxes.

"We'll go over the rules again and again, until they're etched into your brain. I presume you've never fired a gun before?"

"Never."

"First, we'll start you off with a small-caliber pistol."

"Why?"

"It'll have less recoil, and won't scare the life out of you when it goes bang."

He laid the weapon and magazine down again. "Pick up each of the guns, handle them, get a feel for them. Then let's get to work turning you into a crack shot."

51

Carla felt each of the guns, one at a time. The fear, the revulsion was still there, but there was no denying the feeling of raw power the weapons imparted. But it was a power that felt obscene. Guns simply reminded her of death.

Ronnie unzipped the range bag and removed a couple of pairs of shooter's protective earmuffs.

"We'll use these from time to time when we're training so that you don't damage your hearing. But for now, you need to get familiar with the sound of gunfire, up close, with no ear protection." He picked up the black pistol again and slapped the magazine into the butt.

"I've heard gunfire before."

"This time you'll need to get used to it being directed *toward* you— and that's a whole different ball game."

He checked the pistol. "You need to learn to remain calm and focused even when someone's trying to shoot you. We'll be doing some drills to get you familiar with that. It means I'll be firing live ammunition right next to you while you're shooting at your target."

"You're kidding?"

"No, I'm not. You'll also need to get used to using a good, powerful tac light fitted to the rails of the handgun."

"Tac light?"

"A tactical flashlight. If you're operating in the dark, it's vital to help you aim at the target. Wear dark clothes, too. A hoodie, dark jeans or stretch pants, and running shoes. A dark wool hat to cover your hair. No heels, unless you want to get yourself killed trying to escape."

"I'll take your fashion advice."

"One more thing. For now, don't cover your ears when I fire—even if you're tempted to. I want you to get used to the sound of gunfire. We can't have you jumping six feet off the ground each time you hear a gun pop."

He held up the black pistol in one hand. "This here's a Sig 226, in nine-millimeter caliber, with a fifteen-round magazine. One of the best handguns around. Navy SEALs use them, and Homeland Security. They are ultrareliable, and accurate."

He laid his trigger finger alongside the trigger guard, but not on the trigger. "Something else you need to remember. Muscle memory."

"What's that?"

"It means you keep your finger *off* the darned trigger until you're ready to fire. That way you don't kill someone by accident or shoot your own toe off. Now, watch my body stance. I want you to do the same when you shoot, you hear?"

It happened so fast, Carla had no time to react.

In one fluid movement, Ronnie changed his stance, turning sideways, leaning slightly forward. His right hand snapped up, gripping the pistol, his left hand layered over the fingers of his right for support. He fired four rapid shots.

Fifty feet away, four round white-painted metal plates collapsed as rounds slammed into them with a metallic *clink*.

From so close to him, the gunfire sounded like huge explosions going off in Carla's ears. Startled, she hunched her shoulders but resisted the urge to cover her ears.

When the detonations echoed and died, he said, "You okay?"

"Apart from feeling like my eardrums have just burst."

He smiled, nodded to the metal plates. "With any luck, another week and I'll have you shooting like that."

"You're not kidding?"

"If you've got the willpower, anything's possible."

He removed the pistol magazine, checked the chamber was empty, left the slide open, and placed the weapon and magazine on the table.

"You do the same each time you fire while we're on the range, okay? Lay the gun down, magazine out and the slide open. That way we know it's empty."

"Okay."

He pointed to a lighter handgun and magazine.

"This here's a Browning twenty-two. A good pistol to get you started with. We'll shoot it for a while then move on to the guns with a bigger bang and recoil."

"Like the one you just used?"

"That's right."

He picked up the Sig again, placed it in her palm.

"This is the same gun you're going to use to carry out the kills, so you better get used to it. There'll be just one difference."

Holding the hefty pistol sent an anxious tremor down Carla's spine. "What?"

"It'll have a silencer fitted, so it won't make a bang when it's fired. The gun's untraceable, by the way."

"What do you mean?"

"The police won't be able to trace it back to us, unless you're caught red-handed."

"How's that possible?"

"It was bought years ago at a gun show."

"So?"

"There's no paperwork trail, and I'll have the serial numbers filed off. Before you use it I'll clean it completely, the same with the ammo. Use a silicone cloth to wipe it down and there's a not a trace of a print or DNA anywhere on the weapon or ammunition."

"You're sure?"

"Take my word for it."

He took a pair of black shooter's gloves from the Pelican box. "You'll wear these when you execute Shavik and Arkov. They'll help you get a good grip. After the job's done we'll get rid of the gun. Try on the gloves and use them from now on."

Carla slipped them on. The gloves were a tight fit.

"Get rid of the gun how?"

"Throw it into a deep lake somewhere."

Her cell phone chirped a text.

Carla read it. Newark Airport. Arrivals bar. 1 p.m. Wednesday. Okay? A.

Ronnie said, "Important?"

"It's from Angel. She wants me to meet her the day after tomorrow at Newark Airport. I could fly up there and be back here by evening."

Carla texted back: Newark at 1 it is.

"You want me to ride shotgun?"

"It's too risky. If she spots someone watching her, she may leave. I don't fully trust her but I don't think she'd try anything in public."

"I wouldn't count on that. What if she's suckering you, playing a double game? Let me come with you."

"No, Ronnie. I'll be okay. If I get a feeling there's something not right, I'll backpedal like crazy."

"You be very careful, you hear?"

She stared down at the Sig, still in her hand.

"What's wrong, Carla?"

"You know, it's ironic."

"What is?"

"My mother wrote a journal that she hoped would change the world. But instead, the only person it's changed is me."

"How?"

"I never thought I'd see the day I planned on taking a life."

She looked up at him. "What you said—about me executing Shavik and Arkov. It sounds so unreal."

"That's what it amounts to. And it'll be up close and bloody, make no mistake."

He stared into her face. "Maybe I need to remind you—it's never too late to change your mind."

52

Carla saw Angel walk into the bar, every male eye following her.

She wore her dark glasses, the same bangles, and a navy pantsuit that did nothing to hide her combustible figure.

Carla arrived early, feeling anxious, and was skimming a newspaper she'd bought in Knoxville.

Angel left on her shades and ordered a margarita. "Did you take a cab, or drive?"

Carla's dislike toward her hadn't melted. "Neither, I flew."

"Flew?"

"I've been away."

Angel glanced down, her painted nail tapping the *Knoxville News Sentinel* in front of Carla. "Knoxville, Tennessee?"

"Tell me the truth about you and Jan."

"That seems pretty important to you."

"I just can't get my head around Jan being—"

"With someone like me? Some of us can't help being what we are, Mrs. Lane. But trust me, we're alike. Jan saw in me a lot of what he saw in you."

"I somehow doubt that."

When the waitress brought her drink, Angel took a sip. "Jan told me you were at the Devil's Hill."

"Why—why would he tell you that?"

Angel held out both her hands, and her bangles slid down. On each wrist were angry ribbons of faded pink scars.

"When I was thirteen, I was at the Merviak camp."

"I . . . I'm sorry."

"I tried to cut my wrists afterward. The guards used to hold me down and take turns raping me. My mother, my sister, and me. Emotionally, I'm a screwup."

Carla said nothing.

Angel slid the bangles back on her wrists.

"My mother lasted seven weeks there. My sister half that. She was fifteen."

"How . . . how did you survive?"

"The guards were drunk one night. I took my chances and fled."

"So this is personal?"

"You can say that again. Boris Arkov oversaw the Merviak camp before he moved to the Devil's Hill to join Shavik. Arkov was one of the men who killed my sister and mother."

Angel's face tensed with a livid anger. "At first I wanted to kill him. But I realized that wasn't punishment enough, and it wasn't justice."

Carla waited.

"I want to see them all suffer. Arkov, Shavik, all the vermin who ruined so many lives before scurrying away to hide."

"How did you end up in America?"

"Lots of women are brought here by the Russian and Balkan mafias. They bring you into the country illegally and in return you work for your freedom, paying back your debt. It took me seven years. I've been free for five."

"Doing what?"

"Working in clubs and brothels. You know, for years I prayed I'd find the men who killed my mother and sister. I never believed I would. But a year ago I started working in a club in New Jersey. That's where I saw them."

"Who?"

"Arkov first. He looked older, different, his face tighter, as if he'd had plastic surgery. But it was him. I could never forget that animal."

"Did he recognize you?"

"He was drunk so often in the camp, I doubt he'd have recognized his own mother. Another time, I saw Shavik and him drinking together at the club. It's one of many bars and clubs they control."

"What did you do?"

"Nothing at first. I had to be careful."

"Go on."

"I could see that Shavik enjoyed women's company. He often slept with the club's dancers. If he liked them they'd share his bed for a while. So I went out of my way to make sure he liked me."

"And?"

"I pleased him enough that he eventually asked me to move in with him."

"You live with him?"

"You could say that. I come and go as it suits Shavik. Don't look so horrified. It was a tactic, to get close to him, to learn all I could about his operation."

"Where's his home?"

"A big beach house in Jersey. Sometimes I stay for weeks on end. Other times if he's talking business and doesn't want me around, I go back to my apartment."

"How could you sleep with a man like Shavik?"

"Hate can carry you a long way. It can keep you alive, waiting for the right moment to take your revenge."

"On Arkov?"

"Especially Arkov. He's straightforward—a coldhearted, brutal animal without a shred of human feeling. The kind who'd snap your neck in a heartbeat, and feel nothing."

"And Shavik?"

"I don't know what to make of him."

"Why?"

"At times he can be cold and distant. Other times he can be tender and caring."

"I could never imagine Shavik as tender or caring."

"Neither could I have. But believe me, he sometimes is."

"I'm beginning to wonder if we're talking about the same man."

"It's as if there are two people fighting inside him. Like Jekyll and Hyde. I've known times when he's been cold and aloof. Others when he's shown me such kindness."

"Tell me."

"Some nights I've broken down. I have flashbacks to those terrible moments in the camp when Arkov brutalized my mother and sister."

"And?"

"Shavik asked me what was wrong."

"What did you tell him?"

"Nothing. How could I? But he sensed my distress."

Angel paused. "Not that I wanted him to, but often he'd hold me close and stroke my hair until I fell asleep. He didn't use me for sex as most men would. It seemed so absurd, being comforted by a man whose comrades killed my mother and sister."

"What are you trying to say?"

"I don't think Shavik likes himself. I don't think he's a happy person. But don't ask me to explain. It's too deep for me to understand."

"Try to."

"I can't. He's never talked about his personal life. But I get the impression there's a mile-wide scar somewhere deep inside him. I know he's a bad man. But somewhere inside, I sense there was once a good man."

"He killed my mother. And maybe my father and brother."

"I'm sorry, Mrs. Lane."

"Do you have feelings for him?"

"Why do you ask?"

"Call it a woman's instinct."

Angel looked away, then back again. "You've heard of Stockholm syndrome?"

"Yes. It's when hostages identify with their captors. Some hostages can feel sympathy for the people who have harmed them or kept them prisoner."

"I sometimes wonder if I feel that way for Shavik, after he's been tender or kind, or thoughtful. In my line of business, I haven't met many men like that."

"I sense a but?"

"I'm still determined to see them all pay for their crimes."

"What did you plan to do?"

"At first I intended to kill them. I even bought a gun and learned to shoot. Not that I was very good."

"What happened?"

"I came close to shooting Arkov once, when he was in the house, playing cards with Shavik and their bodyguards. I hid the gun in my purse."

"But?"

"Arkov and Shavik are always armed and have at least one bodyguard each. I realized it would have been suicide." Angel toyed with her glass. "Then one night I went to see Jan in concert."

"Why?"

"We came from the same town. My mother taught him music. I hadn't seen him since we were kids. I sent him a note, asking him to meet me afterward."

"And?"

"He was glad to see me. When I told him my ordeal and what happened to my family, Jan was horrified."

Angel looked away, then back again.

"When I mentioned Shavik and Arkov, his eyes lit up."

"Why?"

"It was personal for Jan, too. He learned that Boris Arkov led the paramilitaries who shelled our hometown, killing Jan's parents."

"He told you that?"

Angel nodded. "Yes. Jan also told me about some of the justice groups hunting down war criminals. And that you were a lawyer."

"You told him everything?"

"Yes. We'd meet discreetly after that. Jan wanted to come to the club a few times to try to see Arkov and Shavik for himself. He wanted to be certain."

"Did he go?"

"Yes. And to a few bars in New Jersey I told him about, where the Serb mafia hang out. He started to ask questions. I begged him to be careful. But he asked too many questions, and it got noticed. That's why they killed him, I'm pretty sure of it."

Angel removed her dark glasses, and wiped her eyes with a paper tissue.

Carla felt a stab in her heart. She reached over, touched Angel's hand.

"Keep going, please."

"What exactly do you intend to do, Mrs. Lane?"

"I told you, I'm going to make Arkov and Shavik pay."

"How?"

"The less you know the better."

"What if I told you I know how to destroy them?"

53

"You know what their weakness is, their Achilles' heel?" Angel asked.

"What?"

"Money. It gives them their power. Take it away and you destroy them."

"How do you do that?"

"Shavik keeps a ledger in his home safe."

"So?"

"It contains all the details of his skimming operation and income from the clan's illegal operations. If the feds got their hands on that, Shavik and Arkov and their organization would be ruined. The whole thing comes tumbling down, all the way back to Belgrade."

"Can you get the ledger?"

"No, they'd know it was missing. But I can get photographs of some of the pages. That would get the feds interested, wouldn't it?"

"I'm sure it would."

"You're a lawyer, you could explain it to them, and why they'd need to move quickly."

"Let me think about it. Right now, I don't want you putting yourself at risk. What else can you give me? I need as much insider stuff as you can get."

Angel took a large manila envelope from her handbag and slid it across.

"What's this?"

"Shavik's address in New Jersey. Arkov often stays there when they've got business to discuss, but his home is a penthouse somewhere in Jersey, I don't know where. I managed to take some photographs of Shavik's property and the grounds on my cell phone. It's pretty snazzy, in a place called Cape May."

"I know it. Tell me more."

"The house backs onto the beach, with views out over Delaware Bay. I've put everything in a file folder. Don't look at the shots now. Put them somewhere safe. I'm giving you everything I know."

Carla slipped the envelope into her handbag.

Angel said, "They were meant for Jan. I've also drawn a map of the house, showing many of the rooms."

"What about bodyguards?"

"Shavik and Arkov have one each. Shavik's guy acts as his driver. Arkov's is a big guy called Dobrashin."

"Is there an alarm system?"

"Yes, it's state-of-the-art, and I'm not trusted with the code. But I've been with Shavik many times when he used a back garden gate that leads out to the beach. I made a point of trying to see the code he entered. It was always the same numbers. I took a photograph of the gate and wrote the code on the back. That'll get you access to the house."

Angel hesitated. "Shavik also keeps a memory stick in the safe. I've seen him take it out with the ledger and insert the stick into his laptop. That would interest the feds."

"Why?"

"I'm guessing it's got some kind of encryption software, because he never seems to be able to use the laptop without it."

"What are you saying?"

"That between the ledger, the encryption device, and the laptop, I'm betting there's a ton of commercial information about the clan and its money."

"I'm not a computer nerd. Explain."

"Do you have any idea what organized crime gangs do with all their ill-gotten gains, Mrs. Lane? And no, it's not a trick question."

"You mean from illegitimate businesses?"

"Or legitimate."

"I've no idea."

"What we're really talking about are cash cows. With the mafia, the skim's a way of life. You're were a prosecutor. You know what the skim is?"

"Instead of using a credit card, a customer pays in cash for a drink or a meal, whatever. Cash doesn't have a paper trail. Some of it can be skimmed off."

Angel nodded. "Right. And if you happen to be a crime cartel running dozens of businesses, bars, and clubs you'll have the skim down to a fine art. We could be talking about many millions with Arkov's mafia."

"A year?"

"A month. The trouble is, you bank that kind of dirty cash in the USA and the IRS will get to hear about it, and you're going to jail."

Angel pushed aside her glass. "You can't hide it under the mattress, either, or pretty soon you're sleeping on a mountain."

"So what do they do with it?"

"Move it offshore."

"How?"

"Not electronically, because you're back to using the bank again."

"Tell me."

"Three or four times a year a private Learjet flies in from Belgrade. It's flown in empty and out loaded."

"With cash?"

"Cash, gold, jewels, whatever asset is good for them at the time. But it's not flown back to Belgrade." Angel sipped her margarita, fiddled with the swizzle stick.

"Where's it flown to?"

"Whichever bank is flavor of month. Usually one in the Cayman Islands."

"What about customs or airport security?"

"That's easy. The right officials get bribed."

"Fascinating as all this is, Angel, I'm assuming there's a point?"

"You bet there is, and here it comes. Whenever they fly in, it's like a family reunion. They're all there, the full cast of villains. Shavik, Arkov, the old man."

"Old man?"

"Ivan Arkov. Big daddy himself. He's usually there to make sure his boys haven't tried to rip him off, and to personally supervise the Cayman deposit."

"Where do I come in?"

"The next family get-together is this Sunday."

Across the bar a young man sat reading a newspaper.

The pinhead video camera in his baseball cap and the camera in his cell phone gave him all the pixels he needed.

He managed to get off a dozen shots and grab a good fifteen minutes of video as he pretended to tap his phone's keyboard.

When the two women rose from their table and went their separate ways, he gave it a minute, then followed the darker-haired woman at a safe distance, dialing the number as he walked. The line clicked.

"Yeah?"

"Billy? It's me."

"How's Angel doing for us?"

"Good. They talked for about fifteen minutes. We've got what we needed. I'm following the Lane woman."

"Stay with her. I want to know where she goes."

54

"It's certainly odd. Most odd."

"I wouldn't say odd. More of a surprise."

"These are *all* the children's remains you removed from the closet, Sean?"

"Yes, Pierre. Four in total."

Kelly lifted his glasses back on his head as he hunched over the collection of skeletons and rotted clothing that lay on the four metal tables in front of him.

Among them he saw a girl's shriveled cotton dress and a boy's pair of short wool trousers. As a father, such a sight never failed to distress him.

The forensic expert standing next to him in the autopsy room was Dr. Pierre Bufont, a tall French-Canadian with a wine drinker's blue-veined nose.

"You say you completed the removal of children's remains from the second massacre site?"

"I felt I owed it to Mrs. Lane to speed things up. We took DNA samples of all of the young victims we found."

Kelly handed across a file full of printouts. "None of the bodies from either location match Mrs. Lane's family DNA. See for yourself."

Bufont read the printouts.

"So, it seems we've uncovered something of a mystery."

"We certainly have."

"Will you mention it to Mrs. Lane?"

"I thought it might be wise to let sleeping dogs lie for now. No point in upsetting her."

"Very wise, I think."

Kelly turned to a white-coated attendant who assisting him arranging the remains. "Thanks, Slava."

"You're welcome, sir." The attendant withdrew to a corner of the room, grabbed a broom, and began to sweep the floor.

Kelly said, "In regard to the boy, we found some recoverable DNA in hairs on part of the child's blanket and in his backpack."

"There's no possibility of error?"

"None that I can see."

Bufont looked up from the printouts and scratched his jaw. "You're right. This is strange. Still, all families have their little secrets, I suppose."

The Canadian closed the file, laid it down.

"You say Mrs. Lane is now the only credible witness?"

"That's right."

"The authorities will need her testimony in case a war crimes prosecution ever transpires. Her mother's diary would also help."

"I'll have the prosecutors contact her and take a formal statement."

"What's wrong, Sean? You look bothered."

Kelly rubbed his jaw. "There's always a chance the boy could still be alive."

"You think so?"

"If the shelling or Shavik didn't kill him."

"Shavik?"

"He was in the vicinity. A man like him would have perceived the child as a threat, a witness to be eliminated. And Mrs. Lane told me Alma Dragovich thought she'd heard the boy escape before a shell hit."

"Is the old lady's memory reliable?"

"A hard one to answer."

"I suppose the boy could have survived, even if it seems unlikely. You searched the rest of the buildings thoroughly and found no other remains?"

"That's right. There's another thing that confuses me."

"What?"

"I got the distinct impression from Mrs. Lane that she knew Shavik was alive."

"There hasn't been a sighting of him in almost twenty years. Don't the authorities believe he's dead?"

"Her tone suggested otherwise. Strange, but I sensed as if she had insider information about his whereabouts."

"Interesting."

Kelly crossed to a wall map behind the desk. Tracing a line along the chart, his brow wrinkled in concentration.

Bufont joined him. "You've got that look again, Sean. What's going on in that wild Irish mind of yours?"

"Alma Dragovich told Mrs. Lane that when she became conscious she was in a temporary hospital. And that she was being nursed by a nun. That's when she claimed she saw Carla Lane's younger brother alive."

"Why's that important?"

Kelly tapped the map. "If he did survive, he's another potential witness. I checked, and the nearest temporary hospital back then was in an old convent here, in the mountains toward the Serb border. It's run by an order of Orthodox nuns."

"I've seen the place. It's quite beautiful. Built into the rock face."

"Of course, they don't distinguish between a convent and a monastery in the Eastern Orthodox Christian churches, do they? They're all called monasteries."

Kelly came away from the map. "I hear the nuns still look after the worst of the child victims. Orphans from all backgrounds who were so badly injured physically and mentally, the ones no one wanted."

"What are you going to do?"

"I might take a drive up there and see if they know anything about the boy. Maybe the nuns have records of the patients they treated."

The Canadian smiled, raised his eyes. "You're going back over twenty years, Sean. You're certain it's not just a yearning to see pretty young nuns in habits dating back to your Irish schooldays?"

Kelly gave a hearty laugh. "You know, you could be right."

"Didn't you say Mrs. Lane's family already contacted the refugee agencies?"

"Still, you never know. People slip though the net, Pierre."

Kelly consulted his watch, then flipped through his contact book, next to his desk phone.

"I'll give her the news. But I'll wait another few hours to allow for the time difference. It's going to be another shock. But a hopeful one."

"Will you mention the orphanage, Sean?"

"No, I'll decide after I visit the nuns."

"Why?"

"I don't want to build up her hopes in case they come crashing down."

55

For four solid hours that morning they went through shooting drills, using the larger-caliber handguns, until Carla's fingers felt numb.

The Sig gave a solid kick when she shot it, and a few times the pistol's slide cut into the tender flesh between her thumb and forefinger as she fired, causing her to bleed.

Ronnie adjusted her grip. "Your hand's riding too high up. Keep it lower."

He produced a small black tactical flashlight, fitted it to the guide rails beneath the gun's barrel. He flicked on the flashlight's switch, and a powerful beam sprang on.

"Get used to using the tac light. It could save your life."

He examined her paper targets. "You're doing okay. Most shootouts take place at seven yards or less. If you can learn to hit a target accurately out to twenty-five yards, you'll be doing pretty well."

He corrected her stance and grip again and again—one hand holding the gun, the other hand layered over it, gripping the fingers that held the weapon—until her shooting and aim became faster and more precise.

"Okay, enough for now. We'll keep working on your accuracy and speed." He put away the guns. From the front of the pickup he pulled out a pair of cargo shorts and a pair of Reeboks. "You bring your training sweats like I said?"

"Sure."

"Get them on. You ever run?"

"Not for a while. Can we forget running, Ronnie? I'd need to ease into it with some practice."

"Then let's just take a brisk hill trek. You can change behind the pickup. Getting fit will improve your reflexes."

The sun was out and warm. She changed into her sweats, and Ronnie plucked a couple of bottles of water from a cooler in the truck.

He tossed her one. "It's six miles there and back around that mountain."

"Six miles? *Now?* Walking in this heat? That's pretty tough. I'm not so sure I can do that."

He tore off his shirt. His lean body was tanned, his chest muscled from hard manual labor.

"Sure you can. I'm being gentle on you. I run this trail most days, so just be grateful I'm not asking you to jog."

"Anyone ever tell you that you're wicked?"

"It's my middle name. Bring Angel's envelope with you and let's get moving."

They rested on a hilltop after four miles and sat.

The temperature was over ninety and Ronnie was drenched in sweat. "How are you doing?"

Carla was completely breathless, bent over, the heat and humidity overpowering, her jogging sweats and Nike T-shirt wet with perspiration.

"Scratch what I said about you being wicked."

"Yeah?"

"It's more like a sadistic streak."

Ronnie winked, cracked open his bottle of water, gulped some down. "You'll get used to it."

He stared at the Smoky Mountains in the distance.

Carla slumped on a rock facing him and drank mouthfuls of bottled water.

"You look worried. What's on your mind, Ronnie?"

"Honest?"

"Honest."

"You really trust Angel?"

"Yes, for some reason I do."

"You don't think she'll double-cross you?"

"No, I don't. She was at the Merviak camp. You can't fake hatred, Ronnie. I know she wants to see justice done just as much as I do."

"Let me see the envelope again."

It was clutched in her hand and she offered it across. "I made copies of all the images for you. This one's yours, so you can keep it."

Inside the envelope Ronnie found a green plastic folder containing photographs of a big house, the grounds backing onto the sea.

At least twenty shots of the property inside and out, as well as a hand-drawn map of the interior. "Looks big enough to hold a barn dance."

"Over five thousand square feet, with two double garages."

"Yeah?"

"Did I mention the swimming pool, sauna, and exercise room and cinema?"

"Who says crime doesn't pay?" Ronnie studied the photographs. Printed by a laser printer, the definition was clear enough. "You know this place, Cape May?"

"I've been there a few times with Jan. It's an old seaside resort from the 1800s. Quaint, Victorian. I looked up the address on Google Maps and printed off a few more shots."

"I can see that."

"What do you think, Ronnie?"

He flicked over one of Angel's photographs: of a distinctive wrought-iron metal gate with an eagle's head, inset into an archway in a pink stucco wall. On the back of the snapshot he saw the gate code: "2704 #."

"What else did Angel tell you?"

They had talked for quite a while, but Carla remembered it all. "There's a man named Billy Davix. He's Arkov's nephew. Former marine, a dangerous killer. He works as muscle for the clan. He's the one who killed Jan, on the orders of Arkov and Shavik."

"Angel knows him?"

"She's often seen him in the club."

"Why the family get-together on Sunday at midnight?"

"It's only for a few hours. Apparently old man Arkov flies on to the Cayman Islands just in time for when the banks open on Monday morning."

"That only gives us seventy-two hours. Even less time than I thought."

"I'll do my very best. I promise you, Ronnie."

"Your best might not be good enough. You're a reasonable shot, better than some I've trained, but . . ."

"But what, Ronnie?"

"Sure I can teach you how to shoot even better, how to kill. But Shavik and his kind, they're natural-born killers. You're not ready to go up against people like that, Carla. And maybe you never will, no matter how much time we had."

He clicked his fingers. "They could snuff out your life like that. There are a thousand ways to die, Carla. Painful, torturous ways. People like Shavik are probably familiar with every one of them."

He saw real fear in her eyes.

"Meaning?"

"Everything's too rushed. We haven't even got a solid plan."

"Can't you help me try to figure one out?"

"We'd need you to get access into the property, and deal with any bodyguards without setting off any alarms. That won't be easy. Right now all we've got is a code for the back gate. What if the gate has security camera coverage that Angel doesn't know about?"

He looked at her. "Or what if the back gate sets off an alarm in the main house when it's opened? It's all too complex and doesn't give me confidence. How about you ask Angel for more information?"

"She said that's everything she knows."

"After barely four days of training, and so little information, you'd need a ton of luck on your side, and then some, or else you're going to get yourself killed."

"Are you always this cheerful?"

"As they say in Memphis, just telling it like it is, baby." He pushed himself up off the rock. "Let me think it over some more."

Carla's cell rang.

She plucked it from her pocket, saw the international number, and answered.

"Yes."

"Mrs. Lane?"

"Who is this?"

"Sean Kelly, calling from Sarajevo. Are you sitting down, Mrs. Lane?"

56

The bar in the Serb district was a dark, unwelcoming place with barely a half-dozen tables. It reeked of stale tobacco and coffee.

The owner, a tough middle-aged man with a flattened nose, was leaning on the bar, eating olives from a plate and reading a newspaper.

He looked up as the customer entered. "You look like you've got something on your mind, Slava."

The mortuary attendant no longer wore a white coat. "I could do with a pear brandy. A large one, Yanich."

The bar owner grinned, wiped his hands on his grubby apron, and filled a shot glass to the brim. "A tough day counting bodies?"

Slava swallowed the liquid in one gulp, slapped down the glass, and wiped his mouth with the back of his sleeve.

"It could be worse. I have information that could be worth something to a man like you, with your mafia connections."

The bar owner's grin turned sour. His left hand reached over, grabbed the attendant by the throat, the stranglehold choking him.

"I'd keep that trap of yours shut if I were you. Remarks like that can get a man killed, you hear me?"

"No . . . no offense," the attendant wheezed. "I . . . I'm just trying to do you a favor, Yanich. As old army comrades, like."

The bar owner released his grip. "What favor?"

"There's a witness to what went on at the Devil's Hill."

"I thought there were none. Or at least none any court would listen to."

Slava massaged his throat. "Not anymore."

The bar owner slid a banknote from his wallet and patted Slava's face. "Here, that ought to help ease the pain."

"A hundred? Is that all?"

"Be thankful it's not a fifty. Now tell me the rest."

TENNESSEE

"Kelly's certain he didn't get a match?"

"A hundred percent positive."

They sat there, on the rocks, Carla ecstatic, her heart soaring, her voice laced with excitement.

"It's wonderful news. The kind I desperately needed. I know Luka survived. I just know it, Ronnie."

"Carla, you want a word of advice?"

"What?"

"Don't get carried away."

"Why?"

"I saw the same thing happen so many times in the military when a guy went missing in action. Their family would jump on any glimmer of hope."

"But I told you what Kelly said."

"It's been over twenty years. All you know is that Luka's remains haven't been found. I don't want you to have your hopes crushed."

"I have a strange feeling about this, Ronnie. I truly do."

"Why?"

"I can't explain. Don't look at me like that."

"Like what?"

"That it's a foolhardy hope. I needed this good news. I needed it to get through the days ahead."

"What else did Kelly say?"

"That he'd follow it up and get back to me."

"Follow it up how?"

"He didn't say, and I was too excited to ask. But it makes me even more determined to confront Shavik."

"Why?"

"He was in the building before Luka disappeared. He may have seen him. He may know something."

"Carla . . ."

"I know now Alma was right—that she saw Luka. I know it. Just as I know he's alive."

"Carla, try to keep this in perspective. Don't put all your bets on the one card, or it could really break your heart."

"Don't tell me I'm being foolish, Ronnie. Please, let me cling to my ray of hope. I need to be positive, to have faith. You'd be the same if it was Josh."

He saw the bright hope in her eyes, and it seemed to fill her with energy.

"Maybe you're right. I'm just trying to play devil's advocate here. But I guess anything's possible."

She smiled, really smiled, for the first time since they'd met.

She leaned over, touched his cheek, kissed it. "Thanks, Ronnie. I'm ready to head back if you are."

She stood, and felt a sharp pain in her lower side that made her double up. "Ooh . . . that hurt."

"You okay?"

She struggled to stand. "I . . . I must have pulled something."

"Where's the pain."

"Right here."

"Let me see." He felt around her side and lower back, probing her muscles and tendons. "You're pretty tense and knotted. You think you'll be okay walking back?"

"I think so."

"There's a hospital in LaFollette, another in Harrogate. We can have one of them check you . . ."

He didn't finish his sentence. He stepped away from her but held on to her hand, alarm on his face.

"What . . . what's the matter, Ronnie? Why are you looking at me like that?"

"You're bleeding."

His eyes were fixed on her groin.

She looked down.

Between her legs, her gray sweats were stained with a growing patch of crimson. She stared at the blood in horror.

"What's wrong, Carla?"

"My . . . my baby."

And then all her senses seemed to go, and she passed out.

57

The bar owner had heard the stories about the beautiful old stone house overlooking the Danube.

Rumors about lavish parties, government ministers, and rich industrialists wining and dining in the fifteenth-century prince's residence that belonged to wealthy clan boss Ivan Arkov.

He just hoped Arkov would lavishly reward his loyalty.

The Merc limo and the two bodyguards met him on Belgrade's outskirts. As the car pulled up outside the mansion's entrance, the driver climbed out and opened the door for Yanich.

A dapper, slim man with a Van Dyke beard and a polka-dot bow tie was waiting for him at the top of the entrance steps.

Yanich felt a shiver go through him.

Ivan Arkov looked harmless enough, but he always gave Yanich the creeps. He'd heard stories about the macabre mask fashioned from a victim's facial skin that Arkov kept as a grisly memento in a secret paneled display case in his study. "Yanich. Welcome."

He took the boss's hand, kissed his ring in a token of loyalty. "It's good of you to see me at such short notice, Mr. Arkov."

The old man clicked his fingers, and the bodyguards stepped back, out of hearing distance.

"Come, have some wine from my vineyard. Then tell me what's so urgent about this information of yours."

Arkov sat by the study window, listening.

The paneled walls were polished rosewood, the shelves lined with fancy leather-bound books that looked just for show.

Glass patio doors were spread open and led out to a swimming pool. As Arkov listened to the bar owner, he held his fingers together, touching his lips.

When Yanich finished, the old man sighed and stood. His gray eyes were steady, focused on some distant point, toward the pool.

"This attendant . . ."

"Slava, Mr. Arkov." Yanich sipped the wine and found it hard not to gag. It tasted worse than the slop he rebottled to serve his drunken customers.

"And the forensics expert?"

"His name is Kelly." Yanich offered a sheet of paper. "I wrote the name down so there's no mistake. Also the woman's."

"So, she's a witness?"

"That's what was said."

Arkov thrust both his hands in his suit jacket pockets and stared out at the shimmering pool. "Tell me what else you know about her."

"Her name's Carla Lane. Her mother's family name was originally Tanovic."

A flicker sparked in Arkov's watery eyes. "You're sure of the name?"

"Certain. Kelly mentioned that her young brother may have also survived the Devil's Hill. He intended to visit a hospital run by nuns where the boy was treated."

The bar owner explained all the details.

"You're sure about all of this?"

"Yes, sir. The attendant was in the room when Kelly spoke."

"So, they discussed Mila Shavik?"

"Kelly got the impression the woman knew where he might be."

"What else?"

"That's everything I know. I'd be happy to deal with Kelly, if you like. It could put the brakes on any investigation for a time."

A muscle twitched in Arkov's face, and he offered a razor smile that chilled Yanich to the bone. "Kind of you to offer, but I'll deal with Kelly myself."

"I served with Mila's unit. We always said that he and your son were war heroes for protecting us from those Bosniak scum."

"And what else did they say?" Arkov lit a cigar, and puffed.

"That you've been like a father to Mila. Treated him as if he was one of your own."

"I could do nothing less. His father was my loyal friend. Until a public prosecutor in Konjic put him on trial for his dealings with me. The prosecutor's name was Tanovic, also."

"A relative perhaps?"

"We'll see. But what a waste."

"Sir?"

"The prosecutor had no solid evidence. Mila's father would have waltzed through the trial. Sadly, his nerve must have cracked before he hung himself. I felt it my duty to give his son a good home. The boy needed to belong. To have family around him."

"Your kindness is well spoken of, Mr. Arkov."

"So, you served with Mila?"

"Yes, sir."

"Then you know there was always a certain friction between my son and him."

"Cain and Abel, the men called them, sir. No disrespect intended."

"You know why?"

"No, sir."

"Mila rose so fast in the ranks that Boris felt threatened. Some say Mila is power-hungry. But it's deeper than that. After his father's death, the clan became his family. Mila wants to prove himself worthy of belonging. It's a common striving among orphans, apparently."

Arkov puffed again on his cigar. "He's also got brains to burn. Of course, Boris isn't happy to play second fiddle but that's rivalry for you. Have you spoken to anyone else about all of this?"

"Of course not, Mr. Arkov."

"Good. Then it will remain our secret. And while I hate to remind people what happens to informers, sometimes I must."

From a bookshelf, Arkov picked up a remote control. He pressed a button. One of the rosewood wall panels slid open, and a light snapped on to illuminate a glass display case behind the panel.

For a moment the bar owner couldn't even breathe, the air trapped in his lungs.

Behind the glass was displayed a human face—or at least the remnants of one. The skin had been peeled from a skull and was parchment yellow like a mummy's. It covered a piece of glass made in the shape of a head.

The face looked macabre, bizarre. Like some weird mask that belonged in a freak show. The bar owner wanted to throw up.

Arkov calmly peered in at the face, rubbing the back of a finger against the glass, as if trying to attract some kind of exotic bird perched inside.

"This man tried to sell me out. You wouldn't do that, would you, Yanich?" Arkov's probing eyes never left the bar owner's face, as if he was trying to find his own answer.

"No, sir, never . . ."

"I like to look at it now and then, to tell myself how much I despise informers. Come this way."

Arkov stepped out through the glass patio doors into sunlight, toward the swimming pool table. The bar owner followed.

Arkov removed his wallet, peeled off a handful of banknotes, and laid them in a neat pile on the table. "A token of my gratitude."

Yanich went to eagerly scoop up the notes, sweat beading his face.

He never saw Arkov withdraw a garrote from his pocket—an age-old executioner's weapon made of a length of piano wire, a wooden grip at each end. Arkov slipped the wire effortlessly around Yanich's neck and pulled.

Yanich grunted in pain, eyes bulging as the wire cleaved into his throat, a thin line of blood appearing across his neck.

Arkov whispered into Yanich's ear. "I despise people like you. They'd sell their own grandmothers."

Yanich's face flushed as he struggled to breathe. Arkov pulled harder. The wire cut deeper into Yanich's throat until it severed his windpipe.

He gave a strangled croak.

Arkov let go and Yanich's body slumped forward, splashing into the pool, a gush of blood spraying the turquoise water crimson.

Arkov took out a handkerchief, wiped his blood-spattered hands, and gathered up the banknotes.

"Get rid of this scum and clean up the mess," he told the body-guards.

"Then call the airport and have the Lear fueled. I want it ready to leave."

58

BOSNIA-HERZEGOVINA

It was raining hard as Kelly pulled up outside the convent.

A rumble of thunder sounded as he climbed out of his Renault. He yanked the bellpull and the tinkle echoed somewhere deep inside the darkened archways. As he waited, he looked around him.

The drive into the mountains was treacherous, but well worth the views.

The fifteenth-century Byzantine convent was really quite magnificent, with intricately carved stone windows. Part of it was built into the granite mountainside, a peaceful courtyard beyond solid iron gates, a fountain bubbling away.

He pulled the bell again and a pair of nuns, one young, one old, came striding across the wet courtyard toward the gates. They wore heavy, plain dark habits, and tall wimples covered their heads.

"Do you speak English, sisters?"

The older nun nodded. "Yes, I do."

Around the older woman's waist was a knotted cord from which hung a large wooden crucifix and a bunch of keys. Her face was full of strength, solemn but rather beautiful. "I'm Sister Hilda, the abbess."

Her English was flawless.

"My name's Sean Kelly. I'm working with the International Commission on Missing Persons in Sarajevo." He offered his card and the nun studied it.

"And how may I help you, Mr. Kelly?"

"It's a little complicated, Sister. I'm trying to trace a boy. If you could spare me your time I'll do my best to explain."

Sister Hilda led Kelly under a darkened archway. The nun pushed open a solid oak door and stepped into a vast room.

Kelly shook rain from his jacket and followed her in.

Flashes of lightning exploded beyond the stone windows, and the room looked almost medieval, gilded icons decorating the walls. One end of the chamber had been modernized and looked like a gym-cum-playroom of some sort, complete with physical exercise equipment.

Kelly was greeted by a pitiful sight.

A handful of nuns attended to several dozen patients, young men and women mostly, who looked in their twenties and thirties. Some were missing arms or legs; others slobbered as they hunched in wheel-chairs. Kelly noticed several patients with heavily scarred limbs or faces. Almost all had a vacant look, one that suggested their mental capacity was impaired.

They greeted Kelly with wide-eyed uncertainty. He spotted a hand-some young man with an angelic face standing in a corner, sucking on his thumb.

Across the room a young woman gave him a shy wave with palsied hands.

"Holy God . . ." Kelly said, waving back.

He hated to even admit it, but the scene caused him conflicting threads of emotion. On the one hand it looked almost grotesque, nightmarish. And yet there was a beauty there, too, in the selfless char-ity of the nuns, in the touching innocence of the patients.

"The horrors of war always cast a long shadow, Mr. Kelly. And as always it's the innocent who suffer. Once, every one of these patients was someone's beloved child. They're still loved by God, who entrusts them to our care."

"They're all war victims?"

"Mostly. Some were sexually abused in the rape camps, or were shot or badly injured by shelling. Mentally, some never recovered, especially those who lost their families. Many of the young men and women you see still suffer constant nightmares."

"How many do you have in your care?"

"Almost a hundred."

"That must be difficult."

"Not as difficult as it's been for them."

The handsome young man sucking his thumb sidled up to Kelly.

He gently took hold of the Irishman's hand and rubbed it to his cheek, gazing up at him with a crooked but beautiful smile that brought out the tenderest feelings in Kelly.

He felt so overcome he cupped the young man's face in both his hands. The brown eyes that looked back at him were remote, as if the mind behind them was lost in some other universe. Kelly felt a lump rise in his throat.

"Before I leave perhaps you'd allow me to make a donation to the convent, Sister?"

"That's very kind of you."

"About the records?"

"Please come this way."

59

TENNESSEE

"You visiting?"

"Yes."

"From up north?"

"Yes."

"Get a lot of Yankees down here in fishing season."

The elderly doctor slid the probe over Carla's stomach, slippery with gel, as he examined the ultrasound screen. His smile was friendly but it did nothing to ease her heart-pounding fear.

Anxiety grew in her with every passing second. She could feel her pulse drumming in her ears.

Even the young intern looked worried. After he took the first ultrasound he called in his senior for a second opinion.

"Hill walking, you said?" the elderly doctor asked.

"Yes."

"Better than jogging. You ever wondered why some joggers look so unhealthy?" The doctor had ruddy cheeks and a billiard-ball belly. "Some of them sure look like they're on a mission to kill themselves."

As he moved the probe over her stomach he watched the screen. When he turned back a moment he noticed some scars on her right side. "What happened here?"

"I was injured. There was an explosion."

"How long ago?"

She explained.

"Describe your injuries, if you would."

Carla told him.

The doctor felt her sides, and pressed her stomach. Gently at first, then more firmly. "Tell me if you feel any discomfort or pain."

"No."

"Now?"

"No."

The man's keen eye noticed the long-ago scars on her arm, and the fresh scratch marks on her right hand, in the valley between her thumb and forefinger. He examined her hand. "You shoot?"

"Yes. How did you know?"

"I'm a southerner. I've suffered a few pistol slide bites in my day. Happens if you don't hold the gun the right way."

"Is . . . Is my baby okay?"

"Ma'am, the ultrasound's fine, the baby's heart is beating. The hemorrhaging has stopped but there's something not right, and that's why you've bled."

He wiped off the gel with paper towel, patted her side, and gestured for her to sit up.

"Give me a little while to check your blood and urine samples and we'll talk some more."

BOSNIA-HERZEGOVINA

Kelly descended a winding granite stairway to the monastery cellars, Sister Hilda leading the way. She carried a battery-operated lantern as they passed ornately gilded icons on the walls.

"Tell me about the convent and your order."

"It was built in the fifteenth century by a Serb princess as a place of refuge and reflection, and also to help tend the local sick and destitute. Many of our nuns are nurses."

They came to the bottom of the stairs, and a blackened, ancient oak door with a rusted lock. Sister Hilda inserted a key and pushed hard, and the door creaked open.

"Where are we?"

"This is where we keep our records, Mr. Kelly."

The room they stepped into was large, with vaulted stone ceilings, the floor covered in terra-cotta tiles.

Around the walls, thick wooden shelves sagged with the weight of old ledgers and journals, and bundles of parchments with wax seals. Sister Hilda swung the lantern toward the shelves.

She removed a pair of reading glasses from under her robe and slipped them on. "The boy's name and age?"

"Luka Joran. He was four years old."

"That's not a surname common to these parts."

"His father was American."

"Are you sure?"

"Yes, why?"

"You've brought back a memory. It may be important."

Sister Hilda turned toward a shelf, placing the lantern beside her. She plucked down one of the ledgers and started to flick through the pages.

"The only American we treated was a man brought here one evening with his young son, a small boy about that age. It was snowing, a cold night. I recall it well because both of them were in a bad way physically. And I remember the man's nationality. We never got Americans in this area."

"How do you know he was American?"

"His accent. He was from New York. I once worked there as a young nurse. The two of them were delivered here by car by a Good Samaritan."

"Were they injured?"

She stopped on one of the ledger pages, and pointed to an entry. "It's all here. The boy had suffered shell splinters in his back. They were significant, but they were operable. Also, they both had pneumonia."

Kelly felt his heart quicken. "What else can you tell me, Sister?"

"The child's name was given as Luka. I seem to recall that one of his eyes was unusual; it was milky, an ocular condition he suffered from."

"Please continue."

"There's no family name recorded. I'm not sure we were given one. But let me see . . ."

The nun read the ledger pages, her finger on a line. "It says here David was the father's name."

"Can you tell me what else you recall?"

The nun peered over her glasses. "Only that the father was delirious most of the time, in a bad way with fever. But he never let the child out of his grasp for a moment. He clutched the boy's hand even as they slept."

"Anything else?"

The nun consulted the ledger again. "We treated them both as best we could. They seemed to respond. They had already started a course of antibiotic. We found some in the father's pockets."

"What age was the father?"

She looked back up. "Early thirties, I'd say."

"Tell me exactly how they were brought here."

"A man arrived in a car. He said they were in poor condition and begged us to treat them."

"And?"

"We told him the truth. Our own patients were already dying."

"Why?

"We had no doctor and precious few drugs and medicines. I told him the boy and his father might not live. I told him it would be better if he brought them to a hospital, where they'd stand a better chance. He said he couldn't."

"Why not?"

"The roads were blocked by troops and checkpoints. And he didn't believe they'd survive a trip across the snowy mountains on foot. So he left the father and son with us."

"You treated them?"

"As best we could. We even operated on the boy and removed most of the shrapnel. Things improved. But I knew neither would stand a chance if we couldn't get them drugs. And then a miracle happened."

"What do you mean?"

"The man returned two days later."

"The Good Samaritan?"

"Yes. He looked like a corpse walking. He's been wounded trying to return to us, and was shot in the chest and arm. We had to treat him."

"Why did he come back?"

"To bring us drugs and medical supplies. Without them, most of the patients you saw today would never have survived."

"What about the father and his son?"

"The father's health was deteriorating fast. He needed proper hospital care. I told the man that."

"And?"

"He said he'd try to take them to a hospital. We helped him place the father and son in his car and he drove out of here and I never saw the American or his child again."

"The Good Samaritan, do you know who he was?"

"Yes, I recognized him. He was well known in these parts."

"Who was he?"

"His name was Mila Shavik."

60

What I'm about to do may cost me my life.

Angel inhaled the cigarette and watched the smoke curl to the ceiling.

Lying on the bed, staring up, she knew by heart every tiny crack in the ceiling plaster. Every river and vein her mind conjured up whenever she lay next to Mila Shavik—her eyes open, her heart closed to any feeling except her disgust for what she was doing.

She thought: *Carla Lane was right.*

Hate.

Affection.

It was bizarre, but sometimes those two feelings expressed exactly how she felt about Mila Shavik.

The fact that there were times when her sentiment toward him bordered on a kind of fondness disturbed her. It disturbed her even more because she despised feeling anything toward Shavik other than hatred.

Stockholm syndrome might explain her contrasting emotions. For how could she ignore the times when Shavik was kind and considerate? When he stroked her hair, touched her face lightly with the back of his hand like a tender lover.

Yet she knew it was more complicated: intuition told her that Shavik bore a wound as gaping as her own. Anyone who was half human would always feel pity for another tortured soul. And wasn't that really what she felt for Mila Shavik?

Not affection, but pity.

She no longer tried to fathom the source of his torment. It only distracted her from her purpose.

On the nightstand was an ice bucket filled with crushed ice. It held a bottle of Krug champagne, next to it two polished crystal glasses.

With shaking hands she popped open the Krug, and poured a glass of champagne. There were times when she felt as if she was defiling her mother and sister's memory by being in the company of these murderous criminals.

But long ago she learned to disconnect her mind and her body—they didn't belong to her when she was sharing a bed with someone. She learned to completely separate the woman in the makeup and wig from her real self.

Besides, sharing Shavik's bed had a greater purpose.

One that would allow her to have her revenge.

If she didn't blow it.

What I'm about to do may cost me my life.

For sure, and she knew it.

She crushed out her cigarette, rose from the bed, drew on her silk dressing gown. Moving to the window, she heard a car engine approach the gated driveway.

Fear surged through her body like a stab of electricity as the iron entrance gates swung open.

A black Mercedes with dark-tinted windows rolled up the driveway.

Mila Shavik had arrived.

The beach house on Cape May, New Jersey, had its own impressive grounds.

The swimming pool at the back overlooked Delaware Bay, a wrought-iron gate leading down to the sandy beach, the garden lawns well lit.

The cape had a Victorian feel to it, old turreted homes, restaurants, and yacht clubs, the upmarket neighborhoods a far drive from Jersey's gritty districts infested by drugs and crime.

Angel heard the Merc stop out of view.

She heard the car doors clunk open and shut, the bodyguards climbing out, heard their footsteps enter the hall.

Could she do it?

This one last thing?

A gamble with death?

She had planned every detail. But what if she was caught? What if they tortured her before they killed her, the same ways they tortured her mother and sister?

In her mind, she never forgot the sound of their screams.

Her fear felt like an icy dagger in her spine. She poured the second glass of champagne.

Footsteps echoed out in the hall.

The door handle turned.

And there, in the door frame, large as life, stood Mila Shavik.

61

She forced a smile, made it look genuine. "Try not to look like you missed me."

He came over, a briefcase in one hand, laid it down, and kissed her forehead gently. "I did."

She handed him his champagne. He emptied it in one swallow, put down the crystal. "I wish I could stay but I only came back for some papers. Duty calls."

"What duty?"

"Some work I have to finish at the club. Why don't you relax and watch a movie? I'll be back after midnight. We can have supper, more champagne."

"Promise?"

"Promise."

She put her arms around his neck and kissed him, smelling the faint scent of his aftershave as her lips brushed his. He seemed distracted as usual, and when he drew back she looked into his eyes.

"You're okay?"

He kissed her forehead lightly. "Just tired. Too much work. I need to get something from the safe before I go."

He moved over to the dressing room, stopped in the doorway. "By the way, I have some family business to attend to tomorrow night."

"You want me to stay in my own place?"

A faint smile. "I knew you'd understand."

Five minutes later Shavik was gone.

Angel watched from the window as the tinted-window Mercedes drove out the front gates. The house sounded silent. No one home except the household staff, a Puerto Rican maid and her husband, the chef.

Angel made sure the bedroom door was closed, then took her Toshiba notebook from her bag as well as a notepad and ballpoint pen.

She stepped into Shavik's walk-in dressing room.

The walls were covered in rich, ruby mahogany. Rails of suits, shirts, and casual clothes, neatly stored sweaters, racks of ties. A long mirror and chair.

She pulled apart a rail of suits, to reveal a mahogany panel.

A row of light switches nearby. One of the switches was false: she depressed the bottom right corner twice and the mahogany panel whirred open to reveal a wall safe.

Next, she positioned the chair under the smoke alarm in the ceiling.

She stood on the chair.

Yesterday, she replaced the smoke alarm with another just like it—except hers had a pinhead spy camera inside, pointed at the wall safe. She would replace the original when she finished.

For now, she twisted the alarm casing off the ceiling receiver, stepped down, and plugged a connector between the video camera and her Toshiba.

The video file downloaded.

She fast-forwarded, saw flickering images.

Shavik was onscreen now, his fingers punching the safe keypad. She slowed down the frame speed, observed each inputted number, and wrote them on her pad.

7

6

4

8

0

1

She unplugged the smoke alarm from the Toshiba.

She crossed to the safe. With shaking fingers, she carefully entered the numbers on the keypad. 764801. She touched the pound sign with a lacquered red nail.

A whirring sound erupted and the safe's door sprang open.

Inside was a stack of money and a thick ledger.

"Find everything you're looking for, sweetheart?"

Angel spun round, fear alive in her eyes.

Standing in the doorway was Arkov. Next to him Billy Davix, a weasel grin on his face.

Arkov lunged across the room and grabbed her savagely by the hair.

"Smart one, aren't you? Never underestimate a woman, I always say. But we've been watching you. What are you up to? Answer me, before I break something."

His face was screwed up with rage, holding back a balled fist, ready to strike.

Billy gave a hyena laugh, as if relishing what was about to come.

"You can go to hell." Angel's heart jackhammered against her chest but she stared defiantly at Arkov.

"Who do you work for?"

She spat in Arkov's face.

He lost it then, rage erupting in him. He drew back his fist and punched her face, and there was a sickening noise like bone splintering before Angel passed out.

62

Shavik stood alone at the window smoking a cigarette.

The door burst open and Arkov came in, wiping his face with a paper towel. In his free hand he clutched the smoke alarm camera. "Billy took out the memory card."

He tossed the alarm to Shavik, who examined it. "Where is she?"

"Billy dragged her down to the basement."

"Did she talk?"

"She's still out of it. I punched her so hard I broke her nose."

"I thought I told you not to harm her?"

Arkov grinned. "She needs to know we mean business. Don't worry, she'll talk if she knows what's good for her."

He finished dabbing his face, and tossed away the paper towel. "I never trusted that tart—she tried too hard to get close to you. I was right to keep an eye on her. Clever, planting the camera, but not clever enough."

Shavik flung the camera hard against the wall, smashing it to pieces. "What's she up to? What's she after?"

"Not money. She never took the cash we left lying around. You think she's working for the feds?"

"From the look on her face when she spat at you, it's something much more personal."

"You're right." Arkov cracked his knuckles, enjoying the drama. "Billy's got a hypodermic full of scopolamine. If the truth drug doesn't get it out of her, we'll revert to the old ways."

He stepped over to the door, shook his head. "Looks like you made a big mistake taking her into your bed, Mila."

Shavik crushed out his cigarette. "Don't rub it in."

"My old man called."

"And?"

"When I told him about Angel, he wasn't happy. But it gets worse. He says the Lane woman's a witness."

"To what?"

"The fun and games we had at the Devil's Hill."

"How does he know?"

"He says he'll explain when he gets here Sunday."

"I don't like it. It's too much of a coincidence. First the musician nosing around, now his wife."

"That's what I thought. You think there's a connection to Angel?"

"I've no idea but it wouldn't surprise me."

"I'll get it out of her. It'll be interesting to hear what she has to say once the scopolamine starts to work. Are you coming?"

"In a few minutes."

Arkov grinned again. "What's the matter, Mila? Don't have the stomach for the dirty work anymore?"

Shavik stood there, lighting another cigarette, feeling angry with himself.

He'd let his guard down, been a complete fool. And now he had to deal with Angel. He would do what he had to do.

Kanun and *besa,* loyalty and secrecy.

He should never have invited her into his house, never have trusted her.

Just as his father told him; trust no one.

His father.

Long gone.

It all came back to him in a powerful flash of memory.

He was eighteen. A bright, hopeful young boy with a thousand dreams.

Until one day he came home and found his father hanging from a rope in the basement, still wearing his lawyer's dark suit, his face blue, eyes bulging. He cut his father down, tried to revive him. But even before he put his mouth to the blue lips he knew it was hopeless. Afterward, he had never felt so alone. The man he adored was gone.

He could barely recall his mother; he was five when she died— brown eyes, skin the scent of soap, a ready smile—that was it.

But he never forgot his father.

Why did he take the coward's route?

Why?

He could never answer that question.

He took another drag on his cigarette, looked at his image in the mirror.

Where was that bright, hopeful young boy with a thousand dreams?

Long gone.

Having no one left close to him, did that explain his need to belong?

His desire to be a part of a family, corrupt as it was?

Witnessing so much death, he felt immune to it, and yet always the image of his father hanging from the end of a noose jolted his heart.

He crushed his emotion as he stubbed out his cigarette. He'd learned to do that. Emotions bled you, made you weak.

What happened during the retreat from the Devil's Hill still disturbed him.

The killings, the butchery.

The light died in his eyes, as if at that moment he went to a place inside himself that he shared with no one. Sometimes faces came to him in his nightmares: women young and old, and the small children, the dead and the cries of the dying. A sea of crimson bodies on the snowy ground. And one body in particular, that haunted him.

From his inside pocket he removed the photograph. He racked his mind as he stared at the face in the snapshot.

The Lane woman looked familiar, yet he still couldn't recall where he had seen her before.

Where?

Where did he know her from?

63

"The good news is the hemorrhaging has stopped. And your blood and urine samples are okay. However . . ."

The doctor put down the charts, looked at her more seriously.

Carla felt a jolt of distress in the pit of her stomach. *Something's not right.*

"I'd like you to tell me about this blast, ma'am."

"What do you need to know?"

He spread his hands, shrugged, folded his arms. "Whatever you can tell me."

"It's relevant?"

"It may be."

"My husband was killed."

Faintly startled, the doctor unfolded his arms. "I'm deeply sorry to hear that."

"Why is this important, Doctor?"

"Who checked you out medically, ma'am?"

"The doctors at Mount Sinai."

He left eyebrow twitched. "It's a good hospital. They know their business."

"Is there something wrong? Please tell me."

He gave a sigh, removed his glasses, and rubbed his eyes with his thumb and forefinger a few moments.

"You've had a show of blood. A little more than a show really. A minor hemorrhage. It can happen anytime during a pregnancy. When it does, it's always a concern."

"Will the baby be okay?"

"Your hemorrhage may mean something serious, it may not. You could well proceed to the end of your pregnancy without a further problem. But right now, we want to try to ensure you don't miscarry."

"How?"

"Medication and rest. Any kind of exertion is out. That and we'll need to wrap you up in cotton wool."

"For how long?"

"A week. At the very least until after the weekend."

"I . . . I can't stay here that long. It's impossible."

"So, you're a busy lady?"

"Yes."

"Know what I noticed right away about you when they brought you in here? I mean apart from the fact that you looked half worried to death."

"What?"

"You're exhausted, stressed-out." He glanced at her chart for a moment. "Your blood pressure's up a little, too. Anything been bothering you lately? Anything you'd care to talk about?"

"No."

"Sure?"

"Yes."

"Maybe something that you've been stressing over? You don't have to give me exact details if you don't want. Maybe you've been working long hours, or traveling a lot?"

"I . . . I guess all those things."

"Know what they say? Stress and fatigue don't show up in autopsies."

The doctor slipped back on his glasses.

"In pregnancy, stress can help to induce a hemorrhage like yours. Which is why you really need to kick back your feet and relax. No visitors, just R-and-R. The man who brought you, he's Ronnie Kilgore, right?"

"You know him?"

"I fish out of his dock. He know you're pregnant?"

"Yes. He's a friend. I'm staying at his marina."

"I'll explain to Ronnie that I want you to rest and that we'll monitor you."

"Could I have a few minutes alone with him?"

"Sure you can, but remember what I said about rest."

The doctor winked. "Let's try and turn you into a southern lady of leisure. No more hill trekking. And you can forget about shooting."

"Why?"

"Firing off a few rounds now and then from the back porch to scare off a snake or a bear, that's okay. But blasting away at the range with any kind of regularity, no ma'am. Some studies suggest too much shooting can be a danger to the fetus."

"Really?"

"The noise, the air displacement, the jolt the body receives when you shoot a heavy-caliber round in particular."

"Do you think I'll carry my baby to term?"

"I'm hopeful." He patted her arm. "But I'd don't want you taking any more risks, you hear?"

Bosnia-Herzegovina

None of it made any sense, none at all.

Kelly's mind was turning somersaults as he cruised down the mountain road on his way back to Sarajevo.

Mila Shavik took the boy and his father to the convent.

Then he showed up days later with drugs and medicines.

Shavik, killer, and savior, risking his life to help others. It didn't add up.

A brutal war criminal carrying out an act of mercy.

It puzzled Kelly.

It would certainly puzzle Carla Lane.

He slowed his speed and fumbled in his pocket for his phone. He scrolled to the international number, stabbed the call key, and seconds later heard Carla Lane's voice message kick in.

"Mrs. Lane, it's Sean Kelly. I wonder if you'd call me back as soon as you get this? I have some remarkable information. And I know for a fact Mila Shavik was the last person to have contact with Luka and—"

Kelly heard a car engine roar as it sped up behind him. He glimpsed a flash of blue in his rearview mirror.

The vehicle nudged his Renault.

His body jolted violently.

Kelly lost control of the steering wheel for barely a second but that was all it took. The Renault struck the metal road barrier with a *clang* and a shower of sparks.

"Dear Lord . . . no!"

Kelly screamed as his car smashed through the barrier.

For a split second he floated on air.

Then the Renault nosed down with a sickening sensation, and crashed into the chasm, exploding in a ball of orange flame.

64

TENNESSEE

"Why didn't you tell me before now?"

"I didn't think it would matter."

"Carla, you're ten weeks pregnant. That doesn't matter?"

"I . . . I didn't intend to harm my baby. I guess I've been stressed-out. Blinded by anger, by rage. By my desperation to find Luka."

"But you know now."

"Yes."

"Yet you're still going ahead?"

"Ronnie, don't you see? Luka's like a wound in me that'll never heal."

"You want to know what I see?"

"What?"

"A woman who's torn between the devil and the deep blue sea."

She didn't speak.

He saw the tension around her eyes and mouth, and knew she was struggling to control her emotions. "What about Angel?"

"I haven't heard from her."

"So assuming you don't hemorrhage again, you're going to leave hospital tomorrow and drive to New Jersey, is that the plan?"

"Yes."

"Then what?"

"I . . . I don't know. Try and get in touch with Angel. Find Shavik's house."

"You've got scared written all over your face."

"Of course I'm scared."

"And it's not a plan you've got, it's a death wish."

"I'll try to come up with a better plan."

"The doc said you need to rest up for at least a week."

"I can't stay here that long, Ronnie. As much as I want to protect my baby I can't let this chance slip by. Time may not be on our side. Angel said we've only got a small window. But it's getting smaller, maybe even closing."

She looked back at him. "I just can't go through life not knowing what happened to Luka."

"How long can you stay here?"

"I'll have to see how I feel."

"It's a choice between Luka and your baby. That's really what you're faced with, isn't it?"

"I . . . I don't want to think about it right now."

He saw her lips quiver.

"Carla, you're not even physically well enough to confront Shavik."

"I'm feeling better."

"You're in a hospital, under care. You're bound to."

"Will you stop this?"

"You know what I think? Sometimes you're still that headstrong, resolute ten-year-old girl who survived the rape camp, aren't you?"

"So?"

"You don't get it, do you, Carla? What do you think is going to happen to you if things go wrong?"

"Ronnie, please, I don't need to hear this right now."

"You bet you do. You think Shavik and his friends would let you go? What about your baby, then?"

She stared back at him.

"I promised I'd come back for Luka. I promised to keep him safe.

This could be the only chance I'll ever get to keep to that promise. I owe it to him."

He didn't answer.

"What's the matter? Have you changed your mind about helping me, Ronnie?"

"You want my honest advice?"

"Was that a yes or a no?"

"Suddenly I don't know. Maybe the fact that you're pregnant brought it home. That really you need to consider the life of the baby you're carrying."

"I never stop thinking about it. But what about Luka's life?"

"You don't even know for certain he's alive. And I don't mean to belittle your brother's memory, but Luka's in the past. Your baby's the present. Think about that."

Carla said nothing.

He turned to go. "Regan's outside. She wanted to make sure you were okay."

"You told her?"

"Only that you're pregnant."

"What did she say?"

"She'll be there if you need her. Do me one favor?"

"What?"

"Think hard about what I said. Let go of your hate. Let go of your obsession with killing Shavik and his kind."

"I can't."

He stepped out into the hall. Regan was pacing the floor, drinking coffee from a plastic cup.

"How's she doing?"

"The bleeding's stopped. The doc says she needs to rest up."

"And the baby?"

"Still okay."

"Are you all right, Ronnie?"

"Why?"

"You look mixed-up. Even angry."

"Can you keep an eye on Carla for now?"

"You've got to go?"

"I've got supplies to fetch in Knoxville and won't be back until late. I want to see Josh first."

"He was fine when I left him. I'll make sure he's okay. Go do what you have to do."

"Thanks."

"Looks to me like you haven't slept all night. You ought to get some rest yourself."

"Later."

"You worried about anything in particular?"

He didn't answer, turned to go. Regan put a hand on his arm.

"Hey, big brother, what's really going on with you and Carla?"

"What do you mean?"

"Shooting every day, spending all that time together. What's the deal?"

"Who says there's one?"

"I ain't no dingbat. You spent more time with your truck than you have with a woman in the last four years."

"So?"

"All of a sudden it's like you're coming alive. I saw the way you looked at her at dinner. It's the same look you got now."

"What look?"

"You're concerned. You care about her a lot. Don't you?"

"Regan, the woman just buried her husband."

"That ain't your fault and you didn't answer the question."

He tugged on his hat.

She squeezed his arm as he went to go. "I guess I never thought I'd see the day when Ronnie Kilgore felt something for a woman again. That's a good thing, ain't it, Ronnie?"

The door opened a few moments later and the doctor returned. He checked Carla's blood pressure and pulse.

"Your pressure's still high. Your pulse, too. How are you feeling?"

"Okay, I guess."

"We don't give sedatives to pregnant women, but we'll give you something to lower your blood pressure. You're exhausted, so I'm pretty sure you'll sleep."

"Doctor, I really can't stay here for a week."

"It could be longer, or less. All depends."

"On what?"

He wrote on her chart. "The body's an unpredictable machine. It can rattle on for years, long after someone should have kicked the bucket. Or sometimes the very fit can drop dead."

He half smiled, hung the chart on the end of the bed.

"Not that you're in danger of dying. But simply put, you're in God's hands. Though we'll do our best to tip those hands in your favor. By the way, there was a lady waiting outside, Ronnie's sister. I told her to head on home, you're going to be resting for a while."

The doctor left, closing the door softly. When it opened again the nurse returned with a glass of water and some pills. Carla swallowed them and drank the water.

The nurse left and a little later, Carla felt overcome by exhaustion.

The last thing she saw before she surrendered to sleep was Luka's face staring up at her through a curtain of falling show.

65

When Ronnie let himself into the cabin, it was almost dark.

He heard music down the hall and found Josh asleep on his bed, his wheelchair jammed next to it. His head lay on his pillow, his mouth half open, the bedsheet crumpled in a ball at the bottom of his feet.

His son was still dressed in a T-shirt and an old pair of Dockers cargo shorts, MTV on, the volume low.

Ronnie killed it with the remote. He unfurled the bedsheet, draped it over Josh. He pulled up a chair and sat.

Letting out a sigh, he leaned over and stroked his son's hair.

Next to the bed, a metal support bar curved out from the wall to the floor. Josh had long ago learned the art of hauling himself from the wheelchair.

The room was covered in wall posters just like any normal kid: rock bands, baseball players, and a pouty, pretty young Hollywood actress he could never remember the name of.

The shelves were stuffed, mostly with toys left over from childhood: a bunch of old DVDs and games, a *Toy Story* "Woody" cowboy hat and a grinning, plastic Buzz Lightyear. Furry characters from *Monsters, Inc.*

That was the one difference with Josh: most boys his age long ago discarded such childish things; his son clung to them. Boxes of old toys cluttered the garage because Josh refused to part with them.

As if the happy part of his past, when his mom was alive and his parents together—that time in his childhood when things were clear and bright, happy and safe—was a dream he longed to reclaim.

On the shelves his son still kept photographs of them all together: Josh, Annie, him.

Two were of Annie and Josh when he was an infant. Asleep in a smiling Annie's arms on Myrtle Beach, their first vacation together. Another shot on the dock, five-year-old Josh holding his mom's hand, both of them squinting into the sun, Annie not looking too happy. It was the year he redeployed to Afghanistan.

He stared down at his son's legs, or what passed for them, the scarred and puckered flesh where the surgeons had done their best to re-form the mangled tissue and crushed bone, to at least give him some semblance of a complete body.

At that moment, Ronnie felt drowned by a wave of guilt. It never lessened. Never faded the way he prayed it would. He'd let his wife and boy down, put the army and his country first.

Josh was never going to walk again. He'd come to accept that. There was never going to be any miracle cure—no Lourdes trip that would put everything to rights. All he could pray for now was that he lived long enough to protect his son as best he could, and teach him how to take care of himself.

When Josh was discharged from the hospital, Ronnie had been tough on him. Like a drill sergeant, he'd pushed him to do things almost beyond himself physically, rigging up a set of exercise bars to strengthen his son's upper torso, desperate to prepare for the day Josh would have to survive alone.

There were times after hours of exercise when he'd carry the exhausted boy to bed, and laid him down to sleep. Those times brought him close to tears.

For sometimes when he slept Josh had the face of a young girl, and it was a face Ronnie vividly remembered. Josh looked so much like his mom. The same magnolia skin. The same fine blond hair and full lips.

If he closed his eyes he could still see her the first time they met in Gatlinburg, a girl of seventeen, wearing a pair of worn flat shoes and a faded floral dress she'd sewn badly in places.

She was always a kind of lost soul, Annie.

It was part of what made him want to protect her. Just as he wanted to protect Josh. Was it that same protective streak in him that drew him to Carla?

He felt something for her. He wasn't sure what. It wasn't love; it was way too soon for that, and the timing was all wrong.

But he sensed in her something vulnerable, something lost, a gaping wound so deep within her that it made him want to reach out to comfort her.

Just like him she'd learned that grief and guilt are the hardest crosses to bear.

Looking down now at Josh, he was beset by agony. He leaned over, kissed his cheek. Josh stirred, gave a tiny moan, fell back to sleep, his hands under his head.

He hated going back on a promise—he prided himself on being a man of his word. But Josh needed him, and always would.

With more time, they might have come up with a decent plan, but they didn't have that luxury. As it stood, there were too many obstacles.

He wasn't afraid of men like Shavik. But Carla's plans as they stood didn't stand a chance—except of getting them both killed.

Her couldn't do that to Josh.

He couldn't hurt him again.

No matter how much he might care for Carla, he cared more for Josh, and it couldn't be any other way.

He'd have to tell her that.

He stood, crossed the room, flicked off the light, and took one last look at his son's sleeping figure in the shadowy darkness.

Bottom line, he couldn't risk making him an orphan for a woman he hardly knew. He just couldn't.

From now on, Carla was on her own.

"How are you feeling?"

Carla came awake slowly. Regan sat in a chair next to the bed.

"Drowsy. I . . . I went under as soon as my head hit the pillow."

Regan placed a bunch of flowers on the bedside locker. "For you. I'll get the nurse to put them in water."

"Thanks, Regan."

"Ronnie told me about you being pregnant. But hey, he wouldn't have had to."

"Why?"

"You've sort of got that look on your face all pregnant women get. Bewilderment. Shock. Joy."

"You reckon?"

Regan half smiled. "Yeah. Like the doc stiffed you with a huge medical bill you never expected, but you're still alive and ain't got that incurable disease you thought you had, so you're darned happy."

Regan gave a hearty laugh, the kind that made you want to join in. She looked past the window blinds, parted to reveal lake and mountain.

"Nice view. What's the matter? You look lost as a stray dog."

"The view kind of reminds me."

"Of where?"

"The place I grew up."

"Where was that?"

"A long way from here. A long, long way, and another life, Regan."

"By the sounds of it, wherever you came from wasn't a happy place, was it?"

"No, but it was once." Carla clammed up.

"Hey, I came back a few times to check on you. You know you talk in your sleep? Worse than Dwayne did after a skinful. They give you meds?"

"Why, what did I say?"

"Enough for me to know you've probably been through some heavy stuff."

Carla didn't answer.

"It sounded to me like you were having a nightmare."

"What did I do?"

"You were muttering but none of it made much sense. Something about a boy named Luka. And . . ."

"And what?"

"Seeing bones . . ."

Carla went to speak, but faltered.

Regan patted her arm. "Hey, you don't have to explain, sweetie. You don't have to tell me nothing."

"When I was a child there was a war . . ." Carla's words fell away.

Regan squeezed her hand. "I figured from the way you were squirming in your sleep something bad must have happened to you."

"I'll spare you the details, Regan."

"That's okay. The important thing right now is that you look after that baby, you hear? No overdoing it."

"You never have children, Regan?"

"It came close. I miscarried once, before Dwayne and I split."

"What happened?"

"I was burning the candle both ends—teaching, and working at the dock all hours because Ronnie's wife had died, and helping to look after Josh."

Regan faltered.

"I should have rested up, like the doctor told me. Losing the baby was maybe the hardest thing I ever had to deal with."

"I'm sorry."

"Hey, don't fret, it isn't the same outcome for everyone. But you need to take the doc's advice. Mind if I say something?"

"Go ahead."

"Look, whatever it is you're doing with Ronnie, it's really none of my business. But I know my brother."

"I don't follow."

"When he starts hanging out on the shooting range most days for the first time in years, and trekking up and down those hills like a mountain goat on speed, and with a woman he hardly knows, then there's got to be more to it."

Regan fixed her with a stare. "I mean apart from the fact he likes you a lot. Don't look so shocked. I think you knew that, too."

"Yes . . . yes I did. I like him, too. It's just . . ."

"I won't even go there. But it doesn't take rocket science to fig-ure you and Ronnie are co-conspirators in something, whatever that something is."

Carla bit her lip.

"Now he knows that you're pregnant I bet he's telling you to be careful? Not to take risks with your baby. Giving you advice like he's your personal gyno, right?"

"Yes."

"It figures."

"Why?"

"Because Ronnie's wife was seven months pregnant when she drove her car into the wall. That's why it cut him up real bad. He felt the weight of his wife's death, and their unborn baby. A baby Ronnie really wanted. It was kind of ironic. My brother was trained to kill, yet fate taught him the opposite: that life's so very precious."

Regan's eyes fixed straight on her. "I guess none of us really know the value of a life until it's lost, but then you know that, losing Jan."

Carla faltered. "I . . . I had a young brother. I loved him very much. I lost him in the war I told you about. I never knew if he lived or died."

"I'm real sorry to hear that."

She wanted to say more, wanted to tell Regan everything, but knew she couldn't take that risk.

"I'm . . . I'm sorry, Regan, I think I need to be alone."

Regan pushed back her chair. "Sure. I've got lots to do over in Harrogate. That's why I called in now."

"What time is it?"

"Seven thirty."

"P.m.?"

"A.m."

"I . . . I slept all that time?"

"The nurse said twelve hours. You must have been pretty beat. Stress can do that."

Regan paused at the door, looked back.

"One more thing."

"What?"

"Have you watched the TV news recently or read the stuff in the newspapers about Jan's death?"

"I've seen none of it."

"The cops seem to have hit a brick wall."

"I know."

"They're calling it murder yet they've got no motive. Except I read a piece today that mentioned Jan's past. I'm guessing the cops may want to talk with you about it at some stage."

"What . . . what do you mean?"

"It said he was from Croatia, in the former Yugoslavia."

"What about it?"

"The article mentioned that maybe there was some kind of vendetta, or revenge motive behind his death."

"I know nothing about that."

Regan's left eye arched. "Yet Ronnie's teaching you to shoot? Honey, even if I had the brains of the dumbest sheep I could figure out that something pretty serious was being planned by you two."

Regan's words hung in the air.

"My brother's a good guy, Carla."

"I know."

"That's why I don't want him getting himself into any situation where he might be harmed or killed, you understand? Josh needs him. Needs him badly. Ronnie pledged after Annie died that he'd never do anything to jeopardize his son."

Regan looked at Carla with clear, solemn eyes. There was no mistaking the steel in her voice.

"So whatever it is you're up to, I don't want you putting my brother in harm's way, you hear?"

67

She waited until the door closed and Regan was gone.

She sat there, feeling lost, helpless.

She clutched her stomach, then buried her face in her palms.

What could she do?

If she took the doctor's advice to protect her baby, she might never find Luka.

If she tried to confront Shavik, she risked her baby's life and her own.

Racked by unease, she looked down at her hands.

They no longer covered her face.

She was anxiously folding and unfolding the corner of the bedsheet.

She reached inside the nightstand, and found her handbag.

From a side pocket she took out the big yellow envelope. She removed Luka's blankie and the photograph taken on Dubrovnik beach.

Staring at the image of Luka and her mother and father, she clenched the blue cotton so tightly that her knuckles hurt, turned white. She felt the pain of her conscience. A phone rang somewhere out in the hall. She remembered Angel's promise to call.

She rummaged in her bag, found her cell, and flicked it on. No texts but two missed calls. Neither from Angel, which worried her, but from Baize.

And two voice messages.

The first was from Baize, asking her to call her when she was free.

When the second message played, she recognized the Irishman's voice immediately.

"Mrs. Lane, it's Sean Kelly. I wonder if you'd call me back as soon as you get this? I have some remarkable information. And I know for a fact Mila Shavik was the last person to have contact with Luka and—"

Carla felt her heart thump with excitement.

There seemed to be a moment's time lapse over the line and then came a harsh noise like scraping metal, followed by a scream.

"Dear Lord . . . no!"

A muffled silence followed and the line went dead.

It sounded as if Kelly had crashed his car.

Puzzled, Carla punched her keypad and redialed his number.

It rang out, and switched to answer mode, Kelly's voice telling her to leave a message.

She sat there, agonized.

What was the remarkable information? What about Luka?

Kelly's tone sounded upbeat. As if it was good news.

She would give it a few more minutes and call Kelly's number again. If she got no reply, she'd call the ICMP headquarters in Sarajevo.

When she could bear it no longer she clambered to her feet, gripped by a powerful need to know that she couldn't ignore.

The door opened, a nurse came in, all business. "Ma'am, you need to get back in that bed . . ."

Grabbing her clothes from the nightstand, Carla hurried past her.

* * *

She opened the front door to Ronnie's cabin as the cab drove away.

Josh was sitting by the Yamaha organ, tweaking a few dials. He looked surprised to see her as he pushed his fringe off his face.

"Hi."

Carla joined him. "Hi. Having fun?"

"Just messing with my tuner."

"Is your dad around, Josh?"

"Naw, he had to go out." Josh picked up a McDonald's bag. "He brought some Egg McMuffins for breakfast if you'd care for one?"

"Sure."

"There's a decaf coffee in the other bag that Dad left. You want it?"

"Thanks. How about we zap the food in the microwave?"

She crossed to the kitchen, popped the bag and the coffee in the microwave, figured out the timer, hit the button. When they were done she handed Josh the bag and sipped the coffee.

"How've you been?"

"Fine, ma'am."

He opened the bag, handed her one of the McMuffins.

"Thanks." Carla left it on the table.

"Regan had to go Harrogate. She said she was going to visit you first."

"I saw her before I discharged myself from the hospital."

"Are you okay now, ma'am?"

"I hope so, Josh."

"She likes you."

"Regan?"

"Yeah."

"I like her, too."

He bit on the McMuffin. "She never stops kidding me. But I guess that's kind of like affection, right?"

"Sure it is. Did your dad say when he'd be back?"

"Not until later. He had to drive into Knoxville. Can I ask you a question?"

"Sure."

"Is my dad helping you or something?"

"Why do you ask that?"

"Why are you two working so hard on the range?"

"He's been teaching me how to shoot."

"Why, ma'am?"

"I need to . . . to learn to protect myself, I guess."

"How'd you do shooting?"

"Okay. I think. But I could probably do better."

Josh took another bite, swallowed. "You like my dad?"

"Yes, I do. He's a good man."

"That's what my mom used to say. Except she used to think he loved the army more than he loved her."

"You think he did?"

"I used to, but now I'm not so sure."

"Why?"

Josh shrugged. "Because I know he misses her."

His eyes flicked to the Yamaha.

"Mom used to play while Dad was away in the military. That's really how I started playing. She got bored, so she bought the organ and tried to teach herself."

"Was she any good?"

"Naw, not really. It just gave her something to do. She was sorta lonely."

His head lowered just a little, with the kind of vulnerable purity only a twelve-year-old can show.

"Josh, I need to ask a favor. Where does your dad keep his guns?"

"Why?"

"I need to borrow a Sig he's been letting me use."

"Are you planning on doing some more shooting?"

"Yes, I am."

68

Arkov sat on a basement stool, watching as Billy tied a piece of pencil-thick rubber around Angel's arm.

He slapped the skin, raising a vein. Angel's head lolled to one side, her hair strewn, her makeup and lipstick streaked. Her skirt was half-way up her thighs.

"Another five cc's."

"You're sure, boss?"

"Do it," Arkov replied.

Billy held up the hypodermic in one hand, a glistening dewdrop of scopolamine forming on the needle's pinhead, then he jabbed it into Angel's vein, producing a droplet of blood, and sank the plunger.

"You think this extra shot will work?"

Arkov examined Angel's cell phone in his hand and began to tap the keys. On the table next to him was a silenced 9mm Glock. "With scopolamine, it's hard to judge the right dose."

"What is it with this stuff?"

"They call it Satan's breath. It turns its victims into a zombie. If it works, she can't help but answer our questions."

"What if it doesn't?"

"Then I'm going to enjoy beating the life out of her until I get the answers I want."

Billy grinned, removed the hypodermic from Angel's vein, and yanked off the rubber, a dribble of blood flowing. "Shavik won't like that."

"He's in no position to like anything after the mistake he's made with her."

The door burst open and Shavik strode in.

Arkov grinned. "Speak of the devil. Your timing's perfect."

"Get on with it."

Arkov pinched Angel's face in his hand. "Wake up, it's quiz time."

Her eyes fluttered, and she looked barely conscious.

Arkov grabbed a fistful of hair and shook her head violently. "I said wake up!"

Angel's eyes snapped open.

Arkov grinned, leaned in close to her face. "So, you're back with the living again. What have you got to say for yourself?"

She seemed to come awake then, her senses alert, and she scowled at Arkov as if she was going to spit at him again.

"You cow—"

Arkov drew back his fist but Shavik grabbed it in midair and said, "No. A broken jaw won't help her talk."

Arkov yanked his arm free. "You think you know better, Mila, but you're wrong. We need to go harder on her, not softer."

"I'll be the judge of that. Did you check her cell phone?"

"I'm about to."

"Scroll through her contacts, texts made and received, and all the call lists if they haven't been erased. Make a note of any texts or numbers of interest. Pay attention to the time just before she met the Lane woman in Newark."

"I'm not dumb, Mila. I know what to do."

"Then get it done." Shavik knelt in front of Angel, and her head slumped again. She looked in a stupor, as if she couldn't focus, the drug kicking in.

"Listen to me, Angel. Tell me who you're working for. Tell me that and no one lays another finger on you. I give you my word."

She moaned, a low moan that almost sounded like she wanted to throw up. Shavik let go of her face and she vomited, spraying her clothes, spewing across the floor. Her head flopped to one side again like a rag doll, and she moaned again, in a stupor.

Arkov grimaced. "Terrific."

Shavik examined the discarded hypodermic. "How much did you give her?"

"Ten cc's total. It can take longer to work on some than others."

"For a woman? You want to kill her?"

"Eventually."

"Are you completely stupid?"

Arkov flushed. "You don't talk to me like that, Mila. You'll show me respect."

"When you deserve it. At this rate, that may be never."

Billy grinned, enjoying the confrontation.

Arkov skewered him with a stare. "What do you find so funny?"

"Funny? Nothing."

Shavik tossed aside the hypodermic. "It could be hours before we can get her to talk. Any more bright ideas, you two?"

"Yeah, I've got one." Arkov snapped his fingers. "Billy, I want you to get me something from the car."

Josh wheeled his chair into a storeroom off the hall. Carla saw a big steel gray gun safe with an electronic keypad.

In the middle of the door was a silver wheel lock.

"It's locked?"

"Yeah. Dad's real careful about leaving guns lying around."

"You know the combination?"

"No, only my dad knows that."

"You're kidding?"

"Nope."

"Josh, I need that gun."

"I'm sorry, Miss Carla."

"Josh, please listen to me. If there's any way you know how to open this safe, I really need you to tell me now. I'm begging you."

"Why?"

"Because it's important. Look at me, Josh."

"But . . . why do you need the gun right now?"

"I need to be someplace and it may be dangerous. That's why your dad's been teaching me how to shoot."

"Really?"

"Really."

"How about I call my dad?"

"I don't have that time. You're a smart kid, Josh, but trust me, by the time he drives here from wherever he is it'll be too late. I hate if it seems like I'm pushing you, I honestly do, but this is kind of an execu-tive decision that's all yours."

Josh sat there, uncertain, chewing his lower lip.

"What is it, Josh?"

"I . . . I think the code is in Regan's bedroom."

"You think?"

"I think it's written on a piece of paper on top of her closet."

"You're sure?"

"Pretty much. It's where I can't reach."

"Where's Regan's room?"

He looked serious. "Miss Carla, will I get in trouble for this?"

"Honest? I don't know, Josh. But you can tell your dad I forced you. How's that?"

"You'll back me up? Square it with my dad?"

"Yes I will."

"Will he get angry?"

"Maybe, but I figure he'll understand. Where's Regan's room?"

He pointed left, along the hall.

Carla stepped in. A single closet right behind the door. She pulled up a chair, rummaged on top of the closet, and found a slip of paper with six digits followed by a hash symbol.

Back in the hall, she punched the numbers and the pound key on the safe's keypad. She turned the wheel lock and pulled open the heavy door.

All the guns she'd used were inside.

Boxes of ammo were stored on gray felt-covered shelves, the long guns upright, the handguns racked on wire pistol frames. At the bot-tom of the safe was a plastic tray full of gun cleaning kits, oils, and silicone cloths.

She picked out the Sig with the threaded barrel, took three empty magazines, found the silencer on a shelf, and removed a box of 9mm cartridges.

She remembered to take the silicone cloth to remove all prints from the gun and ammunition. She locked the safe again and replaced the slip of paper on top of the closet.

"Thanks, Josh."

"When are you coming back, Miss Carla?"

Arkov flicked through the road atlas Billy brought from the car.

"Where's this place your guy followed her to?"

"A marina in Union County, eastern Tennessee. He got on her flight, managed to stick a magnetic tracker bug on her car, and followed her there in a rental."

Shavik said, "What are you up to?"

Arkov found Tennessee in the atlas, traced his finger on the page to Union County, then tossed the atlas on the table, a sly grin creasing his lips.

"Making sure our witness is taken care of."

"And what's so funny?" Shavik demanded.

"I've got the perfect plan. Billy, you're on the next plane to Knoxville."

"Yeah? What for?"

Arkov patted his cheek. "Because you're about to play the best role you've ever been offered."

She drove north on Interstate 81 in the rented Ford.

The GPS calculated a grueling seven-hundred-mile drive, through Virginia and Maryland to New Jersey. The estimated trip time was twelve hours. She guessed it could be longer with restroom stops and the drive-through for coffee and food, not that she felt remotely like eating.

To reach New Jersey before midnight would be tight.

Why hadn't Angel contacted her? Had something happened? Or what if Ronnie was right and she was playing a double game?

Her stomach fluttered, not with hunger or cramps, but from fear and tension.

Her overnight case was in the trunk. The Sig, ammunition, and silencer were stashed under her driver's seat. Along with the tactical flashlight, the shooter's gloves, and the silicone cloth. She wore dark stretch pants, a dark navy top, black running shoes. Her navy blue hoodie lay on the backseat, along with a black woolen hat.

She had no plan, none at all, not even an idea of one.

She racked her mind as she drove, trying to come up with a strategy, still terrified of coming face-to-face with Mila Shavik. She tried to focus but the same questions burned inside her head: Where's Luka? What happened to him? Is he still alive?

She tried Kelly's number again. No answer, just voice mail.

What remarkable information did Kelly discover?

One hand caressed her stomach, dreading that her cramps might return.

Over three hours later, she was drinking a cup of McDonald's iced tea as she passed Marion, Virginia, racking her mind trying to come up with a plan.

But nothing came.

At that precise moment Continental Flight 2334 from Newark was touching down at Knoxville's Tyson Airport.

Twenty minutes later, Billy Davix grabbed his bag from the luggage carousel. Using a false ID and credit card in the same name, he rented a Ford SUV complete with GPS from the Hertz desk.

Packed in his luggage case were the clothes he needed, along with a .45 Kimber automatic and silencer. One of the Second Amendment benefits of American citizenship that Davix loved. You could still transport a personal firearm as luggage on U.S. aircraft and nobody gave a Bo Diddley.

He'd stop at a Walmart on the way and buy some hollow-point ammo.

He punched the address for the Kilgore Marina, Union County, into the GPS. Two minutes later he screeched out of the airport parking lot, heading northeast.

It was 1:15 p.m. exactly.

PART SIX

69

Dr. Raymond Leon bit into his sandwich—a thickly filled pastrami on rye with mustard mayonnaise—and waved as he saw Baize totter down the path.

She was smoking a cigarette and he saw the worried look on her face as she waved back. The doctor dabbed his mouth with a paper napkin as she joined him on the bench.

"I appreciate you taking the time to meet, Raymond."

"Not a problem, I had an afternoon slot free. I thought you'd given up those herbal coffin nails?"

Baize stubbed out her cigarette on a garbage bin. "Give me a break, Raymond. It's been another one of those days."

He handed her a paper bag and a bottle of spring water. "This time I got you the Weight Watchers special, no butter, no mayo. Tuna, salad, no cheese, drizzled with light French dressing, in a freshly baked crusty roll."

"You're spoiling me."

Baize laid the bag on the bench and looked out at the park.

Joggers, lost-looking Asian tourists, herds of office and department store workers having lunch on the grass or park benches, milking the sunshine. A quartet practicing, Beethoven soft on the air.

"You coping okay, Baize?"

"It's been a struggle. Sometimes I don't know how I haven't hung myself from a rafter." She unscrewed the water bottle cap. "Want to tell me how it went?"

Leon licked a dab of mustard mayonnaise from his fingers. "Baize, we've been family friends a long time."

"Thirty years."

"You know I can't talk with you about Carla as my patient. Twenty years ago, sure, but now she's all grown up. Now it's doctor-patient confidentiality."

"You don't think her case warrants a little extra consideration?"

"Sure I do. But you want me to get disbarred? Have to move to some hick town out in the tranquilizer belt and start over?"

"I'm not asking to see your every note and record, Raymond."

"Is it what we spoke about the other day in my office? About Carla seeing the remains of her mom and Luka? Because if it is, she hasn't contacted me yet."

"No?"

"No. But when she needs to talk, I'll be there for her, Baize."

"The remains weren't Luka's."

"What?"

"The DNA didn't match."

"That . . . that's wonderful news. Isn't it, Baize?"

"Carla believes Alma saw Luka in the hospital afterward. That he may have somehow survived. There's a chance, but a slim one if I'm to be honest."

"Why?"

"Dan and I tried everything we could think of over the years to try to discover whether David, Lana, and Luka were dead or alive. I'm just praying our hopes aren't shattered again."

"Is that what you wanted to talk about?"

"No, I wanted a general chat, Raymond."

"How general?"

"You could start with how you think Carla might handle what she's learned about her family. Is that nonspecific enough a question?"

Leon held up his palms in a helpless gesture. "It's kind of hard to say at this stage."

"Because she's got so much on her plate?"

"Pretty much. Discovering right after her husband died that she had a completely other life, then seeing her mom's remains, and what she thought were her brother's, is a heck of a lot to deal with. Add to that the fact that she's pregnant. She's suffered overwhelmingly, but it amazes me she hasn't had a complete psychotic breakdown."

"Me, too."

"I guess what people fail to understand is that the trauma is not in the event, but in the body and mind of the victim because of the overwhelmingness. A person can suffer severe injury being attacked by an animal, but if they don't get overwhelmed and are able to kill the animal or run away and escape, they won't end up with any trauma."

Baize sighed as a couple of panting, spandex-clad joggers ran past.

"You know, I used to think love was easy. But it's not, is it, Raymond?"

"No, it's not."

"So much of the time it can be wonderful, warm, fulfilling. Other times it's the most complex and frustrating experience in our lives."

"What is it, Baize? You sounded pretty troubled when you called."

"I'm hopeful about Luka, I'll admit that. But I'm also worried, Raymond."

"Go on."

"Worried because Carla hates Shavik with such a vehemence that it's truly frightening."

"She wouldn't be human if she didn't."

"Anger's boiling inside her like lava, ready to erupt."

"Anger's normal. Anger against the perpetrators and a quest for justice. We'll try to deal with her issues over time."

"That's precisely what worries me."

Leon saw tears at the edges of Baize's eyes. She gave a heavy sigh, struggling with her emotions.

"What are you saying, Baize?"

"I know it's a little late to be admitting this. But all those years ago I didn't tell you everything about Carla."

Leon fell silent, waited.

"Dan and I didn't tell Carla everything about her past, either. Not the whole truth."

"Where's this going?"

"I didn't tell her everything about her past because . . ."

"Because what, Baize?"

"Because I felt it would be way too much for her to handle. But it's been killing my conscience, tearing me apart. Part of me feels it's my duty to tell her. Yet another part of me is afraid of how she'll react."

"What are we talking about here?"

Baize opened her purse, and took out a clear plastic bag containing a sheaf of familiar-looking yellowed pages.

Leon felt the reality sink in. "The diary's missing pages?"

"I removed them, many years ago."

"Why?"

"I didn't want Carla to see them."

"Why not?"

"The pages have to do with Carla's mom and dad."

Leon looked at her, saying nothing.

"Lana was already pregnant when they married."

The doctor frowned. "Was that such a huge deal?"

"Lana was in love with another man. She became pregnant. He let her down. She moved to Dubrovnik to avoid any shame to her father."

"I see. Carla knows nothing about this?"

Baize shook her head. "David and Lana never wanted Carla to feel like she was an outsider who didn't belong in the family. The opposite, in fact. David made a huge effort to make sure she knew that he loved her."

"What is written on the missing pages?"

"Reflections, thoughts, confessions."

"About what?"

"The man Lana once loved. I couldn't let Carla see her mother's words in case she felt hurt."

"Baize, you want my advice? Don't stress yourself about this. David loved Carla like a daughter, and in the end that's all that matters."

"Can you imagine if Carla had to stand up in a court of human rights? I guess that's partly why we didn't pursue a prosecution as vigorously as we should have. Why we didn't want her to visit the past again."

"I'm not with you."

"You still don't get it, do you Raymond?"

"Get what?"

"Why I couldn't tell her."

"Tell her what?"

"That the man Carla hates, the man she despises above everyone else and blames for destroying her life—that man is her real father."

70

"She left?"

"Yeah, in her car."

"When?"

"After ten a.m."

"How did she seem?"

"Okay, I guess."

"You guess?"

"Well, maybe, sorta."

"Maybe, sorta? What kind of answer is that?"

"I don't know, Regan. Maybe see seemed kinda distracted. You think Dad likes her?"

Josh sat in front of the office computer tapping keys, as Regan leafed through a stack of bills on the desk.

"You know your dad. He keeps his cards close to his chest. Ask him yourself. He ought to be back soon."

"I Googled her some more on the Net."

"Yeah?"

Josh turned the computer screen around to show various images of Jan Lane onstage, playing the piano. Others of him and Carla outside concert halls.

"That's her husband. Someone blew up their car. That's what the newspapers said. Weird, huh?"

Regan looked at the screen. "Yeah, I know. I checked, too."

"It made me kind of wonder."

"What did?"

Josh fell silent.

Regan stared at him. "You going to tell me?"

"I didn't want to say it until Dad got home."

"Say what?"

"In case he got angry."

"About what?"

"Miss Carla wanted to borrow one of dad's guns."

Regan slapped a sheaf of papers on the desk, and stared back at Josh. "What did you just say?"

"She . . . she wanted me to open the gun safe for her."

"What for?"

"She said she had to go someplace and it may be dangerous. She said that's why Dad's been teaching her how to shoot. I wanted to call Dad, ask him. But she kind of made me help her. She said she'd square it with him."

"Josh, are you making this up? 'Cause it ain't funny, boy."

"I swear. You can check the safe for yourself. She took a Sig."

"You *opened* the safe for her?"

"Naw, but I told her the combination was on top of your closet. She kind of insisted. Said it was real important, she needed the gun."

"She take anything else?"

"A silencer, a box of cartridges, some gun-cleaning stuff."

"Holy cow."

"You think Dad's going to be angry?"

"I'd say you're in deep doo-doo, buddy."

"Don't say that, Regan."

"What am I supposed to say? 'Well done, here's a medal for ya'?"

A vehicle pulled up outside. Regan peered out.

"Here's your chance to find out what your daddy thinks."

Ronnie strode in, carrying a cardboard box full of office supplies. He slapped them on the desk, looked from Josh to Regan.

"How come you both look like we've been robbed?"

"Tell your daddy, Josh."

71

Ronnie bounded up the cabin steps and yanked open the front door.

Her luggage was gone, the room left clean and tidy.

A faint scent of perfume lingered in the air but that was the only trace of her.

Regan followed him up the steps and inside.

"She left a little after ten?"

"Yeah, about that."

"How'd she seem at the hospital when you saw her?"

"Pretty okay. Why did she check herself out, Ronnie?"

"It's complicated." He took out his cell, called Carla's number.

It rang out. Her voice message kicked in. "It's Ronnie. Call me as soon as you get this." He flicked off his phone.

"You want to tell me what's going on with the gun?"

"Not really."

"Why not?"

"It's complicated, too. Story of my life."

"When I saw her this morning, I told her."

"Told her what?"

"I wasn't dumb. That I sensed something was going on. That I didn't want you involved in anything dangerous because of Josh. You're not going to do that, are you, Ronnie?"

He turned toward the door.

"*Are* you, Ronnie?"

"No."

"Where are you going?"

"I figure she needs to return the rental to Knoxville. There's a flight late this afternoon to New York. She could be planning to be on it. Can you hold the fort?"

"Will she be okay?"

"Maybe. If I can talk some sense into her."

*   *   *

Five minutes later Regan was in the office when an SUV drove up.

A man came in, rapped his knuckles against the open office door. Tall, dark-haired, good-looking. A bad-boy impish smile, his teeth slightly prominent.

He wore a baseball cap, jeans and boots, and a pale blue casual shirt. A couple of bright-colored fishing lures were pinned onto the side of his baseball cap.

On the counter next to him was a dummy grenade, set on a wooden plinth. He picked it up. Inscribed on the plinth it said COMPLAINT DEPARTMENT. Attached to the grenade's pin-pull was a slip of paper that read PICK A NUMBER.

"Funny." Billy Davix leaned against the door frame and looked at Regan.

"That's the South for you. Full of crazy but likable rednecks."

"I thought it wasn't PC to call them that anymore?"

"Not to their faces. Unless you like the feel of a gun barrel up your nose. Appalachian Americans sounds better."

Billy flashed a smile. "Fish biting around here?"

"They're always biting around here, honey. They're like piranha."

"That's what I like to hear." Billy pushed himself away from the door frame. "Got a cabin for a traveling fisherman for a few nights? And a bass boat to hire?"

"Sure."

As Regan got up, Billy winked at Josh, tipped his baseball cap. "Hiya, son. You surfing the Net?"

Josh nodded.

Billy looked down at the screen, saw the images, raised his eyes, tapped it with his fingernail. "Hey, that's Jan Lane. The pianist. He's world-famous. Or at least he was. Wasn't he killed a short while back? I loved his music, especially live."

"You heard him play?"

"Sure, once. In Carnegie Hall, New York."

"Was he good?"

"Yeah, he was a blast."

* * *

"Sweet. All the comforts of home."

"Where's that, mister?"

Regan followed Billy out onto the cabin's veranda.

He raised his baseball cap, showing a full head of jet-black hair, and wiped his brow with the back of his hand. "New Jersey. But I'm a redneck at heart. Name's Billy Lubbock. My folks moved up north from Roanoke when I was a kid. I'll need some fishing lures."

"No problem. How many nights?"

"A couple, maybe more if they're really biting. Anyplace around here a guy can get a beer and a meal in the evening?"

"The county's pretty much dry."

"No bars?"

"A few. You could try the Frog's Rest, ten miles going east down the main road. If you see a sign that says 'Banjo Lessons' you know you've gone too far."

"I'll remember that."

"The beer's good and the company's okay, if you don't mind country and western. Last food orders are at nine thirty."

"You ever go there?"

"Sure. It's about the only place to go around here most evenings." Regan noticed the man wore no wedding ring.

He looked at her. Their eyes met. He flashed the Billy Bob smile.

Something passed between them, he could tell.

Regan felt her face blush. "Let's go pick you out a boat and some lures."

The sun beat down on Billy's neck.

He sat in the boat, a hundred yards offshore. A pack of Marlboro Lights lay on the seat beside him, the lighter stuffed inside the pack. The line was out, nothing biting yet, not that he cared if he caught anything.

No sign of the woman who checked him in but he could make out the boy in the wheelie, sitting on the dock, looking out at him.

The video camcorder in Billy's hand was on, and he panned it left and right, zooming in and out when he needed to, getting shots of the marina from every angle. Details were important. He already had the aerial maps, the road maps, and the waterway route maps.

When he finished he put away the recorder.

He picked up his cell, punched the number.

Arkov answered. "Yeah?"

"I'm here. She's got some connection to the place, for sure. I'll get back to you as soon as I know more."

"Take care of it. I'm counting on you. The woman and the kid, too, if need be."

"You think Mr. Shavik is okay with that?"

"Not your worry, Billy. Just get it done."

"Sure."

"Now tell me everything you've got."

When Billy finally ended the call, he sat back in the boat, studying the marina, trying to figure out his next moves as he lit a Marlboro and inhaled slowly.

72

Shavik sat in the basement, listening to Angel breathing.

Deep, heavy breaths that told him she was completely unconscious. Her makeup was a mess, her head slumped to one side. He gripped her chin, lifted her face. Her eyes were closed, a purple bruise on her cheek where Arkov struck her. "Can you hear me, Angel?"

Nothing.

He shook her face, patted her cheeks. No reaction.

Two hours lost because of the overdose of scopolamine and still no response. He looked over angrily at the discarded syringe, just as the door burst open and Arkov returned, looking pleased with himself. He held a small glass bottle in his hand. "Got it."

"You're sure it'll work?" Shavik asked.

"It depends how bad she is, but it's worth a try."

Arkov unscrewed the cap. A strong smell of ammonia salts wafted on the air. He held the open bottle under Angel's nose. Her reaction was instant.

Her head jerked back, then snapped forward, and she dry-retched, trying to throw up on an empty stomach, but nothing came, only dribbles of mucus and saliva.

When she finished retching, she groaned, blinked, looked up at them, her pupils trying to focus.

Arkov grinned, and screwed the top back on the bottle. "Looks like it's zombie time."

Ronnie walked through the lines of polished rental cars in the Hertz lot opposite the arrivals building at Tyson Airport.

He came to a woman in a kiosk. Her name tag said Peggy.

He tipped his hat, smiled. "Ma'am."

"May I help you, sir?"

"My wife returned a rental this afternoon. White Toyota Camry. She may have left her purse in the car and wanted me to check."

"Your wife's name, sir?"

"Carla Lane."

"One moment, please." Peggy tapped her keyboard, frowned. "You're sure she returned the vehicle to Hertz?"

"Why?"

"I've no record of anyone named Lane returning a rental, sir."

"You sure about that?"

"Absolutely. It's been a quiet day. No white Toyota Camry, either."

"Seems like my wife's been lying to me, Peggy."

He heard the angry roar of a jet taking off as he walked back to the airport parking lot.

Ronnie took off his hat, tossed it onto the passenger seat, and slid into the pickup. He sighed, ran a hand through his hair.

He didn't touch the GPS on the dash. New Jersey was a long drive, at least twelve hours. He'd never make up enough time to catch up with her.

He took out his cell and tried calling her number again.

Her voice mail kicked in once more.

This time he didn't bother leaving a message.

He tossed his cell aside and flicked open the glove compartment.

Inside was the envelope with the copy photographs of Shavik's house in Cape May, and he spread out the images on the passenger seat. He studied them, tapping the steering wheel with his fingers, his mind ravaged.

At the back of the glove compartment was a holstered Glock 26 with a spare clip that he kept for his own personal protection. He took out the handgun, stared at it, and again felt racked by indecision.

And again he asked himself the same question.

Could he break his pledge to Josh?

The same pledge he gave to Regan just hours ago.

And most of all, the promise he made to himself.

On the battlefield and in life he'd seen people behave just like Carla.

Driven by a powerful need to retaliate for the death of a comrade or a loved one, they couldn't see past the red fog.

All that mattered was revenge.

With Carla, it went even deeper once you factored in her brother.

Big question.

How could he protect her? As much from Shavik and his kind as from herself.

As Ronnie sat there, he was conscious of time slipping away. Drops of sweat dripped from his brow onto the back on his hand. He wiped them away with his sleeve, touching his temples, feeling his heartbeat pulsing there.

No matter what, he couldn't break his promise.

He just couldn't, not for the life of him.

Finally, he replaced the Glock in the glove compartment.

He heard the harsh roar of another jet take off.

The big question came back.

How to save Carla from herself?

There was really only one way he could do it.

73

Carla drove off the highway and coasted into a McDonald's drive-through.

She ordered a black coffee, then pulled into one of the parking spaces. She killed the engine, stepped out to stretch her legs, and sipped the hot coffee.

Her body ached after almost nine hours on the road. She turned on her cell. A missed call from Ronnie, and his voice message, asking her to call.

She desperately wanted to call him back, wanted to hear the reassurance of a male voice. Yet in her heart she knew this was her own private battle. It was wrong of her to expect him to risk his life for her, or break his promise to his son.

But the closer she got to New Jersey, the more she realized how bleak her situation was. Fear began to worm its way under her skin. She felt overwhelmed by hopelessness.

Someone like Shavik was too formidable an opponent for a woman like her.

Arkov, his bodyguards, and a property secured by state-of-the-art alarm system made her dread how impossible her task was.

And yet she felt driven—driven to know what happened to the small boy with the milky white eye whose face would haunt her until the day she died.

A razor-sharp memory flashed before her. Of Luka holding on to her, not wanting her to go, his face full of fear as he clutched her dress. Having to pry his tiny, determined fingers away, uncurling them one by one as he cried.

It ripped her heart out. She felt his anguish, his fear and panic and terror all growing within her again.

She closed her eyes, and recalled their pitiful last words.

"*Carla, please . . . Carla don't leave me, please . . .*"

"*I'll come back for you, Luka, I promise. Carla will come back. Don't be afraid.*"

She fought the heartache, opened her wet eyes.

In desperation, she tried put her faith and trust in God, in some vague notion of a divine justice. But it didn't reassure her, no more than it quelled the rising terror that grew inside her like a monster. And yet despite her fear the same desperate need drove her on.

Find Luka.

She climbed back into the car and rested the hot coffee cup in the holder.

One hundred and sixty miles to go, according to the GPS. If she could keep up her speed, and met no traffic delays, she'd reach Cape May in three hours.

She might just make it in time.

It was 9 p.m. exactly.

She restarted the engine.

I'm coming for you, Luka.

I'm finally coming for you.

"Show me the text."

Arkov held out Angel's cell for Shavik to see. Newark at 1 it is.

Shavik considered, then knelt in front of Angel again. "Talk to me, Angel. Tell me why."

"Why?"

"Why open the safe?"

"Ledger . . ."

"But why do it?"

"My mother, my sister."

"What about them?"

Dreamy eyes settled on Shavik, then swiveled, tried to focus on Arkov. The words sounded like a tired but angry snarl. "He . . . killed them."

"Where?"

"Camp."

"What camp?"

Silence.

"What camp, Angel?"

"Merviak."

Shavik's gaze shifted to the faded scars on each of her wrists. The scars she once told him were a long-ago suicide attempt.

He and Arkov exchanged glances.

Arkov went to speak, but Shavik held up a hand for him to be silent.

"Tell me about Carla Lane."

Angel's head rolled on her neck like a ball joint, then jerked upright again.

She looked comatose, as if behind her sluggish eyes there were strange dreams, confusion, delirium. She couldn't help but answer every question. It was as if she were a submissive child, eager to spill secrets.

"Do you know her? Do you know Carla Lane?"

"Yes . . ."

"Tell me about her, Angel. Why did you meet her at Newark Airport? What did you discuss?"

A dribble of spittle slid down the corner of Angel's mouth. Her lips parted, mumbled. "Lots of things."

"Be specific. What did you discuss?"

"Arkov. Shavik."

"What about us?"

Silence.

"Talk to me, Angel. Tell me."

"I gave her . . ."

"Gave her what?"

"Photographs."

"Of what?"

"House . . . photographs."

"Photographs of this house?"

"Yes."

"Is Carla Lane working alone?"

"She was alone."

"I asked, is she working alone, Angel?"

"I . . . don't . . . know."

"Where is she?"

Silence.

"Where is she, Angel? Is she here, in New Jersey?"

"Coming."

"Coming where?"

"Here."

"Tell me, Angel. I want to know everything."

The moon was a big silver ball.

Shavik stood there, on the boardwalk, hearing the waves dragging on the shingle.

He drew on his cigarette, exhaled. He needed air, to escape the stuffy basement. To escape the inevitability of Angel's death.

Her death was so senseless. But out of his hands.

He looked back, knowing the moment was about to happen, narrowing his eyes toward the basement window.

He thought he heard the faint thud of a silenced shot, and the glimmer of a muzzle flash in the darkness.

He felt . . .

What did he feel?

Nothing.

That was always what troubled him.

There were times when he tried to find his heart. The simple boy who long ago had a thousand splendid dreams, a beloved father and good in his soul. But the journey back was too difficult, the road too dark and painful.

For some reason he remembered a summer's day. One of those days his father took him along with him when he drove to Belgrade on business, and they would picnic in the hills above Novi Sad, the views splendid all the way down to the Danube.

Those were the lonely days when his mother was gone and there was just the two of them in the big old house and he felt the sharpness of her loss. The nights when for months after her death he would stay awake to listen for her footsteps on the stairs, but they never came.

On that day looking down at the Danube his father seemed to sense acutely his son's loss. "I know there's just the two of us but we'll get by, Mila. We'll miss your mama but we'll be brave for her, you and I. The way she'd want us to be."

His father winked, squeezing him close, hiding his own sadness, stroking his hair.

Afterward, he'd fallen asleep in his father's arms. He could still remember the peace and serenity of that day. It seemed such a long time since he'd felt that sense of stillness in his heart.

He heard footsteps, and cut off the memory. The less you thought about things that sadden you the better.

Arkov appeared, hurrying down the garden steps and out the wrought-iron gate, his feet echoing on the boardwalk, a grin on his face.

He loved death, that one. Relished killing.

"It's done. We'll get rid of her body."

A long silence. Shavik's face was grim, the light fading in his eyes as he again went into that part of himself that no one could reach.

"You think she told us the truth?"

Arkov clutched Angel's cell phone. "Every word. That's one drug that won't let you lie."

"Talk to our sources. Sound them out gently for any hint of trouble. I want to be sure there's no police involvement. You sent the text?"

"Just like you said: 'Don't call. But all good for tonight.'"

"No reply from her yet?"

Right on cue Angel's cell beeped twice. Arkov studied the illuminated blue screen and hit a button. His face sparked.

"Seems like we're in business. It says: 'On the way.'"

"Give it to me. Let me see."

Shavik took the phone, stared down at the text.

"We'll be waiting for her."

74

UNION COUNTY, TENNESSEE

The bar was all neon beer signs, cheap plastic seats, and dim lighting.

Billy guessed he was the only guy in the place who had showered and shaved, let alone dabbed on some aftershave.

This was a place of tattoos and missing teeth.

Guys huddled over beers, mumbling to each other. A few wearing cowboy hats and boots, or grubby overalls, others wearing Mossy Oak camouflage deer-stalker outfits, some with depressed-looking wives who sat sipping beer and gazing blankly at the walls, as if they wanted to cut their wrists, or had at least considered the option before venturing out with their partners that evening.

A selection of deer antlers hung on one wall; on another was a glass case with a huge, shiny preserved bass fish the size of a small shark. A blue-and-white neon Miller Light sign glared above the bar mirror.

Entertainment was provided by three overweight beards playing guitar, keyboard, and banjo, and crucifying a Willie Nelson song. A band that sounded like the only notes they cared about were the ones the bar owner slipped them at the end of the night.

Billy sipped his Bud. Too bad he'd left his gun in his luggage; otherwise he'd have shot every last one of them.

What made it even worse was that almost every dish on the menu was some kind of fried catfish.

He chose the only other unhealthy option, a Cajun cheeseburger, fries and a beer, and a Jack Daniel's chaser.

He needed it to chase away the greasy taste of the burger—had just knocked it back when in the bar mirror's reflection he saw the door snap open and three women come in. Pretty, their nails and hair done, war paint on.

He saw Regan whisper with her girlfriends before they all went to sit in a corner booth.

The place wasn't that busy for a Friday night, no hooting-hollering, yee-haws, or line dancing—or did they still do that these days? He sipped his beer, took another bite of the burger, wanted to spit it out.

"Hi . . ."

He swallowed as he saw her approach in the mirror, felt the tap on his shoulder, swung round in his bar stool, and the smile that had always been one of his best features lit up his face. "Hi, Regan."

"So you decided to risk it?"

"Life and limb. Must be a gambler."

"How's the burger?"

"A grade up from shoe leather."

"I should have warned you."

"Funny thing is, the sign outside says Bar and Grill, except there's nothing grilled."

"This is the South, honey. It's deep-fried all the way. Then deep-fry it again and cover it in gravy. Just to make sure you've killed the taste."

He nudged away the plate. "No harm done. Buy you a drink?"

Her neck seemed to flush, even in the neon light. "I'm . . . I'm here with a couple of friends, Billy."

He tipped his baseball cap, with a hint of the shy, little-boy-lost kind that most women liked. "No problem. Hope you don't think I'm being forward?"

"No . . . no, not at all. Maybe a little later, when I've had time to talk with my friends?"

"Sure. I'm not going anywhere."

She turned to go. "How's the fishing?"

"Pretty good; they're biting, that's for sure."

The band was playing a Dolly Parton number. "Nine to Five." Had Dolly been there, angel that she was, she still would have thrown up, then probably blasted the suckers with a double-barrel.

"Is it always this good?" Billy asked, ordering another round. The band finished murdering the song and took a beer break.

Regan sipped her margarita. "Midweek they've got open season for new bands to try out."

"Yeah?"

"Those are the nights I wish I was deaf."

He grinned. She had a sense of humor, this one. Her skin was dusky, her bare shoulders golden brown.

Regan toyed with the straw in her glass, flicking it with a pink glossed nail. "So what brought you to Union County Marina?"

"I was passing through, thought I'd try it. This time of year I usually take a couple of weeks' vacation, drive south with my son, go fishing or hunting. Matt's fourteen. My only boy."

"His mom doesn't mind you two boys haring off like that?"

"Not these last ten years. Left us for a car salesman she had a fling with. The guy took my trade-in and my wife. We've never seen her since."

"I'm sorry to hear that."

"Don't knock it. Best deal I ever got. She and I were already on the slippery slope. Matt's staying with my sister and her kids in Lexington this trip. It's getting to the point when it's no fun for him vacationing with Dad no more. It's all about kids his own age."

As he turned back to his beer, Regan noticed his profile, took a sip of her margarita, and said, "You know, you look like that actor, Billy Bob Thornton?"

He slipped off his cap, laid it on the bar, running his hand through his full head of hair. "You're being kind, or else you're shortsighted. What about you? You married? I guess not, being out with the girls Friday night."

"Once. Water under the bridge."

"How'd you end up working the dock?"

"It's a family business. My brother runs it, I help out."

"The boy yours?"

"My brother Ronnie's. Josh. He's a great kid."

"He looks it. I didn't see Ronnie around, did I?"

"He's in town on business, but he'll be back."

"Yeah? Maybe I'll get to meet him later?"

"You never know with Ronnie; he keeps his own hours."

He nudged away the empty chaser, wanted to make sure he didn't ask too many questions right away and make her suspicious. "Well, I guess I better let you get back to your girlfriends, Regan. Time to hit the road."

"You're heading back to the dock?"

"I promised to call my boy, and I got some work calls to make."

"What kind of work you do?"

"I kill things for a living."

"You what?"

"Licensed to kill, that's me. I've got my own pest extermination firm. Bugbusters. Want to hear my slogan? Pest in Peace."

She giggled. "How's business?"

"Always in demand. Folks always got something they need rid of."

He picked up his cap. "It's been good talking to you, Regan, enjoyed it. And I don't mean this to sound like a come-on, I really don't, but if you feel like a nightcap later, I'd be glad if you joined me. I'll be on my porch, admiring that lake view of yours."

"It does."

"What?"

"Sound like a come-on. But I just might take you up on the offer."

75

Billy parked his SUV outside his cabin and switched off the engine.

The sound of crickets cluttered the warm night air. Walking up to his front door, he looked back.

Regan's cabin was dimly lit, the blue flicker of a TV on inside. He saw a curtain flutter and a head appear, then it disappeared and the curtain settled. The kid, probably up watching TV, and checking out the engine noise.

Billy noticed no extra vehicles parked outside Regan's place.

He turned the key and let himself into his cabin. He opened his suitcase. The .45 Kimber automatic was there, and the silencer, along with the hollow-point ammo he bought on the way. Next to it was a brown bag with a bottle of Jack Daniel's. He took out the bottle, grabbed two glasses from the bathroom, then moved out onto the veranda and sat at the wooden table.

The dusky Milky Way glittered, the water glassy calm. A faint sound of laughter and music drifted, someone having a party in one of the houseboats.

He sat on the veranda a few minutes, smoking a Marlboro Light, thinking things through.

A hundred yards along the boardwalk the dock office loomed, its pale vinyl siding a blob of gray in the darkness. Stubbing out his cigarette first, he removed his boots and socks, and stood up in his bare feet.

Easing himself over the veranda, he padded toward the office.

The door was locked.

A sign stuck on the paintwork said: NO CASH KEPT HERE. He moved around the back, where he'd noticed the second entrance. Halfway there he stood on a sharp pebble and recoiled, shuffling around on one leg until the jolting pain in his foot eased.

He tried the back door. Locked, too.

He took a lock-pick set and pencil flashlight from his pocket. It was one of those fancy tactical flashlights with different settings. He switched it to the dim blue ultraviolet light. He got the door open in less than a minute.

He hesitated before entering the darkness.

The office had no hardwired alarm—he'd checked when he stepped in that afternoon. But he shone the blue light about to make sure there were no motion sensors or battery-operated devices that he might trigger. His practiced eyes saw none.

He inched over to the desk and filing cabinet. No need for the picks this time; the top drawer slid open with a squeak. He searched, found nothing except a few filed letters from a veteran's organization—

interesting, Ronnie Kilgore was ex-military, special forces. But he hit pay dirt when he slid out the second drawer.

The guest book was inside, the brown covered one he'd filled in that afternoon. He sat at the desk, the ultraviolet light hard on his eyes as he flicked back through the pages.

It took a him a few minutes but then he grinned as he saw the signature, the name and address in block letters.

"Hey, baby, looks like we're in business."

76

The Learjet entered New York airspace at 11 p.m. after its long haul across the Atlantic, skimming above the clouds at thirty-four thousand feet.

After a brief fuel stop in Shannon, Ireland, and another in Boston to clear U.S. customs and immigration, it carried on with its filed flight path to the five-thousand-foot runway at Cape May.

Sitting in a leather passenger seat, Ivan Arkov was stretched out, dozing beneath a blanket.

One of his bodyguards came through the cabin, waking him. "The captain says twenty minutes, sir."

A groggy Arkov felt the Lear sink on its descent. He's slept badly, tossed and turned. Conflict raging inside his head, his problem niggling him all during the flight.

He yawned, sat up. He was still in reasonably good shape for seventy-two but every time he woke his body seemed to ache with more pains. Old age, someone once told him, was like frying bacon naked. You knew it was going to hurt, you just didn't know where.

More and more his thoughts turned to a successor. And there lay his conflict.

Two contenders. Boris or Mila?

Blood or brains?

He buttoned his shirt, tied the knot on his silk tie. Below, New York's dazzling blaze of lights. The aircraft banked to port, descending toward New Jersey and Cape May.

Arkov rubbed his face in his hands.

Mila Shavik, highly capable, still hungry for power.

But Boris was his own blood.

Really, it all came down to *kanun,* unswerving loyalty to the clan.

And Arkov had devised a final test to decide his successor.

It would be the ultimate test of loyalty.

He smiled, amused by the irony.

He heard the landing gear whir into place.

Minutes later the Lear touched down with a squeal of rubber.

The Lear taxied to the end of the runway, and the engines died with a whine.

A polished black Escalade SUV waited on the apron. The jet's passenger door opened with a pneumatic hiss, and the cabin flooded with the salt air of Delaware Bay.

Shavik was there, waiting as Arkov came down the steps. He kissed the old man on both cheeks. "Ivan."

"Boris didn't see fit to greet his father?" Arkov said grumpily.

"There's been a development."

The Escalade cruised at a steady sixty.

They sat in the plush rear leather seats, Shavik next to the old man.

"Tell me about this Angel."

"It was personal. She was at the Merviak camp. She made contact with the musician, Jan Lane, after she recognized Boris and me in one of the clubs."

"That's how it started?"

"So it seems."

"It seems you also made a bad choice in women, Mila. What about Lane's wife?"

"It appears she wants to avenge her husband's death. Right now she's on her way to my home." He explained about the text to Angel's phone.

"She's working alone?"

"That's the way it looks."

"Explain."

"She's an amateur, driven by revenge."

"That doesn't mean she hasn't involved the authorities."

"If she had, we'd know about it by now. But our sources have heard nothing."

Arkov pursed his lips, considered, then ran a hand over his face, his tiredness showing after the long Atlantic crossing. "There's still more to it, Mila."

"How so?"

"An irony. How long have we know each other?"

"Over thirty years."

The old man laid a clawlike hand on Shavik's arm. "You remember the day I taught you the meaning of survival? And of loyalty to your family?"

"What about it?"

"Your father was working in Pristina and you stayed with Boris and me. Already I saw great potential in you. A bright boy, quick to learn. I wanted to teach you an important lesson. The same one that was taught to me as a child."

Shavik listened, unspeaking.

"I gave you a baby goat. After a month, you grew fond of it, as any boy would."

Still, Shavik said nothing.

"Then I made you slit the animal's throat. I explained that otherwise the household would have no food."

Arkov looked at him. "It taught you a vital lesson about loyalty, be it to your family or your clan. And that to survive you need to have the courage to kill something dear to you. That's the sign of a true man."

"Why do I get the feeling this isn't just about a goat, Ivan?"

"Perceptive as always, Mila. Your father died because of that prosecutor, Tanovic. That's why you hate the Bosniaks. I always told you they were scum. That Milosevic was right. We had to finish them off like vermin."

"Is there a point to all this?"

"Be patient. There was another reason why I made you kill the goat."

"Why?"

"I sensed you had a soft heart. A soft heart that had to be hardened if you were to survive in our world."

"Where's this going?"

Arkov's thin lips parted in a slit of a grin. "Aren't you sometimes amazed by life's odd quirks of fate, Mila? As if there's a strange logic to this universe we don't comprehend? You made another bad choice in women years ago. With that Bosniak, the prosecutor's daughter you knew."

Shavik fell silent.

"Carla Lane."

"What about her?"

"She's not just a witness who can destroy us all."

"What do you mean?"

"Her mother was Lana Tanovic . . ."

77

A thin fog rolled in from the sea as she turned off Exit 0 on the Garden State Parkway.

Ahead lay the coast, and Cape May's slim white lighthouse stabbing the night sky. Quaint, gingerbread houses with picket fences, a vast array of Gothic and Victorian villas and mansions. The last place she'd expect someone like Shavik to live.

She drove east, toward an inlet with rows of impressive houses overlooking Delaware Bay. Stopping in a parking lot near a beach, she switched off the engine. She sat there, trying to calm herself.

She felt her hands shaking violently. Out of fear, she was tempted to simply to call the police, but she didn't doubt Angel's warning. Shavik would be gone before they arrived. She rolled down her window.

Fluorescent pools spilled from walkway lights. Was it her imagination, or was the fog getting thicker?

A salt tang on the air, but no breeze, the only sound the surf dragging on the beach. A sound she and Jan loved to listen to at night.

It made her think of him. She put a hand to her stomach. No cramps. But anxiety gnawing at her so much it made her feel nauseous.

Wherever you are, Jan, please try and protect our baby tonight.
Please.

For some reason a thought resurfaced: What had happened to her in Shavik's office all those years ago? Would she ever know? Did she even want to?

She shivered, tied back her hair with a band, and slipped on the black woolen hat.

Her hands shook as she reached under her seat for the Sig. Laying it on her lap, she fitted the tac flashlight and retrieved the silencer and the box of cartridges.

She slipped on the shooter's gloves and used the silicone cloth to remove the cartridges one by one from the box, loading the magazine, and the two spares. Her hands shook so badly she dropped at least half a dozen cartridges and had to scramble for them on the floor.

Three magazines of fifteen rounds each.

She felt her blood pounding in her temples. Would she really have the courage to kill Shavik? A surge of doubt threatened her, but a powerful memory crushed it.

In her mind she saw the faces of the camp victims: tormented women and children. The fathers and youths torn from their families to face certain death.

Then she saw again the shriveled remains in the closet and a livid rage took hold.

Her shaking stopped. A strange calmness came over her.

She stepped from the Toyota and pulled on her dark zip-up hoodie. Her body ached after the long drive. Slipping the Sig into one pocket and the silencer into the other, she shut the car door, flicked on the alarm, and tucked the keys into her jeans, along with the spare magazines.

A sandy inlet lay ahead, a thin swirl of fog misting the air like smoke.

Somewhere out there was Shavik's residence.

In her mind, she heard Luka's voice again, calling out to her.

She dug her hands into the pockets of her hoodie and started to walk toward the inlet.

Her feet dragged in the sandy soil.

A few hundred yards on she saw it. Pale stucco. A private board-walk with neon lights on above the jetty, a huge, sleek black powerboat tied up, its lacquered paintwork gleaming.

Even in the dim lunar light she could make out the shape of an eagle in the wrought-iron gate, the faint blue glow of an electronic key-pad next to it.

She approached the gate. She saw steps leading up to a swimming pool. A few dim lights on inside the house. Her heart hammered again in her chest, so hard she could hardly breathe. She took deep breaths, and pulled out the Sig.

With trembling hands, she screwed on the silencer.

She fingered the gate keypad, carefully entering the code—2704—and hit the pound sign.

The gate solenoid sprang open with a buzzing sound, drowned by the wash of waves. She cocked the Sig and flicked off the safety catch.

As she pushed at the gate, it gave a tiny squeal. She gave it a few moments before she moved inside.

The Sig was outstretched in her hand but she didn't dare yet to turn on the tac light. Moving up the steps past the pool, she came to patio doors. Darkness lay beyond. She heard a scraping noise behind her.

She spun round and a fist slammed into her face.

She staggered back and fell to the ground, dazed, dropping the gun. It clattered on tile as rough hands dragged her to her feet and powerful security lights blazed on.

Facing her was Boris Arkov, a baseball bat in his hand, a grin on his face.

Two muscular bodyguards held her arms.

Arkov grabbed her savagely by the hair. "Thought you were being smart, didn't you?"

He punched her again, this time hard in the left temple.

Carla felt a pain blossom in her skull.

And everything went out of focus and she passed out.

78

Billy was sitting on the porch, his boots back on, his feet up on the table.

A bucket of crushed ice from the refrigerator stood next to them. A yellow citronella candle he'd found in one of the drawers glowed, keeping the mosquitoes away. As he lit a Marlboro in the candle flame he saw Regan pull up in a white Dodge Durango.

She peered over toward his cabin but went up the steps to her own place and let herself in.

He waited, flicked on his portable radio-CD player, kept it low, and the strains of Itzhak Perlman playing Beethoven seemed just made for the star-filled night. Five minutes later the front door opened again and she strolled down to join him.

"Beautiful night." He stood politely.

"We get a lot of them around here."

"Jack Daniel's and ice okay? Or I've got beer in the fridge."

"Jack's good."

"Will Josh be okay on his own, or is your brother back? I hate to think of Josh being left on his own."

"Ronnie ought to be back soon. But Josh'll be okay. Don't let that wheelchair fool you. He's able to take care of himself."

She sat across from him. He could smell her perfume. He splashed the bourbon into her glass, scooped in some ice.

"Your friends all gone home?"

"They decided to hang on."

"Don't tell me they're the band's groupies?"

"They're not that desperate." Regan sipped, giggled. "But you never know. There isn't much else to do around these parts. It's either the bar or the lake."

Hands behind his head, Billy looked up at the stars. "Know what you mean. Still, a man could get used to this life."

She nodded to the CD player, Perlman's silky violin in the background. "You like that kind of music?"

"I like any kind of music that's good. Classical especially."

"You don't look like the type."

"Looks can be deceiving." He smiled. "I work hard at looking like a pest controller. Truth is, I studied music for two years. Wanted to play the oboe real bad."

She giggled again. "You're kidding? The oboe? Why?"

"I have a soft heart. I felt it was a much-neglected instrument that needed some affection."

She pointed a varnished fingernail, smiling. "Now that there's a definite lie. Tell the truth."

"Okay, I played the banjo."

Her giggle rippled, and she put a hand over her mouth.

"What about you?"

"I don't play. But Josh does. Me, I like anything, really."

"Jan Lane was pretty good—Josh had a pic of him up on the computer screen. I've got a few of his CDs. You should listen to his stuff. Talent like that is rare. Tragic that he died."

"I'd never heard of him until a little while ago."

"No?"

Regan put down her glass. "It's a real coincidence. You mentioning Jan Lane like that . . ."

"Yeah?"

"His widow Carla was here recently."

"You're kidding?"

"Nope."

"How come?"

"My brother Ronnie served in the military with her grandfather."

"Guess it's a small world. Why'd she come?"

"To see Ronnie. You really like it here?"

"What's not to like? I'd give my left leg to live in a place like this. Peace, fishing, scenery. More critters than a pest controller could deal with in a lifetime."

A bee buzzed round them, then landed on the table. Billy raised his right palm, waited with the hard-eyed patience of a hunter, then slapped the table fast, squashing his target. "It doesn't pay to bumble with the B."

Regan put a hand over her face and almost snorted a laugh, leaning forward, and putting down her glass. "Either you're funny, or I've had too much to drink."

Billy wiped his palm with a paper tissue, leaned a little closer, too, scooped more ice into his glass. In the citrus light he saw expectancy glint in her eyes. Her lips were moist from the bourbon.

He figured she wanted to be kissed, but he was uncertain if it was such a good idea.

His hand came up, softly caressed her blond hair. For a moment, she seemed to go with it, and her mouth opened as she bit her lip, but for some reason she pulled back, the moment lost.

"Sorry. I . . . I don't usually do this."

"With strangers, you mean? So soon?"

"Something like that."

"That's okay. I understand. On a night like this. The stars, a few drinks, pleasant company . . ."

"I guess. Well, I better be heading to bed. Early start tomorrow."

She finished her drink, stood.

"Billy."

"Yeah?"

"I enjoyed talking tonight."

* * *

CAPE MAY

Fog everywhere.

In the few places where it was lighter, stars glittered through the smoky haze.

Shavik stood on the boardwalk, a brandy glass in his hand, his shirt open at the neck. Silence, except for the ceaseless sound of distant waves.

He was in that place again, the place inside himself that he shared with no one. For the first time in a long time he felt . . . what?

A kind of dread?

He recalled what Ivan Arkov said:

"Her mother was Lana Tanovic . . . from your hometown. Do you remember her?"

Shock lit his face the moment he heard the words, before he replied, "I . . . I knew I saw her before. But her name—her name was different."

"Saw her where?"

"In the camp."

Now Shavik stood there, breathing deeply, and took a sip of brandy.

She was a stranger to him, this young woman.

Yet could he kill her? Knowing who she really was?

His own flesh and blood?

He took a long swig from the bottle.

Conflict building in him, he could feel it.

He could never forget what happened that day more than twenty years ago in the camp office.

Never.

And the secret he told no one.

It haunted him.

He heard footsteps on the boardwalk.

Old man Arkov ambled down, looking pleased. "I took a look over the Cayman deposit."

"And?"

"A good haul this time, Mila. You did well."

"You're staying long?"

"That depends on how long the fog lasts. You look troubled."

Shavik took another swig. "There are people she may have confided in."

"That muddies things."

"I'll take care of it."

"Boris said the woman's pregnant."

"So we believe."

"Exploit that weakness. Do whatever you must to make her talk. Then send her the way of her mother."

The old man left, his footsteps fading to a hollow echo.

Shavik waited until he'd gone, then he flung the glass onto some rocks, and heard it shatter. He'd make her talk. But he knew what he was dreading.

The journey back into the private hell of his past.

A past he preferred to forget.

What monstrous dreams awaited to ambush him? What terrifying gargoyles lurked in the dark belfry of his mind?

He flexed his fingers, as if to prepare himself, then started to walk back toward the house.

Kilgore's Marina
Union County, Tennessee

Billy watched Regan stroll back to her cabin and step inside.

Billy smirked. Billy Lubbock. Pest controller. It gave him a kick, role-playing. Like his acting days. He blew out the candle, grabbed the bottle of Jack and the glasses, and brought them back into his room.

He slid out his cell and called the number. While he waited, the cell cradled between his cheek and his neck, he pulled the Kimber .45 from under his mattress, felt the solid weight of it as he screwed on the silencer.

Arkov answered.

"It's Billy. She's been here. Her name's in the guest book."

He had the book in front of him. Had taken it from the office and he'd get rid of it. He didn't want his signature anywhere. He popped two spare loaded magazines in his pocket as he filled Arkov in.

"You did well, Billy. We've made progress, too."

"Yeah?"

"Angel talked, and we've got the Lane woman."

"How?"

Arkov explained everything. "We'll deal with her. What about the guy who runs the dock?"

"His sister says he ought to be back tonight."

"I'll find out how much the Lane woman told her redneck friends. Can you can handle things your end if you need to?"

"Sure."

"I'll call you once we know. With luck, an hour or two at most."

The line died. The Kimber .45 was still in Billy's hand. He flicked out the magazine. Loaded, ready to go. He slammed the mag back into the butt and it made a familiar *click*. Man, he loved that sound.

He felt his adrenaline kicking in, his palms beginning to sweat, the way they always did before a kill.

He didn't particularly like the idea of wasting the boy in the chair, but if he had to, it was a done deal.

Pest controller. He sure liked that. A nice touch. All those zingers just came off the cuff. Bugbusters. Licensed to kill. It doesn't pay to bumble with the B.

Darn, he was good.

Another hour or two.

At most.

Then it would be time to say adios to some pests.

Buenas noches, roaches.

79

Carla jolted awake, a caustic smell piercing her nostrils.

It drifted down into her lungs like poison gas and her head snapped back, eyes wide open. She took a deep breath, felt a razor-sharp pain knife her lungs, so hard that she gasped in agony. Her hands were bound behind her back and she was seated in a wooden chair.

"Welcome back. Feeling better, sweetie?"

Boris Arkov grinned, knelt down to face her, patting her stomach. "How's the baby?"

Carla felt her blood chill.

Arkov winked, shaking his head. "Didn't the doctor tell you that pregnant women should pay attention to their health? You ought to have been more careful sticking your nose in where it wasn't wanted. Too late now."

Carla's heart sank quicker than a stone.

Arkov picked up a hypodermic syringe and filled it with the clear liquid from a small bottle. "Time to feel Satan's breath."

He grabbed her arm, painfully hard. She struggled as he went to jab the needle into her vein.

"Leave it! No drug this time."

Mila Shavik emerged from the shadows, a bottle of brandy in his hand.

His shirt was undone a few buttons, his tie loose. "Get out, Boris . . ."

"But the drug will be quicker loosening her tongue . . ."

"It could also kill her. Leave us."

"Going easy on her will get us nowhere. Her kind only respond to brute force."

"I said get out. Now."

An enraged Arkov tossed the syringe on the table and stormed out, banging the door after him.

"Boris doesn't like taking orders. He also has a fondness for violence that seems to run in his blood."

Carla said nothing.

"You know who I am?"

"Mila Shavik."

Without a word, Shavik knelt in front of her. His right hand reached out, touched her stomach as if to feel the swell there. He almost looked mesmerized.

"It's true that you're pregnant?"

Carla didn't speak, an icy shiver flooding her heart with terror.

Without a word, Shavik moved behind her, and loosened the ropes. She looked at him in disbelief, and rubbed her arms and hands.

"Boris wanted to do it the hard way. I thought first we'd just have a friendly talk, and see if we can work things out." He switched a moment to Serbo-Croat. "Do you still speak your mother's tongue?"

"No. How did you know I was coming? Angel?"

Shavik slipped his hand into his right pocket, took out two cell phones, held them up. "Easy. You gave yourself away."

"Where's Angel?"

"Not your concern."

"Is she dead?"

He didn't reply as he pulled up a chair, and slipped the cell phones back in his pocket. He sat facing her and produced a pack of Marlboro. "You're a defiant one, aren't you? Ever since that day on the camp parade ground. You haven't changed."

Now that Carla was close up to Shavik, oddly she felt nothing, no rage, no revulsion. But there was another feeling there, buried deep. She tried to divine it. Was it a kind of pity? It felt strange.

"You . . . remember me?"

"It took a while, but yes."

"And now you're going to kill me?"

"That depends."

"On what?"

"Your answers. And they better be honest. You came here to kill me, didn't you?"

"Among other things."

"Such as?"

"You have information I want."

"Really? We'll come back to that. First, these people you've been hanging out with at the marina. I need to know what you've told them."

"Why, so you can kill them?"

"No, but we may have been seriously compromised."

"Enough to make you flee?"

"I'm afraid so. Well, what did you tell them?"

"Why don't you amuse yourself thinking about that one on cold winter nights?"

He took a drag on his cigarette, tapped ash on the floor. "You want information. So do I. Let's be civilized and trade a fact for a fact. I'll tell you anything you want to know, and you tell me. Agreed?"

"Anything?"

"Anything."

Carla's gaze was steady. "I want to know about my father, David Joran. And my brother. His name is Luka. He was four years old when we were in the camp. I know you were the last person to see him alive."

"What makes you think that?"

"I'm right, aren't I? Where are they? What did you do with them? Did you kill them? The way you killed my mother and my husband?"

Shavik's face looked blank, impossible to read.

For no reason at all, he reached out, touched her hair gently, and let it fall about her face.

She struck him hard across the cheek, and the cigarette fell from his hand onto the floor.

Calmly, he crushed it out with the toe of his shoe. Wiping his mouth with the back of his hand, he stared at the splash of blood.

Carla went to lash out at him again.

This time he reacted instantly, caught her hand mid-flight, forced it down.

"Spirit *and* defiance. You think you got that only from your mother?"

"What are you talking about?"

"Do you know who I really am?"

"I just told you. Mila Shavik. A war criminal, a butcher."

"It's time you knew the truth."

80

Arkov stormed into the study, his face crimson, and slammed the door with a terrible fury.

He headed straight for the bar and grabbed a bottle of bourbon.

His father was already there, seated at a lacquered table, a meal in front of him. Salad, a selection of cold meats, some fresh fruit. Shavik's Puerto Rican housekeeper, a plump, handsome woman, was pouring him a glass of red wine.

The old man dabbed his mouth with a napkin, waved a hand dismissively, and the woman left.

"Another disagreement?" He lit a cigar, inhaling slowly, enjoying the aroma.

His son splashed bourbon into a crystal tumbler and downed it in one swallow. "Is it ever any other way?"

His father scowled. "Nothing changes, does it?"

"You find it funny, Father?"

"No, I find it rather pathetic. My blood may be in your veins, Boris, but unfortunately my brains are not in your head."

"Saying I'm stupid now, are you?"

"Calm yourself, and get sense. I'm saying you and Mila should be working together, not fighting like pit bulls. How many times do I have to tell you that?"

A sneer lifted the corners of his son's mouth. "That's a joke, considering you never stopped pitting us against each other. As if we were prizefighters, you enjoyed watching us trying to beat the life out of each other."

The old man blew out another cloud of cigar smoke. "Survival of the fittest, nature's most important law."

"You make me sick, Father."

"That's the drink talking. Show respect." The old man stood, hitched up his trousers. "What's happening?"

"He won't let me use the drug. He thinks it might kill her."

"He has a point."

Arkov took a swig, and his mouth twisted with scorn. "Brute force is the only way to deal with the clever kind. He'll get nowhere talking."

"You're right, but that's Mila's problem. These people Billy's watching. You think they know something?"

"The woman's a lawyer, not an assassin. Yet she was carrying a silenced Sig. She's also been visiting the former special forces guy at the marina. It's too much of a coincidence."

"I agree."

"That means he's a risk."

"Then deal with him."

"What about consulting with Mila?"

"It's my decision." The old man crushed out his cigar in a crystal ashtray, buttoned his jacket, and stepped toward the window with a worried look. Fog hung in the night air like a thin pall of smoke.

"What's wrong?"

"It might be wise if I left. If this fog gets any thicker, I could be stuck here. What about the airport?"

"Still open. I checked. They're expecting some private traffic."

"Good. Then I'll leave you a little earlier than I planned. Have your driver take me right away, Boris."

The old man moved to the door. "Let me know when it's all been dealt with, and make sure Mila finishes off the woman when he's done. Or that pleasure may be yours."

"And the others?"

"Have Billy solve the problem."

"Permanently?"

"As the coffin lid closing. Tell him to make it look like some kind of domestic dispute."

Boris cracked his knuckles, a sudden excitement sparking, the very thought of violence stimulating him. "All of them?"

"It's better that way—no loose ends. You think Billy's capable of that?"

"He knows what he's doing."

* * *

"Do you remember the day I summoned you to my office?"

"Yes."

Shavik took a long swig of brandy, as if he was trying to steel himself. "You recall what happened?"

"No, I don't."

"Why?"

"I was ten years old. Like every other woman and child who suffered the brutality you meted out in the camp I was traumatized. Don't you remember what you put us all through? Or are you going to claim you were just following orders."

"I was."

"Liar."

"You don't recall anything of your visit to my office?"

"I've learned the mind has a defense mechanism that helps it bury trauma. In my case, I was one of the lucky ones."

"Then tell me what you do recall."

"You can go to hell."

"Fact for a fact, remember?"

"First tell me what happened to my father and brother."

"It's complicated. But I'll tell you the truth. You have my word."

"Are they alive? Please, you have to tell me . . ."

"First, I need to know what you remember."

"Why's that important?"

"You'll understand after I explain."

"I told you, nothing. Did . . . did you harm me?"

"That depends by what you mean by harm."

"Did you . . . did you touch me?"

"Yes, I touched you."

He looked at her, her eyes meeting her stare. "Just as I touched your hair now."

Carla's eyes felt suddenly wet. "Did you rape me?"

Shavik looked strangely horrified. "Of course not."

"Why can't I believe that? You and your men raped women daily, and killed them. You killed my mother."

"Look at me. You're wrong. I oversaw the camp, yes. But I never personally harmed a woman or child. The men I commanded killed and raped, because they were encouraged to do so by those above me. Yes, I slept with camp women. But killed them, no. Nor did I kill your mother."

"I don't believe that."

Shavik's jaw tightened as if he was jolted by a sudden pain. "What do you know about your mother's past? Before she met your father."

"She was from Konjic. A quaint town in the mountains between Sarajevo and Mostar, where Muslim and Christian lived side by side for centuries. Until war changed it all."

Shavik took another slug of brandy, a distant look on his face, as if he were in another place. "Let me tell you a true story."

"I don't want to hear your stories, Shavik."

"You'll want to hear this one."

81

"My father was a lawyer."

Shavik took another mouthful from the bottle. "Not entirely an honest one, but a good father. Let's just say he dealt with clients from the shadier side of life. The shadiest of them all was Ivan Arkov."

"What's this got to do with me?"

"Your mother's father was a public prosecutor. My father and he crossed paths in court many times. They were rivals."

"I asked what this has to do with me."

"It's important to know the secret that was kept from you. That day in the office I simply told you the truth."

"What secret? What truth?"

"One day in a café in the old town I saw your mother. We were eighteen. I sat beside her. I asked to buy her coffee."

"You . . . you knew my mother that well?"

"Yes, I did. That first day I met her I learned she loved Shakespeare, and wanted to be a writer. I told her I wanted to be a lawyer, like my father. She was kind and wise, funny and intelligent. We enjoyed each other's company. I knew who her father was. She knew of mine. We didn't care that our knowing each other would be frowned upon. Our family rivalries had nothing to do with us. So our relationship went on like that for many months, secretly."

Carla was aware of a coldness seeping into her, a quickening of breath.

"Don't look so surprised. We were young and innocent, from different sides of the ethnic divide. My father despised Bosniak Muslims. Your grandfather hated Christian Serbs. It's been going on like that in parts of the Balkans for hundreds of years. Christian hating Muslim, Muslim hating Christian. But your mother and I, we didn't care about the past, only the present."

Carla didn't reply, shock still sinking in.

"We were just two young people who wanted to do what young people did—talk, laugh, have fun, fall in love."

She stared at Shavik, felt her stomach heave with disbelief. "My . . . my mother *loved* you?"

"She used to say that we were like Romeo and Juliet, victims of our families' feud and bigotry. And she was right."

"I . . . I can't believe what I'm hearing . . ."

"When our parents found out, we were forbidden to see each other. But that didn't stop us. We defied them. Until things took a sinister turn."

"What . . . what do you mean?"

"My father was due to face a corruption charge that would have ruined him. The charge was brought by your grandfather. The night before the trial my father hung himself. My mother was already dead. I had no one else. My only brother died when he was three. Ivan Arkov took me in, gave me a home, food, and shelter.

"He told me that your grandfather was responsible for my father's death. That Prosecutor Tanovic harassed him because I refused to stop seeing his daughter. That he would never allow her to marry a Serb like me."

"Marry?"

"We talked about it, your mother and I. But after that, I hated your mother's people. From that day on, I wanted my revenge."

"What about my mother?"

"I wrote and told her it was over. That I couldn't see her again, not after what happened. There was too much hate in my heart."

"What did she say?"

"She wrote back, a final letter, telling me how much she still loved me. But I couldn't let go of my hate. It was too deep, too bitter."

"What . . . what happened?"

"I heard she left for Dubrovnik soon after, and I never saw her again."

"Never?"

"Until that day in the camp when I hardly recognized her, and it all came flooding back."

"What did?"

"Emotions, feelings, regrets, for the life we'd lost."

"She . . . she went to offer herself to you, to plead for the lives of our family."

"She begged me for medicines for your father and brother. I promised to get them for her."

Anger raged in Carla's voice, her tone hard. "Why?"

"Because I still loved her. Because . . ." Shavik faltered.

"Not because she offered you her body in return?"

"No."

"You're telling me you didn't harm her?"

"Never."

"That doesn't add up. My mother wrote a diary. I remember some words she wrote after she went to see you, and what they said."

"Tell me."

" 'I've paid a terrible price for seeing Shavik.' There were other lines. 'It's done. I did what I had to. What Shavik did makes me cry.' My mother's words exactly. What did she mean by that? What made her cry? What did you do to her?"

"Perhaps the price she paid was knowing me again. Resurrecting old feelings she wanted to forget. What did I do to her? Nothing. I simply made her a promise."

"What promise?"

"That I'd try my utmost to save her and her family."

"Why?"

"I think I answered that question already."

"Did she believe your promise?"

"I'm not sure."

"You wanted nothing in return?"

"I wanted to speak with you."

"Me? Why . . . ?"

"I was curious."

"About what?"

"You made an impression the day you defended the old woman. There's a lot of your mother in you. You still don't remember our talk, do you?"

"I told you, I remember nothing. If you didn't kill my mother, then who did?"

"Arkov was in charge of evacuating the prisoners. As they were driven off in the trucks I saw Lana standing in the back. I realized you and your brother were missing. I saw your mother stare back toward the camp building. I sensed something was wrong."

Shavik paused. "I ran back into the camp, looking for you and your brother, but couldn't find you. The shelling got worse. Then I heard shooting . . ."

Shavik's voice broke off. "I left the camp and caught up with Arkov. I found the women and children dead or dying."

Carla didn't speak.

Shavik went on, "Some of the prisoners tried to escape. Arkov shot them and all hell broke loose. The men had been drinking for days, and all reason went out the door. It was a bloodbath."

"Arkov killed my mother?"

"He denied it, but I never believed him."

Carla felt her hands shaking with revulsion, and an icy coldness in her stomach.

"What . . . what happened to my father and brother?"

"I returned to the camp one last time. I found the boy lying wounded in the rubble, but there was no sign of you. I tended to his wounds as best I could. Then I took him to the Omarska camp where your father was kept."

"My . . . my father was still alive?"

"Barely. I drove them to a field hospital run by some nuns. The nuns were unsure they'd survive. But I'd made a solemn promise to your mother that I'd try to save you all."

"What did you do?"

"I left them with the nuns and tried to make it to my own lines. Once there, I loaded up a car with medical supplies. On the way back I was wounded."

"But you returned?"

"By the time I got to your father and brother they had deteriorated. But the nuns said there was still hope. They treated my wounds and said if I could make it over the mountains that night to a hospital, they'd survive."

"What happened?"

"There was a snowstorm. My car got stuck. In the freezing cold your father faded fast. I tried everything I could. But he passed away, holding your bother in his arms."

Carla was ashen. "What . . . what about Luka? Tell me."

"He was crying for his father. Crying and growing weaker by the minute. Seeing him cling to your father's body it . . . it reminded me of the way I clung to my own father when he died. It seemed the first time in years I registered any kind of emotion."

"What happened then?"

"I wrapped him up warmly, built a fire, gave him more drugs. I tried everything I could. But once your father died the life seemed to go out of your brother and a little after midnight he passed."

Carla broke down. Her body convulsed with sobbing.

She seemed to lose all control then, all reason, and with a terrible fury she hit Shavik about the head and chest using her fists.

He stood there, not moving, taking it all, and when her energy was spent and she was still sobbing he put his arms around her.

She could smell the male scent of him, expected to feel a powerful sense of revulsion, but it was the strangest thing—she felt nothing,
except an odd kind of pity that was frighteningly close to forgiveness.
Aware of it, she drew herself back with a sudden loathing.

"What did you do with their bodies?"

"Next day a local farmer helped me deliver them to a morgue in
Mostar. I later learned they were buried in a grave site near the town."

"I can't even pretend to understand you, Shavik. Not ever. How did
you grow to hate so much that you'd allow women and children to die?
How? When did you cross that line between good and evil? Whenever
I saw you in the camp, your eyes were so full of hate."

"I have no answer. Except that in my mind, I was avenging my
father. In my part of the world, the code of the vendetta is always absolute. The man who does not take vengeance for the wrong done to his
own was himself cursed, if that makes sense?"

"You call that an answer?"

"No. But I remember something your mother said in her final letter
to me."

"What?"

"She said that good and evil, like love and hate, are so close that
they're chained together in the soul. That we can unleash whichever
one we choose. Perhaps she was right. I chose to unleash hate."

He stared back at her, remorse in his eyes. "You know, I've never
got her out of my blood. Not ever. The only time I seemed to find
peace was when I was with her. She made me feel alive again. She was
a remarkable woman."

A fraught look ravaged Carla's face, as if she was close to the edge
of things.

Shavik fell silent.

The silence went on forever.

Shavik went to reach out, as if his hand meant to touch her hair, a
strange kind of look in his eyes, but then he drew back warily.

"I'm not the beast you think I am. There's something else. Something I didn't know until that day your mother came to see me in the
camp . . ."

"No, I've heard enough."

"It's important."

"I don't care."

From somewhere in the house came a gunshot, quickly followed by another.

Carla startled.

A burst of gunfire stuttered in reply.

Shavik jumped to his feet and said to Carla, "Don't move."

He wrenched out a pistol and crossed the room. Opening the basement door, he peered up the stairs. Almost immediately an alarm went off inside the house, a high-pitched bleating that felt as if it was rupturing their ears.

Shavik heard noise and stepped back. Moments later footsteps clattered on the stairs and Arkov appeared, wielding a machine pistol, sweat drenching his face, his left hand and shoulder bloody, a briefcase under his other arm.

"We've got trouble. Get down to the boat dock, now!"

82

Miriam Flores scrubbed the dishes and lay them on the sink to dry.

She wiped her hands on the dish towel and looked at the wall clock.

Five past midnight.

These meetings sometimes went on late. Very late if she was unlucky. The old man and the two others, her boss and the weirdo one, the old man's delinquent son with the cold stare of a killer.

Talkie-talkie. Yap-yap. Babble-babble.

In a language she didn't understand or care to.

The people she worked for were scumbags.

Rich scumbags.

Hardly ever talked to her and her husband. With luck, she'd get to bed at 3 a.m., and be up again at seven to cook them breakfast.

They never thought about the little people who had to wait on them hand and foot. Little people were nobodies.

Miriam sighed. Time to unwind. She poured herself a glass of Chardonnay from the refrigerator. Licking her lips, she opened a cupboard. Nuts and an apple. Great way to the curb the appetite. She took a packet of almonds from the cupboard, then plucked a plump red apple from the fruit bowl on the kitchen table. Grabbing a paring knife in the drawer, she hit the TV remote.

Reruns. *America's Got Talent* or *Jerry Springer*?

She preferred the Springer.

Pure lowlife theater. Dumb, crazy people beating the tar out of each other and washing their dirty linen in public. She sipped her Chardonnay—pretty good. Munching a handful of almonds, she peeled a cut of crunchy apple, and upped the TV volume. She chomped a few mouthfuls, and stopped, feeling something hard touch her jaw.

Not an almond.

Cold steel.

A gun barrel, pressing into her right cheek, like a toothache.

She gave a tiny cry and a split second later a hand slapped over her mouth.

"I don't want to hurt you, but if you make a sound I will."

A man's voice. In the brushed, stainless steel of the refrigerator Miriam glimpsed a figure in black.

Holy Mother.

The hand came away, hovered about an inch from her mouth.

"What's your name? Speak softly."

"Miriam."

"Remember, not a sound, Miriam. Got that?"

She gave a terrified nod, perspiration beading her brow.

The hand moved away from her mouth. The figure spun her round.

She was face-to-face with a man wearing a black ski mask, black clothes, black sneakers, holding a black gun. Brown eyes in the slits of a balaclava.

The man held up a roll of wide gray tape. "Know what this is?"

Miriam stared at the tape roll, pure dread in her face.

"It's duct tape, Miriam. Silence on a roll."

She looked at the man, not understanding, but had a feeling what was coming next; she'd be bound. Maybe raped or shot. She was sixty-eight next birthday. She had read about weirdoes assaulting older women.

But the man must have sensed her fear, and said softly, "You do as I say and I promise you don't get hurt. Yell, call for help, and it's a different story. You understand me, Miriam?"

Another nod. She wondered if deranged killers spoke like that just to lull you?

"I just need to ask you a few questions."

"Questions?"

"About your employers. Then I want you to be nice and quiet while I lock you in the pantry with that bottle of wine of yours for company, okay?"

83

Arkov stood at the window, watching the Escalade carrying his father back to Cape May airport move out through the front gates.

As the red taillights vanished into the fog, his mind lingered on a perverted thought. He hoped he'd have the pleasure of dealing with the woman himself. A tingling anticipation coursed through his loins, a feeling that was almost sexual in its intensity.

He'd take a stroll down to the basement and see how Shavik was getting on. Better still, he could watch using the cameras from the privacy of the security room.

He put his hand under his suit jacket, removing the Glock from its holster. He racked the slide, chambering a round, before replacing the weapon.

Then Arkov snapped open his phone and hit the number.

Billy answered on the second ring. "Yeah?"

"Do it. Kill them all."

Dobrashin, Arkov's bodyguard, zipped up his pants, flushed the toilet, and waddled back into the security room.

All 320 pounds of him slumped into the swivel seat and it creaked in protest. He needed to oil that thing, man. A sumo wrestler's build had certain advantages—like getting instant physical respect—but swivel seats that squeezed your butt like a zit were not on the reward list.

Arms swollen with energy, he reached out to fiddle with the console buttons and scan the screens.

All clear. Every image as it should be. Except one: the guy Shavik, in the basement, talking with the female intruder. He didn't know what the heck was going on there but it wasn't his business and he didn't care.

More than a dozen infrared cameras covered strategic locations both inside and outside the house and he could switch between any of them.

Infrared beams out there in the garden, too.

Anything moved, he'd see it, or if he didn't, the alarms would sense it and go off. Which was how they caught the woman.

Nobody could get past those beams or cameras, and even if they did they still had to face him. *And* the Heckler & Koch MP5—a short-barreled machine pistol lying on the console.

Dobrashin reached down and grabbed what looked like a small violin case by the console. He snapped open the catches. Inside was a ukulele.

Fact of life—everybody had a day job *and* they had a dream.

His dream was to be like that Hawaiian guy with a quivering voice who had a massive hit with "Somewhere over the Rainbow." Dobrashin wanted to make it onto a show like *America's Got Talent* or *American Idol*. Make it big. Forget the bodyguard stuff; he wanted big bucks, not to get wasted for some rich moron.

Dobrashin's folks came to the United States when he was three and he played the ukulele since he was eight. He did a pretty good impression of the Hawaiian guy, could hit the high C's no problem, even modulate his voice to get that quivering sound. Dobrashin started to strum the ukulele, got the song going, pitching his voice high.

Oooo, oooo, oooo . . .

Oooo, oooo, oooo . . .

C, E minor, F, then C.

"Somewhere over the rainbow, way up high . . ."

"Hey, that's pretty good."

Dobrashin stopped strumming, felt something hard touch his right ear.

He went to turn, and the chair squeaked. He glimpsed a guy dressed in black, black balaclava, Glock in hand.

"Don't move again. You ever think of playing professionally, son?"

Dobrashin was struck dumb.

"Well, did you?"

"Yeah."

"I'd give it some serious thought. You've got a voice."

Dobrashin almost said, "Thanks," but stopped himself.

"I'm looking for a lady. I think she came here. Her car's parked not far away. You know who I'm talking about?"

Dobrashin nodded.

"Where is she?"

"The basement."

"Alive?"

Dobrashin's eyes shifted to the bank of security screens.

Ronnie followed the bodyguard's gaze, saw Carla seated in a room, another man standing, talking to her. Shavik?

"I guess I'm a little late to change her mind. Is she in any immediate danger?"

Dobrashin shrugged.

"Lay the instrument on the console, and keep those palms down, away from the MP5. Then slowly—and I do mean slowly—bring your hands round behind your back. No tricks, or you're going to screw up the coroner's weekend."

Dobrashin laid down the ukulele. Slowly, deliberately, he put his beefy arms behind his back. He felt a couple of hard plastic ties slip over his wrists and get pulled tight. He couldn't move his arms.

Duct tape was run tight around his mouth. Dobrashin snorted.

"I'll take the tape off when I want to ask you some questions, so relax. For now, sit still while I put another set of ties on your ankles. You're going to get hog-tied, buddy. It's still a lot better than getting shot . . ."

Dobrashin glimpsed a movement in one of the cameras.

Arkov.

Calmly walking down the hall, heading to the security room.

The intruder behind him was too busy fiddling with the plastic ties to notice the screens because the moment the stout metal security door opened on its return springs and Arkov appeared, the intruder startled.

Dobrashin twisted round in the chair, saw it all unfold.

Arkov, shock registering, wrenching out his gun.

The intruder went to reach for his but didn't make it in time, Arkov firing first, two rounds smacking into the plaster wall above the intruder's head.

The intruder moved fast, grabbed Dobrashin's MP5, rolled on the ground and fired, stitching the walls with rounds, hitting Arkov in the left hand and shoulder.

Arkov staggered back out the way he came, and the return spring slammed the security door shut with a metal *clunk,* the steel two inches thick.

Then there was only silence and the smell of cordite from spent ammunition, Dobrashin watching the camera screen as a wounded Arkov scurried back down the hall . . .

* * *

Arkov staggered toward the bedroom, knowing exactly what he had to do.

The basement exit route led to the dock, but first he had important things to do. Sweat drenching his face, agonizing pains stabbing his chest and shoulder, he yanked out his cell as he moved, and fingered the number, frantic.

A voice answered. "Felix."

"It's Boris. We're abandoning the nest. We'll use the boat. You know the plan, stand by to meet us."

The call took six seconds, and as Arkov ended the conversation he reached the bedroom. Every second counted, all his instincts honed to survival.

He lurched into the walk-in dressing room, tearing away the clothes-laden hangers to get to the safe. A black briefcase lay below it. On a shelf next to him was a loaded MP5.

Blood dripped down his arm where a bullet shattered bone, the pain excruciating, but it didn't stop him from stabbing at the keypad with a finger.

The safe sprang open.

He grabbed the ledger, the laptop, and the decoder, stashing them in the briefcase.

He hit an alarm button near the wall safe and a high-pitched siren shrieked all over the house. Holding the briefcase under his arm he grabbed the MP5, then stumbled out of the room and down the basement steps, the alarm still sounding, his wounds on fire.

In all, it took him less than forty-seven seconds from the moment he exited the security room.

Shavik already had the basement door open as Arkov staggered down the stairs.

"Get down to the boat, now! We've got trouble!"

84

The boardwalk was swallowed up by fog as they hurried from the basement exit. It led to the rear gate, and they moved out toward the lit pier.

Neon overhead lights lit the way, but barely illuminated the board-walk. The black powerboat was out there somewhere, lost in the mist of fog.

Shavik dragged Carla by the hand, urgency in his voice. "Move. Don't stop."

Carla was sure she heard police sirens, and then came the low but distinct throb of a helicopter in the distance.

She could barely walk, her legs trembling with fear. It all felt so unreal, like a dream: Shavik urging her on, Arkov staggering behind, grasping the briefcase and a machine pistol, his bloody arm bent like a stroke victim's.

"You hear that? They're coming closer." Arkov's voice sounded strained with fear.

They reached the black powerboat, its sleek polished body complete with cream leather seats. Shavik let go of Carla and frantically untied the mooring ropes. The sound of sirens and the chopping noise grew louder.

Carla saw her chance. She turned and started to run.

She had barely gone five yards when Arkov stretched out his foot, tripping her, and she fell forward onto the boardwalk.

Arkov tossed the briefcase onto the boat. "She'll only slow us down. We finish this here and now."

"No!"

But Arkov ignored the command and raised the MP5, his finger tightening on the trigger.

"I said no!" In an instant Shavik crossed the distance between them and struck Arkov hard across the jaw, sending him reeling backward

onto the boat, his head bouncing off the floor, the machine pistol glid-
ing across the wood.

"Start the engine, and be quick about it . . ." Shavik ordered.

Arkov groaned, tried to sit up, but then he collapsed, his head
slumping to one side. He looked out of it.

The sirens grew even louder.

Shavik's face was lit by rage as he grabbed the MP5, then took hold
of Carla's arm and hauled her up . . .

Ronnie tried the steel security door. It was locked solid. He pounded
the metal with a fist, then turned to Dobrashin, tore the duct tape from
his mouth, and wielded the MP5. "Get that door open, fast."

"There's a security feature, man. It's time-locked. I can't."

"There's got to be an override switch. Where is it?"

Dobrashin fell silent.

Ronnie aimed the MP5 between Dobrashin's legs.

"If I have to ask you again, you'll be hitting those high C's even higher."

TENNESSEE

Billy watched the cabin from his veranda.

All the lights out now, except one.

Flickering, faint, like a TV. Was somebody still up?

He couldn't wait all night.

Get in, get out, fast.

That was his rule.

He slipped his legs over the veranda railing and strolled toward
Regan's cabin, not a sound except the crickets. The .45 and the silencer
were in his jeans pockets, along with the tac light. At the bottom of the
cabin steps he slid off his shoes.

Better to move in his stocking feet. He inched up the stairs, keeping
to the side. A tiny creak here and there, but nothing more. He reached
the front door, and tried the handle.

Unlocked.

He grinned. Some idiots were still too trusting in these parts.

The kind of trust that could get you killed.

He slipped the .45 from his right-hand pocket and removed the silencer from the other. He screwed it on the barrel, then flicked off the safety catch, but left the hammer uncocked.

Opening the door gingerly, he was met by darkness, except for the faint flickering of a TV, somewhere in the back, one of the bedrooms maybe?

He heard muffled music, or voices, he couldn't tell which.

He moved inside, readying the .45. Flicking on his tac light, the low blue beam washed the walls.

He was in a living room.

The sound of music or voices, still muffled.

He could make out the source of the flickering light down the hall. A TV screen illuminated from a crack in an open door. Billy padded down the hall, not making a sound, and approached the door.

He peered in through the crack. A bedroom. The boy was asleep on the bed, almost looking like a girl, his hands under his head, MTV on, some band playing crap.

Billy looked farther down the hall, saw other doors. Regan's room had to be down there. He got a voyeuristic kick out of her not knowing he was in the cabin, and with it came a feeling of power.

Which first? The boy or Regan?

Get the dirtiest job over with first.

He stepped into the boy's bedroom . . .

85

Shavik untied the last mooring rope and hustled Carla on board.

He turned on the engine, lights flashing on the console. The bleating sirens sounded closer, somewhere along the inlet now, the lights of the police vehicles lost in the heavy fog.

"What are you going to do with me?"

Shavik's brow glistened with sweat as he tossed the MP5 aside and started the engine, which idled with a steady throb.

"Nothing. On second thought, it's better that you stay."

"You're not going to kill me?"

"That wasn't my intent."

"I don't understand."

"Maybe someday you will. Meantime, I can only ask your forgiveness."

"I can never forgive someone like you."

"Stranger things have happened." He took hold of her arm, lifting her gently out of the powerboat and onto the jetty.

"You'll be found, no matter where you run to, Shavik."

"No doubt." He looked at her, as if he meant to say something, but seemed to think better of it. "This is where we must say our goodbye. Your mother was right, you know."

"What do you mean?"

"About good and evil, love and hate. That we can unleash whichever one we choose. And in the end, we'll all pay the price of our sins."

"You said there was something I should know."

"Did I? I think you know it all now. So whatever it was, it must have been of no consequence."

Carla thought she saw the strangest thing, a swell of emotion in Shavik's eyes, as his hand reached out to touch her face, but she pulled away.

He let his hand fall. "No matter what you think of me, I wish you a long and happy life."

He took a cell phone from his pocket, as the sound of heavy footsteps came running down the jetty, the sirens very close now, the noise static, as if they'd pulled up at the house.

"By the way, there's a man renting a cabin at the marina. He goes by the name of Billy Lubbock. Tall, dark, about thirty. He may try to kill your friends. Call and warn them, and tell the police. But be quick, there may not be much time."

He tossed the phone at Carla just as the running footsteps came closer, and Ronnie appeared out of the fog, a machine pistol in his hand.

The moment he saw Shavik he roared, "Get down, Carla!"

She ducked, sliding away, and Ronnie opened up, stitching the boat with rounds, gouging lumps out of the fiberglass.

Shavik weaved and ducked, moving behind the controls as the gunfire erupted.

A split second later the powerful Mercury engine snarled to life like an enraged animal, and with a tremendous surge the boat roared off into the fog.

TENNESSEE

The cell phone on Regan's nightstand vibrated on silent.

A silky hum that shook the phone at least a dozen times, shaking the glass of water next to it.

When no one picked up, the noise ceased.

Moments later, the cell started to vibrate again.

It seemed to go on forever, trembling on the nightstand, but no one answered . . .

DELAWARE BAY, CAPE MAY

Ten minutes out to sea, in thick fog, Shavik had the weather radar on, knowing the marker buoy was near.

He throttled back, killed the engine, and then there was only a deep silence, the boat drifting, the sea all around him choked by a wall of fog. He took a cell phone from his pocket and was about to punch in a number.

"All things come to those who wait, remember?"

He spun round. Arkov stood there, supporting himself by the side of the boat, the MP5 in his hand. He looked pale as death, a vengeful sneer twisting his face.

"Don't they, Mila? It's hard to kill a bad thing."

"You never spoke a truer word."

"Where's the woman?"

"Gone."

"Where?"

"A long story, as they say."

"You let her go?"

"Yes, I did."

A terrible rage lit Arkov's face. "You fool. She's the last witness. Are you insane?"

"You could be right. But I think I lost my reason long ago."

Arkov raised the MP5, his finger flexing on the trigger, but then he seemed suddenly confused, aware of his surroundings as he stared wildly around him at the wall of thick fog. "Where the devil am I?"

"A question I've often asked myself, Boris."

"Don't be smart."

"We're waiting at the buoy marker. I was about to call Felix to make sure it's safe to proceed. Or did that bump on your head make you forget our plan?"

The boat was drifting. Out of the fog Shavik spotted an old rusting marker buoy looming ahead. It jutted at least eight feet out of the water, bobbing on its float, rocking with the motion of the sea. The powerboat bumped hard against it.

Arkov lurched.

Shavik saw his chance and kicked Arkov below the knee and he grunted with pain. A fist cracked into Arkov's jaw and he went down, his body slamming against the boat's gunwale.

Shavik wrenched away the MP5 and heaved a dazed Arkov up by the arms, dragging him onto one of the leather seats.

"It's time for you and me to have a serious talk."

Arkov defiantly spat his reply, blood staining his lips. "About what?"

"Lana Tanovic, among other things."

TENNESSEE

As Billy moved into the boy's bedroom, something flickered past him.

What the . . .

A moth. His heart skipped, and he almost pulled the Kimber's trigger.

Even for a pro, he had to remind himself: muscle memory. Finger off the trigger until ready to fire. Swearing, he moved over to the bed.

He stared down at the sleeping boy.

One shot.

One shot and the kid would feel no pain, his cortex severed.

The darn moth flew past again.

Get lost!

He placed the gun barrel close to the back of the boy's neck.

Gently, he cocked the hammer.

Sweet dreams, amigo.

In the silence after he cocked the hammer, Billy heard it, a low throb, like a cell vibrating. It rang and rang.

Then came another sound.

Distinct.

No mistaking that sound.

Another hammer cock.

Right next to him.

Then he felt it.

A cold barrel prodding the base of his neck.

"Uncock your gun, mister."

He glanced behind him, felt the sweat already drip from his brow.

Regan.

In a silky nightdress.

A silvered revolver in her hand.

He didn't expect that.

"Who are you? What are you doing here?"

Billy didn't answer.

"You've sure got a way with words, mister. But I guess so do a lot of lying thieves. Are you a thief, here to rob? Because if you are, there's nothing to take. I already deposited the day's takings."

Billy avoided the questions. "How did you know I was here?"

"I was watching you from my window. I saw you creep over here. *Creep* being an apt word."

"Why'd you watch me?"

"What is this, forty questions? Because I liked you. Because I felt a little lovestruck. Big mistake. But just as well I watched. Now what do you think you're up to, mister?"

Billy grimaced. Another mistake, hitting on her. But not one he couldn't recover from. He thought fast, every nerve in his body taut as violin string.

"Take that gun away from my neck or I'll kill him, I mean it."

"You'd really do that? Kill a child?"

"Try me."

"It doesn't make sense. Why kill a child just to rob me?"

Pause.

Billy was losing patience. "You ain't listening, are you? I said do as I say or he's dead."

"I guess it really doesn't pay to bumble with the B, does it?"

Billy almost smiled. He liked her. Pity. "Nope. That was a good line."

"Easy to fall for a good line."

Billy's fingers felt greasy on the .45. He was ready to squeeze the trigger. Regan wasn't moving. She had guts, facing him off, he'd give her that.

The boy stirred in his sleep, gave a soft moan.

Billy nervously licked his lips. "One *last time*. Take the gun away. Or else they'll be scraping the kid's brains off the wall. That's a promise. Now I won't say it again."

He could almost *feel* the silence. Heavy, racking.

Nothing happened.

Billy moved his arm just a touch, tightened his finger on the trigger, a hair's breadth away from pulling it. She must have seen it.

"I *mean* it. Don't test me."

More silence.

At last, Billy felt the pressure of the gun tip ease off his neck.

She was doing what he told her. He almost let out a sigh but held it in.

"Lay the gun down, Regan. On the bed, next to me."

"Who *are* you?"

"Just do it."

He glanced out of the corner of his eye. Regan laying the gun down.

Billy saw her hand move, and he turned slowly, keeping the .45 on the base of the boy's skull.

As she lay her gun down, Billy tensed, brought up his .45 quickly now, all in one fluid motion, and aimed to shoot her.

But the woman was quicker.

The revolver came up again out of nowhere and exploded, the .38 round hitting Billy in the temple, drilling out the other side of his skull, making an abstract painting on the wall with his brains.

Josh startled awake, recoiling in the bed, already screaming with shock, just in time to see Billy slump on the floor, his body twitching, blood fauceting from his head wound.

Regan clasped Josh, her arms going around him, hugging him close, trying to calm him. "It's okay, baby, it's okay."

She let her revolver fall to the floor and saw Billy, eyes wide in death, staring up at the ceiling.

A moth danced across his face, became trapped on the silky wet blood.

She stared down at his wide, lifeless eyes.

"Know what? It doesn't pay to bumble with a redneck, either, mister."

86

The sea fog was no more, just a cool breeze, a vast ocean.

Seagulls shrieked as the Coast Guard cutter killed its engine and drifted alongside the rusted marker buoy.

The officer scratched his head, mystified.

A guardsman held out a grab hook and pulled them closer, securing them to the marker buoy, bobbing in the gentle swell.

Weird, thought the officer.

Really weird.

He'd seen a few sights in his day but this one sure beat them all.

The man's body hung from a rope tied to the top of the marker buoy. His shoulder was caked in dried blood, his blue face bloated.

He'd been shot, maybe badly beaten, too. Tied to the dead man's chest was a briefcase, a rope laced through the handle and strapped securely around the body.

"Can you get the briefcase?" asked the captain.

A guardsman used a knife to cut through the rope securing the case. It took a while before he got it free and then he handed the case to the officer, who found it locked.

One of the men handed him a crowbar and he broke open the locks.

Inside was a ledger of some sort, a handwritten note taped to the cover. A Mac laptop below it, and something small, protected in bubble wrap and sealed with scotch tape.

The officer pulled off the scotch tape and tore at the bubble wrap.

A memory device inside.

As he read through the note taped to the ledger, his skin tone bleached almost white. Stunned, he looked back up at the guardsman.

"Get me the Cape May police on the radio."

87

BELGRADE

It was late afternoon that same day when Mila Shavik's plane touched down at the city's Nikola Tesla Airport.

He carried a briefcase and a Samsonite overnight bag, his false passport in the name of a British businessman. He passed through immigration, entered the arrivals hall, and was met by two muscled thugs who escorted him to a waiting black Mercedes. An hour later it pulled up outside the entrance to the private mountain estate in Novi Sad.

Ivan Arkov came out. He looked under stress, his sour face haggard in the sunshine. "Boris?"

"He didn't make it."

The old man's mouth pursed, a flicker of emotion in his watery eyes, red from lack of sleep, but other than that he displayed no outward sign of grief, as if his son's death were simply an unpleasant cost of doing business. "You have what's important, Mila?"

Shavik held up the briefcase. "It's all here."

They sat at a table by the far end of the pool. Two bodyguards on duty at the other end, out of earshot.

The old man massaged his temples. "Boris's body?"

"He died at sea. I was lucky to make it out alive."

"And the woman?"

"She escaped. It was all over the TV."

Shavik looked at the old man. "It seems the cops have put everything together. The bomb, our rackets. How we tried to kill her and the others."

Arkov's thin lips tightened with displeasure. He looked out at view of the Danube, peaceful scenery all around.

"We'll still take care of her. This time I'll arrange it myself and there will be no more mistakes. You disappoint me, Mila."

"It won't happen again."

"I'd like to believe that."

"It won't happen again because you and me are over, Ivan."

"That tone in your voice. It's disrespectful. I don't like it."

"You're not meant to."

Arkov stared back, not used to insolence. "Be careful with your manners. With Boris gone, you're my successor. You're about to have what you always wanted. Don't throw it away, Mila."

"You can keep it. Do you know something else? For the last thirty years I feel as if I've been someone I was never meant to be. Does that make sense?"

"What's wrong? Did Boris's death hit you hard?"

"Hardly, I killed him."

Arkov's eyes lit with rage.

Shavik's left hand was in his pocket in an instant, something pointing from it, the outline of a gun barrel. "Take the garrote from your pocket, Ivan. And that Walther automatic you like to carry in your inside jacket."

"Have you lost your mind?"

"Actually, I think I've found it. Lay them on the table. Speak one word or make a sudden gesture and I'll put a bullet between your eyes, and that's a promise."

Arkov considered, then did as he was told, laying the Walther down first, then the garrote.

"What's your game?" Arkov demanded.

Shavik moved the garrote aside, took the Walther, and laid it on his lap, out of view of the bodyguards. "Shall I tell you what I know?"

"About what?"

"My life. How you destroyed everything dear to me. How you killed my father. You were afraid he'd tell the truth in court and ruin you. So you made it look like suicide."

"That's a lie."

"Boris told me. Don't deny it. He told me how you ordered him to kill Lana Tanovic along with the others at the camp. You even wanted me to kill Carla Lane . . ."

"The women, yes, we're talking about Bosniak scum, but not your father—"

"Tell me the truth. Speak it now. Or I'll kill you this instant."

There was no mistaking the steel in Mila Shavik's voice. His eyes looked infinitely dangerous. He leaned closer, his finger on the Walther's trigger, as he said in a hoarse whisper, "I said tell me the truth."

"You father would have ruined me. I could have had you killed, too, but I chose not to, Mila. I've always had a fondness for you. Always."

"For that I'm supposed to be grateful?"

"You're a better man than your father. He was weak."

"He was an honest man."

"All honest men are fools."

Shavik smiled. It was the coldest smile the old man had ever seen. "Then you'll appreciate what you're about to see. Open the briefcase."

Arkov opened it.

Inside was a red brick. The old man's complexion turned bone white.

"What's the meaning of this?"

"That one way or the other, Ivan, you're going to hell."

Openmouthed, Arkov stared back at him.

"Everything's gone to the feds. We're finished, Ivan. But I'll give you a choice. You can go to hell now, or you can go later, when the authorities are done with you. Your choice."

"You don't know what you're doing."

"I know more than you think. Carla Lane is my daughter. You wanted me to kill her."

"What are you talking about?"

"Don't play the innocent, Ivan. You're too old for that game. You knew Lana Tanovic had my child, didn't you?"

"Of course I knew."

"You don't miss much, do you?"

"It was my business to know once you joined the clan. But I must say, you having a brat by that Bosniak whore surprised me. Killing her would have been the ultimate test of your loyalty."

"I may be past the point of no return, but you're sick, Arkov. The sickest of them all."

"Did you tell her the truth, about her being your daughter?"

"Why burden her with hate and anger? Why destroy her life the way you destroyed mine? I'm right—you don't miss much. And here's another thing you won't miss."

"What?"

"The bullet that's about to kill you."

"You're deranged, Shavik. You'll never leave this house alive."

"That was never really part of my plan."

Rage lit the old man's face, a ferocious anger that sounded like a snarl as he grabbed for the gun.

Shavik shot him in the face.

Arkov lurched backward. Shavik shot him again, in the heart. As he slumped sideways in the chair, blood everywhere, the bodyguards were already moving.

Shavik spun in his seat, aimed, and shot the first man in the chest from twenty-five yards across the pool.

The second man managed to get off one shot, clipping Shavik's shoulder, before he fired twice in return, punching the bodyguard back, hitting him in the chest, killing him instantly.

Shavik stood and walked over to the first bodyguard, picked up his weapon. The wounded man went to sit up, reach for his weapon. Shavik shot him in the heart.

The gunshots echoed and died like church bells, and then came stillness, complete stillness, the beauty and peace of the hills and gorges of Novi Sad all around him, the view splendid in the sun, as always, all the way down to the Danube. The way it always looked when he was here with his father.

There was a surreal quality to it all. As if he were underwater, everything happening in slow motion. He was in that place again.

The place inside himself that he shared with no one. But this time he felt a kind of calm he had not felt since he was a child, like one of those moments when he was falling asleep in his father's arms.

It was like a stone dissolving inside him.

For the first time in a long time, he smiled, really smiled, and at the same time he felt his eyes become wet.

Other noises now. More bodyguards rushing out from the house, guns drawn.

Standing there, staring out at the peace and the tranquility around him, Shavik felt the remarkable peace seep within him.

Two bodyguards rushed forward, thirty yards away, raising their handguns.

Shavik didn't give them a chance.

He raised the pistol.

Touching it to his left temple, he squeezed the trigger.

88

You breathe in deeply, let it out.

Water laps the lakeshore.

A hot sun warms your skin. You feel at peace.

The kind of peace you could only dream of. Like waking after a long and restful sleep.

The spring air is as soft as the old cotton blanket you sit upon. Regan and Josh are on the dock, painting a houseboat. They wave. You wave back and dip your hand in the cool water, trailing your fingers.

It feels good.

Nine months have passed.

So much has happened.

You look down at your sleeping baby. A mosquito net covers her crib, and you can hear the soft and comforting murmur of her breathing. You lean in close, inhale the scent of her skin.

With her plump cheeks, angel lips, and dimpled smile, she has laid claim to your soul, and to Baize's. You both marvel at the circle of life but you know it's far deeper than that. A creator's magic, a glorious mystery that is far too profound for any of us mere mortals to comprehend.

And you think this is how it must have been for your parents all those years ago when they gazed in wonder at you and Luka, all of you huddled close together for warmth in Mr. Banda's apartment.

You understand. Understand the bottomless depth of their love and the enormity of their pain when they could not protect you from evil. You prefer not to dwell on that pain, for it disturbs you so.

No more than you want to dwell on what happened to you in Shavik's office, for there are days when that thought creeps into your mind like an intruder, firing your imagination with worrisome conjecture. All you know for certain is that for some reason you believe what Shavik said, that he never harmed you or your mother.

And that you hate him no more.

But you do not dwell on such thoughts, either.

You prefer to live in the present.

Ronnie strolls down from the cabin carrying a warmed baby's bottle. He hands it to you, sits beside you on the blanket, crossing his legs.

Your baby cries as you lift her from the cradle until you touch the bottle to her hungry lips, and you hear her suck. You've called her Lana.

Ronnie whispers to her, his eyes locking with yours as you look up, and something passes between you, a question asked but not spoken. *Happy?*

The answer lies in the touch of your hand upon his face. *More than I ever thought I'd be.*

Whatever is between you, it goes deeper than desire. You are grief's survivors, soul mates, friends.

You know Jan would have liked this man.

For when he holds you in the stillness of the night you know he holds you out of love. And even if it isn't love for you just yet, then it comes close, and that's enough right now. You'll be patient, give it time.

Ronnie hands you a white envelope from his back pocket.

"A present. For Momma."

You feel the outline of something folded. "What is it?"

"Look inside."

You tear open the envelope. You see the printed travel documents. The journey you've wanted to make. And you look into Ronnie's eyes and say, "When?"

"Whenever you feel ready."

There are many ways to reach the grave near Mostar.

You can drive by car up through resin-scented woods, or travel by bus or by train, then walk across the bridge over the bluest river in the world, and climb the hill that overlooks the sixteenth-century town.

There are many ways but on this sunny day you drive from Dubrovnik in a rented car.

You know these streets. You have traced their narrow ways on colored maps on your computer screen. You know, too, that on warm days young men still come to Mostar bridge, undress their supple bodies, and dive into the ice-cold water to earn the title "Mostari," just as they have done for over three hundred years.

You park near the cemetery, a long meadow scattered with butterflies.

Ronnie's lips brush your cheek; you let go of his hand and step out of the car.

"If you need me, I'm here, Carla."

You nod.

But you know he will meet you later.

For this is something you must do alone.

You walk among the headstones, carrying a bunch of daffodils.

A gardener pruning an olive tree nods as you wander to the simple marble stone. Under the blistering sun, you sit on the grass next to their grave. It makes you feel closer to your departed.

You touch the warm marble, feel the inscription. The words you've chosen to remember them by. Words you want the world to know. Are they not true? The truest words ever spoken?

The marble's heat seeps into your fingertips.

You weep.

For in your deepest being, you feel the presence of those you love who lie here now—your father, your mother, Luka.

You look from the blue sky to the white stone, whispering to them, telling them that you miss them, that you think of them lying here in the cold and snow of winter and the scorching sun of summer.

You tell them that you will always miss and love them. That you can never forget them.

A wind gusts. Like a warm tongue, it licks around the cracked, centuries-old stone of the town's cobbled streets.

You hear voices.

You hear them call your name, like a whisper on the breeze.

From your pocket you take the piece of frayed blue cotton—that comforting square of Luka's blanket that granted him peaceful angel sleep on so many restless nights—clutch it gently as if it's made of precious golden thread, before you touch it to your lips.

Do you hear me, Luka?

I know this comforting square of cotton will soothe my baby. Just as I know that here on this earth there are sweet and blissful days that lie ahead of me.

Wondrous days when I will walk down to the sea with my child, and we will rush together into blue waves, and scoop out armfuls of cool water and whoop with joy. Just as I know that although you and I are no longer one flesh, we have never stopped loving.

You kiss their stone.

You lay down the daffodils, but keep a single flower.

You place the piece of blue cotton in your pocket and say goodbye, but only for now, for you know you will come here again.

And you tell them what you want to tell them.

That one fine day when your last hour comes, when your heart has reached its journey's end, when you sigh your last breath, you know that you will come here to be with them.

But not yet.

But not yet.

You stroll the narrow streets toward the old town.

The olive tree your father carved upon is no longer there but you stand on the edge of rebuilt Mostar bridge and gaze down.

Blue water rushes below you.

You think of your mother and father whose lives entwined here. And you know that this bridge is what it has always been, a link, a symbol of hope.

You have prepared for this moment. Waited for it, even though fearful.

As you stand there, a handful of youths stroll down the street in their bathing suits, talking and laughing, before they climb onto a parapet and plunge their bodies into the cold blue waters.

They surface and wave at you from the water, laughing.

You remove your top and jeans, your bathing suit beneath.

Young men stare. Some protest and warn you of the danger. But you climb onto the parapet and gaze down at the water far below, still clutching the flower.

You are doing this for Lana, your mother.

This is her promise kept.

Without thinking, you jump.

You feel the air rush in your ears. You enter the water with a huge splash, hands out a little, to slow your fall. When you surface, you take a great deep breath. You feel invigorated.

You're drenched, and laughing.

This is how your father must have felt that day, when he handed your mother his heart.

You swim lazily toward the shore, toward the winding walkway where Ronnie is waving, waiting to meet you on the riverbank.

You take slow and idle strokes, for you enjoy the cool freshness of the water as it soothes your body like a balm.

Like that day in the river with Luka.

Little Luka with his pretty, mischievous smile and his way of laughing and joking as he giggles and runs away, teasing you to chase him, saying: "No, no kisses. No kisses for you today." And then: "Well . . . well maybe just one if you are good?" before you catch him and his giggling explodes and he plants a kiss on your cheek with tender cherub lips.

How can you ever forget him?

Your heart is still broken. It can never heal. It will never stop weeping.

And yet there is hope, for another life has grown inside of you.

You let go of the flower in your hand. In a flash of yellow it floats downstream.

You find comfort in such small things.

In the ceaseless flow of nature, and in the life of your baby. In the knowledge that a timeless ritual goes on.

You find comfort in the truth that existence has an unquenchable power all its own, one that hate or pain or dark shadows or the evil brutality of men cannot destroy.

Because you know in the depths of your being, just as we all know, that we can unleash love or hate, whichever one we choose. And that hate perishes the moment you stop feeding it; but good lives on long after it dies.

And suddenly they come to you, those profound and yet simple truths: that life is greater and stronger than all the shadows. That nothing loved is ever truly lost. And whatever evil wraps its arms around us, its embrace is only momentary, a fleeting thing.

And you remember your mother's words, the same words you have inscribed upon her gravestone. You can still feel their chiseled outline beneath your fingertips, as deeply as if they're engraved upon your soul.

Listen to them—please listen to them—for we all know these words to be true:

How can evil destroy the light of goodness that shines within us?

How can it ever?

When there is not enough darkness in the world to quench the light of one small candle . . .

AUTHOR'S NOTE

Story seeds can begin in so many unexpected ways, and this one was no different.

Some years ago, one spring morning I sat on a café terrace in Croatia's beautiful, ancient walled city of Dubrovnik, overlooking the Adriatic Sea. Bullet scars still gouged the walls from the Yugoslav wars that had once plunged the region into the kind of cruel genocide not seen since the Nazi holocaust.

A young woman sat down nearby. She was pretty, with long dark hair and sensitive brown eyes. We talked. Let's call her Marina—not her real name—and her harrowing tale was not one I expected to hear on such a beautiful spring morning.

I learned that America was Marina's adopted homeland, and that her parents had met in Dubrovnik in the early 1980s, fallen in love, and married.

What happened in Yugoslavia over twenty years ago, the world knows about—a genocidal war that cost a quarter of a million lives.

Marina, then eleven, and her mother and beloved younger brother were rounded up and forcibly separated from their father by Serb paramilitaries. Imprisoned, the family endured the unspeakable horror of a rape camp for many months, in conditions as cruel as those in Auschwitz.

The day the camp was finally liberated, Marina was found wandering the outskirts of a nearby town by U.S. Special Forces—a lost survivor, alone, and so badly traumatized that she was unable to speak for days.

Later adopted by one of the U.S. officers who found her, she had come back to her mother's homeland hoping that a sample of her

DNA would find a match to any of the many thousands of bodies discovered in mass graves, among them her family.

Much of *The Last Witness* borrows from Marina's tragic story.

Much more again is based on real events that occurred at a time when the world, despite its pledge, allowed genocide to happen once again.

ACKNOWLEDGMENTS

The writer's life would be ideal were it not for all the writing.

Thankfully, the research is a lot easier because no writer has to do it alone.

To those who helped me along the lonesome trail—and you all know who you are—my grateful thanks.

I would particularly like to single out Ian Hanson, in Sarajevo, who has my greatest admiration for doing a vital forensics job that truly only the chosen can do.

And in Ireland, David Lillie, trauma therapist, who has explored the dark shadows that lurk within the human heart, and who helped me understand the minds of those who suffer the brutal distress of abuse and war.

Any inaccuracies in either of their fields of expertise within this book, deliberate to suit the story or otherwise, are mine and not theirs.

To Fiona O'Connor, for her invaluable help.

To Rheagan, one of my favorite southern belles among the wonderful Redmond clan—having kept my promise, I just hope you forgive the name change.

To Dan and Dolly Kilgore—for allowing me to borrow Union County Marina, in the beautiful hills of East Tennessee, as a setting.

To the three amigos: Lukie, Nealo Bambilo, and Kimmy K.

To my family and fellow "Waltons": Tom, Diane, and Elaine.

And to our mom, Carmel, because she deserves all our thanks and because we love her.

Gratias to all.

KEEP READING FOR AN EXCERPT FROM

THE SECOND MESSIAH!

THE SECOND MESSIAH

A THRILLER

I

EAST OF JERUSALEM
ISRAEL

Leon Gold didn't know that he had two minutes left to live and he was grinning. "Did anyone ever tell you that you've got terrific legs?" he asked the drop-dead gorgeous woman seated next to him.

Gold was twenty-three, a tanned, good-looking, muscular young man from New Jersey whose folks had immigrated to Israel. As he drove his Dodge truck with military markings past a row of sun-drenched orange groves, he inhaled the sweet scent through the rolled-down window, then used the moment to glimpse the figure of the woman seated next to him.

Private Rachel Else was stunning.

Gold, a corporal, eyed Rachel's uniform skirt riding up her legs, the top button open on her shirt to reveal a flash of cleavage. She was driving him so crazy that he found it hard to concentrate on his job—delivering a consignment to an Israel Defense Forces outpost, thirty miles away. The road ahead was a coil of tortuous bends. "Well, did anyone ever tell you that you've got terrific legs?" Gold repeated.

A tiny smile curled Rachel's lips. "Yeah, you did. Five minutes ago, Leon. Tell me something new."

Gold flicked a look in the rearview mirror and saw sunlight igniting the windows and the glinting dome of a fast-disappearing Jerusalem. There was only one reason he stayed in this godforsaken country with its endless friction with the Palestinians, high taxes, grumbling Jews, and searing heat.

The Israeli women. They were simply gorgeous. And the Israel Defense Forces had its fair share of beauties. Gold was determined that Rachel was going to be his next date. He shifted down a gear as the road twisted up and the orange scent was replaced by gritty desert air. "Okay, then did anyone ever mention you've got seductive eyes and a terrific figure?"

"You mentioned those too, Leon. You're repeating yourself."

"Are you going to come on a date with me or not, Private Else?"

"No. Keep your eyes on the road, Corporal."

"I've got my eyes on the road."

"They're on my legs."

Gold grinned again. "Hey, can I help it if you make my eyes wander?"

"Keep them on the *road*, Leon. You crash and we're both in trouble."

Gold focused on the empty road as it rose up into sand-dusted limestone hills. Rachel was proving a tough nut to crack, but he reckoned he still had an ace up his sleeve. As the road snaked round a bend he nudged the truck nearer the edge. The wheels skidded, sending loose gravel skittering into the rock-strewn ravine below.

Alarm crept into Rachel's voice. "Leon! Don't do that."

Gold winked, nudging the Dodge even closer to the road's edge. "Maybe I can make you change your mind?"

"Stop it, Leon. Don't fool around, it's crazy. You'll get us killed."

Gold grinned as the wheels skidded again. "How about that date? Just put me out of my misery. Yes, or no?"

"Leon! Oh no!" Rachel stared out past the windshield.

Gold's eyes snapped straight ahead as he swung the wheel away from the brink. A white Ford pickup appeared from around the next bend. Gold jumped on the brakes but his blood turned to ice and he knew he was doomed. His Dodge started to skid as the two vehicles hurtled toward the ravine's edge, trying to avoid a crash. The pickup was like an express train that couldn't stop and then everything seemed to happen in slow motion.

Gold clearly saw the pickup's occupants. Three adults in the front cab, two teenagers in the open back—a boy and a girl seated on some crates. The smiles on their faces collapsed into horror as the two vehicles shrieked past each other.

There was a grating *clang* of metal striking metal as the rears of both vehicles briefly collided and then Gold screamed, felt a breeze rush past him as the Dodge flew through the air. His scream combined with Rachel's in a bloodcurdling duet that died abruptly when their truck smashed nose-first into the ravine and their gas tank ignited.

Fifteen miles from Jerusalem, the distant percussion of the massive blast could be heard as the army truck's cargo of antipersonnel mines detonated instantly, vaporizing Gold's and Rachel's handsome young bodies into bone and ash.

The Catholic priest was following two hundred yards behind the pickup, driving a battered old Renault, when he felt the blast through the rolled-down window. The percussion pained his ears and he slammed on his brakes. The Renault skidded to a halt.

The priest paled as he stared at the orange ball of flame rising into the air, followed by an oily cloud of smoke. Instinct made him stab his foot on the accelerator and the Renault sped forward.

When he reached the edge of the ravine, he floored the brakes and jumped out of his car. The priest saw the flames consume the blazing shell of the army truck and knew there was no hope for whoever was inside. His focus turned to the upturned white Ford pickup farther along the ravine, smoke pouring from its cabin. The priest blessed himself as he stared blankly at the accident scene. "May the Lord have mercy on their souls."

His plan had gone horribly wrong. This was not exactly what he had intended. If the pickup's occupants had to die, so be it—the priceless, two-thousand-year-old treasure inside the vehicle was worth the loss of human life—but he hadn't foreseen such awful carnage.

He moved toward the pickup. A string of deafening explosions erupted as more mines ignited. The priest was forced to crouch low.

Seconds later his eyes shifted back to the upturned Ford pickup. He could make out the occupants trapped inside the smoke-filled cabin. One of them frantically kicked at the windshield, trying to escape. Nearby the sprawled bodies of a teenage boy and girl lay among the wreckage.

When the explosions died, the priest stood. His gaze swung back to the burning pickup. The desperate passenger had stopped kicking and his body had fallen limp. As thick smoke smothered the cabin, the priest caught sight of the leather map case, lying wedged inside the windshield.

He knew it contained the ancient scroll that had been discovered that morning at Qumran, and that the pickup was on its way to the Antiquities Department in Jerusalem with its precious cargo. But the priest was desperate to ensure that the scroll never reached its destination.

His orders from Rome were clear.

This was one astonishing secret that had to be kept hidden from the world.

Flames started to lick around the map case. "Dear God, no."

He scrambled down the rocks toward the wreckage.